THE
CABAL

THE
CABAL

DAVID HAGBERG

A TOM DOHERTY ASSOCIATES BOOK

NEW YORK

THE CABAL

Copyright © 2010 by David Hagberg

A Forge Book
Published by Tom Doherty Associates, LLC
175 Fifth Avenue
New York, NY 10010

www.tor-forge.com

Forge® is a registered trademark of Tom Doherty Associates, LLC.

ISBN 978-0-7653-2020-9

First Edition: July 2010

Printed in the United States of America

0 9 8 7 6 5 4 3 2 1

This book is for Lorrel.

At the end of days in the Roman Empire, foreign influences and lobbyists took practical control of the government, leaving the senators to do little more than snipe at each other, much like Washington today.

PROLOGUE

Fall

It was well past midnight when the cab dropped Kirk McGarvey off in front of the Hay-Adams Hotel across Lafayette Square from the White House, and one of the doormen met him. "Good evening, sir."

McGarvey, the former director of the CIA, hesitated. He was dead tired. It seemed like months since he'd slept last; now in his early fifties, he didn't bounce back as quickly as he used to. Yet his mind was alive with a thousand separate possibilities and desperate situations.

He was tall, with the build and moves of a rugby player. His hair was thick, brown but graying at the sides, and he had a wide honest face that his wife, Kathleen, had always found attractive, and deep eyes that, depending on his mood, were either green when he was at peace with the world, or gray when he was in the field and operating at top speed. He had done things, and seen things, that most people couldn't know or understand. He had killed people.

And he was just coming off an assignment in which even more people had died at his hands, which he felt would never come clean no matter how often he scrubbed them. For a long time now he had wanted it to end. He had come out of the field into an uneasy retirement that never lasted for more than a few months at a stretch, and he was getting tired of the game.

So far the FBI had been unable to find the forty kilos of polonium-210 that had been smuggled across the border from Mexico. The news that the situation had been arranged by a high-ranking Chinese intelligence officer was never made public, but the fact that the highly radioactive poison hadn't shown up anywhere had the White House puzzled. Perhaps it had never existed in the first place.

And over the past days another Chinese situation had come up when one of their high-ranking officers had been assassinated in North Korea. A nuclear war had very nearly been touched off, until the blame was traced to a former Russian KGB officer by the name of Alexander Turov, living in Tokyo, with a connection to Howard McCann, who, until Mac's son-in-law, Todd Van Buren, shot him to death, had been financing the Russian.

The problem was that no one knew where McCann, the CIA's deputy director of operations, had gotten the money to finance the polonium or the assassinations.

But McGarvey had a start, provided to him by Turov's laptop courtesy of Otto Rencke, the Company's resident wizard. Two names, one of them McCann's. McGarvey had not brought them up during his meeting at the White House with the president. He'd wanted to give the CIA a head start before the administration got all over it.

"I have to take a walk, first," he told the doorman.

"It may not be safe at this time of the evening, sir."

"That's okay, he knows how to take care of himself," Mac's wife, Kathleen, said, coming out of the lobby. She linked her arm with her husband's and they headed down the driveway and crossed the street to the park, the White House lit up like a jewel.

"Is it over, Kirk?" she asked.

"The dangerous parts."

"No war?"

"No war," McGarvey said.

They stopped under a light and she studied his broad, honest face. "But there's more, isn't there."

"There's always more, sweetheart," McGarvey told her.

PART

ONE

Six Months Later

ONE

□

The George was a trendy newly rebuilt art deco hotel one block from Washington's Union Station, its restaurant busy this Wednesday noon with a few congressmen, a number of television and print journalists, and well-heeled tourists who liked to be in the middle of things.

The noise level was surprisingly low, as if what everyone was discussing was confidential. The service was as crisp as the April weather, which, after a long damp winter, was energizing. The elections were over, a new president sat in the White House, and an optimistic mood had begun to replace the pessimism since 9/11.

Seated at an upper-level table that looked down on the first floor and entryway, Todd Van Buren sat nursing a Michelob Ultra, waiting for Joshua Givens, a buddy from the University of Maryland, where they'd both majored in political science. Todd had minored in international law and languages—French, Chinese, and Russian—and had been immediately hired by the CIA, while Givens, who'd minored in journalism, had started work for the *Minneapolis Star,* and over the past six years had worked his way up to a well-respected, if junior, investigative journalist with the *Washington Post.*

When he had called this morning and left a message on Todd's voice mail, he sounded frantic, almost frightened.

At twenty-nine, Todd was the youngest person ever to run the CIA's training facility, known unofficially as the Farm, with his wife, Elizabeth, at Camp Peary near Williamsburg, 140 miles south of Washington on the York River. His father-in-law was Kirk McGarvey, former director of the agency. He and Liz both had a fair amount of field experience, much of it alongside Liz's father, who'd arguably been the Company's finest field agent, bar none. They'd practically gone to school on his tradecraft, and once their covers had been blown they'd been recruited to run the training facility. Something they'd been doing with a great deal of success for the past three years. And after the first three months no one ever questioned their ages.

Givens knew that Todd worked for the CIA, just as he knew who Todd's father-in-law was, which made his message this morning all the more cryptic.

"Trust me on this one, Todd," Givens had said. "Don't tell anyone we're meeting. No one. Not your wife, and especially not her father."

Noon at the George, it was ten after that now, and Todd was beginning to regret driving all the way up from the Farm, and lying to his wife in the bargain, though that had been easy because she was spending the day on an exfiltration exercise with the new class. Tomorrow would be his turn, pushing the twelve field officer trainees as close to the breaking point as he could. He and Liz were hands-on administrators.

He would explain to her where he'd been when he got back. They'd been spies, but they had never lied to each other. She'd made him promise before they got married. She loved her father, but he'd been gone for almost all of her childhood because he had not been able to tell the truth to his wife, and she'd kicked him out of the house. Todd's relationship with Liz was the most important thing in his life, not just because he loved her but because of their two-year-old daughter, Audrey. He owed both of them at least that much.

Givens appeared in the doorway from the hotel's lobby, spotted Todd sitting upstairs, and came up. He looked out of breath and flushed, as if he had run all the way in from the *Post*. Unlike Todd, who was tall, solidly built with a broad, pleasant face, Givens was short and whip thin, his movements quick, almost birdlike. In college Todd had lettered two years as a running back on the football team, while Givens had lettered all four years in cross-country. He'd been incredibly fast with the endurance of an iron man, and it didn't look as if he'd changed much.

"Thanks for coming," Givens said, sitting down across from Todd. He laid a computer disk in a jewel case on the table and slid it across. "Don't hold it up, don't look at it, just put it in your pocket."

"Okay," Todd said. He slipped it into his jacket pocket as their waitress came over.

"Iced tea, with lemon," Givens said. "I'm not staying for lunch."

"So, here I am," Todd said. "And I'm curious as hell."

Givens glanced down at the entryway, and then at the other diners on the lower level, before he turned back. "Listen, for the past five months I've been investigating a power broker group called the Friday Club. And what I'm finding out is scaring the crap out of me. Everything I've come up with so far is on the disk."

"Robert Foster," Todd replied. Everyone in Washington knew of the so-called club whose ultra-conservative members called themselves American Firsters. Lobbyists, a number of high-ranking aides and advisers to some key senators and congressmen as well as at least one White House insider, and others. All men, all of them with power.

"He's the top dog," Givens said. "And when I started looking it didn't take me long to find out that some of his lobbyist pals represented people like the Saudi royal family, the Venezuelan oil minister, the deputy director of Mexico's intelligence service."

"What were you looking for?"

Givens hesitated. "This is going to sound far-fetched. But one of the guys on the list was your deputy director of operations, Howard McCann, who got my attention when he turned up dead in the line of duty."

Todd kept any hint of emotion from his face, but alarm bells were jangling all over the place. McCann had been a traitor who'd financed the hit on a Chinese general in Pyongyang, and before that was the money-man behind a scheme to smuggle forty kilos of polonium-210 across the border with Mexico. When Todd's father-in-law confronted the man in a safe house just outside Washington, the DDO had pulled out a pistol and it had been Todd who'd opened fire, killing him. There'd been a lot more to it than that, of course, but to this point they'd not been able to figure out where McCann had gotten the money. It was a puzzle.

"You have my attention, Josh," he said carefully.

"I'm in the middle of something really big. Maybe even a shadow government. These guys have influenced elections, got federal judges removed from the bench, made sure some top banks and big financial companies got federal backing—bailouts just like what happened to Chrysler and just about everyone else a couple of years ago."

"Planning a coup?"

Givens shook his head. "Nothing so messy or dramatic as that. I think they've already accomplished what they set out to do. They're running things right now. Or at least the important stuff. Guys from the Federal Reserve are in the club, along with a couple of four stars from the Pentagon. This cuts right across the board."

Givens looked away for a moment, apparently overwhelmed by what he was saying. When he turned back he'd come to some decision.

"What?" Todd prompted.

"Could be the bastards engineered nine/eleven."

This was getting over the top for Todd. "Do you know how crazy that sounds? Just another conspiracy theory. Our guys deal with that kind of shit twenty-four/seven. Doesn't get us anywhere."

"Look what they've accomplished," Givens said.

"Tell me."

"A direct reduction of our civil liberties, for one. For Christ's sake, libraries and bookstores are supposed to inform the FBI what fucking books we're reading. Now you tell me who's crazy?"

"What do your editors over at the *Post* have to say about it?"

Givens dismissed the question with a gesture. "These aren't the Woodward and Bernstein days. We don't run partial stories hoping the exposure will make other people come forward. Everyone's gotten too smart."

"Who have you shared this with?" Todd was having a lot of doubts.

He and Givens hadn't been close, but the guy had never seemed nutsy. And his investigative pieces in the *Post* had seemed first rate. But this now made no sense.

"No one. Not even my wife, Karson. Not until I have everything nailed down."

"Okay, I'll look at your disk," Todd said. "Then what?"

"How did McCann die? What was he working on?"

Todd spread his hands. "Even if I knew something like that, which I don't, I wouldn't be able to talk about it."

"Especially not with a reporter."

"Something like that."

"Give it to your father-in-law then. From what I hear he still carries some weight." Givens looked down at the entryway again, as if he was expecting someone. "Hell, I don't have anything solid yet. All I have are a lot of disconnected facts. Sudden changes in government policies, resignations of some key people here and there, upset elections in two dozen key states over the past couple of years. It's all on the disk."

"I'll see what I can do," Todd said. "But I can't promise anything. You've gotta understand that, Josh."

"Do what you can," Givens said. "What you think is right."

His iced tea came, and he drank some of it then got up. "I trust you, man. I think you're the only person in the world I can trust."

"I'll call you if I come up with something," Todd said.

"Not at the paper," Givens said. He handed Todd a business card. "Call me at home." He gave Todd a long, hard look then turned, went downstairs, and left the restaurant.

T W □

□

Tim Kangas, thirty-one, medium height and build, thinning light brown hair and ordinary brown eyes, laid a twenty-dollar bill on the downstairs table after Givens hurried past and left the hotel. His partner, Ronni Mustapha, picked up the nylon sports bag on the chair between them and casually reached inside and switched off the shotgun microphone's recording circuit. They'd heard everything.

They'd been following the *Washington Post* reporter for three weeks, waiting for the tipping point, which had apparently happened just minutes ago. An article in the newspaper would have meant next to nothing, but his meeting with a CIA officer, especially one with Van Buren's connections, could possibly be devastating.

"Get the car," Kangas said, and Mustapha, an ordinary-looking man in his late twenties with deep-set dark eyes and an easy, pleasant smile when he was in public, took the bag and left directly behind Givens.

No one would suspect he'd been born in Saudi Arabia; when he was five his parents had immigrated to Atlanta, where he'd completely assimilated, down to a soft Georgia accent. Nor would he be pegged as a CIA-trained NOC, non-official cover, field officer, the same as Kangas, who'd been born and raised in southern California. Both of them knew how to lie, how to fit in, how to fade into the woodwork, how to be anyone at anytime.

They had been picked for the program because both men had been born with a fiercely independent streak, exactly what the Company wanted. But after six years in the field, Kangas in Central America and Mustapha in Syria, Lebanon, and Iran—his parents had insisted that he learn Arabic as a child—they'd become too independent, which was all too common. And they'd also gotten fringe, over the top and in the end too brutal. Each was credited with half a dozen or more unauthorized kills of Enemies of the State and the Agency had pulled them in, offered them citations, and generous severance packages.

Kangas had left the Agency two years ago, and within five days he'd been offered a position with Washington-based Administrative Solutions—Admin—a private contracting firm second only to Xe, formerly Blackwater USA, in revenues, prestige, and the occasional missteps. S. Gordon Remington, an Admin vice president, had known just about everything in Kangas's CIA file, which had been nearly as impressive as the six-figure salary he'd offered.

The job had been boring most of the time, guarding high-ranking businessmen in Iraq and Afghanistan, making the occasional hit when it was needed, and usually as part of a firefight, which was ridiculously easy to engineer in countries where almost every male between the ages of twelve or thirteen and forty was armed and carrying a serious grudge—usually religion-based.

Mustapha had been recruited last year, and had joined Kangas in Afghanistan where they'd become partners. Their tradecraft was similar, their ambitions were about the same—hurt people and make a lot of money doing it—and they knew how to cover each other's back.

Van Buren was getting up, as Kangas took out his encrypted cell phone and speed-dialed a number that was answered on the first ring.

"Hello," Remington answered, his British accent cultured.

"The meeting has taken place."

"We're you able to record their conversation?"

"Yes."

"Is there damage?"

"Yes, sir. Just as you suspected, our subject handed over a disk."

Remington was silent for several beats, and although Kangas had never had much respect for anyone, especially anyone in authority, he did now have a grudging respect for Admin's VP. The man knew what had been coming, and he'd been prepared.

"The situation must be contained," Remington said. "Are you clear on your mission?"

"Both of them?"

"Yes. And they must be sanitized as thoroughly and as expeditiously as possible. This afternoon, no later than this evening."

"Give us twenty-four hours and we can cut the risk by fifty percent," Kangas said. Running blindly into any sort of a wet operation was inherently dicey, even more so in this instance because of who Van Buren was; his background was impressive.

"This is top priority," Remington said. "All other considerations secondary. Are we clear on that as well?"

Van Buren was coming down the stairs.

"Standby," Kangas said, and he avoided eye contact as the CIA officer passed by and left the restaurant through the hotel lobby to the valet stand.

Kangas got up, and left by the front door, which opened on the street, just as Mustapha pulled up in a dark blue Toyota SUV with tinted windows.

"We're in pursuit now," he told Remington. "But with the weapons we're carrying this won't look like a simple robbery."

Remington chuckled, which was rare so far as Kangas knew. "You've been out of the country too long to understand what the average bad guy carries."

"Yes, sir."

"Call when you're finished."

Van Buren was waiting at the curb, and as Kangas broke the connection, pocketed his phone, and got into the Toyota, a valet parker brought a soft green BMW convertible around and got out. Van Buren handed the man some money, got behind the wheel, and took off.

"Don't lose him," Kangas said.

Mustapha waited for a cab to pass, then he pulled out and, keeping the cab between them and Van Buren, started his tail. "Is it a go?"

"Yes, but right now this afternoon. Both of them."

Mustapha gave him a sharp look. "That doesn't make a lot of sense."

"That's what the man said. ASAP."

THREE

☐

Lunchtime traffic west on Constitution was even heavier than normal because of a huge art show on the Mall. Todd had to pay attention to his driving until he passed the National Museum of American History and turned south toward I-395, which would take him across the river to I-95 and the two-and-a-half-hour drive to the Farm. Because of the sunny weather, tourists seemed to be everywhere, most of them without a clue where they were going.

Across the river, the Pentagon off to the right, traffic thinned out enough for him to phone his father-in-law in Florida, but after the fourth ring he got his mother-in-law's soft West Virginia voice on the answering machine.

"Hello. We can't take your call now, but after the beep please leave a message and number and we'll get back to you. Have a nice day."

"Hi, Mom, it's Todd. Have Dad give me a call on my cell. I came up to Washington to meet an old friend for lunch and I'm on my way back to the Farm now. It's quarter to one."

Ten miles later, through Alexandria, traffic thinned out even more as the highway branched off to I-95. Todd took the disk out of his jacket pocket and looked at both sides, but Givens hadn't written anything on the disk itself or on the jewel case. Whatever was really going on had no business being in the *Post*, especially not any sort of a connection to McCann's death. That was one can of worms that would probably never see the light of day. Some things were much too dark even for the Freedom of Information Act.

In any event, McCann's death was still a part of the ongoing investigation that his father-in-law had gotten involved with last year. Already plenty of people had died because of it, and before it was over more would probably go down. If anything of what Givens had told him was true, which Todd was having a hard time believing, then shit would truly hit the fan big time.

They had never figured out what McCann had been up to or who had been directing him, and now this. Todd tossed the disk on the passenger seat and concentrated on his driving.

Forty minutes later his cell phone rang. It was his father-in-law.

"Hi, Todd, what's up?" Kirk McGarvey asked. "Is Liz with you?"

"Nope, she was busy when I left, and I didn't have time to mention I was coming up to Washington. This has something to do with McCann."

McGarvey hesitated for a beat, and Todd could see him standing, probably in the kitchen of the Casey Key house on Florida's Gulf Coast south of Sarasota, looking down at the IntraCoastal Waterway.

"Okay, you have my interest."

"Does the name Josh Givens ring any bells?"

"Vaguely. He's a reporter with the Post?"

"An investigative reporter, and not too bad," Todd said. "He and I went to Maryland together, and were pals for a while. He called this morning and asked me to have lunch, he had something important for me."

"He mentioned Howard by name?"

"He did. Said Howard had been involved with a lobbyist group called the Friday Club."

"Robert Foster."

"The same," Todd said. "Josh was talking all sorts of shit about a shadow government, and a lot of disconnected stuff that was all over the place. Sounded crazy."

"Did you believe him?"

"I don't know. But I'm sure that he believed what he was telling me, and that he was afraid. He gave me a disk, which he said had everything on it."

McGarvey hesitated for a moment. "Give Otto a call, see what he thinks." Otto Rencke was the CIA's director of special operations and the resident computer genius. He was a friend of the family and the nearest thing to a son for McGarvey and an uncle for Todd and Liz.

The Interstate cut through rolling hills, some of them heavily wooded, Fredericksburg behind him to the north and Fort A. P. Hill Military Reservation, where military units were given advanced field training, was off to the east. He and Liz had both spent six weeks there in search-and-evade training with the Green Berets.

"I'll call him when I get back to the Farm."

"Call him now," McGarvey said.

That got Todd's attention. "Do you think it's that important?"

"If it involved Howard, then yes, it could be."

"I'll call him right away," Todd said, an oddly disquieted feeling rising in his gut.

He broke the connection with his father-in-law and glanced over his left shoulder as a dark blue Toyota SUV pulled up beside him. The windows were so deeply tinted he couldn't make out who was inside, and the SUV just hung there.

"Shit," Todd muttered, his internal alarms ringing all over the place.

The Toyota's passenger-side window powered down and Todd only had a split second to see that a dark-skinned man was aiming what looked like a small automatic weapon of some kind.

Todd glanced in his rearview mirror to make sure no one was on his bumper and jammed on the brakes to get him back to the SUV's rear quarter where a nudge from his left bumper would send the bigger vehicle into a spin. But the other driver anticipated the move and also jammed on his brakes.

Todd yanked the wheel hard to the right sending his car toward the ditch and the woods off the road, when something very hard slammed into his shoulder and he was thrown sideways against the seat-belt restraint, losing control of the car.

He frantically reached for the pistol holstered high on his right hip, but several rounds slammed through the sheet metal of the door like rivets through soft steel, hitting him on his left side, then in his shoulder again and finally his neck, and suddenly he was drowning in his own blood, the world beginning to fuzz out as his BMW slammed into a small tree, tilting to the right over a drainage ditch before it came to a complete stop.

All he could think of were Liz and their daughter, how they were going to react to his death.

He tried to fumble for his pistol for what seemed like minutes when the face of the dark man appeared in the driver's window and it was all Todd could do to look up into the muzzle of what he recognized was a Knight PDW, compact submachine gun, and a billion stars burst inside his head.

Mustapha lowered the weapon, and went around to the passenger side of the BMW, opened the door, and unlatched Van Buren's seat belt, allowing the body to tumble out of the car. It took him a precious thirty seconds to search the body, taking a wallet and the pistol, but there was no disk.

Kangas had parked on the side of the highway blocking the view of anyone passing, and watching for the Virginia Highway Patrol. Their position here at this moment was precarious.

Givens had given the CIA officer a disk, and Kangas had seen Van Buren put it in his coat pocket.

The front seat was a mess of shattered glass, blood, and bone fragments, and it took a full sixty seconds before Mustapha found the disk up on the dashboard in plain sight, and the cell phone they'd seen Van Buren using wedged between the seats. He pocketed them, and tossed the disk Remington had given them inside. He wore latex gloves so he left no fingerprints.

First making certain that no one approaching on the highway could see what he was doing, he put one round into the back of the CIA officer's head.

Insurance. That's how you survived.

FOUR

"Where'd you go, Kirk?" Kathleen McGarvey asked her husband.

It was coming up on eight of a soft, south Florida Gulf Coast spring evening, and they were just finishing their dinner of broiled lamb chops and light salads, with a half bottle of Greek retsina wine on the pool deck of their Casey Key home. McGarvey looked up out of his thoughts and offered her a smile.

"Sorry. Wool gathering, I guess."

"You've been doing that a lot lately," Katy said. She was slender, with short blond hair, a bright oval face, and smiling eyes. "Something sneaking up on us again?"

She'd hated every assignment that had not only taken McGarvey away, sometimes for weeks at a time, but that had put him in mortal danger. On more than one occasion he'd come home on a stretcher, with IV tubes dangling from his arms and an oxygen mask covering his mouth and nose. But even more than his injuries, she mostly hated the fact that he killed people—bad people, but human beings nevertheless— and hated herself for at least half-understanding the necessity of what he did. America had enemies, and very often he'd been this country's last line of defense, sometimes its only viable line of defense.

Also troublesome to her was her husband's almost preternatural awareness that something or someone was lurking just around the corner, coming their way, and he often showed this understanding by becoming moody, withdrawing into his own shell, which he realized he'd done ever since Todd's call this afternoon.

"I don't think so, sweetheart," he told her, and he reached across the table and squeezed her hand. "Todd called this afternoon with something. I told him to let Otto take a look."

"But?"

McGarvey shrugged, something tickling at the back of his head. "I thought I would have heard from one of them by now."

"It probably wasn't important," Katy said, but then she frowned. "Don't you think?"

"I don't know."

"Well, for goodness sake, call them."

They had switched the house phones off, which they often did when they wanted to have dinner undisturbed. "Pour me a little more wine," McGarvey told her. "Be back in a minute."

He went in to his study on the other end of the house, switched on the phones, and speed-dialed Otto's roll-over number, which would reach him wherever in the world he was.

Rencke answered on the first ring, all out of breath, as he usually was when something big was happening or about to happen. "Oh, wow, Mac, I've been trying to get you for the past two hours," he gushed. "I was gonna send someone from the Bureau in Tampa."

"What's wrong?" McGarvey felt hollow in his stomach. He glanced out the windows where he could just make out Katy in the reflected blue from the pool lights.

"Are you okay? You had the phones off."

"We're fine. What the hell's going on, Otto?"

"Shit, shit, shit. I don't know how . . ." Rencke said. "Is Mrs. M right there?"

"She's out by the pool," McGarvey said. A terrible sense of dread wanted to overcome him. "Is it about Todd and the disk Josh Givens gave him this morning?"

"Yeah, the cops gave it to me, and I'm running it on my laptop right now. We're on our way down to the Farm. Louise is driving. I don't know, it's just too much."

McGarvey had never heard his old friend like this. Never, not even in the worst of circumstances, and there'd been plenty of those over the years. "Tell me," he said.

"Todd was shot to death sometime after one on I-Ninety-five just south of Fredericksburg."

All the air left the room, and McGarvey closed his eyes. Bright strobes were popping off in his head, like old-fashioned camera flashbulbs. For just a beat he could see Todd and Liz hunched down on the dock here below the house, their two-year-old daughter Audrey in a bright yellow bikini standing between them. With an absolute clarity he could see the pride on his son-in-law's face; I done good, he was saying.

He could see Liz the night, early in her marriage, when she'd shown up at their house in Chevy Chase after she and Todd had a terrific fight. She never cried, or never let anyone see that she cried, but tears had been streaming down her pretty cheeks that night. "I love him, Daddy," she had blubbered. "But I don't know what to do."

"What happened, sweetheart?"

The strangest look crossed her face, as if she was trying to think of something to say. But then she shook her head. "I don't know," she'd said in a small voice, her tears drying up. "I must have forgot on the way over."

Then Todd had shown up, anguish in his eyes, near total devastation, and he and Liz had embraced and had left together. McGarvey had never found out what they'd argued about. But he could see them now, see their faces, hear their voices as clearly as if they were standing right here in front of him.

"Has Liz been told yet?" he asked, coming out of himself.

"No. That's why we're headed down now. She's going to need someone next to her when she finds out."

"Start at the beginning and tell me everything you know," McGarvey said, desperately pulling himself together, but it was like swimming upstream against an impossible current.

"The Bureau has taken over from the VHP. His body was found beside his car. He'd been shot several times right through the window glass and the sheet metal on the driver's side door, probably from a car next to his. His wallet was gone, but once the tags were run, they came up with Todd's name and the CIA security notification number. Blake downstairs called me a couple hours ago, and I had him put a total lid on it. No one is to be told anything."

"It wasn't a drive-by shooting or robbery," McGarvey said.

"The Bureau's seeing it as a professional hit."

"Witnesses? I-Ninety-five is a busy highway that time of day."

"None have come forward so far," Rencke said. "But maybe later when we go public someone will make the call."

McGarvey was starting to settle down a little, his experience kicking in. Someone had assassinated his son-in-law for so far an unknown reason or reasons that most likely had something to do with Howard McCann's connection to Robert Foster and the Friday Club and whatever it was Givens had uncovered. "What's on the disk?"

"Nothing believable, Mac," Rencke said. "Honest injun. It's like the ravings of a maniac, or someone on a bad acid trip. The Friday Club has supposedly come up with a plan to overthrow the government by force, arresting the president and his cabinet and putting them on trial for treason."

"When?" McGarvey asked, for want of anything else to say. Rencke was right, it was crazy beyond belief, but then so had crashing airliners into tall buildings.

"That part doesn't matter. The guy leading the army is Howard McCann in hiding somewhere nearby, gathering an elite strike force of disaffected SEALs, Delta Force, and Bureau and Company field officers."

"McCann is dead."

"Yeah. Which makes the disk worthless."

"Somebody must have thought differently," McGarvey said.

"His cell phone was missing too, and if they can crack the encryption algorithms they'll have his phone book. Lots of important numbers."

"My number will come up," McGarvey said. "Todd called just before it happened." Christ, he didn't know how he was going to tell Katy. He didn't know about his daughter. Hell, he didn't even know about himself, what he would do once he caught up with Todd's killers. But he was sure they wouldn't live to see a court of law let alone the inside of a jail.

"One of our Gulfstreams is on the way down for you. Should be at SRQ within the hour."

"Get Liz to All Saints. She'll need someone with her. Maybe Louise." All Saints was the hospital in Georgetown that the CIA and most of the other intelligence agencies in the area used. Everyone on the staff had secret or better clearances and there'd never been a leak from the place, no matter the circumstances nor how high the patient's profile might have been. "I assume Todd was taken there."

"Yeah," Rencke said. "And you'll have some muscle."

"For the time being," McGarvey replied, a little distantly now that he was ramping up to go back into the field. "Send somebody over to pick up Givens. Give it to the Bureau for now, but I want him brought out to the Campus and secured." The Campus was the cluster of buildings, above- and belowground, at the Agency's Langley headquarters.

"Pushing a *Washington Post* reporter around could get a little dicey, kemo sabe."

"Do it," McGarvey said. "We'll see you at the hospital."

"Right," Rencke said and broke the connection.

McGarvey looked out the window but Katy was gone, and when he turned around she was standing in the doorway a stricken look on her features.

"Who's going to All Saints?" she asked.

"Liz," McGarvey said and he started toward his wife, but she held up a hand.

"How bad is she?"

"It's not her."

Katy's eyes narrowed. "Not Audie. Is it Todd? Has there been an accident?"

He had dreaded this moment for his entire career, but it was the nature of the business that casualties would occur. It was war, us against them. Only when the star that would be put up in the lobby of the Old Headquarters Building, anonymous, no name, representing a fallen agent you were close to, was the burden next to unbearable.

"Todd was shot to death this afternoon."

Katy went pale. "Dear God in heaven," she said softly, and she looked deeply into her husband's eyes. "Assassinated?"

"Yes."

"Has Elizabeth been told yet?"

"Otto and Louise are driving down to the Farm right now. He called me from the car. They'll be there for her, and they'll chopper up to the hospital. Todd's body is there."

"Why?" Katy asked, her voice plaintive, pleading.

"I don't know yet, but I'll find out."

Katy hesitated for just a beat. "I'll pack if you'll clear the table," she said, and she turned and left.

And so it begins, McGarvey thought, rage already building up inside of him.

FIVE

Givens's town house was in Berwyn Heights, northeast, just within the Beltway, in a pleasant brick and redwood complex, with a pool, clubhouse, and playground for the kids. Thousand Oaks was home to mostly young, upwardly mobile couples, near to a good private prep school, shopping malls, and a couple of decent restaurants. His town house was a three-bedroom—one for him and his wife, one for their only child, Larry, four, and one for an office where he was trying to work on a novel.

The dark blue Toyota SUV backed into a parking spot just at

eight, and Kangas doused the headlights and shut off the engine. They would have made the hit earlier, on the road as they had with Van Buren, but their instructions had been to contain the situation. It meant they needed access to the newspaperman's personal computer, so they'd waited until Givens had left the *Post* and had driven home.

They watched as he went up the walk and entered his apartment.

It was a matter of timing. It was unlikely that the CIA would have allowed news of the assassination of one of its officers to go public, at least until it was known why the kill had been made. That meant Givens would not know that the man he'd met for lunch was dead, and that he was likely to be next.

But sooner or later the Company, probably through the FBI, would be sending someone over here to have a word with the *Post* reporter, even though approaching someone in the media in that fashion was considered extremely risky.

"Let's do it," Kangas said.

He and Mustapha, dressed in jeans and dark Windbreakers, got out of the SUV, crossed the parking area, careful to stay out of the direct spill of the streetlight, and went directly to Givens's town house. No one else was around, though traffic on University Boulevard/Highway 193, below, was steady. Nor did it appear that anyone was sitting on one of the balconies, or looking out a window.

At the door, Mustapha pulled on latex gloves, drew his silenced 9mm Austrian-made Steyr GB, and stepped aside as Kangas put on his gloves then rang the doorbell.

A few seconds later Givens answered the intercom. "Yes?"

Kangas held a CIA identification card in a leather wallet directly in front of the peephole. "Sorry to bother you, sir, but Mr. Van Buren sent me. It's about your meeting this noon, and the disk. He has a question."

"I told him to phone."

"Yes, sir. But considering the nature of the information, he thought it might be safer this way."

"Oh, all right," Givens said, and a shadow moved away from the peephole. Moments later the deadbolt snapped back and the door started to open.

Kangas pushed hard, bulling his way into the town house, shoving Givens back against the hall closet door, and charging the rest of the way into the apartment.

"What the fuck—" Givens shouted.

Mustapha stepped into the apartment, closed the door behind him, and fired one shot into the middle of Givens's forehead at point-blank range.

A young, attractive woman in shorts and a T-shirt, her feet bare, was at the kitchen counter when Kangas, a pistol in his hand, appeared in the doorway. She was looking up, surprise and fear in her eyes, her mouth pursed, as he fired one shot, catching her in the bridge of her nose, driving her back against the stove, where she crumpled to the floor.

A small, slightly built boy with tousled brown hair came around the corner, and before he could comprehend what was happening Kangas shot him in the head, killing him instantly and driving his body back out of the kitchen, blood splattering on the wall.

Mustapha came in from the living room and glanced indifferently at the bodies of the woman and boy. "I have his BlackBerry. I'll take the study," he said.

Kangas nodded. Mustapha was the computer expert, and the clock was clicking. Time was precious.

Careful not to step in the blood, Kangas went down the corridor to the master bedroom furnished nicely in Danish modern, and quickly searched the closet, where he found an old military .45 autoloader, but nothing in any of the clothing; then he checked the chest of drawers, rifling through the shirts and shorts and a small box with a few pieces of cheap jewelry, the armoire, again checking pockets and finally the two nightstands and the drawers beneath the bed, which contained only extra blankets, pillows, and sheets.

The framed pictures on the walls looked like family photos, and quickly taking them apart revealed nothing hidden. Nor did his search of the master bathroom, or of the child's messy bedroom at the back of the town house, turn up anything useful.

Mustapha was buttoning up a laptop computer when Kangas came back. He looked up. "Anything?"

"No. You?"

"Everything's in his computer," Mustapha said. "Names, dates, places, transcripts of interviews, and lots of photographs."

The study had been taken apart, books down from the shelves, drawers opened and emptied, framed photographs and certificates taken apart. It looked as if the place had been randomly searched, which was their intention.

"Nothing else?" Kangas asked.

Mustapha shook his head.

Kangas took out a plastic envelope that held a dozen strips of sticky tape each holding a fingerprint or partial print and transferred the prints around the apartment—doorknobs, countertops, and the woman's purse and Givens's wallet, which were first emptied of money and credit cards.

The entire operation had taken them less than seven minutes before they cracked the door to make sure that nothing moved in the parking lot, and then calmly walked back to the SUV and drove off, Mustapha behind the wheel this time as Kangas got on the cell phone.

Remington answered on the first ring. "Yes."

"The problem has been taken care of."

"Both problems?"

The question was more than rude, putting in doubt his ability and judgment, and Kangas bridled, but he held back a sharp answer. Remington might not have proper manners, he was a Brit after all, but he did know what he was doing, and the pay was good. The problem was Kangas had never much cared for taking orders. And he certainly never liked smug bastards who didn't show proper respect. It was one of the reasons he'd left the Company, which was about little more than suits giving orders, many of which never made any sense because the bastards giving them either didn't know what the hell they were talking about, or they'd had their noses so far up someone's ass they couldn't come up for air.

"Yes, sir, both problems," he said after a brief hesitation.

They were back out on University heading toward the Beltway, traffic very light, when a pair of unmarked cars moving very fast passed them and pulled into the driveway of the apartment complex.

FBI, Kangas figured, and he glanced at Mustapha. They had cut it close this time.

"Do you have a delivery?" Remington asked.

"Yes," Kangas said. "When?"

"Morning. Seven o'clock."

Kangas wanted to ask why the delay if the operation had been important, but again he held back from the question. "As you wish," he said.

"Make damn sure you come in clean," Remington ordered brusquely. "No fuckups."

The day would come, Kangas promised himself, when Remington would apologize for his incredible rudeness and lack of respect. It would be the last thing he did before he died.

"Yes, sir," he said.

SIX

It was four a.m. in Washington when the CIA's executive Gulfstream touched down at Andrews Air Force Base and quickly taxied over to a hangar well away from operations, and then inside, where its engines spooled down.

Katy had taken a light sedative just after they'd left Sarasota, but she hadn't managed to get much sleep, and now she looked like hell, her hair a mess, her makeup smeared, and her eyes red and puffy. But she didn't seem to care about her appearance or anything else, and McGarvey was worried about her.

"We're here, sweetheart," he said; she looked up at him but didn't say anything.

A half-dozen Company security officers in dark blue Windbreakers were waiting with a pair of Cadillac Escalade SUVs inside the hangar. One of them was speaking into his lapel mike when the flight attendant opened the hatch, and McGarvey helped Katy to the steps.

"Thank you," he told the young woman, who'd been solicitous but not intrusive on the flight.

A ground crewman opened the cargo bay hatch and took out the McGarveys' hanging bag and overnight case, which one of the security officers took and placed in the back of the lead car.

It had been fifteen years ago, maybe twenty, when McGarvey had returned from an assignment that had gone bad in Chile, when Katy had given him her ultimatum: either me or the CIA. It hadn't mattered that he had assassinated a woman—the wife of a general—who he'd thought was innocent, that he had blood on his hands, that he was battered physically and emotionally; he hadn't been given the time to explain and ask for help. So he'd walked out and had run to Switzerland, throwing away his marriage and young daughter. Because he had been too proud, and because he'd had nothing to give at that moment.

But now it was his turn. Katy was battered beyond anything he'd ever endured in his life, and she needed him more than he'd ever imagined anyone could need someone.

"Easy now," he said, taking her arm and helping her down the boarding stairs.

One of the security officers came over, while the others, their heads on swivels, stood in a half-circle between the aircraft and the hangar's open doors.

"Karl Tomlinson, Mr. Director, we're here to get you to All Saints."

"Is my daughter there yet?" McGarvey asked.

"Yes, sir, along with Mr. and Mrs. Rencke."

They crossed to the lead SUV and McGarvey helped Katy step up and into the backseat. She was like a zombie, moving only when he helped her to move.

As soon as they were strapped in, the driver, with Tomlinson riding shotgun, took off and headed at a high rate of speed across the ramp to the main gate, where they were waved through, then directly up to Suitland Parkway and into Washington proper. At this time of the morning traffic was very light, and the driver only slowed for red lights, the chase car right on their tail.

"Anything new as of the last few hours?" McGarvey asked. Katy was staring out the window, apparently with little awareness of what was going on around her, otherwise he wouldn't have asked the question.

Tomlinson looked over his shoulder, a hard expression on his square, solid face. "It was no drive-by shooting, sir. They were professionals."

"They?"

"Someone called in, said they saw a man come around from Mr. Van Buren's BMW and get into the passenger seat of a dark-colored SUV—possibly a Toyota or Nissan—a second man was behind the wheel." Tomlinson glanced at Katy for a reaction, but she didn't look up. "No descriptions or tag number, but it was a professional hit. Todd had apparently reached for his pistol, but never managed to draw it."

Knives were stabbing into McGarvey's skull; he kept seeing images of Todd and Liz and the baby, and of Todd in action. The kid had been damned good. Steady, reliable, and the hell of it was that he hadn't needed the job. His parents had been wealthy and he'd inherited a lot of money and a big house. He'd come to work for the CIA out of ordinary patriotism, something that was a lot less rare, even in these times, than the average American realized.

"Did the Bureau pick up Josh Givens, the Post reporter?"

"He and his wife and child were shot to death in their apartment, a few minutes after eight last night," Tomlinson said. His accent was East Coast, maybe Connecticut or New Hampshire, and crisp. He was a professional in the middle of an assignment he found distasteful. "It was meant to look like a robbery. Money and credit cards missing."

"Not likely," McGarvey said, trying to see a reason. The stuff on the disk that Givens had handed over to Todd made absolutely no sense, and yet Todd and Givens had both been assassinated. The only common thread was the disk.

"We're cooperating with the Bureau. They've agreed to keep a lid on it, and Mr. Adkins has agreed."

Dick Adkins had been the deputy director of the CIA when McGarvey had been the DCI, and now he ran the show. He was a good administrator but not much of a spy.

Another thought suddenly struck McGarvey. "Was there a computer in the apartment?" he asked. "Maybe a laptop?"

"It wasn't mentioned, sir," Tomlinson said.

"Find out."

Tomlinson turned away and said something into his lapel mike. It took a couple of minutes for the reply before he turned back. "No computer."

"The disk in Todd's car was not the one Givens handed him in the restaurant," McGarvey said, at least one part of the assassination of his son-in-law and the reporter clear. "It was a fake. It's why they had to get the computer."

"I'll pass that to the Bureau—"

"Not yet," McGarvey said, his mind still spinning. If the disk was a fake, it meant the assassins may have been at the restaurant and witnessed the hand over. But it also meant that whoever had directed the hit had to know what Givens had been working on; had to know enough to manufacture the bogus disk so that it could be planted in Todd's car after he'd been murdered.

Not only did they have the original disk and Givens's computer that contained whatever it was the reporter had gathered about the Friday Club, but they had Todd's cell phone from which they would have found out that his last call just before the murder had been to his father-in-law.

It made him the next best target. Exactly what he wanted.

. . .

All Saints Hospital was on a quiet side street not far from Georgetown University Hospital, in an undistinguished four-story brownstone with the emergency entrance at the rear. No sirens were ever used, and the brass plaque next to the gate in front read *Private*.

Security in the main lobby was outwardly low key, one plain-looking man, who happened to be a weapons and martial arts expert, behind a desk. In the facility's forty-plus years there'd never been any sort of an incident, nevertheless everyone—doctors, nurses, aides, security officers—were on their toes. Always.

The two Cadillacs drove through the electrically operated gate to the back, where the security officers got out first to make sure the parking area and emergency entrance were secured before they allowed McGarvey and his wife to get out of the lead car and hustle them inside. They were met by one of the nurses, a no-nonsense, severe-looking woman.

"Good morning, Mr. Director," she said. "Would you like something for Mrs. McGarvey before we go up?"

"No," McGarvey said. "We want to see our daughter."

"Yes, sir. She's on the fourth floor in the waiting room."

McGarvey motioned for his security team to stay behind and he helped Katy back to the elevator and up to the fourth floor and the waiting room just across the corridor.

A stricken Elizabeth, dressed in jeans, T-shirt, and sneakers sat on a couch, Rencke's wife, Louise, holding her shoulders. She looked up when her parents appeared in the doorway, and for a moment it seemed to McGarvey that she didn't recognize them. But then she got up, slowly, like a tired old woman and came to them.

McGarvey folded her into his arms and held her, silently, for a long time.

"Oh, Daddy," Elizabeth said softly, her voice husky, all the way from the back of her throat. "He looks so bad."

"Where's Audie?"

It took Liz a few moments to answer. "At the Farm, this is no place for her."

Katy had come out of her trance, and she moved McGarvey aside. "Go see to him," she said.

"He was assassinated," Liz said. "Was it something he was working on? Do you know, because he didn't say anything to me? Otto said he called you. But he never left a note. I was out on a field exercise, but I could have come into town with him. Maybe if I'd been there it could have been different."

"It was something new, but he didn't know anything about it until he got up here," McGarvey said. "He was just coming up to see an old friend for lunch."

"Who?"

"Josh Givens. They were friends in college."

The name didn't mean anything to Liz, and she shook her head. "Is he in the business?"

"He was an investigative reporter with the Post."

Liz caught the past tense and her eyes hardened. "Did they get him, too?"

"Yeah," McGarvey said, a sudden great weariness mixing with a deep rage that wanted to consume his sense of reason.

Liz and Katy and Louise were all staring at him. "Get the bastards, Daddy," Liz said, the corners of her mouth down turned; a very hard look in her eyes.

"I willl," he said. "In the meantime I want you to get back to the Farm. Audie needs you and you'll be safe there."

"I'll go, too," Katy said. "Will you be coming along?"

"Right behind you. We'll set up the debriefing there."

Otto was just coming down the corridor when McGarvey left the waiting room. He looked like he hadn't slept in days, his long red hair flying everywhere, his jeans tattered, and his CCCP sweatshirt dirty, sweat stains at the armpits. He'd been crying, his eyes red, his cheeks still wet.

"I'm sorry, Mac. Honest injun, but I can't go back in there," he said. "The doc's waiting for you."

"Bad?"

Rencke's eyes were downcast. "Yes." He looked up. "We tried to stop Liz from seeing him, but couldn't."

"Nothing you could have done differently," McGarvey said. "I'm going to talk to the doctor, but in the meantime I want you to send Liz and Katy back down to the Farm with one of the teams that brought us in from Andrews. Have the other standing by, because soon as I finish here, I'm heading down. I'll want a debriefing team standing by, and I'm going to need you to back stop me."

Rencke's eyes were round. "What've you got in mind?"

"The Friday Club, but first the second name on the disk I brought back from Tokyo."

"The Friday Club has to be a dead end. The disk was way too weird. Over the top."

"It's a fake. The real stuff was on Givens's computer, which was missing from his apartment."

"That means they knew what Givens was up to," Rencke had said. "A story in the *Post* would have done nothing—just another conspiracy theory, background noise—but handing over shit like that to somebody like Todd was too big to ignore."

"Get Liz and Katy out of here, I'll be back in a few minutes."

SEVEN

Todd's body, covered in a white sheet stained with blood, was lying on a table in one of the operating rooms where he had been taken fifteen hours ago. As soon as it was released an autopsy would be performed downstairs in the morgue, but Elizabeth had insisted no one was to do a thing until her father showed up.

The on-duty chief of surgery, Dr. Alan Franklin, had come upstairs when he'd been informed that the former director had arrived, and when McGarvey walked into the small well-equipped room, he turned away from the window that looked down on the rear courtyard, came over, and shook hands.

"Good evening, sir," he said. He was an athletically built man in his late fifties, with a hound-dog face and eyes that drooped. He'd worked on McGarvey a couple of times in the past, and he was damn good at what he did—saving the lives of CIA officers who were brought to him in serious condition.

"Was he DOA?" McGarvey asked.

"Yes. But even if we'd been right there, we couldn't have done a thing for him. He'd been shot several times in the upper body, once in the left leg, and again in the left side of his neck. The bullet severed his carotid artery and he'd probably been very close to bleeding out when he took a bullet to his forehead." The doctor glanced at Todd's shrouded body. "But that wasn't enough. Your son-in-law was dead, lying on his face on the grass beside the car, when they put a final round into the back of his head at point-blank range."

"Insurance," McGarvey muttered. His killers were professionals who'd been ordered to make the hit, and before they walked away they had made sure that their mission had been accomplished.

"I'd like his body released for autopsy, Mr. Director."

McGarvey nodded, thinking about the first time he'd met Todd. Liz had been shy about bringing him to the house until she'd introduced him to her father—in the CIA's Starbucks on the first floor of the Old Headquarters Building. A less intimate setting, though she'd learned later that for Todd the meeting had been the toughest thing he'd ever done; meeting the legendary CIA agent who'd risen to the directorship on the seventh floor had been way over the top, even for a young man as self-assured and in love as Todd had been.

"Let me see him."

The doctor went around to the opposite side of the table from McGarvey and pulled the sheet away, revealing Todd's marble white face.

The wounds in the forehead and neck were massive, either one in themselves totally devastating, without a doubt lethal.

"All of him," McGarvey said softly. He was distressed to the core that Liz had insisted on seeing her husband like this, but he understood her need for closure.

The doctor pulled the sheet all the way off Todd's body, and even McGarvey, who was hardened to seeing death, was momentarily taken aback. This man was his son-in-law, the father of his grandchild, not just a dedicated, capable CIA officer who'd been shot to death in the line of duty.

McGarvey looked away. "Okay," he said. "It'll be a closed-coffin funeral unless his wife says differently."

"Do you want to see the autopsy report?"

"Not unless you come up with something that doesn't fit."

"Yes, sir," Dr. Franklin said. "Get the bastards who did this, Mr. Director."

McGarvey looked him in the eye and nodded, then turned and went back down the hall to the empty waiting room. He sat down on the couch, an old western on the television, but the sound had been turned off.

After the debriefing, which would take place at the Farm, Dick Adkins would want him to come up to Langley to personally warn him from getting involved. Since it was possible that this somehow included some powerful men in Washington, McGarvey would have to be careful with what he said. He couldn't afford to go head-to-head with the Company or with the Bureau, too much was at stake. He needed a free hand. Yet he needed the incident to be out in the open. I'm coming for you, and he wanted the message to be crystal clear.

It was at least a fair bet that whatever Givens had uncovered that had led him to call Todd to a private meeting not only had something to do with the Friday Club, but to the Mexican polonium thing and the Pyongyang assassination, and whatever else was coming next. To this point, according to Otto, neither the CIA nor the Bureau had come up with anything solid in their investigations. It had taken a *Washington Post* reporter to do that.

The hospital was quiet at this hour, though he thought that he could hear the murmur of voices somewhere down the corridor, but then that faded away, and the only sounds were from some machinery somewhere. The problem was that he had been alone with his innermost thoughts for most of his life, or certainly all of his career with the CIA, and he'd lost much of the normal ability to share his feelings. Sometimes even with himself.

But just now, here at this time and place, he was able to see his hate and rage, and in a way it frightened him more than anything or anyone had ever frightened him.

Seeing his daughter's face and then seeing Todd's body had scraped away some last vestige of civilized behavior; erased that bit of humanity in him that sometimes made him hesitate to pull the trigger when there was just a hint of ambiguity. Shoot a suspect in the kneecap to disable him, not in the head to end his life—though that had very often been necessary.

This time ambiguity meant nothing. He was going after whoever was behind this, one by one, no matter who they were, no matter who ordered him to stop, no matter if his actions would be against all reason, all sanity, no matter the consequences to him.

He got up and went back out into the corridor when Todd's body was rolled out of the operating room and to the elevator. The autopsy would take place in the basement morgue, and afterward his remains would be zippered in a rubber bag and placed in a refrigerated chamber until it was transferred to a mortuary for preparation before the Arlington burial.

McGarvey could see all of that, every step of the way.

The two attendants rolling the gurney didn't look up until the elevator doors closed, and then they avoided McGarvey's eyes. This was no normal killed-in-the-line-of-duty, if such a thing was ever normal, this involved the son-in-law of the former DCI, a man who was admired by most and feared by many.

The fourth floor settled down again, leaving McGarvey with his dark thoughts until ten minutes later Rencke came back up, and sat down across from him.

"They're off," he said.

"What about Louise?"

"I sent her back to work. I think she'll be more useful to us on the job. That way we won't have any trouble getting satellite time if we need it."

"Did you tell them I would be right behind them?" McGarvey asked.

Rencke nodded. "The Bureau is working on it, and so is the Virginia Highway Patrol, but except for the one call no one's heard a thing."

"Todd told me that Givens apparently had proof that Howard was connected with the Friday Club," McGarvey said. "Which makes Foster and that crowd one of my best bets."

"Lots of heavy hitters, Mac."

"They'll have a weak point. Someone on the edge, someone new, maybe someone's whipping boy, someone with a grudge, someone in trouble who might be willing to make a trade."

Rencke nodded. "I'll see what I can do. In the meantime do you want me to come down to the Farm with you?"

"No, I want you at the Campus. Before this is over I'm going to need some serious backup."

Rencke looked like he hadn't slept in days, and he looked as if he were on the verge of tears, but he nodded. "How do you want to start?"

McGarvey had thought about it. Going up against Foster and the others in the Friday Club would be dicey at best. One word from them and he'd be in trouble. The Bureau would almost certainly try to come after him, which would slow him down. Something he didn't want to happen. When he went up against them he would be looking for reactions, but not until he was ready. For that he needed more information.

"I'm going to need whatever you can come up with for the second name on Turov's computer, Roland Sandberger. His deep background, his associates, his connections, money trails, that sort of thing, as well as a list of his current contracts."

"He's president of Administrative Solutions, but you knew that. Former Army Delta Force operator who was on the front lines in both Gulf Wars and Afghanistan. Got out four years ago as a bird colonel and started his contractor company. He pays his people very well—too well—which means his troops are super-loyal, but which also means he started with bags of money. Source unknown at this point. He gets the best people, he gets the best results, and he gets the best contracts."

"Find out if he has any connection with the Friday Club. I'm betting he does," McGarvey said. "Could be one of his sources for contracts."

"That shouldn't be too tough to find out," Rencke said.

"And I want a running tab on his itinerary. I want to know where he is right now, and where he's going, when he's going, and who he's going with or to meet. Tap his phones, hack into his computer, whatever it takes. When I go after him I want to know what I'm up against."

Rencke nodded uncertainly.

"I especially want to know when he's out of the country."

"Shit," Rencke said softly.

EIGHT

It was just getting light when McGarvey went downstairs and got into the car with Tomlinson and the driver who had brought him in from Andrews. Work traffic had started up across the Key Bridge, then south down the Jefferson Davis Highway where, past the Pentagon, they picked up I-395.

Already it had been a long day and even longer night, and McGarvey laid his head back with his dark thoughts, unable to close his eyes let alone get some sleep. He kept seeing Todd's body. His death—the manner of his death—had been more than an assassination, it had been a message: Don't fuck with us; we're capable of and willing to strike back to protect our interests.

Administrative Solutions certainly had the manpower and the expertise for a hit like that. It wasn't clear if they had the motive, the name of the contracting firm's founder and president had been in Turov's computer, and that was a start.

It was certainly possible that the Friday Club had hired Admin; there had been a link between Howard McCann and the club, and McCann, through Turov, with the company. But it did not mean that the Friday Club had ordered Todd's assassination and the murders of Givens and his family. The links were there, but they weren't strong enough to take to the Bureau or for McGarvey to take any action.

Yet.

"Have my wife and daughter reached the Farm?" he asked.

"They're about five miles out," Tomlinson said.

"No troubles?"

"No, sir. Would you like to talk to Mrs. McGarvey?"

"That's not necessary," McGarvey said. "Just make damn sure that the perimeter is clear and stays that way."

"Yes, sir," the Company security officer said, and he began relaying the orders via his comms unit.

The interstate south was in fairly good shape, most traffic was heading into the city, not out, and by the time they reached the large wooded reserve of Quantico that was home to a Marine Corps Unit, a cemetery, and the FBI's training center, McGarvey had finally been able to shut down enough to close his eyes and drift into a restless sleep.

His cell phone vibrated against his hip, waking him instantly. He sat up and looked out the window not immediately recognizing where they were, except traffic had increased and they were obviously on the outskirts of a fairly big city. Probably Richmond, he thought, which was only a half-hour from the Farm.

He answered on the second ring. "Yes."

"Mrs. M and Liz got there okay," Rencke said. "Where are you?"

"Outside Richmond, I think," McGarvey said, the cobwebs clearing. "What do you have for me?"

"Foster and his Friday Club are big, kemo sabe. I mean really big. The White House has been using the group to float new policy issues. Don Hestern, he's Frank Shapiro's assistant, is one of the regulars." Shapiro was the president's new adviser on national security affairs.

"Anyone from the Company since McCann?"

"Not that I've found out so far, except I'm sure it's not Dick. I've got his Fridays covered since McCann went south. But considering Foster's reach I wouldn't be surprised if we had somebody over there."

"Give it to security, see what they can find out."

"I don't think that's such a hot idea, Mac," Rencke said. "Look, if Adkins or Whittaker or someone else upstairs gets wind that we've started an internal investigation—a rogue investigation—a lot of shit's going to hit the fan. And it'll point toward you, something I don't think you want right now."

Rencke was correct. "Then you'll have to look down everyone's track on your own. But if someone stepped in for McCann, it'll have to be one of the top people in either Operations or Intelligence."

"Or someone on Dick's staff," Rencke said. "Someone close enough to the DCI's office to know policy developments." Rencke was silent for a moment. "And you know what that would mean."

"That McCann had the cooperation of someone else inside the Company," McGarvey said. "The point is what the hell do they want?" McGarvey said.

"Foster is pushing the conservative movement. After Bush it's become an uphill battle. So these guys are serious."

"Yeah, but to what end?" Mac said. "What the hell are they after that's so important they'd gun down a CIA officer in broad daylight on a major highway? And what about Mexico City and the polonium, and the Pyongyang assassination? Because if there's a pattern in there I don't see it."

"Neither do I," Rencke said heavily. "Neither does anyone else. But killing Todd for whatever was on the real disk Givens gave him is connected."

"Who else is involved with Foster?"

"Everyone, Mac, honest injun. Their fingers are in just about every pie—Treasury, Justice, DoD, Interior, Homeland Security, you name it. Not only that, but some of those guys have been accused of illegal shit, like fund-raising, influence peddling, even tampering with elections all the way down to the county and local levels in some of the key states."

"Garden variety Beltway white-collar crooks," McGarvey said, even more bothered than before Rencke had called. "But not terrorists. Not assassins. Which leaves us with Administrative Solutions and Roland Sandberger. Where is he right now?"

"Baghdad, I think. Admin has a big contract bid coming up, personal security for our embassy people and other civilians, Halliburton and the like, and I suspect he'd want to be on the ground over there."

"Find out," McGarvey said, unable to keep a hard edge from his voice. "Who's running the offices stateside?"

"His VP and chief of operations. A Brit by the name of S. Gordon Remington. I've dug out a few basic facts on him, and so far he comes up clean. I'll keep digging, but something curious is going on with everyone in the company—contractors in the field as well as the front-office people. I've had no problem getting names and addresses, dates and places of birth, marriages, kids, that kind of stuff. Even social security and passport numbers, but if I had to write a résumé for Sandberger or Remington I'd draw a blank. Both of them served in the military—Sandberger in our Delta Forces; Remington in the British SAS—but I can't come up with their service records."

"Encrypted?"

"No, just blank," Rencke said. "I mean, SAS has a record that Remington served for fourteen years, and was honorably discharged as a lieutenant colonel two years ago, but there's nothing on where he served, or even what he did for them. And it's the same with Sandberger. Someone erased their pasts."

"Convenient," McGarvey said. "But you're talking about computer records, right?"

"Right."

"Find somebody they served with and see if they can tell us anything."

"That's my next step. And I'm also looking a little closer at Admin's personnel. There has to be somebody who's got a grudge about something. A pissed-off contractor who quit or got fired, who might be willing to talk."

"How're you going to find them?"

"Tax records. One year's return shows an income from Administrative Solutions, and the next year it doesn't. Easy."

"Let me know if you come up with something," McGarvey said. "In the meantime, have there been any rumbles from the seventh floor?"

"Not a word," Rencke said. "I think they're waiting to see how it goes with the debriefers, and what you'll do next."

"Who are they sending?"

"Dan Green and Pete Boylan."

McGarvey knew them both. "Good people," he said.

"They'll be fair."

NINE

Rock Creek Park cut a broad diagonal across the northwestern section of Washington, separating Georgetown from the rest of the capital city. Joggers, hikers, Rollerbladers, and bicyclers were almost always present, lending the area an anonymity. It was Washington's Central Park, with trails, a golf course, an amphitheater, a nature center, and picnic areas with tables and grills dotted here and there, a lot of them along Beach Drive, which more or less followed the winding course of the creek until it emptied into the Potomac.

The dark blue Toyota SUV pulled off to the side of the road just after it crossed to the east bank of the creek above the golf course and Kangas cut the engine. It was seven and still fairly early, but the park was unusually empty, though two young women in jogging outfits passed by; a few moments later, a deep blue Bentley Arnage pulled up and parked a few yards away.

"We play it straight. Money's still good," Kangas said to Mustapha. "Agreed?"

"For now," Mustapha conceded, but he was of the same temperament as Kangas. Neither man liked taking orders, especially orders they thought were stupid, which was one of the many reasons both men were single. Women were for screwing not for living with. And while they both had a great deal of respect for Remington, they also agreed that something was going on with Admin that did not bode well. The center was beginning to fall apart.

The two men got out of the SUV, Kangas carrying a small canvas bag with Givens's laptop and BlackBerry from the apartment, and the disk and cell phone Mustapha had taken from Van Buren's car, plus the recording of the conversation in the George restaurant, and they walked over to the Bentley and got in the backseat.

S. Gordon Remington, solidly built, rugged shoulders, a refined but bulldog face with thick bushy eyebrows and a Sandhurst drill-sergeant mustache, sat in the far corner of the car, up against the driver's side rear door, an unreadable expression in his slate gray eyes. The smoked glass partition over the rear of the front seat was closed and nothing could be seen of the driver/bodyguard.

"Good morning, sir," Kangas said, laying the things on the floor between them.

Mustapha closed the door. "Sir," he said.

"Tell me," Remington said without preamble.

"The situation has been sanitized but at some risk," Kangas began.

"Van Buren is dead and the disk was replaced with the one you supplied us. We took it and his cell phone from the BMW."

Remington said nothing, and Kangas held his temper in check. Push came to shove they would go over to Executive Services no matter what confidentiality agreement they'd signed. The money might not be as good, but word in the industry was that Tony Hawkins ran a tight ship and protected his people. Of course they would first have to do a little cleanup work on their background jackets, but that wouldn't be impossible.

"The disk wasn't a problem, sir," Mustapha said. "But Van Buren's cell phone might be. He made a call just before our hit. To Casey Key, Florida. To Kirk McGarvey, his father-in-law."

"Was there a record device on the phone?" Remington asked, a flicker of interest in his eyes, his voice soft, refined, upper-class British.

"No, sir," Mustapha said. "There is no way we can know the substance of their conversation, but considering Mr. McGarvey's background it's a safe bet they discussed the meeting with Givens and the fact he'd been given a disk."

"Which by now the CIA undoubtedly has, and has read, and pronounced utter nonsense. Exactly as planned." Remington looked at them. "Is there a problem?"

"Yes, sir," Kangas said. "Mr. McGarvey and his freak friend in the Company are likely to suspect the disk is a fake."

"You're referring to Otto Rencke, the Company's resident oddduck genius."

"They have a formidable history together."

"Look, Mr. Remington, if McGarvey gets involved we could be in some deep shit," Mustapha said, but Kangas held him off.

"Won't be easy, but it's nothing we can't handle, sir. It'll just take time and finesse and maybe some force."

Remington looked out the window at the creek for several moments, and when he turned back he smiled. "For the moment Mr. McGarvey is my problem, and no concern of yours. Tell me about Mr. Givens and his family."

"They've been eliminated," Kangas said. "We took his laptop and BlackBerry and left behind the trace evidence you suggested. There'll be no repercussions except for the connection between Givens and Van Buren, which McGarvey will almost certainly look into."

"As I said, Mr. McGarvey is not your problem, for the moment," Remington repeated. "In fact, I'd hoped that Mr. Van Buren would get his father-in-law involved. It makes the next step that much easier."

"Sir?" Kangas asked. He was sure that despite Remington's high-profile American wife, the man had to be a faggot. All the signs were there; the soft, dreamy speech patterns, his dress, his manners.

"Mr. McGarvey will be taken care of, trust me, gentlemen. You've done a fine job, and you will be suitably rewarded. But stay close, there'll most likely be more to do."

"We'd rather be back in the field," Kangas said. He was uncomfortable with these kinds of assignments. The ethics and especially the freedom of the battlefield, where skill and tactics counted more than finesse, more than screwing around with civilian targets, were more to his liking.

Remington pursed his lips. "Are we clear on this, gentlemen?" he asked, his voice gentle.

"Yes, sir," Kangas said. Bastard.

"Yes, sir," Mustapha agreed.

When they had driven off in their SUV, Remington powered down the divider. "Let's go to the office, Sarge."

"Full day, sir?" Robert Randall replied, his accent Cockney. He'd been a top sergeant at Sandhurst and in fact had been one of Remington's chief instructors in the old days with the SAS. They had their own history, and Remington had a great deal of respect for the sergeant.

"Nothing more than the usual," Remington said, glancing down at the laptop and other things Kangas and Mustapha had collected. They were becoming a problem, just as Roland had predicted they would.

"Think of them as a disposable tool," Sandberger had told Remington. "Use them once or twice and then dispose of them." He had smiled faintly, and now, sitting in the back of his car, Remington had remembered that conversation in full detail.

"They could give us considerable trouble."

"Of course they could, and will," Sandbergber had agreed. "So we put them where we wouldn't put anyone else. In the shitholes where the air is bad and the odds are stacked against them. If they succeed, all well and good, we'll give them a bonus. If they fail . . ." Sandberger had shrugged indifferently. "They're history."

Remington had seen the logic, and just now they were the perfect pair for not only what had already transpired, but for what would probably develop over the coming days.

The serious problem at hand, the one Roland had assigned to him, because in his words S. Gordon had the finesse to pull it off, was the issue with the Friday Club and Admin's contract with Foster, vis-à-vis Kirk McGarvey.

And the ultimate solution was mostly Sandberger's, but partly Remington's, who understood true British virtue, that truth was far less important than perception, something they'd perfected in their colonial days.

Certainly not Foster himself, but Admin would suggest that certain members of the Friday Club begin a quiet campaign to accuse Kirk McGarvey of treason. The charge had been made in the past but had never managed to stick for reasons unknown, except that the man had the reputation of being physically dangerous. But that was exactly the quality in a man that Admin most understood, and admired, and that the firm knew how to manipulate.

President Langdon had been elected on a platform of trust—the revitalization of American values—and chief among his goals was the transformation of U.S. intelligence gathering methods. Places like Guantánamo and the old Abu Ghraib—now Baghdad Central Prison— were to be dismantled, and dinosaurs like McGarvey were to be finally retired for the good of the nation. Torture and interrogation under drugs were to be eliminated, and terrorists and religious fanatics were to be given the civilian rights of private citizens under the aegis of a recognized national governments.

So much bullshit, Remington thought. In his estimation only a complete idiot would stick to methods of honor when his enemy was sending airliners into buildings or children into the streets with explosives strapped to their frail bodies. Washington did not have the stomach to fight the real war; it's why companies such as Administrative Solutions were hired to do the tough bits, the morally ambiguous actions. And it was for that very reason that the Friday Club was not only necessary but owed its existence.

Kirk McGarvey had been marginally useful to the nation for a portion of his career, but he could no longer be trusted. He was a madman who had to be eliminated or at the very least be kept behind bars for the remainder of his life.

The death of his son-in-law had unhinged him. Made him mentally unstable. Made him extremely dangerous.

T E N

McGarvey was housed in the visiting VIP wing of the BOQ across the yard from the two-story brick-fronted headquarters building. It was assumed that his debriefing would run through the afternoon, perhaps longer, and he would stay at the Farm overnight at the very least to keep him out of harm's way until the situation could be stabilized. No one knew what might be coming next.

Tomlinson and Bob Dingle, the other security officer who'd driven down here with him from Washington, had been assigned as his bodyguards. They waited at the Charge of Quarters station in the front hall while Mac splashed some water on his face, and joined them. It was a few minutes before noon.

"They're waiting for us, Mr. Director," Tomlinson said. He was cool; everyone had a great deal of respect for McGarvey, but the Company was under siege. A CIA officer had been gunned down in broad daylight and his father-in-law knew something about it.

"How about my wife and daughter?" McGarvey asked.

"Mrs. McGarvey was given a sedative, and she's resting now in the infirmary. Mrs. Van Buren is in the conference room. She won't start without you."

"I see," McGarvey said, his heart torn between wanting to go to Katy to make sure she was okay, and being with Liz to get the debriefing over with as soon as possible, and with as little additional emotional damage to his daughter as was possible under the circumstances.

The Farm was in lockdown for the remainder of the day and all of tomorrow until a new sitrep was prepared; no one was in the Yard when McGarvey and his bodyguards walked across past the center circle, the flag at half-staff, over to headquarters and upstairs to the camp commandant's briefing room on the third floor.

Double-paned windows, with electronic white noise continuously transmitted in the gap between the glass panels, looked down the hill through the woods toward the York River, the firing range, and the starting block of the confidence course, deserted now.

Elizabeth sat hunched in a chair on one side of the conference table that had places for fourteen people, her head down, her hands clasped between her knees. She was still dressed in the same jeans and plain sweatshirt she'd worn to the hospital and the mop of short blond hair on her head was a mess.

The debriefers, Dan Green, a little person shorter than four-six, with a broad head, hawklike nose, wide, soft brown understanding eyes, and oddly shaped hands and distorted fingers sat across from her, next to his partner Pete Boylan, who was a vivacious woman in her early thirties, short dark hair, vividly blue eyes, and a voluptuous figure that could have landed her a place in Hollywood. Everyone back at Langley was afraid to approach her; the men because she was beautiful and they figured they wouldn't have a chance, the women because they felt they would appear frumpy next to her, and the clients whom she debriefed because they instinctively felt she would know when they were lying. But she had a reputation of being friendly not aloof, and kind not harsh. She and her partner were people who understood things, and were sympathetic.

"Mr. Director," she said, looking up when McGarvey came into the room.

Green simply smiled sadly, an expression of near absolute devastation on his face. Their method was simple: Pete was the interrogator and Dan was, in the end, the priest to whom you confessed.

Liz looked up at her father and managed a weak smile. She'd finished crying, and now she seemed determined, the beginning of anger and raw hate starting to show up in the set of her mouth and eyes.

McGarvey sat down next to her. "I don't think my daughter knows anything that might be of use at this point."

"Yes, sir," Pete agreed. "But she asked if she could remain."

"I want to know what's going on," Liz said. "No one's told me why he went to Washington, except to see a friend who you told me had been killed. But why?"

"We don't know yet, sweetheart," McGarvey said.

"Have you had a chance to take a look at the material on the disk that was found in Mr. Van Buren's car?" Pete asked.

"His name was Todd," Liz said sharply. "Let's just start there, okay?"

Pete nodded, her eyes not leaving McGarvey's.

"I've not seen it, but Otto Rencke filled me in."

"What do you think?"

"Nonsense, of course."

"Of course," Pete said. "Not worth killing a CIA officer for. But your son-in-law, Todd, telephoned you from his car apparently less than a minute before the incident. What did he say to you?"

"That he had a meeting with Josh Givens in Washington, a friend of his from college, about some sort of conspiracy involving the Friday Club."

"Did he say how he felt about the information he'd been given?"

"He thought it was unlikely, but he told me that Givens apparently believed it."

"What was your advice to him?" Pete asked.

"I told him to discuss the situation with Mr. Rencke."

"Was there any urgency in your instruction, Mr. Director," Dan Green asked, gently, as if he was hesitant to interrupt. "I mean to say, was Todd to return to the Farm and, say, mail the disk to Langley, or perhaps send it by courier, or perhaps encrypted e-mail?"

"I told him to call Otto immediately."

"Why was that, Mr. Director? Why the urgency?"

McGarvey had thought about that very thing after he'd hung up from Todd's phone call. "I thought that Mr. Givens was a respected member of the press, with a good reputation, and I didn't suspect that he would waste his time chasing after nonsense, nor would he have called on a friendship with someone inside the CIA with Todd's . . ."

"Connections?" Pete asked.

"Yes, with my son-in-law's connections unless he thought it was important. Todd said that Givens was deeply frightened."

"By the Friday Club?"

"Yes."

"But the disk was mostly nonsense, something a man of Mr. Givens's experience would have understood," Pete said. "How do you see that?"

McGarvey glanced at his daughter, who was hanging on his every word. The expression of feral anger in her eyes was something new, and disturbing to McGarvey. He'd seen the look before in the eyes of field officers who'd been caught out and were in a fight for their lives— kill or be killed—but such an emotion in his daughter's eyes wasn't right, and there was nothing he could say here and now to help her.

"The disk found in his car was a fake. His killers took the real one."

Green nodded thoughtfully. "That would have to mean whoever

was behind this had been closely monitoring Mr. Givens's activities for a period of time long enough to suspect what might be on the disk he passed to your son . . . to Todd."

Green exchanged a sympathetic glance with his partner, who pursed her lips. It was obvious that they were being cautious, perhaps overly so, for reasons McGarvey could not know. But he suspected that some instructions had been passed from Dick Adkins on the seventh floor. *Whatever the hell you do, don't provoke the son of a bitch.*

"I'd think it would have to be more than one man; an organization large enough to conduct a decent surveillance operation," McGarvey suggested.

"A government organization?" Pete asked pointedly. She was being leading, and making it obvious. Left hanging in the air: the CIA?

"I don't think so."

"Or, don't hope so?"

"That, too," McGarvey said, not willing to be drawn in, and yet wanting to help because he couldn't cover everything even with Otto's help. He wanted the Company to follow some leads, just not the same ones he was going to chase.

"You're aware, of course, Mr. Director, that Mr. Givens, his wife, and small son were murdered last night," Green said, his voice soft, sympathetic. "But you might not be aware that several sets of fingerprints were found linking two known felons who've done time for breaking and entering, strong-arm, drug trafficking and use, activities of that nature."

"Found on Mrs. Givens's purse, Mr. Givens's wallet, perhaps places around their apartment where money or something worth money might have been hidden?"

Green conceded with a gesture.

"The place was searched."

"Yes," Green said, leading McGarvey down the path he'd chosen, leading McGarvey to make the conclusions.

"Trashed?"

"No, the apartment wasn't trashed in particular."

"Professionals leaving behind fingerprint evidence, but probably no DNA traces."

Pete glanced at her partner as if to say: I told you so. "The Bureau did find traces of talcum powder in a few spots," she said.

"Rubber gloves. Is that how you see it?"

"It's likely."

"Nothing useful was found in Todd's car."

"No," Pete said, and this time she glanced at Elizabeth who'd closely followed the exchange.

"I know about the bullet to the back of his head after he was already dead," Liz said. "So we're all agreed these were professional hits. By whom and for what purpose?" But before she waited for an answer from anyone, she added: "By what Agency?"

"We don't know that, sweetheart," McGarvey said.

"But you do, Daddy," she shot back. "You goddamned well have a good idea. Connected with Mexico City and Pyongyang? Is that it?"

She had caught all of them flat-footed, especially McGarvey. Officially Liz hadn't been in the need-to-know loop for either operation. But her father had not only been the DCI, he had been involved in both, and the closest friend of the family was Otto Rencke, the Company's director of special operations. If she wanted to she could learn just about anything she wanted to learn.

"Would you care to explain, Mr. Director?" Pete asked.

"You'll have to get that from Mr. Adkins."

Pete nodded. "Will you be staying here this evening?" she asked. "I mean to say that we will have a few more questions, and in any event since Todd's telephone was taken, we have to assume that his killers know he spoke to you last, presumably about his meeting with Mr. Givens and the disk. Makes you a prime target."

"I'll stay until morning."

"And then what, sir?" Green asked, his eyes drooping as if he just heard the saddest thing in his life. "Will you give us a heads up, because frankly we're at a loss as to what is happening, or as Mrs. Van Buren rightly demands: why and by whom and for what end purpose?"

"Of course," McGarvey said, and everyone, including the distraught Elizabeth, knew he was lying.

ELEVEN

□

Remington's Empire-style house with white Romanesque columns was on Whitehaven Street between the Danish and Italian embassies. Its furnishings were straight out of an *Architectural Digest* article on how the British gentry lived. The money for almost everything, including the Bentley, came from his wife, Colleen, of the New York Moons, whose fortune though slightly smaller than Donald Trump's was of longer duration; she was the great-granddaughter of one of the turn-of-the-century robber barons.

She'd married her husband because of his British title—his father had been the ninth Earl of Paxton—and because of his accent, which she considered pure class. And he had married her because of her money; his father had squandered on gambling what little money the family had left, losing the country mansion finally to back taxes when Gordon was ten. He'd been sent to an uncle in London and had been forced to work his way through Oxford, mostly by a series of illegal but brilliant scams, including a numbers racket, the details of which he'd learned from watching old American gangster movies. If anything, he'd always been a quick study.

It was shortly before five in the afternoon when he emerged from his bedroom suite in his brocaded dressing gown to find his wife heading out the door. She came back and pecked him on the cheek.

"Don't wait cocktails for me, I'll be in town."

"Kennedy Center?" he asked indifferently. Because of her family she was on several boards, including the Kennedy Center Foundation, which was the money-raising arm of the center. Tall, for a woman, slender with a narrow face but wide, chocolate eyes like Audrey Hepburn's, she had conquered the Washington social scene within the year after she and Roland had married and moved down from New York.

She nodded with just as much indifference. "Don't forget we're at Senator Worley's reception at eight and afterward we need to pop in at the Chinese embassy, their new ambassador has arrived."

Her unspoken message was for Gordon to behave himself and stay at least reasonably sober. At fifty he was already beginning to develop one of the vices that had led to his father's downfall; drinking every day, starting usually around noon, sometimes earlier, but normally not to such an extent that he was falling down drunk. Not yet anyway.

"Sure," he said. "See you in a couple of hours."

She nodded then left.

Remington stood in the vestibule for a long moment, alone as in reality he'd always been since his father's death, listening to nothing. The cook and housekeeper did not live in the house and were off for the evening and he had two hours alone now to invent some sort of strategy for the next stage of the damage control, the tone of which would depend on what was in Givens's computer.

He headed back to his study, hesitating for just a moment at the wet bar in the alcove between the kitchen and living room. Today, or at least this afternoon until he talked to Roland, he needed his wits about him. All his wits.

The primary parts of the problem—Josh Givens and Todd Van Buren—had been taken care of in a totally satisfactory manner, which had given him some much needed time. Today at the office his day had been consumed by the Baghdad contracts, which Roland was on site to finalize, so he'd had no chance until this moment to look at the things Kangas and Mustapha had brought him.

Sitting down at the antique Rosewood desk that his mother had liberated from the estate and from whom he'd liberated it after she'd been placed in a public dole nursing home outside London, he unlocked a bottom file drawer and took out the *Washington Post* reporter's laptop and BlackBerry, plus the CIA officer's cell phone and the disk Givens had handed over at the hotel, as well as the digital recording of the conversation between the two men.

He began with the recorded conversation at the hotel, sitting back and listening to it several times to make sure he missed nothing, especially not the reactions of the young CIA officer.

If nothing else Administrative Solutions under Sandberger had the well-deserved reputation for thoroughness. No messy shoot-outs in which innocent bystanders were gunned down. No trips to the Hill to answer intrusive questions by some congressional subcommittee. No tax audits by the IRS. No complaints from any foreign government. And damned few disaffected employees walking out the door threatening to *tell all*. In fact, Admin had remained beneath the radar of the media. Until now.

He'd argued against taking on Foster's Friday Club as a client, but Roland had been adamant to do just that, arguing that the club's powerful members and connections would lead to a lot of lucrative contracts.

"We can't lose," he'd promised.

Except that the media was all over the club and Admin was starting to come into the reflected glare. Something they didn't want or need. Look what all the media attention had done for Ron Hachette and his company Task Force One. Some of his people had been brought under indictment for murdering supposedly innocent civilians in Baghdad. And Hachette himself was still under intense security by Justice.

What Givens had told Van Buren at the restaurant was as bad as they thought it would be, based on the information they figured the reporter had managed to gather over the past several months.

But Remington felt the first sense of buoyancy listening to the young CIA officer's reaction. Van Buren had been, at the very least, skeptical, as he had every right to be. What Givens had told him was nothing short of fanciful—except of course for the fact that everything he'd said, plus much, much more, was true. He'd not yet stumbled upon the most important aspects of the Friday Club's activities, especially not the reasons for what had been done and what was being done, nor the ultimate goals.

Science fiction, had been Remington's initial reaction when Sandberger had brought him into the Friday Club's fold. And even at that Remington suspected that he hadn't been told the half of it.

Setting the recorder aside, he fiddled with the reporter's BlackBerry, but after a few minutes finding only a long list of telephone numbers with nothing more than cryptic notations after each, along with several dozen Web sites, which he didn't want to bother looking up at this point, he moved on to the laptop.

It was a high-end Toshiba, slim, lightweight, and wide open. After booting up, then hitting the file manager, Remington's mouth dropped open. He was inside with no encryption program, not even a simple password to block access, which told him that Givens was either a man highly confident in the power he wielded as a newspaper reporter, or incredibly naïve, or terribly stupid, or all three.

Out of more than three hundred documents, fully one third of them had the notation "FC" in front of them: FC: Foster; FC: Weitman; FC: DoD; FC: Pentagon; FC: Homeland Security; FC: Atlanta—which Remington realized were files that involved the Friday Club and its members and associations.

Opening the FC: McCann file, he was struck dumb after the first page or so and he sat back in his chair to catch his breath. Givens had somehow stumbled onto payments made to the now deceased CIA deputy director of operations by the club to a Cayman Islands account from something called Littoral Associates, Ltd., which had been suggested by Sandberger two years ago.

The FC: Pentagon file contained similar lists of payments to several important generals in various accounts, mostly in Switzerland.

The FC: Atlanta file contained a detailed account of a highly complex and still ongoing program of gerrymandering that to this point had resulted in swinging seven of Georgia's districts from solid Democrat to Republican. The manipulations had not helped in the last presidential election, but there was little doubt in Remington's mind that given time the political climate in the state would change. It was about the long term, something Remington and Sandberger had not discussed in any detail. Admin's job, vis-à-vis the Friday Club, was to provide security. Keep the media at bay. Keep the walls unbreached.

Keep a lid on investigators like Givens and his friend Van Buren.

But this now, this information in the reporter's computer went beyond the pale. Givens had gotten far too close.

Remington telephoned Sandberger's sat phone, which was answered on the second ring.

"Yes."

"It's Gordon, we need to talk."

"Trouble?" Sandberger asked without hesitation.

"It has the potential."

"I'll be at the Steigenberger, first thing in the morning."

"See you then," Remington said, and he phoned his night office number to arrange for his travel to Frankfurt in such a way that he would not miss Senator Worley's reception or the do at the Chinese embassy.

TWELVE

It was ten in the evening when McGarvey's cell phone vibrated silently in his pocket. Katy had been transferred to one of the rooms in the visiting VIP building and he'd been sitting next to her bed for the past three hours watching her troubled sleep. He wanted to reach out to her with more than just a touch; he wanted to let her inside his soul so that she could see exactly who he was. No artifice, no hiding of any truth no matter how ugly, just his real self with all the complexities and contradictions of a man who had lived the life he had.

He went out into the corridor and answered the call, the ID was blank but he knew that it was Otto. "What do you have for me?"

"How're Mrs. M and Elizabeth?"

"Both sleeping."

"How about you?" Otto asked, an edginess to his voice. He was worried, just as everyone was, which way McGarvey was going to jump. Because Mac was going to jump and everybody knew it.

"Impatient," McGarvey said. He was being short with his friend, but he couldn't wait around down here much longer. He was on the verge of exploding, and yet he knew that he had to hang on; when the shit started to happen it would have to be done right. He wasn't going to lose his life because he had blinders on and was rushing things.

"Sandberger's in Baghdad, but his pilot filed a flight plan for Frankfurt. Apparently it's a layover, because no flight plan has been filed beyond that."

"Any idea where he'll be staying? Or for how long?"

"He's been to Frankfurt four times in the past two years. Twice he's disappeared into the city, apparently staying someplace other than a hotel, and the other two times he's stayed at the Steigenberger Airport Hotel, each time for one night only."

"Bodyguards?"

"He almost always travels with muscle, and over the past eighteen months or so it's been the same two. Carl Alphonse, who was a New York City SWAT team commander until he retired to go to work for Admin, and Brody Hanson, who was kicked out of Delta Forces for reason or reasons unknown, except that he was discharged an E-7 under other than honorable conditions. Both men had the highest grades for marksmanship, hand-to-hand, infiltration, and exfiltration—about what you'd expect from guys like these."

"Any idea why he's flying out to Germany all of a sudden?" McGarvey asked. "Meeting someone?"

"My guess would be Remington, but I'm not coming up with any air reservations yet," Otto said.

"How about flight plans?"

"Admin has only the one Gulfstream. So if it's Remington he'll be traveling commercial. Maybe under an assumed name. Anyway my babies are chewing on it." Rencke's babies were his computers and some of the most sophisticated programs on the planet.

Now that it was beginning, now that he was preparing to go back into the field, he began to calm down; his nerves had been jumping all over the place since he'd gotten word of Todd's assassination, but now they were steadying out. He held out his right hand, palm down, his fingers spread, and he was rock solid.

"I need to get over there by morning, at least before noon. Non-commercial. A clean diplomatic passport, no questions asked by anyone on the seventh floor, at least not until I'm finished. Shouldn't take more than a few minutes."

"To do what, Mac?" Otto asked. "Lean on Sandberger? The guy's a tough son of a bitch. And if the German federales catch you carrying—or worse, if you shoot someone—it'll get back to Adkins at the speed of light."

"And he'd have to sit up and take notice," McGarvey said. "We're talking about the murder of my son-in-law. The son-in-law of a former CIA director. That carries some weight."

"Yes, it does," Rencke said. "From both sides of the fence. Your shooting days are supposed to be over. You're too personally involved this time. It's expected that you'll back off and let the Bureau handle it."

"I've always been personally involved," McGarvey said, bitterly. "All my life." And he knew that he should be asking himself if it was worth it, but at this moment the question was moot.

Rencke was silent for a long time, and when he came back he sounded sad, resigned, as if he knew that no matter what McGarvey did, no matter what action his old friend took, he would be there for him, as he had been for years now. Mac was family, and except for his wife, Louise, his only family.

"A Gulfstream and crew will be ready at Andrews within the hour. Your passport will be aboard. What else do you need?"

"Give me one hour on the ground in Frankfurt, then call Dave Whittaker and tell him I might need some backup." Whittaker, who was a stand-up guy, was the deputy director of operations when Mac was the DCI. Now, under Adkins, he'd become the deputy director of the agency. His was a steady if stern hand, and although he'd never completely approved of McGarvey's tradecraft, he'd always supported his boss one hundred ten percent.

"Shit, Mac," Rencke said after a long moment. "You're not thinking straight. Honest injun."

"You're probably right," McGarvey agreed. "But I didn't create the situation." The hard edge was back in his voice, and in his heart.

He shook his head, and the only thing he could think of were the bastards, the dirty rotten bastards. And he could see the son of a bitch putting the insurance round into the back of Todd's head.

"I didn't start it," he said bleakly.

"I'll be here for you."

"Thank you," McGarvey said and he broke the connection. And for a long time he stood in the semidark corridor, the only light coming from the exit sign at the door to the stairs, and thought frankly about his life, about his contributions to the safety of the United States. Thinking about his career that way seemed almost filled with hubris, and yet he was proud of what he had done—or most of what he had done. And now he was back at it, only this time his motives were a whole hell of a lot more personal.

Katy was still sleeping when he went back into the room, took a small leather satchel, about the size of a dopp kit, out of their luggage, and went across the hall to one of the empty rooms where he switched on a nightstand light after he'd closed the door.

She had watched him open the floor safe in their bedroom back in Florida as she was packing and pull out a 9mm Wilson semiautomatic pistol with custom grips and sight, three spare magazines of ammunition, and a suppressor.

He holstered the pistol at the small of his back and, turning out the light, went back across the hall and returned the kit to their luggage.

For a long time he stood near the bed, watching his wife's sleeping face. She didn't look exactly at peace, but she was finally getting some rest. He hoped she wasn't dreaming.

Leaning down he kissed her lightly on the cheek, took his small overnight bag from the closet, and went downstairs.

Liz was waiting in the darkened dayroom, sitting in the corner smoking a cigarette, something she hadn't done for a long time.

McGarvey held up across the room from her. "What are you doing, sweetheart?" he asked.

"Waiting for you," she said.

"What about Pete and Dan Green?"

"I sent them back to Langley. They were done here and they knew it. So I didn't get any argument." Liz stubbed out her cigarette. "Anyway, you don't have to keep watching over your shoulder for them. They won't be there. They understand the score, and in fact Pete said to wish you good luck."

McGarvey put down his bag by the door and went across to her. "I'm so sorry. I wish—"

Liz looked up at him with so much anguish and such total devastation written all over her face that she took his breath away. "When we raised our right hands and took the oath, we understood the risks," she said. "You know this probably better than anyone else." She didn't avert her eyes. "How did you handle it?"

"Sometimes not very well," McGarvey replied, thinking back to the day Katy had given him her ultimatum—me or the CIA—and he had run away.

She looked away for just a moment, finally, maybe seeing some of the anguish and devastation on his face. "Do you know what's keeping me on track? The only thing?"

"Audie?"

She looked up at her father and a brief smile passed her mouth.

"Her too. But it's you, Daddy. And Mother." She shook her head. "Christ, there never was such a couple, or ever will be."

McGarvey had no idea what to say. But he leaned over and brushed a kiss on her cheek.

"The gray Chevy van, government plates, out front. No one will notice. Keys are in it."

McGarvey nodded. "Keep your head down, sweetheart, this is bound to get ugly."

Her eyes tightened. "Oh, I hope so."

And McGarvey left.

THIRTEEN

The airport shuttle dropped Remington off under the sweeping portico of the five-star Frankfurt Steigenberger Hotel around two in the afternoon. Although he had slept reasonably well in first class on the Lufthansa flight over, he'd been restive, worried about what was coming next.

With Kirk McGarvey now in the mix, the assassinations of Van Buren and Givens would have to be explained to the satisfaction of the FBI, and of course the CIA, which was one of the objects of the exercise in addition to silencing the nosy reporter. And he needed to impress on Roland what was at stake for both of them, for Admin's continued existence, even for their personal freedom. He had no desire to end up in a federal prison somewhere because Roland refused to keep his eye on the ball.

He carried only a small overnight bag with a clean shirt and underwear and his toiletries—because he was only staying the night, taking the morning flight back—plus his laptop with all the material from Givens's computer and a BlackBerry, encrypted. He figured there would be little danger crossing borders with the material; he was just an ordinary businessman who'd popped across the pond for a meeting. No one bothered with commerce.

He spotted Sandberger seated across the lobby, reading a newspaper, but went directly over to the front desk where he checked in and sent his overnight bag up to his suite with a bellman, whom he tipped well, but not so well that the man would remember him.

The hotel wasn't terribly busy at this hour, though more guests were checking in than out, and heading across the expansive lobby he spotted Roland's bodyguards, sitting fifteen feet away from their boss; Alphonse with his back to the elevators, and Hanson with his back to the lobby doors. Their attention constantly shifted, though not so noticeably unless you were looking for it. Nor did they stand out physically. Both men were of average build, with pleasant faces, neatly trimmed hair, expensive if casual European-cut clothing—open-necked shirts, khakis, and double-vented sport coats—but they were well-trained killers. They were among Admin's best and highest paid operators, and therefore the most loyal.

Sandberger, too, was a deceptive man, with narrow shoulders, slight build, sparkling blue eyes, ash blond hair, and a pleasant small-town smile and demeanor. But he was a steely-eyed businessman with an astute understanding not only of the American political scene but of international affairs. And like his bodyguards he was a killer.

Remington had been with him two years ago in Kabul to interview three local recruits, all of whom had served as President Hamid Karzai's personal bodyguards, but were looking for fatter paychecks—or so they'd claimed.

They were supposed to meet in a tea shop in the area known as the Wazir Akbar Kahn a few blocks from the National Bank of Pakistan, across the street from an alley with rug, silver, and copper merchants, but Sandberger was spooked and he told the three that the shop was not acceptable, that they would have to meet tomorrow in another place, to be specified.

Almost immediately Remington sensed something was wrong, not only from Sandberger's body language but from the sudden rise in tension in the three men, and he stepped back, his hand automatically going under his jacket for his Beretta 92F.

"If this all works out for us, you'll have a nice future right here in Kabul, if that's what you want," Sandberger said, pleasantly, his voice betraying nothing of what Remington damned well knew was about to go down.

They hadn't taken their seats yet and were standing around the small wrought-iron table under the striped awning, traffic busy on the anonymous street. The three were flustered, and one of them—Remington couldn't remember his name except that he was a tough-looking bastard who wasn't to be trusted for all the tea in China—glanced to the left toward the merchant's alley, and it was at that moment Sandberger moved, lightning fast, decisive, and final.

Before Remington or the three Afghans could move, Sandberger had whipped out his razor sharp KA-BAR, slit the nearest man's throat ear-to-ear with an almost casual backhand swipe, pivoted lightly on his heel to plunge the broad combat blade into the second man's right eye socket, burying the weapon to the hilt, and even before the first man had crumpled to the dusty floor stuck the knife into the heart of the third man.

Remington, who was fully combat trained, had never seen anything like it in his life, not even in the Sandhurst training films, or from visualizing the field ops his sergeant had told him about. And he'd always considered his reflexes reasonably good, but at that moment he knew that neither his reflexes nor his killer instinct were up to Sandberger's.

"Let's get out of here," Sandberger had said, calmly as if he were suggesting they go catch a bus.

He wiped the blood from his knife on a paper napkin, sheathed it, and, smiling pleasantly at the horrified tea shop patrons, sauntered up the street to where they had parked their Range Rover.

Remington at his side—then as now.

Sandberger looked up from the *Hochster Kreisbatt* newspaper, a big, friendly grin on his pleasant face, his eyes lit up as if he were seeing an old friend for the first time in years, and it was always the same with him. "Gordon, good of you to fly over on such short notice."

"We needed to talk," Remington said, taking the chair across the broad coffee table from his boss. Very often, when they met away from the office like this, Sandberger chose hotel lobbies for their anonymity, or if he were stateside they would meet at Admin's training camp in the low mountains of northern New Mexico.

"Would you like some tea or coffee?" Sandberger, always the gentleman, asked.

"No." Remington booted up his laptop and when he'd opened the FC files, turned the computer around and pushed it across the table. "Take a look at this first. This is how far Givens managed to get."

Sandberger gazed at Remington, almost paternally. "I know now why I chose you as my partner. You're the detail man, something I've never been, as you well know. I like field action, and you like keeping all the balls up in the air. Never a misstep, right?"

"You need to keep your eye on this ball, Roland, before it jumps up and bites us on the arse."

Sandberger chuckled. "Mixed metaphor, old man," he said, but then he drew the laptop closer and started going through the files.

Remington glanced over at Alphonse who was staring directly at him. The bodyguard was Sandberger's, not Admin's, personal pit bull, as was Hanson, and he had no doubt that if he made any sort of an untoward move they would be all over him in an instant. Alphonse smiled pleasantly, and Remington got the impression that he was looking into the eyes of a cobra, swaying, distracting its enemy before pouncing.

Good men Roland had recruited and continued to recruit. Classy, like their boss.

Sandberger had gone through several of Givens's FC files and he looked up. "Is the rest of this stuff more of the same?"

"For the most part, yes."

"You haven't shared this with Robert or any of the others, have you?" Sandberger asked, referring to Robert Foster and members of the Friday Club.

"I wanted to talk to you first, give you the heads up. But they will have to be warned. No telling what'll happen next with McGarvey on the loose."

"All in good time, but it's exactly how we planned it, Gordon. McGarvey is considered to be a loose cannon by the CIA, the Bureau, and any number of congressmen—actually, the sort of man I'd like to hire."

"He'll make a move, and it's bound to be dramatic."

"The more dramatic the better." Sandberger glanced at the computer screen. "He doesn't have this material, thanks to your quick action." He smiled. "Actually, you were brilliant, you know. But there's more."

"You still want to go through with it?" Remington asked. "We'll have to kill him and there will be repercussions."

"Indeed."

Remington had no real idea why he'd come over here, except that he thought he had more respect for McGarvey than Roland did. They'd read the same files on the man's impressive career, and had come to the same conclusion that he would have to be neutralized in such a way that he would be no further threat to the Friday Club. That had been Foster's demand. McGarvey had already caused them enough grief—even though he probably wasn't aware of it—and Foster wanted the man to be muzzled. Permanently.

"We can't just shoot him down in public," Remington had argued. "It wouldn't be easy. He was the DCI, for goodness sake, and he's sharp as a tack. As good or better than any two of our people."

"Oh, I don't know about that. He's in his fifties. A bit long of tooth for the lightning-quick reaction. Killing him could be done."

Remington looked away for a moment. He had a great deal of respect for Roland, but he often had feelings about things. Hunches. A tickling of the hairs at the back of his neck, warning him that something was coming his way. But Roland was a straight-forward, stand-up guy who relied on three things: his own intellect, his own experience, and the collective intelligence and experience of the people he surrounded himself with. Admin's staff at the Washington office as well as out in the field numbered nearly two hundred. And every single one of them, from Remington to the data-entry clerks, had an open door to the boss, 24/7. Sandberger formed his own opinions, but he listened to everyone.

"Now give me a précis of everything you know," Sandberger said. "And hold nothing back."

FOURTEEN

The CIA's Gulfstream had flown east across the Atlantic at thirty-four thousand feet, the ride smooth enough for McGarvey, whose mind was seething with possibilities, to actually get a few hours' sleep. When he'd finally opened his eyes the former Northwest Airlines attendant Debbie Miller was there pouring a cup of coffee from a carafe and adding a dollop of a good Napoleon brandy.

He smiled wanly. "Evidently my reputation has preceded me."

"We were instructed to take very good care of you, Mr. Director," she said, her smile radiant. "Would you care for something to eat? Breakfast?"

"What time is it?"

"Just coming up on eight-thirty in the morning in Washington, and two-thirty in the afternoon in Frankfurt."

McGarvey glanced out the window. He could see what looked like farmland interspersed by wooded areas. They were descending, he could feel it in his ears. "How far out are we?"

"Less than twenty minutes."

He held up his coffee cup. "This'll do for now. And thank the flight crew for a smooth ride."

"Our pleasure, Mr. Director," she said and she went forward to the galley, as McGarvey looked out the window at the German countryside.

He'd been here, many times before, but the Germany of his youth was different from the combined Germanys now, deeply into the worldwide recession, Berlin looking inward rather than global, more concerned about the economy than some hot or cold war with the Russians.

That was in a much simpler, if more deadly past. Now the major threats to much of Europe from Germany east, and especially north-east, were the encroachments by Muslims who by and large refused to assimilate into whatever culture they landed in the middle of. Holland and Denmark and Germany were supposed to change their centuries-old traditions and mind-sets to accommodate the immigrants from the east; upheaval and insensitivity were the new watchwords.

Against that background noise, McGarvey was fighting his own battles that most recently had begun in Mexico City, then Pyongyang, and now Washington.

Two names had been on Turov's laptop; McCann, who Todd had shot to death and who had very probably been connected to the Friday Club, possibly financially, and Sandberger, whose Admin perhaps only supplied security.

Mac intended to push the man in public, because men of Sandberger's persona very often reacted badly under that sort of pressure, and how they reacted could say reams about their real agendas.

If he was correct in his thinking, Givens had been assassinated because he'd gotten too close to Foster and the Friday Club, and Todd had been murdered in part because of his contact with the newspaper-man, but also because of his father-in-law. They were trying to neutralize a thorn in their side. Of course that logic only worked if there was a connection between Mexico City, Pyongyang, and now this.

And that connection eluded him.

His sat phone burred softly in the pocket of his jacket, hung up forward. Debbie brought it back to him on the third ring and re-treated as he answered.

"You gotta be close," Rencke said.

"Fifteen minutes. Did you find out where Sandberger's staying?"

"He's back at the Steigenberger, just for the one day and night," Rencke said. "His crew filed a flight plan back to Baghdad for first thing in the morning. And Remington is there, too, staying for just the night. Got in late on a Lufthansa flight that was supposed to touch down at eleven-forty, but didn't actually get there until around one-thirty."

"Anyone with him?"

"No. And I woulda found out sooner, except he's traveling under a work name—Donald Higgs—on a damned fine Canadian passport. First-class work. I was impressed, and I'm looking down a couple of tracks to see how he managed, 'cause there's really a Don Higgs in Ottawa, a lawyer, same description, similar UK background."

"So it's just Remington and Sandberger and two bodyguards."

"Right."

"One hour on the ground then call Whittaker," McGarvey said, and he broke the connection and laid the phone on the seat next to him.

He wasn't going to shoot anyone this time, unless he was given no other choice, nor did he want to damage the four men. That would come later. He was counting on the eventual need for it. For now he just wanted to get their attention, and hopefully the attention of the German Federal Police. Make it official so it would be tough for his coming to Germany to be swept under the rug later.

It was a starting point, an important one, because for once in his career he had absolutely no idea where this was headed. But no power on earth could turn him away from taking it to the finish.

They touched down at Frankfurt and taxied over to the terminal routinely used for state visits by members of foreign governments, and McGarvey hesitated at the open hatch. The pilot and copilot were looking at him.

"If you don't hear from me within two hours, go back to Washington," he told them.

"We can wait here for as long as you want, Mr. Director," the pilot said.

"I appreciate that, Captain. But if I'm not back aboard by then, it'll mean I'm probably in jail."

"Does this have anything to do with your son-in-law?"

"Everything to do with it."

"Then good hunting, sir," Debbie said.

Two stern-faced customs officers in uniform were waiting for him just inside the terminal, that just now was empty, and they scrutinized his diplomatic passport that identified him by his actual name. "Can you tell us the nature of your visit, Mr. McGarvey?" the older of the two asked.

"It's routine State Department," McGarvey said. "I've come over to have a word with the president of an American contractor firm doing business in Baghdad. Administrative Solutions. Guy's name is Roland Sandberger."

Both customs officers stiffened, their change in attitude barely perceptible, but there nonetheless. "Do you expect any difficulty?"

"I don't think so."

"Where and when will this meeting take place?"

"At the Steigenberger as soon as I can get a cab over," McGarvey said.

"The shuttle will take you. Will you be staying the night?"

McGarvey had left his overnight bag aboard the aircraft. "No. Just an hour, perhaps less."

It was perfectly clear that the customs officers were nervous, especially the older one, who probably had more field experience than his partner, and perhaps because he knew McGarvey by reputation. The one action they could not take, because of his diplomatic immunity, was search him for a weapon.

His passport was returned to him, and the officers stepped aside. "The shuttle is just in front. We hope your visit is as productive as it is dull."

"Me too," McGarvey said, and he went outside and got into the Steigenberger van, which headed immediately for the hotel.

On the short ride over from the VIP terminal he'd made a conscious effort to get out of his head the image of Todd's shot-to-hell body lying on the gurney in All Saints. He wanted to go into this meeting with clear eyes, and steady nerves, or else it would be next to impossible for him not to take someone apart.

The lobby was not particularly large, though well appointed, and not very busy at this hour. The front desk and concierge services were to the left, and pausing for just a moment, he spotted Sandberger and another man he took to be Remington seated across a broad coffee table from each other. Sandberger's muscle were seated a short distance away, left and right, in positions to cover the front desk and elevators from one direction, and the main doors to the portico from the other.

The one facing the doors said something, and Sandberger looked up, startled for just a moment, but then his expression and manner turned wary, but curious, as McGarvey walked over. Remington looked as if he were a deer caught in headlights, but for just a brief instant, recovering nearly as fast as his boss had. He, too, was guarded.

One of the bodyguards started to rise, but Sandberger motioned him back.

"Good afternoon," McGarvey said.

"You come as something of a surprise, Mr. Director," Sandberger said pleasantly, but cautiously. "No coincidence, I suspect."

By now the customs officers had contacted their superiors, who would be querying the Federal Intelligence Service, the BND, as to what the former director of the CIA was doing in the country on a diplomatic passport. And what information did they have on the American contractor company Administrative Solutions, and what one or more of its officers were doing here.

"No," McGarvey said. He sat down in one of the easy chairs facing the two men, as well as the front entrance. He was wearing a kahki sport coat and he made a show of unbuttoning it, in part to convey the message that he was armed and ready to use his weapon, and in part to distract himself for a second so that he didn't just jump up and take all four of them apart.

"What are you doing here, then?"

"I want to know who killed my son-in-law."

Sandberger and Remington exchanged a quizzical look and Sandberger spread his hands. "I'm sorry, I don't know what you're talking about. But if you've lost someone in your family, I'm sorry. Was he in the business?"

"A *Washington Post* investigative reporter and his family were also murdered, after he'd spoken to my son-in-law."

Sandberger did not respond.

"It had to do with an investigation of the Friday Club. I'd like to know what connection you and your company has with Robert Foster."

"Sorry, I don't know what you're talking about."

"You're a liar, of course," McGarvey said, letting a sharp edge into his tone. "And a murderer."

Sandberger had been drinking coffee. He leaned forward, picked up his cup with a steady hand, and eyed McGarvey as he took a sip. "You're retired, aren't you? A little old to be running around accusing people of things. One of these days your reflexes will go bad, be a little off, and something will jump up and bite you in the ass."

"How about Alexander Turov? That name ring a bell?"

Sandberger said nothing, and Remington was holding himself in check.

"He knew your name," McGarvey said. "I took it from his laptop after I killed him in Tokyo."

Sandberger just shook his head, but it was obvious to McGarvey that Turov's name was familiar to him.

"The Russian was an interesting man. He was an expediter, nothing more, while your firm fields some of the shooters." McGarvey looked pointedly at the bodyguards. "I killed him because it was my job, nothing more than that. But when I find out who assassinated my son-in-law, it'll be more than a job."

Remington started to say something but Sandberger held him off with a gesture.

"Thanks for the warning, if that's what it was. But I had nothing to do with your son-in-law's tragic death."

A pair of husky, Teutonic-looking men, square, solidly chiseled features, one of them completely bald, both of them wearing suits cut a little large in the middle to conceal the bulges made by weapons carried in shoulder holsters, came in from the portico. They were obviously federal cops.

"Watch your backs, gentlemen," McGarvey said. "Every time you look over your shoulders I'll be there, until one of you fucks up and then I'll kill you."

As the BND officers started over, McGarvey took out his sat phone, snapped photographs of Sandberger, Remington, and Sandberger's muscle, then hit speed dial for Rencke's number.

The cops were five feet away when the connection was made and McGarvey transmitted the photos. "Call Dave," he said, and he laid the phone on the coffee table, stood up and spread his arms and legs, all the while smiling at Sandberger.

FIFTEEN

□

"That won't be necessary, Herr McGarvey," the bald officer said, his English accented but good. He offered his ID booklet, which identified him as Hans Mueller, Bundesnachrichtendienst embossed around a stylized eagle.

He was a desk jockey and not an actual spy, or shooter, and Mc-Garvey relaxed. "What can I do for you?"

"Just a few questions," Mueller said. He glanced at Sandberger and the others. "I assume that none of you have carried weapons into Germany."

Sandberger shook his head.

"I'm armed," McGarvey said, and the cops zeroed in on him. He had their attention.

"Will you surrender your weapon at this time?"

"Of course," McGarvey said pleasantly. He took his Wilson from its holster at the small of his back, ejected the magazine and carefully levered the one round out of the firing chamber, and handed the pistol over handle-first, then the magazine and bullet.

Mueller glanced at the weapon. "You know that you have broken German law by bringing this here."

"You might want these, too," McGarvey said, glancing at Sandberger, as he took the spare magazine and suppressor out of his jacket pocket and handed them over along with his sat phone.

Mueller wasn't happy, but the other cop acted as if he were confused, and neither one of them seemed to know what to do with the pistol and especially not the silencer.

For a seeming eternity no one moved, and McGarvey kept asking himself why these idiots weren't taking the next step, and frisking Sandberger and Remington and especially Sandberger's bodyguards. The fact that Sandberger's muscle were shooters stood out like a neon sign. Stupid lapses like that could get a field man killed in a hurry; it was why they were desk jockeys. Most BND officers McGarvey had met were damned good.

He glanced over at Sandberger and the others and he could see that they were thinking the same thing.

But the moment ended when Mueller handed his partner the pistol, ammunition, and silencer. "You'll have to come with us now. Your diplomatic passport does not cover this."

"No, I suppose not," McGarvey said.

"You're not going to cause trouble, sir?" Mueller said.

"You have my gun," McGarvey said, and he turned again to Sand-berger. "As I said, watch your backs, because I'll be there."

McGarvey rode in the backseat of a slate gray Mercedes C350, the younger BND officer driving, traffic heavy as they skirted downtown and headed up to the north side of the city.

Mueller turned and looked back. "What is your relationship with those four men in the hotel lobby, Herr McGarvey?"

"I came over to ask them a few questions."

"Concerning what?"

"The assassination of my son-in-law, who was a CIA officer. He and my daughter ran the CIA's training center."

Mueller's eyebrows rose. "The Farm. Yes, I know of this place in Virginia. And we know that he was shot to death outside Washington. And you came to Germany because you think Herr Sandberger's company had something to do with it?"

McGarvey's opinion of the BND desk jockeys went up a notch. They might not have been field officers, but they had done their homework before coming over to the Steigenberger to find out why the former chief of the CIA had come to Germany on what was likely a fake diplomatic passport.

"It's possible they might have information I need."

The cop digested this for a moment. "And what exactly was meant by your comment for those men to watch their backs, you'll be there."

McGarvey looked out the window. They'd left the skyscrapers be-hind and had turned off the busy autobahn into a pleasant area of apart-ment buildings, some new and some old probably dating back to before the war. "Did you know that two of his men were probably armed?"

"I asked you a question."

McGarvey turned back. "So did I, and that'll be 'sir' to you." They were leaning and he was leaning back. He had wanted to make two points here: one was putting Sandberger on notice, and the second was to place his suspicions into the record of at least one government's law enforcement or intelligence apparatus so that when he came into the CIA's spotlight, dealing with him would no longer be a simple matter of the dismissal of a grief-stricken father-in-law.

A bleak expression came into Mueller's eyes, as if his hopes of an easy assignment had just been dashed, and he turned around to face forward.

They finally turned down Homberger Landstrasse, another reasonably pleasant tree-lined street of some apartment buildings, and what might have been small government installations or military barracks, called *Kaserne*, but of the old-fashioned sort, and McGarvey suddenly knew where they were taking him.

"I didn't know the BND was using the Drake Kaserne," he said. The series of mostly low buildings behind a tall iron fence had first been occupied in 1930 by the German army. After the war, from 1956 to 1992, the U.S. Third Armored Division had headquartered here, until the German government took it back using it to house various agencies, including the customs unit of the Federal Border Police.

He'd been here once, before the Germanys were reunited, when he had stalked a Russian KGB general hiding out in East Berlin. It was a bad period, which he didn't care to remember, except that it had stuck in his mind then as now that Germans, at least at the governmental level, were still trying to live down the Nazi era, and never knew quite how.

"Yes, you were here, I saw that in your record," Mueller said. "So, you have a very good memory, which will be excellent for our purposes."

They pulled up to a gate at the *Kaserne*, which was opened by a uniformed civilian guard with a sidearm under the watchful eye of another guard just at the doorway to the security office.

"May I call my consulate here in Frankfurt?"

"I'm sure that whoever you sent those photographs to will have already notified your people," Mueller said. "And we'll find out who you called."

McGarvey couldn't help himself, and he smiled. "I don't think so."

"We have some pretty good people on this side of the pond, too, you know, you arrogant bastard."

Another little bit of the puzzle dropped in place for McGarvey. "What exactly is it that Administrative Solutions does for the German government? Can you at least give me a hint?"

But Mueller said nothing, until they stopped at a nondescript, one-story building near the rear of the installation, and he and his partner got out and Mueller opened the rear door.

McGarvey got out and went into the building, which looked very much like a military interrogation and holding center, and was led down the corridor to a small room furnished only with a metal table and two chairs. The walls were bare concrete, the floor plainly tiled, with a single dim lightbulb set into the ceiling and covered with wire mesh.

He sat down at the table and Mueller sat across from him; his partner leaned against the wall beside the door.

"Shall we begin with why you came to Germany under a false passport, but aboard a CIA aircraft?" Mueller said.

"To talk to Roland Sandberger, as I've told you."

"Why did you bring a pistol?"

"I always travel armed. Have for years."

"And what about the silencer?" Mueller asked. "Were you planning on killing Herr Sandberger?"

McGarvey shrugged. "Only if I felt that it was necessary."

"What would have constituted a necessity?"

McGarvey took a moment to answer. "I had a reasonable expectation that either he or his bodyguards would have tried to assassinate me."

Mueller glanced over his shoulder at his partner then turned back. "I see. And now what are your expectations, Herr McGarvey?"

"That you've just run out of questions. That you'll be reporting this to your superiors in Pullach. That you will not interfere with the movements of Sandberger or his employees. That this incident has been reported to the consul general here in Frankfurt, and most likely via some old-boy connection to Langley. And that sometime tomorrow someone will show up to fetch me."

Mueller was not happy.

"Have I left something out?"

"Fuck you," Mueller said, and he and his partner left the interrogation cell.

"And the horse you rode in on," McGarvey added.

SIXTEEN

It was around two the next afternoon when David Whittaker, the deputy director of the CIA, showed up at the Drake Kaserne and McGarvey was fetched from his VIP guest suite.

Since he'd not brought an overnight kit, he'd been supplied with pajamas and toiletries, had been fed a good wiener schnitzel with boiled potatoes and several bottles of dark Lowenbrau for dinner, and an equally good breakfast and lunch. Other than that he'd been left alone, though the morning English edition of the *International Herald-Tribune* had shown up at his door, and he'd had a television to watch, but no telephone.

Whittaker was dressed, as usual, in an old-fashioned three-piece suit, bow tie, and wingtips; his eyes wide behind his wire-rimmed glasses. He was the most moral man McGarvey had ever known, and stern because of it. His was just about the last of the old-school East Coast Presbyterians, the kind who had ruled the roost since the OSS days of World War II.

"You've become something of a problem," he said when McGarvey was brought to the dayroom, and they shook hands.

"I always have been," McGarvey said. When Mac was the DCI, Whittaker ran the Directorate of Operations, and had done a fine job. Now he had risen to his highest level in the Company; it wasn't likely that he would ever become the DCI, because he was too low key, not political enough. The U.S. was one of the few countries in which the top spy wasn't a professional intelligence officer, only an appointed, well-connected amateur, and for a long time morale at the CIA had been low. Especially these days when more than fifty percent of the Agency's employees had less than five years' experience.

"The Germans have released you into my custody," Whittaker said. "As you might guess a lot of strings had to be pulled at the highest levels."

"Thanks."

Whittaker gave him a bleak look. "So far this incident has not reached the White House. At least not officially—"

"Which incident is that, Dave?" McGarvey interrupted sharply. "My arrest here or Todd's assassination?"

"The Bureau has identified Todd's killers. They were Muslim extremists, members of one of al-Quaida's splinter cells in Laurel, Maryland."

"Bullshit," McGarvey said. He was trying to put a cap on his almost blind anger, and it was taking everything in his power.

Whittaker overrode him. "They were targeting CIA officers. It was the same group who made the hit just outside our main gate a few years back. Todd just happened to be in the wrong place at the wrong time."

"Arrests are expected any time now?"

"No," Whittaker said. "One of their bomb makers apparently screwed up yesterday and blew up the storefront mosque where they were at afternoon prayers. The rubble is being sifted for clues as to who was directing them."

"What about Givens?"

"He and his wife and child were killed in a home invasion, a simple robbery."

McGarvey tried to interrupt, but Whittaker held up a hand. "Two pairs of fingerprints were found in the apartment and the suspects are already in custody."

"They admitted it?"

"Not yet."

"They have alibis?"

Whittaker conceded the point. "It was to be expected. But they'll eventually come around."

"Unless they die under mysterious circumstances," McGarvey said. "Maybe they'll hang themselves in their cells." He shook his head. It was worse than he expected. "Christ."

"Todd's funeral is the day after tomorrow at Arlington. You'll be allowed to attend, of course, but before and afterward you'll be kept in custody."

"What am I being charged with?"

"Treason," Whittaker said, solemnly. "And that comes from the Justice Department."

McGarvey almost laughed.

"I'm told that President Haynes tried to hold you back; he even warned you. More than once. And he liked you. The new president does not." Whittaker shook his head. "Sorry, Mac, it's out of my hands."

"Are we talking about North Korea?" McGarvey asked. Last year a high-ranking Chinese intelligence officer had been assassinated, apparently by North Korean police in Pyongyang. China was threatening to attack, and Kim Jong Il was promising to launch three of his twelve nuclear weapons on Beijing, Seoul, and Tokyo. Millions of people would have died.

In desperation a North Korean intelligence officer had been smuggled into the U.S. where he'd come to ask for McGarvey's help proving that North Korea didn't order the assassination. And McGarvey had done just that, despite warnings from the White House not to get involved.

Whittaker nodded. "You made a lot of enemies."

"I stopped a war."

"That's up to the diplomats. It was felt at the time, and still is, that had you not interfered, our position in the region would have been strengthened."

"They were willing to risk a nuclear war for the sake of points?"

"Some of the president's advisers made a case for it."

McGarvey nodded after a long moment. "At least I'll get my day in court."

"In *camera* with no jury because of the sensitive nature of the material."

"What about Katy and Liz?"

"They're safe at the Farm," Whittaker said.

"Safe from who, Dave," McGarvey shot back. "Todd's killers were blown up, and the guys who killed Givens and his family are in jail. Who's left?"

Whittaker sidestepped the question. It was clear that he was extremely uncomfortable. He was doing his duty; he didn't have to like it. "Otto and his wife have disappeared; nobody knows where they are."

Somewhere in or near Washington, McGarvey guessed. With his laptop and a secure access to the web. Otto would want to stick around in case Mac needed help.

"Did you bring someone from housekeeping with you?" McGarvey asked, his anger rising. "Do you want to take me back in cuffs and shackles?"

Whittaker almost stepped back. "No," he said.

"They'll never prove treason against me, and you know it. In the meantime we still have a problem that's somehow connected between Mexico City and Pyongyang."

"The material on the disk we found in Todd's car was simply too fantastic to believe. You saw it; you can't tell me that you put any validity to what Givens was claiming."

"It wasn't the disk Givens gave my son-in-law."

"That would admit a conspiracy—"

"Right," McGarvey said, but suddenly he was tired, and he didn't give a damn. All he wanted now was to get back to Washington for

Todd's funeral, to be with Katy and their daughter, Liz, and with their granddaughter, Audie.

It was obvious that Whittaker felt essentially the same; he, too, was tired of this assignment, which probably seemed to him to be a waste of time.

"If it's any consolation, the Company will do everything within its power to defend you. I'm behind you, and so is most of the senior staff."

McGarvey nodded. "What does Carleton think about my chances?" Carleton Patterson was the CIA's general counsel and had held that position for at least ten years. His was always a reasoned opinion.

Whittaker shook his head. "Not good."

Left unsaid was that this was a hell of a way to end a distinguished career.

SEVENTEEN

□

At Andrews Air Force Base the CIA's Gulfstream with the same crew that had brought McGarvey over to Frankfurt in the first place taxied over to the government hangar and inside and the engines spooled down.

"Good luck, Mr. Director," Debbie said as McGarvey hesitated for just a moment at the hatch.

He nodded to the pilot and copilot and winked at the girl, then went down where a pair of U.S. marshals was waiting for him, badges hanging out of the lapel pockets of their suit coats. They were large men, alert, their jackets unbuttoned, earpiece comms units and sleeve mics.

For an awkward second or two the four of them, including Whittaker, stood at the bottom of the stairs. It wasn't every day that a former director of the CIA was taken into custody, and especially not a man of McGarvey's experience and reputation, and everyone was taking this seriously.

The larger of the two—square-jawed, with a no-nonsense look about him—stepped forward. "Mr. Director, I'm Deputy U.S. Marshal Ansel." He nodded toward his partner. "Deputy Marshal Mellinger. Sir, at this time we are placing you under arrest on a federal warrant on a charge of treason. Do you want your Miranda rights explained to you?"

"No."

"If you'll give us your word that you'll cooperate, there'll be no need for handcuffs."

"You have my word. Where are you taking me?"

"To the D.C. Superior Courthouse annex for booking," Ansel said. "Afterward you'll be transported to Langley until your trial."

"We need to finish your debriefing," Whittaker explained.

And it was about what McGarvey figured. He would be treated with kid gloves until after the funeral, everyone knew that he wouldn't make a move until then. "Whatever I tell you will be used against me at my trial. That about it, David?"

"You know the drill, Mac. You've been in these sorts of situations before. The more you tell us the easier your life will be."

"I don't think you're going to like what I tell you. And it's not very likely Dick will pass my version along to the White House. It's something none of them will want to hear."

He and Whittaker had spoken only a few words on the long flight back from Germany, amounting to little more than conveying the entire Company's sympathies about Todd's death.

"He was a good man, Mac."

"Too good," McGarvey had said, and after a moment Whittaker had turned away to stare out the window at nothing.

After a dinner of lobster, a light salad, and French bread with a good pino grigio, and coffee and brandy, McGarvey had gotten a few hours of sleep, waking only briefly when they'd landed at Prestwick, Scotland, to refuel, the sun chasing them as they headed west.

Standing now in the hangar at Andrews, McGarvey turned to tell Whittaker that none of this was the CIA's fault, but the DDCI had walked away to an armored Cadillac limousine, at least in a symbolic way washing his hands of the entire affair for the moment.

"Sir?" Ansel said, politely.

McGarvey went with the two deputy marshals and got into the backseat of a Cadillac Escalade SUV, with no access to the door locks, which snapped into place once they headed out.

The base was fairly busy this afternoon, and Air Force One had been trundled out to the apron, where people were beginning to gather. Mellinger was driving and he stayed well away from the security zone around the blue and white 747.

"Where's the president heading off to?" McGarvey asked.

Ansel half-turned in his seat and looked back. "I don't know, sir," he said. But then he shook his head, his face long as if he'd just thought of something disturbing. "Some of us had a lot of faith in you."

"Maybe the charges against me are wrong."

"Personally, I hope so. But the consensus is otherwise."

"Guilty till proved innocent, that it?" McGarvey asked. He was on the verge of lashing out, but he held himself in check. Consensus was almost always more important than just about anything else. It was the basis for nearly all the principles of a democratic government. Except that an important lawyer of the sixties and seventies once said that the Constitution hadn't been written to protect the masses from the individual, be he a criminal or not, but to protect the individual from the masses.

"We're just doing our jobs," Ansel said, and turned forward.

And that was the problem, McGarvey thought, too many people just doing their jobs and nothing more. It was a philosophy he'd never understood. It was, in his estimation, a coward's way out.

They were admitted through the sublevel sally port into the booking and holding area of the courthouse, where McGarvey was taken directly into a small room where a technician took his fingerprints with an electronic reader under the watchful eyes of Ansel and Mellinger who were behind a bulletproof window.

Afterward he was stood against a wall with inches and feet marked on a scale and photographed in right profile, face on, and left profile.

In an adjacent room he turned out his pockets onto a counter where a uniformed clerk inventoried his things—wallet, watch, some money, and a compact, razor-sharp knife in an ankle holster, which the Germans had not caught, and which raised an eyebrow here. His things were bagged in a large manila envelope, but instead of being logged into the property room the bag was turned over to Ansel.

"Anything else we should know about?" the deputy marshal asked.

"I gave you my word, and that'll have to be enough, unless you want to do a full cavity search," McGarvey said.

"No, sir," Ansel said, but he was wary and it was obvious he wanted nothing better than to get rid of his prisoner.

Mellinger had stood to one side through all this, his hand inside his jacket.

McGarvey looked over at him. "Tell your partner to take his hand off his pistol. It makes me nervous." He looked into Ansel's eyes.

"Listen here, pal—" Mellinger said, but Ansel cut him short.

"We don't want any trouble, believe me."

"No, you don't."

Twenty minutes after they arrived, they were back downtown and headed across the Roosevelt Bridge and north up the busy Parkway toward the entrance to the CIA campus.

"What have you heard?" McGarvey asked, breaking the silence once they were across the river.

"Treason," Ansel said. "Something to do with an incident in North Korea a few months ago. Apparently you went head-to-head with President Haynes over it, and he may have backed down, but President Langdon doesn't agree."

"No, I didn't expect he would," McGarvey said. "What else?"

"The word on the street is that your people are going to the mat for you."

"You mean the CIA?"

"Yes, sir," Ansel said. "We were given word that you were to be treated with kid gloves, and that was at the request of Langley. Specially Mr. Adkins."

Dick Adkins had been promoted to DCI by President Haynes after McGarvey had left, and he'd been kept on an interim basis by the new president until a replacement could be found. In the past six months no one suitable had been named. And in fact a lot of high-level staff positions in Washington had yet to be filled.

"It's shaping up to be a fight between the CIA and the White House."

"Right," McGarvey said. "And we know who'll win that one."

They were stopped at the main gate where the CIA's general counsel Carleton Patterson was waiting in the parking lot with his white Mercedes S550. He got out when the U.S. marshals pulled up, and walked over.

"I'll take it from here," he said. He'd been the Company top legal beagle for almost ten years, coming down to Washington from a prestigious New York law firm to help out three presidents ago, strictly on a temporary basis. He was tall, slender, silver-haired, and as well put together as one would expect for a man in his position. He and McGarvey had respect, if not friendship, toward each other.

"Good luck," Ansel said.

But Mellinger shook his head. "Prick," he said half under his breath, and Ansel shot him a dirty look but said nothing, and the two of them got back in the Escalade and drove off.

"I don't think he likes me," McGarvey said, getting in Patterson's car.

"A lot of people in this town don't care for you," Patterson said. "You're old school. Hell, you even approved of Guantánamo."

"I even participated," McGarvey said. "We gave them a better chance than they gave us on nine/eleven."

They were waved through the gate and headed up the drive in the direction of the Old Headquarters Building, but turned off before they reached the OHB's circular drive and parking lot.

"Say that in front of a judge and you'll be dead in the water," Patterson said, eyeing him.

"If it gets that far," McGarvey said. "You putting me up in a safe house here on the Campus?"

Patterson hesitated a moment. "If you promise not to run. Green and Boylan want to finish your debriefing, and Dick would like to have a word."

"My son-in-law's funeral is tomorrow. I'm going nowhere."

Until afterward, was the unspoken finish to the sentence, but McGarvey didn't amplify and Patterson thought it better not to pursue the matter. McGarvey was cooperating, and for now that was enough.

EIGHTEEN

□

The safe house was a small, two-story colonial in the woods away from the OHB, the white paint on the exterior peeling in places, and some weeds growing in spots in the gravel driveway indicating either that the place hadn't seen much use lately, or that even the Company was lacking in nonessential maintenance tasks because of the economy. McGarvey expected both.

"Will I have minders?" McGarvey asked when they pulled up.

"Green and Boylan will be bunking with you for the time being," Patterson said, and as he said it Pete opened the front door of the house, and smiled.

"Pretty girl," McGarvey said.

"Yes, she is. And bright." Patterson turned to him. "They have your jacket, your *entire* file from day one, so it won't do any good to try to hide some of your . . . more disagreeable . . . outcomes."

McGarvey got out of the car but hung back for a moment. "They were called assignments, and the outcomes were what I had been ordered to accomplish. You might want to get that idea straight in your head, Carleton. Could be important. Soon."

Carleton gave him a bleak look, and started to say something, but then thought better of it and drove off.

"Mr. Director," Pete said. "They sent your things over from the airport, and we brought some spare clothes for you from your suitcase at the Farm. We want you to be comfortable."

"How are my wife and daughter?" McGarvey asked on the broad porch.

Pete stepped aside to let him go into the house, then followed him and closed the door, making a show of not locking it, which wouldn't have mattered in any case. "As well as can be expected, sir."

"May I call them?"

"We'd appreciate it if you would hold off. Just until tonight. Dr. Sampson is with them this afternoon."

Leonard Sampson was the company's chief shrink, a bright, dedicated man. McGarvey couldn't think of many people he'd rather have with Katy and Liz just now. "Anything from Otto yet?"

Pete's eyebrows knitted. "We were hoping you might be able to shed a little light on his whereabouts."

"I've been out of the country."

"Yes, sir," Pete said not pushing the query.

The house was in much better shape inside than out, with nice furnishings, but it smelled unused and musty, closed in for a long time. To the left was a living room with a river rock fireplace that someone had stupidly painted white, an enlarged inauguration photograph of President Langdon above the mantel, surprisingly with no halo. A dining room to the right was furnished with a cherrywood table, seating eight, and a breakfront filled with nice stemware. A number of thick files had been placed at the head of the table. Beyond the dining room, McGarvey assumed, was the kitchen through swinging half-doors. A guest bathroom was tucked into the stair hall that led back to perhaps the den.

Dan Green showed up at the head of the stairs and came down, a curious expression on his face, as if he had just heard something that he'd never even guessed at, likely something he'd read in McGarvey's file that he was having a little trouble reconciling with what he'd thought he'd known.

"Good afternoon, Mr. McGarvey," he said, and shook hands. "I trust you had a reasonably pleasant flight back. A spot of trouble in Frankfurt, or so I heard."

"Nothing much," McGarvey said.

Green's left eyebrow rose, and he was about to speak, when Pete stepped in.

"Well, would you like some coffee, before we begin, Mr. Director," she asked. "Are you hungry? Maybe you'd like to get a couple hours of sleep. Flying through time zones can wear a person to a frazzle."

"Let's just get started."

"A beer?" Green asked.

"Sure," McGarvey said, and he followed Pete into the dining room as Green went back to the kitchen.

"Would you like to clean up, splash some water on your face?" she asked. "Your things are in the front bedroom upstairs, first door on the left."

"No," McGarvey said. He took off his jacket, hung it over the back of a chair, and sat down at the opposite end of the table from Pete and the stack of files.

She hesitated for just a beat, but then sat down. Like Green she was dressed in jeans and a light pullover. They could have been coordinated, but the look was meant to be relaxing, not intimidating: "Hey, *we're just ordinary people who've dropped in for a chat. No reason to be intimidated by us. Really.*"

Green came back with the beer but no glass, again an old pal over for a barbecue in the backyard, and did a slight double take when he saw that McGarvey had chosen to put as much distance between himself and his interrogators.

He handed McGarvey the beer, and went to the window where he looked out at the driveway and the wooded hill in the distance on top of which one could see the antennas and satellite dishes on the roof of the OHB.

"Could we begin with the circumstances that led you to accept a job of work for North Korean intelligence?" Pete said. "It's not quite clear from the incident file you provided us."

"I'm under indictment for treason," McGarvey said, but Pete waved him off, a horrified expression on her pleasantly round face.

"Heaven forbid, Mr. Director, it's nothing like that at all. You've been charged, but certainly not indicted. This is merely a fact-finding session. I mean, we have most of the details, we're simply trying to put everything into some sort of perspective. You understand."

"No, I don't," McGarvey said. "Because whatever I have to say to you, will end up on the seventh floor, and by the time it gets to Justice, or the White House, it'll all be sanitized to fit whatever the current preconception is."

Dan Green turned around, a scowl on his oddly proportioned face. "Is that what you think this is all about?" he demanded. "We're to accept your spin, and none of the rest of us have any other opinion?"

McGarvey looked at him. "Your opinions don't count, Dan. Only mine do. That's the drill they want to use to hang me."

"Who?" Pete asked. "Who wants to hang you?"

"And why?" Green added in his quiet manner, all traces of his previous hostility gone, replaced by an oddly out of place neutrality. Studied. Scripted.

"The disk found in Todd's car was not the one Givens handed over to him in town."

"You've already said that."

"Nor was his murder a random act. Nor were Givens and his family murdered in a home invasion gone bad."

"You've also said that," Green continued. "Assuming you're correct, who murdered them and why?"

"Very likely by someone working for Administrative Solutions, under the orders of the Friday Club, probably through an intermediary. It's why I went to Frankfurt to confront Roland Sandberger, tell him what I knew and get German intelligence involved, officially."

"I don't get that part," Pete said, genuinely puzzled. "Come to us with your suspicions, why the Germans? Specifically. What's the BND's involvement?"

"In your opinion," Green added.

McGarvey thought that he could dislike the little man, but it was just a job. "It has nothing to do with the Germans."

"Now I'm confused," Pete said.

"If he'd been in the UK I would have involved the SIS, if it had been in Pakistan, the ISI. Didn't matter where I confronted him, I just wanted the local intelligence apparatus to sit up and take notice."

"Good heavens, whatever for?" Pete asked, still puzzled.

"Don't you trust your own government?" Green asked.

McGarvey shook his head. "No."

ПIПЄTЄП

Remington sank down on the bench in Rock Creek Park, weary from his trip to Frankfurt. He'd expected the German authorities to ask them about McGarvey, but Sandberger had seemed indifferent, talking instead about the Baghdad contracts, which in the end would be worth millions—tens of millions, now that Task Force One was out.

That evening they'd had a good dinner at the hotel, and Sandberger had left around midnight to return to Iraq, leaving Remington to stew in his own juices until his afternoon flight back to Washington.

Last night at home hadn't been much better for him. He and Colleen had a social engagement at the British embassy, that she insisted they keep, but he had begged off and she'd left angry. He'd slept in the guest bedroom last night, and she'd been gone before he'd gotten up this morning.

Sandberger called on the encrypted number shortly before noon, and he was abrupt.

"He's back in the States, under house arrest, but he hasn't been indicted yet. Do you understand?"

"It's only a matter of time," Remington had replied, trying to work out what Sandberger wanted him to understand, while full well knowing what the next step would be. They had discussed his last, extreme measure at some length.

"The funeral is tomorrow. Make it happen."

"Is it necessary?" Remington had asked. He wasn't exactly squeamish, but McGarvey had tracked them down to Frankfurt, armed, and if they missed he would come after them.

"Yes," Sandberger said. "For Christ's sake he actually came after us in Frankfurt."

Remington had looked out the window at the river. "Let's not underestimate this man."

The line had been silent for a long moment, and when he came back Sandberger was cool at best. "Don't underestimate me, Gordon."

"Of course not," Remington had assured his boss, and the connection had been broken, leaving him to seriously wonder what the hell they'd gotten into with the Friday Club.

He had stewed about Roland's call the rest of the day, and even now he had to wonder where the hell they were headed, and if they were going in a direction that made the same sense that Admin had made to him when he had joined.

"In for a penny, in for a pound," his father had told him when the last of the family's fortune had been gambled and drank away. The pater had been a fatalist; whatever happened was supposed to happen. It was life. A man's future was determined at birth. Before birth. But Gordon had not believed in it; look what that sort of belief had done to the old man.

Remington glanced at his watch, which showed a minute before four, as Kangas and Mustapha in jogging outfits came around the curve in the Parkway just south of the Massachusetts Bridge.

They stopped a few feet away and did their stretching exercises. Other people were using the park, and the air smelled of charcoal grilles and was filled with the sounds of laughter and children's cries. Normalcy in a world Remington figured had been going mad for as long as he could remember. It's how he made his living.

"You handled the situation with the CIA officer and Givens very well and Mr. Sandberger is pleased, especially with how you covered your tracks. He's approved a healthy bonus for you."

"Thank you, sir," Mustapha said. "Did you want us here this afternoon to tell us that? Or is there more?"

Remington held his temper in check. He and Sandberger had discussed what would eventually have to happen to them, and he felt the sooner the better.

"It's become necessary to go to the next stage," he said. "The funeral is tomorrow at Arlington. Can you be ready by then?"

"Of course," Mustapha said. "But this will be even more dangerous than the other day. Much more dangerous."

"I agree," Remington said. "But this project has the personal interest of Mr. Sandberger, and he's the guy who signs your checks."

Mustapha straightened up and looked directly at him. "We appreciate that, but we'd like to make a suggestion."

"Are you getting cold feet?"

"Not at all," Mustapha said. "But taking him out will be tough."

"Your point being?"

"We'd like to use an IED. In the road. After the funeral. Easier to blame on the ragheads."

Remington had considered it, and had even discussed the issue with Roland. McGarvey was truly dangerous, taking him out with long guns would be preferable to taking a chance that he would survive an explosive device. And Sandberger had agreed.

He took out an electronic security detector, about the size of a flip phone, pointed it first at Kangas then at Mustapha. If they'd been wearing a wire or any sort of recording device the ESD would have picked it up. But they were clean and he pocketed the device.

"If you have the chance, take it," he said. "But only if you can get out clean. Absolutely clean. Because if you don't, Mr. Sandberger's next order will be to have you eliminated."

Both men nodded.

"Are we absolutely clear on this point?"

"Yes, sir," Mustapha said.

"And on the further point that we never had this discussion?"

"Right," Mustapha said.

Remington got up and headed to where he'd parked his car without looking back. It either ended tomorrow, or it would just be getting started.

TWENTY

After an early dinner of pizza and beer, Dan Green and Pete wanted to continue with the debriefing, but McGarvey refused. They'd gotten to the part when a North Korean intelligence officer had shown up at McGarvey's home in Casey Key, and Mac's decision to help. The going was slow because they'd wanted every detail: the time of day, what everyone was wearing, what, if anything, Mac's wife had overheard, or what he had told her, the make and model of the North Korean's car—presumably a rental—and its tag numbers, even its general condition.

"No dents, or scuffs, or perhaps mud around the wheel wells?" Green had nitpicked. "We just want to get a sense of this colonel's fastidiousness, his attention to details, if you will. Little lapses like those might translate into what sort of an officer he was: sloppy or neat, a dreamer or an itemizer."

"Paranoid or assured," Pete added.

"Later," McGarvey told them. "I want to call the Farm."

"We'll be at it until late tonight," Green said a little crossly. They were in their element doing this sort of thing, and they had just hit their stride and didn't want to quit.

"Whatever. But first I'll have a word with my wife and daughter. I want to find out how they're doing."

Pete shrugged. "We have a lot of ground still to cover," she said. She took a cell phone out of her jeans, handed it to McGarvey and motioned for Green to leave the kitchen with her. "We'll give Mr. McGarvey his privacy."

"It's on record in any event," McGarvey said, and he dialed his daughter's number in her private quarters as his debriefers left.

Liz answered after three rings, and she sounded all out of breath, as if she had been crying all afternoon, which she probably had been. "Yes."

"Hi, sweetheart, it's me. How are you and your mother doing?"

"I think it's just starting to sink in," she said. "But it's so unreal. I even thought that maybe you were Todd finally calling, and I was all set to be pissed off at him for being late and not letting me know." She hesitated. "I was worried."

"I know. I feel almost the same thing."

The kitchen was modern, with new appliances and bright wallpaper, homey, a place that was meant to seem comfortable. No threats here. Just friends in a pleasant situation talking about old times. No need for secrets. And it was true, he almost expected Todd to be coming through the front door to find out what the hell all the fuss was about.

"How are you doing, Daddy? Any progress?"

"Some, but it's still early going," McGarvey said. "I'm beginning to put a few things into place."

"Anything you can talk about?"

"We're being monitored."

"Of course," Liz said after a brief hesitation, and McGarvey could see the field officer in his daughter kicking in, checking all the angles, looking in all the corners, considering all the possibilities.

"How's Audie?"

"She was a little fussy earlier, but she's in bed—" Liz stopped short. "Mom's right here. We're outside having a cup of tea. I'll put her on."

A moment later Katy came on, her voice nearly unrecognizable. "Kirk?" she said. "Can you come get us?"

"Not tonight. But I'll see you tomorrow."

Katy hesitated. "Oh, at Arlington."

"Yes. And afterward I'll take you home."

"I'll stay here until you're done. You're not finished yet, are you?"

"No."

"Then I'll stay here," Katy said. "I think I hear the baby crying. I'm putting Elizabeth back on."

Liz came back. "Mother's staying here for the time being, but I don't know how much help I can be for you."

"Stay with your mother, and tomorrow—I know it'll be almost impossible—keep your eyes open. And whatever you do, don't make a move without your minders."

"I understand."

"Try to get some sleep, sweetheart," McGarvey said.

"I'll try," Liz said and she was gone, leaving McGarvey holding for a long time before he pushed the end button and laid the phone down on the dining room table.

A minute later his interrogators came in, Pete apologetic, Dan Green a little angry.

"We didn't listen in, Mr. Director," Pete said. "On that you have my word."

"It doesn't matter," McGarvey said, suddenly more than tired; he was weary, mentally as well as physically. And tomorrow loomed large in his mind, because he would not be able to do anything until after his son-in-law had been buried. What made tomorrow even worse for him was the thought of leaving Katy and Liz again, just as he had done for more than twenty years.

"Can we get you anything else before we pick up where we left off. The North Korean intelligence officer come for a chat with you."

"No," McGarvey said, getting up. "We're done for the night. I'm tired."

"The hell we are," Green said. "You have a lot to answer for."

"Yes, I do," McGarvey said and he turned to leave when Green started to step in front of him.

"Leave it, Dan," Pete cautioned. "We're all tired."

Green stepped aside but said nothing.

"You'll continue to cooperate this evening, Mr. Director?" she asked. "Can we have your word on it?"

"Yes, for tonight," McGarvey said.

"What about tomorrow?"

"That'll depend."

"You're charged with treason," Green said angrily, and McGarvey got the impression that the man's anger wasn't real, it was a part of his and Pete's dog and pony show.

"If that were the case, they would have put me someplace a hell of a lot more secure than here, don't you think?" he said.

He walked out into the stair hall and Pete came to the door. "How did Sandberger react when you showed up?" she asked.

"He wasn't happy," McGarvey said.

"I would have given anything to have been a little bird in the corner," Pete admitted. "We'll be with you tomorrow."

"Who else?"

"Federal marshals in the car with you and nearby. Just in case Todd's assassination wasn't a random act."

TWENTY-ONE

First thing in the morning Kangas and Mustapha parked their untraceable Buick LeSabre near the Tomb of the Unknowns in Arlington National Cemetery, and walked a quarter of a mile back down the hill in the general direction of the South Gate, crossing Porter, Miles, and then Grant drives. A few people were out and about, but not many; a hush seemed to hang over the place.

Neither man had ever wanted to be buried here, even though they'd been career government employees, because neither of them saw themselves dying in service of their country. It was an old line from Patton, something like: Let the other son of a bitch die for his country. They considered themselves to be too professional to be killed because of stupidity.

"Nice day for a funeral," Mustapha said.

"For someone else," Kangas replied, and he laughed.

They reached a spot from where they had a decent line of sight to the driveway that opened to Southgate Road, that in turn led to Columbia Pike or South Joyce Street away from the cemetery. After the funeral, which would start in a few hours, the procession would pass through the gate, according to Remington's intel, which had never been wrong before. The guy might be a prick, but he knew what he was doing.

Right on time a blue-and-white panel van without windows, marked Fairfax County Highway Department, pulled up about twenty feet down the driveway from the gate and parked in the middle of the road, almost on top of a storm sewer lid. Two men, dressed in blue coveralls and wearing hardhats, got out of the truck and placed a few traffic cones blocking the lane that led out of the cemetery. No one from the gate came down to ask what was going on.

"Considering what's been happening, and who's going to be here soon, you'd think security would be tighter," Kangas said.

"Makes you wonder about the Bureau," Mustapha agreed. "And Homeland Security."

"And the Company. The Van Buren kid was one of theirs."

The men were Islamic jihadists from the Ramila Mosque, Abu al-Amush who'd been born and raised in Baghdad, and Richard Hamadi, who'd come over to Detroit with his parents when he was a child. Al-Amush had been radicalized during the tail end of the Saddam Hussein regime and then in the war with the Americans, learning to hate whatever side was in power. And he had brought his message first to Detroit where he'd recruited workers from the auto assembly lines, and finally here two years ago, bringing Hamadi with him, when he'd been lured by the Ramila's imam, to carry the message of hatred to the young men raising money for the cause.

And carry out the occasional assignment.

Mustapha had been the lead contact man with the mosque, which had been moved in secret from its storefront months ago, leaving behind only the shell that had been destroyed in the explosion after the deaths of Van Buren and Givens. And convincing the imam and his followers had been relatively easy; they were all fanatics whose attention was totally focused on only two things: hatred and money. Kangas was the influential American businessman with deep pockets who'd been taken in by Mustapha, a true believer and a dedicated jihadist himself.

This assignment today, for a further contribution of ten thousand dollars to the cause, was right up al-Amush's alley, who'd learned all there was to know about IEDs, especially cell phone controlled IEDs, in Baghdad so that he could have written an instruction manual on the subject, except that he was practically illiterate, as were many of the so-called freedom fighters.

Kangas and Mustapha moved to a grave site a little closer to the driveway, from where they could watch the maintenance workers without appearing to be paying any attention.

"Fucking rag heads," Kangas muttered.

"At least they have a cause," Mustapha said. "Something we don't."

Kangas looked over in surprise. "Give me a break." He nodded down toward the two men who'd pried the storm sewer lip up and were rolling it back to the truck. "Tell me about them. What service do you suppose they're providing?"

"At least they think they know who their enemies are. We've been over there, we know the drill on the streets. They get their heads so filled with shit in the mosques that they practically think they can walk on water. They look forward to dying."

"Which leaves us, contracting to protect the good guys," Kangas said.

"Up until now, Tim. 'Cause I'm telling you that this shit just ain't right, and you know it as well as I do. Bagging bad guys in the field is one thing, this is something different, and I don't know if this is why I signed on."

"The money's goddamned good."

"Fuck the money."

"I'll take your share," Kangas kidded, worried for the first time. He wasn't about to walk away from Admin, not until shit began to happen, not until the center started to fail, which wasn't quite happening yet. But he'd never had an inkling until now that Ronni might be developing a conscience.

"That's not what I'm saying."

The maintenance workers loaded the heavy forged iron sewer lid into the van, waited a few moments as a car came up from Southgate Road, the driver steering around the cones and stopping at the gate, then unloaded another sewer lid, this one six inches thicker, with an unusual starfruit shape on the underside. They quickly manhandled it the short distance and carefully placed it over the two-foot diameter opening in the road.

By the way they handled the replacement lid it was obvious even at a distance that it was much heavier than the original. But their movements had been masked by the van from anyone at the gate, and in the short interval the new lid had been visible from anyone on the road below the gate, or from inside the cemetery where Kangas and Mustapha watched, no one had shown up. It was the one bit of luck they'd counted on.

The contingency plan had been to blow the IED now.

Kangas withdrew his hand from the cell phone in his jacket pocket, and the maintenance workers removed the traffic cones, got in their van, did a U-turn, and drove off.

When the correct car approached the sewer lid, Kangas would key a telephone number into his cell phone, omitting the last digit until just before the front bumper of the car reached the lid. It would only be a matter of a second before the call was connected, and a signal sent to the IED attached to the underside of the lid. It was a shaped charge, and the new sewer lid had been ground down in such a way that when the Semtex went off the blast would send a firestorm of lethal shrapnel and super hot gases upward, blowing apart anything directly above. No one would survive, even if they were riding in an armored limousine.

It was only a few hours now until the funeral.

They turned and headed back up to the LeSabre. "There's more here than we're being told," Mustapha said. "You've figured that out, haven't you?"

"I don't give a shit," Kangas said. "I'm given an assignment and I do my job. Just like I did in the Company."

That wasn't entirely true and both men knew it, but Mustapha said nothing.

"Look, you don't want to do this shit with me, I'll take care of it myself."

"Mustapha shook his head. "No. We're in this together, just like from the beginning. We're a team. Doesn't mean I have to like what we've been handed."

"I don't much like it either, and it doesn't have anything to do with wiping out a couple of incidentals, whoever's with him in the car. It's McGarvey I'm worried about. If we don't take him out this afternoon we could be in a world of shit."

"Then we'll just have to make sure we do the job right."

TWENTY-TWO

The afternoon was almost too bright, the sky too clear, the air too balmy for a funeral, as McGarvey walked out to the same Cadillac Escalade that had brought him over from Andrews. He'd been handcuffed, at the request of the federal marshals—it was standard procedure—his sport coat over his shoulders, and Pete and Dan Green were on either side of him.

Steve Ansel and Doug Mellinger were waiting at the SUV, all four doors open, their jackets unbuttoned. No one wanted trouble today.

"Just a minute," Pete said, and she produced the key for the handcuffs. "No trouble, Mr. Director?" she asked. "Your word?"

"My word," McGarvey said.

"This is bullshit, Pete," Green objected.

"It's his son-in-law's funeral, goddamnit," Pete said and she glanced at the federal marshals. "Any objections?"

Ansel shrugged. "You drive. We'll sit in the back with Mr. McGarvey, just to make sure."

"Afterward we're coming back here. We're not finished with the debriefing."

"You have him for as long as you want," Ansel said. "That was the interagency understanding."

Only a part of McGarvey had listened to the exchange, but it had registered with him; he understood the bureaucratic bullshit-speak that was a separate language not only in the District of Columbia and most of the Beltway, but for the isolated center here and there, like the CIA, or Quantico, or Fort A. P. Hill and the Farm, of course. But he'd been a part of the establishment, or sometimes on the fringes, for so long that he understood not only what was being said, but what was meant between the lines. Unofficially the CIA and just about every other intelligence or law enforcement agency had been at odds for years, not sharing intel, not really cooperating, and now a pair of federal marshals had most likely been ordered to give the Company enough rope to hang itself—or at least cause an embarrassment.

"Fine," Pete said, and they all got into the SUV, with her behind the wheel, and headed down the hill and along the long sweeping curve past the OHB, the front parking lot nearly full.

They passed through the front gate and headed down to Washington. Traffic was light, nevertheless the pair of deputy marshals in the back with McGarvey had their heads on swivels. No one wanted an incident, but Mac did have a reputation; wherever he went trouble seemed to materialize.

Pete glanced in the rearview mirror. "It's not being made public that Mr. McGarvey has been charged with anything, or is under arrest."

Neither marshal commented, and McGarvey got the impression that they couldn't care less. A pair of LE officers simply doing their duty, doing what they'd been tasked to do.

"In any event it's our call," Pete said. "If this became public there'd be a firestorm. The media would come down on us like a ton of bricks. Nobody wants that. The fact a former DCI is in custody for treason is spectacular. It's not every day something like that happens."

It came to McGarvey that Pete was up to something, and he could see that Dan Green was wondering the same thing, because he was giving her an odd look. But Ansel and Mellinger weren't getting it, or didn't give a damn.

"Do you think there'll be a trial?" McGarvey asked, and Pete glanced at his image in the rearview mirror and their eyes met.

"That depends on what you give to us over the next few days or weeks," she said, and her partner gave her a double take. "We'll have to keep you in isolation to run down all the facts here. But no one wants to rush into anything blindly, right?"

Ansel glanced at McGarvey and then at the back of Pete's head. "What are you talking about?"

"Well, it's classified for now, I'm afraid," Pete said. "Need to know, and all that. You understand. And trust me we appreciate your help. Taking responsibility for Mr. McGarvey's security as well as his safety. It takes the burden off us."

Ansel was getting angry. "What the hell are you going on about?"

Pete glanced over her shoulder. "Hey, listen, we're just following orders like you guys. Doesn't mean we have to like it. Right?"

Mellinger said something like *She's fucking with us*, or at least that's what it sounded like to McGarvey and he gave Pete a brief smile. She'd just told him that she was going to cut him some slack.

"Actually it's about Administrative Solutions," McGarvey said. "The contracting company that took over from Task Force One in Iraq. They're probably working for someone right here in D.C., and I've probably gotten a little too close."

McGarvey was a well-built man in obviously good shape, but Ansel and Mellinger were like fullbacks while he was like an aging, former college quarterback. They weren't taking him seriously, and were making no bones about it.

"We don't need your bullshit, Mr. McGarvey," Ansel said. "As soon as we can get you back to the Farm, we'll be out of your hair. And I don't give a shit what happens after that."

"No, I don't suppose you do."

"What was that?" the deputy federal marshal asked, angrily.

"You're just doing your job."

Ansel hesitated a second. "Right. But I'm warning you not to try anything stupid. If you do I'll personally come down on you hard. I don't like traitors."

"Accused traitor," McGarvey corrected him. "No trial yet."

He glanced up at the rearview mirror and Pete was watching him, a quizzical expression in her eyes. She'd given him an opening, but she had no idea what he had just done with it.

Ansel was rising to the bait, and it was clear he wanted to say something else, but Mellinger gave him a knowing shrug—this shit doesn't matter—and Ansel settled down. But the exchange would end up in the reports they would file later this afternoon, and would become a part of the official McGarvey File, just as the encounter he'd had with Sandberger and Remington in Frankfurt was.

They came down the GWM Parkway passing Theodore Roosevelt Island on their left, the afternoon now even brighter than it had been up at the CIA, and got off at Arlington Memorial Drive, and it struck McGarvey again why he was coming to this place, his mood deepening.

Todd had once told him in confidence that in some ways he was intimidated by his wife. "Sometimes she's more macho than I am. So what the hell am I supposed to do? I don't know what to say, how to react when she gets like that."

"It's a defense mechanism," he'd advised his son-in-law. "I wasn't around when she was growing up, and she built up this heavy-duty fantasy in her head about me as a superman. Something she figured she had to live up to as best she could. There were a few years there in grade school and junior high that she was getting into fights just about every day. She wanted to be just like her father. Katy told me that the worst thing any of the kids at school could call her was feminine, or girly girl. And she's probably still fighting that chip on her shoulder."

"She's in competition with me now?"

"Yeah," McGarvey'd said smiling. "You just inherited the problem."

"What the hell do I say to her?"

McGarvey remembered laughing out loud, even though his son-in-law had seemed so forlorn. "Tell her that you love her, and make sure you mean it. It'll take the wind out of her sails."

Apparently that tactic had worked, because McGarvey had never heard another complaint from Todd. And now his son-in-law was gone, and Liz had no one to compete with on her level.

TWENTY-THREE

Kangas pulled into the parking area at the Tomb of the Unknowns from where they would be able to watch Todd Van Buren's funeral procession arrive and depart. "You okay?" he asked Mustapha.

"I'm steady, I just don't have to like it. But if we can take McGarvey down it'll make my day. Give me the phone."

Kangas considered for a moment, but then handed his partner the cell phone they would use to trigger the IED. Mustapha was more of an explosives expert than he was anyway, and the logical choice as point man, and for now, at least, he seemed to have all of his shit in one sock.

Scuttlebutt during their old CIA days was that McGarvey had started his career as a serious kick-ass black ops officer, who'd probably been responsible for more field actions that had resulted in eliminations than any other officer back to, and including, the OSS during the big war. And even though he was an old man now, in his early fifties, he was still a formidable force. Someone to be seriously reckoned with.

If you take a shot at the bastard, whatever you do, don't miss. He'd heard that before, too.

The funeral was due to begin at two, and the front-end loader the gravediggers had used to open up the plot on the other side of Porter Drive headed away around one, a pair of groundsmen covering the mound of dirt with a tarp and setting up the electric device that would lower the coffin. A few minutes later a small flatbed truck showed up and four workmen set up several rows of chairs on the opposite side of the grave from where an Army chaplain would conduct the service.

A number of people came to visit the Tomb of the Unknowns, some of them taking a few pictures and then heading off, while others lingered. A few glanced down at the funeral preparations, but then turned away. The reminders of death were everywhere here, of course, but no one wanted to be reminded of any sense of immediacy. Whoever was going into the ground down there had died very recently. It was difficult to think about.

For a while after the chairs had been set up, and the workmen had driven away, only the occasional visitor passed on the road in front of the open grave, until fifteen minutes before the hearse with Van Buren's body was due to arrive. At two, a plain blue Chevy pulled up and the chaplain, in uniform, showed up and walked down the hill to the grave site.

Others started arriving in singles and pairs, at least a dozen and a half cars, most of them civilian, until a Lincoln limousine showed up, and Kangas and Mustapha sharpened up. A pair of large men dressed in dark business suits, obviously bodyguards, got out of the limo, and looked around for several long seconds before one of them opened the rear door, and a slightly built man with thinning hair, also dressed in a dark business suit, got out, and the three of them joined the others waiting at the side of the road.

"All the big dogs will be here," Kangas said. The man from the limo was Dick Adkins, director of the CIA, and supposedly close with McGarvey.

"Maybe we should take them all down."

"What're you crazy?" Kangas said. "Christ, what the fuck's the matter with you, man?"

"I'm steady, so just take it easy."

"What the fuck are you talking about, then?"

"Just a thought, don't have a fit," Mustapha said. "The Company screwed us. Payback works for me. I mean, if we're here and we've got the hardware, why not do a little something extra for ourselves?"

"Then what?"

Mustapha was gazing at the people gathered down the hill from them, a crazy look in his eyes that worried Kangas, who'd seen the same shit-faced expression on a kid in Baghdad a couple of years ago, just before the bomb went off, killing twenty Iraqi police recruits. Like the kid, and now Ronni, was seeing the face of Allah, or something. Paradise. It was all nuts.

"I don't know," Mustapha said, and he relaxed a little. "Maybe I'm just yanking your chain."

"You're a crazy son of a bitch."

Mustapha laughed. "And you aren't?"

For a second Kangas wanted to say something, thought he should say something, but then he turned away and shook his head. Just then the funeral procession, led by the long black hearse, came past on Memorial Drive. A few people turned to stare, but most turned away.

"Okay, here we go," he said.

Following the hearse, a black Lincoln limousine pulled up above the grave site, a pair of bodyguards got out and helped two women out of the backseat. From photographs Kangas recognized them as McGarvey's wife and their daughter—the wife of the CIA officer they'd taken out.

Four other cars pulled up, and people got out and joined the two women, and Kangas felt a brief pang that the funeral party was so small. But then he figured that his own wouldn't be any larger, because besides Ronni there weren't a whole hell of a lot of people who gave a damn. He hadn't spoken with his ex-wife in nearly five years, they'd had no children, his mother was dead, his stepfather didn't give a shit, he had no siblings and only a handful of aunts, uncles, and cousins, none of whom he'd spoken to for a long time.

"No McGarvey," Mustapha said.

"Not yet," Kangas said, and a Cadillac Escalade with government plates came down the hill and pulled up at the end of the line. The windows were so heavily tinted that Kangas couldn't make out who was inside, but then a woman got out from behind the wheel, and a very short man got out from the other side.

They stood there for a moment or two, looking at the group gathered near the hearse. The rear doors opened and a pair of large men got out, one from either side, followed by Kirk McGarvey, on the passenger side.

"Bingo," Kangas said, half under his breath. Yet he was a little disappointed, because the former DCI didn't look like much after all.

TWENTY-FOUR

Liz had insisted that there be no church or chapel service, Todd would not have wanted it. What ceremonies were to be performed and what words were to be said, would take place graveside. She'd also insisted that his name as a CIA officer not be placed in the public record, instead she wanted only the anonymous star on the marble wall in the lobby of the OHB at Langley.

"He belongs there with those heroes," she'd instructed. "He was one of them. He'd feel at home there."

Nor had she wanted a big crowd, though all the instructors at the Farm and many students of Todd's wanted to pay their respects today. She hadn't wanted to share her grief or theirs with them.

"Stay here, please," McGarvey told the deputy marshals and his CIA minders. "You have my word I won't try to run."

Ansel and Mellinger didn't like it, but they nodded, and McGarvey walked past the line of cars to where Katy and Liz were standing near the hearse. The chaplain had walked back up the hill, but stepped discreetly aside.

Katy was holding on to their daughter, and she looked awful, her hair and makeup a mess. He'd never seen his wife this way, but Liz was practically catatonic with grief.

"It wasn't just a robbery, was it?" Katy asked, her voice trembling, and barely audible.

"No," McGarvey said, kissing his wife on the cheek. "Where's the baby?"

"At the Farm."

Liz suddenly focused, and she looked from her father to the hearse where the funeral director and his assistant had opened the rear door and withdrew the flag-draped coffin out onto a wheeled stand, and she almost collapsed.

"Easy, sweetheart," McGarvey said, taking her arm.

"It's not real," she whispered. "This is not real."

She was trembling, but not crying, and McGarvey's heart broke not only for Todd, but because he couldn't do a damn thing for his daughter when she needed him more than she'd ever needed him.

"Is it someone we can find and punish, Daddy?" she asked, her grip tightening on his arm.

"Yes," he said close to her. "I'll find them, I promise you."

"No trial."

"No trial," he said.

Six men who'd come up from the Farm to represent everyone there, took up positions on either side of the coffin as pallbearers, and Liz turned to look at the people gathered on the side of the road, waiting to follow the coffin down the hill.

"We have to wait," she said. "Otto and Louise aren't here."

McGarvey looked around, but she was right, and a tiny worry began to nag at the back of his head. "They're probably hung up in traffic. They'll get here, but we need to start now."

Liz glanced at the people waiting, then up into her father's face. "Okay, Daddy," she said.

McGarvey nodded at the pallbearers, who gently lifted the coffin off the trolley, and with the chaplain in the lead they started down the hill, Liz's and Katy's bodyguards nearby, reminding everyone that this business was far from over.

Dick Adkins and Dave Whittaker held back, even though it would be up to Dick to present Todd's widow with the flag, and McGarvey suspected they wanted to distance themselves from him until they saw which way he would jump. After Germany they were treating him like something volatile, nitroglycerin ready to explode at the slightest mishandling.

When the mourners were seated, and the coffin placed on the lift's framework over the open grave, the chaplain began, and when he spoke Todd's name out loud, Liz squeezed her eyes shut. Todd's parents were dead, and only a few distant relatives had shown up. He'd once explained to McGarvey that his family was filled with odd ducks. They had sacks of money, but no one much cared for one another. It was one of the reasons he'd fallen for Liz. For as long as he could remember he'd wanted a wife and children, loads of kids and in laws and people who cared.

The chaplain was speaking about service above self, love of country, dedication, bravery, and finally the ultimate sacrifice of a man in his prime; platitudes, but comforting, except McGarvey was having a tough time settling down.

He glanced over at the two bodyguards from the Farm, and they acted nervous, too, their heads on swivels as if they expected something to happen at any moment. Adkins and some of the others seemed ill at ease, though Whittaker was apparently paying attention to the service.

None of this made any sense to McGarvey; not Todd's death, not the obviously fake disk, not the murders of the *Washington Post* reporter and his family, not Sandberger and Administrative Solutions, especially not the Friday Club, because if there was a pattern he wasn't seeing it. Yet everything within him, all of his senses, all of his experiences, his entire hunch-mechanism, if that's what it could be called, were singing. Trouble was here and now, and he wasn't armed.

. . .

The funeral was short, and after Adkins presented Liz with the folded flag he and Whittaker, who'd avoided eye contact with McGarvey, headed back up the hill to their limo, Dick's bodyguards preceding them. The chaplain came over and shook hands with Liz and Katy and McGarvey and he, too, left, the other mourners stepping over to where Liz and Katy were seated to pay their respects.

Neither Katy, nor especially Liz, was engaged in any of it; they were in a different world, which made McGarvey feel all the more helpless. Senseless; so goddamned senseless, and yet there was a reason for Todd's assassination.

When the last of the people were finally gone, McGarvey helped Liz and Katy to their feet, and walked back up the hill with them, their bodyguards never more than a few feet away.

At the road, he helped them into the CIA limo that would take them back to the Farm until the situation was resolved one way or the other, or until in McGarvey's estimation it was safe for Katy to take their daughter, with bodyguards, back down to their home on Casey Key.

McGarvey stood at the open door, and touched his wife's cheek. She was looking up at him, her eyes large and moist. She hadn't cried during the service, she'd already shed her tears, and there would be more to come, but for now she was holding on.

"I can't go with you now," he told her, and she nodded.

"I understand," she said. "And I know it's foolish for me to say it, but be careful."

"I will."

"Hurry back to me, darling," she said. "I miss you terribly."

He reached in and kissed her. Liz looked at him. "Take care of Audie," he said. "For now, that's what's important." But she didn't respond.

No one said a thing to McGarvey when he walked back to the SUV and got in the backseat, Ansel and Mellinger beside him, and Pete behind the wheel with Green riding shotgun. They were subdued, and the deputy federal marshals knew enough to keep their peace, and McGarvey was happy for it. He didn't want to start any trouble, but the funeral, and being with his grief-stricken wife and daughter, had put him right at the edge.

The hearse had left immediately after the coffin had been carried down to the grave, and the chaplain and mourners were all gone now, leaving only the CIA's Lincoln limousine a half-dozen car lengths up the road.

Pete started to pull out, but McGarvey stopped her.

"Let's follow them," he said. "I want to make sure they get out of here okay."

"Yes, sir," Pete said, and although the marshals didn't like the delay they continued to hold their silence.

Something heavy was in the air, McGarvey could feel it, feel that something wasn't right. He powered down the window and looked out, but except for the Tomb of the Unknowns up the hill no one was at any of the other graves or monuments within sight.

"That's bulletproof glass, Mr. Director," Ansel said, but McGarvey ignored him.

It was nothing but an imagination that was severely overworked, he told himself, as the Lincoln started down to the South Gate, and Pete fell in behind.

"They'll be okay," Pete said. "They have good minders who know their business. And once they reach the Farm no one will be able to touch them."

"They have to get there first."

Pete glanced over her shoulder. "Something wrong?" she asked.

"I don't know," McGarvey said. "I want to follow them down to the Farm."

"No way," Ansel said, but Dan Green looked over his shoulder at McGarvey.

"I think it's a good idea, Mr. Director," Green said. "Just to be on the safe side."

TWENTY—FIVE

The limo with the two women followed by McGarvey's Cadillac SUV headed down Miles Drive that connected with Grant and then Clayton to the South Gate, at the same time Kangas got behind the wheel of the Taurus, Mustapha riding shotgun with the mobile phone detonator, a dreamy expression on his face. They had switched from the LeSabre, they had used before as an ordinary tradecraft precaution.

"Watch the delay," Kangas said, pulling out of the parking area onto Memorial Drive, heading as quickly as was prudent in the direction McGarvey and his women had gone.

"The numbers are in," Mustapha said. "All it wants is the nine."

Kangas suddenly had a sharp premonition of doom, almost like the battlefield hunches that your time was numbered. He was spooked, in part because he'd temporarily lost sight of the two CIA cars around the curve, and in part because although McGarvey hadn't looked like much in person, the man's reputation was nothing short of fearsome.

"There they are," Mustapha said, and Kangas saw the SUV through the trees below and to the left.

He started to turn onto McPherson Drive, which led straight down to Grant, when a Toyota SUV with a man behind the wheel and a woman riding in the passenger seat suddenly appeared out of nowhere, and he had to brake hard to avoid a collision. When the Toyota passed he pulled in behind it, but they were going too slow, and he was conscious only of the possibility that if they missed McGarvey this afternoon they'd have to try again. It was a prospect he did not relish, especially if someone discovered the IED under the storm sewer lid. McGarvey would put it together and realize that someone was gunning for him.

"Get around them," Mustapha said. "We won't make it in time."

"We don't want to get stopped."

At the bottom of the hill where Grant met Clayton Drive, Kangas spotted the limo and McGarvey's SUV through the trees approaching the South Gate. They'd run out of time. Except for some blind stupid bad luck they would have been in perfect position by now.

Mustapha was fingering the cell phone's keypad. "What do you want to do?"

It was a matter of seconds before the two cars would go through the gate and pass over the IED.

"We'll have to take the shot from here," Kangas said, making the only decision that was possible.

The car they were following turned onto Clayton, evidently heading to the South Gate, and just past the intersection Kangas slowed nearly to a halt, no cars behind them or ahead of them at that moment.

Their view of the gate, and especially the driveway beyond it leading to Southgate Road, was mostly obscured by a line of trees. But it was the best they were going to do for now.

"What the hell am I supposed to do?" Mustapha demanded. "I can't see a fucking thing."

"Get ready with the nine," Kangas said. "I'll tell you when."

"Goddamnit . . ."

"Stand by," Kangas said as the limo passed through the gate. "Okay." With a two-second delay from the time the last number was entered and the signal went to the IED, the timing would be tight. But they had no other choice.

He could just make out the hood of McGarvey's SUV passing the gate.

"Now," he said sharply.

Mustapha pressed the nine, but almost instantly a large explosion hammered the quiet afternoon, blowing branches off several trees directly in their line of sight.

No delay, the single thought flitted across Kangas's mind.

TWENTY-SIX

One moment Katy's limousine was there and in the next instant it was replaced by a bright flash, followed immediately by an overpowering bang and a millisecond later a concussion that knocked all the air out of McGarvey's lungs.

Glass seemed to be flying everywhere inside the SUV, which swerved sharply to the left, slammed into the ditch at the side of the driveway, and stopped at an odd angle, its front bumper stuck in the upslope of the swale, throwing everyone inside forward against their restraints.

The front airbags had deployed but a large piece of smoldering metal had blasted through the windshield on the passenger side, slicing the airbag and decapitating Dan Green in a spray of blood that splashed McGarvey and the two federal marshals.

Pete Boylan had been shoved back by the airbag, and she was pawing at the material, but she seemed to be in a fog, not really aware of what had just happened.

McGarvey could just make out what remained of the Company limo, the wreckage lying on its side. Nothing was left of it except the engine block and some twisted lengths of metal attached to the badly distorted frame, which couldn't be recognized as being a part of a car just a moment ago. Very little of the cabin was intact, nor were any bodies visible, though four people had been inside the car. Flames and dark, greasy smoke rose from the wreck.

All of that came to McGarvey in the first second or two after the explosion, the horrible thought crystallizing in his mind that his wife and daughter had been killed right in front of his eyes. Not twenty feet away from him.

Every part of his body ached; it felt as if he'd been run over by a truck, and sounds were distorted. It was as if he were in a dream state where he couldn't make his arms and legs function.

Ansel on his left had pulled himself up and he was saying something impossible to understand. And Mellinger had been shoved aside, and lay doubled over on the floor up against the right rear door.

McGarvey managed to reach over him and yank the door handle, but the car's frame was bent and the door jammed. He braced his back against Ansel, who was struggling to come to his senses, and kicked at the door, once, twice, and on the third time it screeched open.

Ansel was trying to grab for him, but McGarvey scrambled over Mellinger, who was starting to come around, and tumbled out into the ditch.

He got to his feet and for another second stood, drunkenly swaying, until he was able to climb up onto the driveway and totter toward the burning wreck. But the intense heat and thick black smoke stopped him from getting close.

And it hit him, fully hit him, Katy and Liz were dead. There would be no bringing them back, nor would there be much of anything left to bury.

He raised his right hand to shield his eyes against the brightness of the flames, wanting to see his wife and daughter, their remains, but nothing was there. The blast had come up from the road, blowing out the bottom of the limo that had apparently been an ordinary VIP vehicle, and therefore unarmored.

In the far distance he thought he might be hearing a siren, but then it was gone, and he wasn't sure he'd heard anything.

In pieces now it was really hitting what had just happened, and more than that, why it had happened, and he focused on two names: the Friday Club and Administrative Solutions.

He saw the expressions on Sandberger's and Remington's faces in Germany.

He heard Todd's voice on the cell phone.

He felt his wife's body against his as he'd hugged her before the funeral, and saw the devastated look in Liz's eyes.

And Otto and Louise not showing up.

Nothing was making any sense to him, and it was driving him nuts.

He paced a few feet to the left, and then to the right, like a caged animal seeing its freedom just beyond a fence. For this moment he was hammered into inaction, if not submission, so overwhelmed by what had happened even he was having trouble fully comprehending the situation. The fear that his family would someday pay the price for what he was had always preyed on his mind; in fact, he had left Katy early in their marriage in what he'd come to believe was a false hope of saving her, or removing her from danger.

And now he asked himself if he'd been right to come back, and that burden was the most terrible thing he'd ever faced in his entire life. He was mad at himself and afraid for what might happen next. What he might do. What self-control remained after Todd's assassination had been erased.

Someone was shouting his name, and he turned in time to see Ansel coming across the driveway, his pistol drawn, Mellinger just a few paces behind. For a split second he had no idea what they wanted, and what Ansel was shouting, but then it came to him in nearly the same force as the explosion, that he was their prisoner, and they were going to take him into custody.

Todd's death had been hard enough on him, but this, now, was devastating, and there was no telling what a former black ops officer, an assassin, might do next. The safest thing would be to get him someplace safe, under lock and key until he could be calmed down and this mess sorted out.

"On the ground," Ansel shouted. "On the ground now!"

McGarvey watched the big man charging across the driveway, his pistol coming up.

"On the ground," the federal marshal shouted again.

Mellinger had drawn his pistol, but he looked a little shaky.

At the last moment, McGarvey stepped aside out of the line of fire, kicked the side of Ansel's left knee, which caused the man to stumble, and twisted the Glock 22 out of his grip.

Ansel reached out and tried to break his fall, but McGarvey shoved him aside with his knee, and turned to face Mellinger, pointing the pistol at the federal marshal's face.

Mellinger pulled up short eight or ten feet away, almost losing his balance. He was still shaky and he knew it.

"Throw your gun away and get on the ground."

"I can't do that, Mr. Director."

"I don't want to shoot you, but I will," McGarvey said, conscious that he was running out of time here. He could definitely hear sirens in the distance now, and there was no way he was going to give himself up.

"You're under arrest for . . ."

"You saw what just happened here, goddamnit!"

"Mr. Director, you are my prisoner," Mellinger said doggedly. "And I am taking you in." He started to raise his pistol.

"I'm sorry," McGarvey said, and he shot the man once in the left thigh, knocking him to the pavement, and before the federal marshal could react McGarvey was on him kicking his pistol away.

"You son of a bitch," Mellinger shouted.

"I didn't kill you or your partner, remember that," McGarvey told the federal marshal.

He backed away and looked again at the remains of the Company limo, a black rage threatening to consume him. All he could think about was getting away from here. The sirens were getting much closer now.

He turned as a Toyota Land Cruiser SUV pulled up, and raising his pistol he hurried across to the driver's side.

The window powered down, and Otto was there, dressed in a black suit, the tie correctly knotted, his long normally out of control hair neatly brushed. He was gripping the wheel with both hands, tears streaming down his cheeks, and he was trying to talk, but couldn't.

His wife, Louise, leaned over from the passenger side. "Get in the car, Kirk," she shouted.

He hesitated for just a second, not sure how he could go on. But then he knew how he was going to do it, and he knew why, and he yanked open the rear door and jumped in.

TWENTY-SEVEN

On Jessup Drive, above the South Gate, Kangas had seen everything, pulling up just after the explosion. He hoped to see McGarvey's car destroyed, but instead the limo bearing the man's wife and daughter had gone up in a flash, with no possibility that anyone inside could have survived.

McGarvey had jumped out of the Escalade and had taken down two men, both of them armed, and had even shot one of them in the leg, before he'd commandeered the Toyota SUV.

"Maryland plates," he shouted, as the Toyota sped away as if the driver had been there just to pick up McGarvey and get him away. But that made no sense.

"Did you get a number?" Mustapha asked.

The few other cars that had been coming down either Clayton, Jessup, or Patton drives had all made hasty U-turns moments after the explosion and were speeding away. No one wanted to be in the middle of what obviously was some sort of terrorist attack.

"Niner-two-peter, two-romeo-peter."

"Get us the hell out of here," Mustapha said, writing the number on a scrap of paper.

Kangas headed up Jessup, which would take him to the cemetery's main exit on Memorial Drive and then across the river back into the city in the opposite direction that the authorities would be coming. But he figured it would be only a matter of a few minutes before somebody wised up and stationed squad cars at all the gates.

"Son of a bitch, that was close," Mustapha said.

Kangas glanced at him. "You missed."

"I didn't have a clear line of sight."

"Well we're in some deep shit now. And we're going to have to clean the mess ourselves before it gets totally out of hand."

Mustapha was silent for a moment but then he shook his head as if he'd come to some decision. "Either that or we bug out and take our chances somewhere else."

"We're going to finish this, Ronni."

"Did you see that bastard take those two guys down? It was a walk in the park for him."

"They weren't expecting him to come at them like that."

"Bullshit. They drew their pieces."

"Now we know what to expect," Kangas said. "We won't make the same mistake they did. Anyway he didn't kill them. Which means they're probably Company security, or maybe Bureau muscle or federal marshals."

"It looked like he was in custody."

"But why?" Kangas said.

They reached the exit on Memorial Drive, traffic panicky as it came out of the cemetery, and when they got to the bridge across the river Kangas speed-dialed Remington's encrypted number. It was a call he didn't want to make, but if they weren't going to bug out, as Mustapha had suggested, they'd have to come clean.

Remington answered on the first ring as if he'd had his cell phone in hand and was waiting for the call. "Yes?"

"There's a problem."

"Tell me," Remington said.

"We got hung up behind some traffic on the way out after the funeral and had to guess when to push the button. We got it wrong. McGarvey survived but his wife and daughter were killed outright."

"What happened next?" Remington asked, and it didn't sound as if he were the least bit concerned.

"McGarvey was like a crazy man. He took down two armed men—probably CIA security or maybe federal LEs—shot one of them in the leg and then jumped in the backseat of a dark Toyota SUV and took off. We got the Maryland tag number. You can run it."

"Give it to me."

Kangas repeated the number.

"Did you manage to get away clean?"

"Yes. There was a lot of confusion. Nobody was paying attention to anything except getting the hell away."

"Where are you now?"

"Just getting off the Arlington Memorial Bridge," Kangas said. "I'm going up to Rock Creek Park in case you need to meet up."

"No," Remington said. "I want you to go to ground for now, until I can figure out something."

"Sorry, sir. But if we'd been given more time to plan—"

"I don't want to hear excuses," Remington shot back. "This isn't over, nor is your involvement. McGarvey is still a problem. He's still your problem. But for now you're to keep out of sight until I can work out what comes next."

"Mr. Sandberger—" Kangas said, but again Remington cut him off.

"Will not be bothered with this for the moment."

"Can you tell me if McGarvey was under arrest, because the two guys on his ass sure didn't act like bodyguards?"

"He's been charged with treason."

It wasn't what Kangas had expected to hear. "Holy shit," he said half under his breath. "Why not let the FBI do our work for us? At the worst he'll go to prison, at best he'll get shot to death trying to escape."

"There are other considerations," Remington said. "None of which are any of your business at this juncture. For now keep your heads down, but keep in touch. There'll be more."

"Treason for what?" Kangas asked. "If we're going to continue to put our asses on the line and either get arrested or taken down by the crazy son of a bitch, we ought to know exactly what we're dealing with."

"What you're dealing with is a million-dollar bonus. For each of you."

Kangas's breath was taken away. "Yes, sir," he said. "We're going to ground."

"Good man."

TWENTY-EIGHT

The house on Whitehaven was quiet, Colleen had gone to a meeting of one of her charity events and the cook and cleaning lady had the afternoon off. Remington had poured himself a large snifter of a good Napoleon brandy after the call from Kangas and he stood now at the window of his study turning over the possibilities in his mind.

He would have to call Roland with this, of course, but before he did so he needed to think things through. Kangas and Mustapha had screwed up, that much was clear, and there was no question now that they had become expendable. In fact, they might even have become liabilities, depending if anyone had seen them near the scene.

But beyond that they would have to deal with a man who couldn't be more highly motivated to strike back at whoever he suspected had killed his wife and child. He'd come to Frankfurt to confront Roland, whose name he'd told them was on Alexandar Turov's computer in Tokyo, which meant the former CIA director had at least part of the puzzle, and it meant that he would probably come after Admin, especially Roland.

And he turned that over in his mind. It was possible that McGarvey would even manage to take Roland out, leaving Admin without a CEO, which was a role Remington had always seen himself filling.

But this had to be done carefully, subtly, because Roland was nobody's fool. McGarvey as a tool, as a weapon, was a difficult, interesting possibility.

Remington drained the last of the brandy, and at his desk brought up a nationwide LE search engine, and entered the Maryland tag number Kangas had given him. The vehicle came up as a 2008 dark blue Toyota SUV, registered to Pierre Alain, MD, with an address up in Baltimore, with no wants or prior violations.

The Baltimore address turned out to belong to a UPS package service and the American Medical Association had two Alains, one Rudolph and the other Michael, neither of them with practices on the East Coast.

Following a hunch about the name, Remington tried the French National Medical Association directory, and came up with Pierre Alain, a GP with Medicins Sans Frontiers, present location unknown. But when he checked the Doctors Without Borders directory, no Pierre Alain was on the roles.

The name Otto Rencke came to Remington's mind, McGarvey's computer freak friend in the CIA. He would have the wherewithal to fake an identity with little or no problem, especially one that would be bulletproof. Which meant with Rencke's help McGarvey would be safe from rearrest for the moment.

But a man like that would not go to ground for very long, especially not with his motivation, and especially not if he were offered an enticing target. Something that might show up on Admin's Website, and something that Rencke would be sure to see.

It was two in the afternoon here but eleven-thirty in the evening in Baghdad when Remington poured another brandy then got through to Sandberger's encrypted satellite phone. It had been less than one hour since the botched assassination in Arlington, but nothing had shown up on any of the online news sites, except that an explosion of unknown origin had taken place at the cemetery's South Gate, casualties were likely. To this point no witnesses had come forward, though an unnamed source suggested a pair of federal government vehicles may have been targeted.

"I take it that the explosion at Arlington I'm hearing about involved our boys," Sandberger said, and Remington thought he was hearing music in the background, and perhaps a woman's laughter.

"Yes, but there was a mistake."

"Is McGarvey dead?"

"No, and he's on the loose," Remington said.

Sandberger said something away from the phone, and the woman stopped laughing and a moment later the music stopped. "Tell me everything."

Which Remington did, leaving out nothing but his speculations about Otto Rencke getting word to McGarvey that Sandberger was back in Baghdad, sections of which were essentially still lawless. In his present frame of mind it was no stretch to expect that McGarvey would go to Iraq to try to take Roland out.

"Killing his wife and daughter, as you say, in front of his eyes certainly gives the man the motivation to come after us. But why didn't Kangas and Mustapha finish the job? That was damned sloppy on their part; when this business is done with I want them eliminated. Erased from the face of the earth as if they'd never existed. Clear?"

"Clear. But trying to take McGarvey down just then would have put them in extreme jeopardy, and not simply from McGarvey himself. If they'd been taken into custody at the scene, the fact that they were Admin contractors would have come out. In fact, they probably did the right thing getting out of there before the authorities arrived."

"Failure is never the right thing, Gordon," Sandberger said harshly. "I want you to find out who actually owns the Toyota that picked up McGarvey. It'll give us a lead as to where the man's gone to ground. Once you have that I want him taken down, no matter the cost of the resources. Am I clear on that as well?"

"Perfectly," Remington said. "But there may be another possibility you might want to consider."

"I'm listening," Sandberger said, coldly.

"Too many things have been happening here in the Washington area. We need to allow things to cool down before this comes back to us, especially to you, from someone other than McGarvey."

"If you're talking about my name and McCann's on Turov's laptop, if the CIA had any proof of my involvement don't you think they would have come after me by now?"

"But if a connection is also made between you and the Friday Club, Foster might send someone after you."

"Bullshit, Gordon. We're Foster's personal contractor service. Do you think the bastard would dare try to hire another service to take us down? We have safeguards, and he knows it. Something happens to Admin and the backlash would end up in his lap."

"I wasn't thinking about Admin, Roland. I was thinking about you personally."

Sandberger fell silent for a few seconds. "You're even more of a devious son of a bitch than I thought, and I like it. What do you have in mind?"

"One other consideration. Back to Foster and why he hired us in the first place. I don't really care what sort of a deal you signed up for, what I'm more interested in is what Foster did *before* he came to us. Before he felt the need to come to us. Do you see what I'm driving at?"

"Perfectly. But the only deal, as you put it, was simply that he felt someone in the media might be putting together a hatchet job on him and his pals and that might make it to the Bureau, and he wanted us to find out what was going on, and if the rumors were true nip it in the bud. But none of us thought it would involve the CIA."

"There was McCann, and I think it's a safe bet that he wasn't killed in the line of duty, but because of his affiliation with Turov. Another safe bet would be that McGarvey was somehow involved, and when it was over he handed it to someone inside the Company and walked away."

"You're probably right again. So taking out his son-in-law might not have been the right thing to do. But I don't see that we had any other choice."

"Neither do I. But now he's become our problem, and we have to deal with him. But not here in Washington. Maybe if he turns up back in Florida, or somewhere out of the country."

Sandberger laughed. "Maybe he'll come here," he said. "It would be the perfect solution."

"You'd want that?" Remington asked, smiling. Maneuvering Sandberger was getting easier with each try.

"Absolutely."

"How much longer will you be in Baghdad?"

"A few days, maybe a week."

"Let me see what I can put together. I'll give you the heads up."

"Yes, do that," Sandberger said.

TWENTY-NINE

At the brownstone in Georgetown McGarvey paced up and down in the kitchen, stopping from time to time to look out the window at the little garden in back that Louise had planted. But he wasn't actually seeing anything except for Katy's face in the back of the funeral car, looking up at him with trust and love, and then the terrible flash. And it was over.

Louise came over to him, her eyes still wet. "Can I fix you something to eat? Maybe a drink?"

He looked up at her. "I'll have to do something for Audie."

Louise's voice caught in her throat. She was a tall, slender woman, whose hair was normally just as out of control as her husband's. And though she wasn't as smart as Otto, she was a genius in her own right. And sweet, kind, thoughtful, considerate, and Otto and everyone else who'd ever come in contact with her, including McGarvey, thought the world of her. Katy and Liz had loved her.

Otto had come in from parking the Toyota in the back. "We're taking her," he said. "Louise and I can't have children of our own, so we'll adopt her, if it's okay with you."

A look of wonderment and pure joy came into Louise's round face, and her eyebrows shot up, as she looked from her husband back to McGarvey. "Is it possible, Kirk?" she asked. "I mean, Otto and I haven't discussed it or anything—there was no need for it—but I think it's a fabulous idea. I know it's way too soon—"

McGarvey had seen the logic and the love in Otto's offer the moment the words came out of his friend's mouth. And he could see that Louise was so happy she was frightened. They wanted children.

He nodded. "Liz would have liked that," he said, a tremendous burden, one of many on his shoulders, lifted. "So would have Todd."

"She'll stay at the Farm for now," Otto said. He'd poured McGarvey a snifter of cognac and brought it over. "Sit down now and drink this. We have a lot to talk about. Somebody wants you dead, because sure as hell that was no accident, nor were Mrs. M. and Elizabeth the targets. You were. Which means someone was shitting enough Twinkies they thought they could get away with assassinating not only a CIA officer and a newspaper reporter, but a former director of the Company. A man who'll probably come under indictment for treason over the Pyongyang thing."

McGarvey leaned back against the counter and took a drink. Too soon, he wanted to say. Time to run, this time for good. Maybe back to Greece. Bury himself so that he could start to heal.

He didn't know if he could stay here now and yet he knew damned well it was too late for him to turn away. It had been too late after the polonium thing in Mexico, and far too late when he had killed Turov in Tokyo and when Todd had put a bullet in McCann's head at the safe house up near Cabin John. All that had happened over the past year, and yet it seemed like a century ago.

And here he was, and it still wasn't over.

His grip tightened on the brandy snifter and he looked down at what he was doing, his knuckles white, and with the most supreme effort of his life, he loosened up, took another drink, and put the glass down with a steady hand.

"What is this place?" he asked.

Otto exchanged a relieved glance with his wife. "We bought it about six months ago, just after the incident with Turov and Howard. I wasn't picking up anything solid about what had been going on, but I thought there was a possibility that more would be coming down the pike. So I figured one of these days we might need a safe house off the Company's books. Totally untraceable as are the utilities and taxes and the car. Sort of a hideout but right in the middle of things, you know what I mean?"

"Why weren't you at the funeral?" McGarvey asked. "Liz asked about both of you."

"Otto had a hunch that if something were to happen, Arlington would have been a good place for it," Louise said. "I've learned to trust his instincts."

"Why not more security officers?" McGarvey asked.

"I don't know who to trust, Mac," Otto said. "Honest injun, I can't find anything, but I know something's there. Anyway, it wouldn't have mattered. We didn't know about the IED."

"Someone had to be within a sightline to push the button. Did you see anything, did anyone see something?"

"There were lots of cars, and all of them got out of there in a big hurry after the blast. The shooters would have probably been among them." Otto spread his hands. "I don't know yet if any security cameras picked up something, but I'll check on it this afternoon."

"I'm not turning myself in," McGarvey said. "Not until this is resolved."

Otto nodded. "What do you want to do?"

"I'm going after Roland Sandberger, this time for real."

"That's wrong, Kirk," Louise said. "There's no proof he ordered this thing. You've killed people, like a soldier on the battlefield. But not this. Not execution style."

McGarvey ignored her, his grief changing into a black rage he was having trouble controlling. "I want to know where he is right now."

"After Frankfurt he went back to Baghdad, and Remington came home," Rencke said. "But Louise is right, we have no proof that Admin was involved."

"I'll get the proof just before I kill him."

Again Rencke exchanged a look with his wife, and spread his hands. "He always travels with two bodyguards. Tough guys. Well trained and highly motivated to keep the guy who signs their paychecks alive. They won't be easy. And Baghdad's still a dangerous place. Accidents happen all the time."

"Works both ways," McGarvey said, his bitterness barely below the surface.

"What happened to Dan Green and Pete Boylan?" Louise asked, trying to defuse McGarvey's anger.

"Dan is dead, but I'm not sure about Pete. I think her airbag might have deployed in time to save here. I don't know."

"We should check on her," Louise told her husband.

"I'll need a weapon, whatever air marshals are carrying these days, probably Glock twenty-threes, and a Galco shoulder holster, some clothes, an ID, and a couple hundred dollars cash. And a sat phone. Encrypted."

"You're not getting to Baghdad like that," Rencke said.

"Orlando, and I'll need a rental car there."

"You're going home," Rencke said. "But you don't have to do anything like that. I can get everything you need from here."

"I don't want you and Louise involved more than you already are."

"No shit, Mac, don't do that to me—to us. You can't just turn your back."

"Goddamnit, I don't want anyone else to get hurt!" McGarvey shouted coming away from the counter. "It's enough. It's . . . enough."

Rencke nodded. "Okay, kemo sabe. I'll get you to Orlando, but you gotta know that the federal marshals or at least the Bureau probably have someone watching your house."

"I'll deal with it."

"You're not going to hurt our own people," Louise said, angrily.

"No," McGarvey said. "Not badly."

"When do you want to leave?" Rencke asked after a beat.

"Tomorrow afternoon. First I have to get some rest."

"In the meantime what about me?"

"Find a connection between Sandberger, McCann, and the Friday Club. Someone funded the polonium-210 in Mexico and the hit in Pyongyang. Find the money trail, and maybe we'll find out the why."

THIRTY

The director of Central Intelligence Dick Adkins sat in the backseat of his armored Cadillac limousine heading up 17th Street to the White House wondering what the hell he was going to tell the new president that made any sense. Except for the fact he'd once worked with and then for McGarvey before becoming DCI himself, this briefing would have landed in the lap of Madeline Bible the director of National Intelligence.

But President Joseph Langdon had asked specifically for Adkins, and although he'd been in office six months no one in Washington had really taken his measure yet. Everyone, including the media, was still being cautious, and Adkins wasn't looking forward to the meeting.

At five-eight with a slender build, thinning sand-colored hair, and a pleasant if anonymous face, Adkins had never aspired to run the CIA. Unlike McGarvey he was more of an administrator than a spy, and unlike most of his other predecessors he'd never been politically connected. He'd just inherited a job that no one seemed to want when McGarvey left the Agency. He'd been stuck with it through the previous administration, though he had the feeling his tenure was about to come to an abrupt end.

They went up West Executive Avenue and stopped at the guardhouse, but were immediately waved through; Adkins's face was a familiar one.

The president's national security adviser Frank Shapiro, a hawk-nosed ultra-liberal, met him at the West Entrance, a sour expression on his narrow face.

"You're late, Mr. Director."

"Unavoidable," Adkins said, not rising to the bait. Within ten days after the new administration was in place, he and Shapiro had gone head-to-head over a National Intelligence Estimate in which Adkins had argued for the retention of the prisoner and interrogation facility at Guantánamo Bay.

"Over my dead body," Shapiro had said flatly, and Adkins remembered wishing for just that.

They headed to the Oval Office, the West Wing bustling with activity this afternoon, and Adkins girded himself for what he knew was coming.

"You didn't bring any briefing materials with you?" Shapiro asked. "The president has a number of serious issues he wants to discuss."

"No, I brought nothing."

"Top of the list is Kirk McGarvey. The man has become a menace, and the president wants him brought in."

"Not such an easy job."

"The CIA won't be asked to handle it, we're leaving it to the Bureau. But the president will want to have your advice. You know the man better than I do."

Adkins almost called him a prick. "I wasn't aware that you'd met him."

"I never did," Shapiro said. "But you know what I mean."

Maybe asshole would have been a better word, Adkins decided.

President Joseph Langdon, a tall, ruggedly built man with features and mannerisms reminiscent of Lyndon Johnson, was seated at his desk in shirtsleeves, his tie loose, the directors of the FBI Benjamin Caffery and the National Security Agency Air Force Major General Warren E. Reed across from him. He looked up, a stern set to his mouth.

"I'm glad you're here, finally. Now we can get started." He nodded for Shapiro to join the meeting and to close the door.

No other chair had been set in front of the president's desk, so Adkins was forced to remain standing. It was an insult.

"I want to know why better control wasn't kept of McGarvey?"

"That was up to the Federal Marshals Service, Mr. President."

"But he was in the custody of the CIA at Langley for debriefing. And prisoners accused of high crimes against the nation are generally not permitted to attend funerals. Especially uncuffed."

"It was his son-in-law's funeral."

"It's unfortunate. I'm told that Mr. Van Buren was an outstanding officer. But it changes nothing."

"McGarvey is not guilty of treason."

"Justice informs me otherwise," the president said. "He will be brought in, and he will be prosecuted. Which is why you're here. We want your input. You've worked for and with him for a number of years. Where has he gone? What will he do next?"

"I don't know," Adkins said. And he didn't, though he had a fair idea that wherever he'd gone to ground it involved Otto Rencke, who'd also disappeared.

"Who killed his wife and daughter?" Caffery asked. He was a large man, with a round face and a WWII haircut, who in his six short months as the FBI's director had already begun to develop the reputation of a man you never wanted to cross. A modern-day J. Edgar Hoover.

"Muslim extremists," Shapiro answered for Adkins. "Roadside bombings have finally come to America. Although I don't think anyone believes the target at Arlington was anyone other than McGarvey himself."

"I agree, Frank," Adkins said. "But it brings up the interesting question of just why your Muslim extremists wanted Kirk McGarvey dead?"

"Any number of reasons," Shapiro shot back. "But the CIA would know more about that than I do. What's the man been up to lately? I've seen no reports on his recent activities."

"He was retired."

Shapiro wanted to press the argument but Langdon held him off. "I'm sorry for Mr. McGarvey's loss, but he's brought many of his problems onto himself by his reckless actions."

"In service of his country, Mr. President," Adkins said, his voice rising. "Have you read his record, sir? His entire record?"

"You forget yourself," Shapiro practically shouted.

"Do you people understand what sacrifices he's made for his country?"

The president eyed him coldly then turned to Caffery. "How soon will you have McGarvey in custody?"

"It's hard to give you an exact time table, Mr. President, but it will be soon. We believe he's still in the Washington area. All public transportation venues are being watched twenty-four/seven, as are car rental companies. His photograph has been sent to every law enforcement agency within a one-hundred-mile radius of Arlington, and all of his known friends and associates are being tailed. We've requested wiretaps for a few of his acquaintances here and in Florida, which we should have within a few hours. We'll bring him in."

"Someone is bound to get hurt," the president said.

"That's a possibility we've considered, but when we have him located, we'll go in with an overwhelming force."

Adkins couldn't believe what he was hearing. "His wife and daughter were killed in front of his eyes, for Christ's sake. But he didn't kill the marshals who wanted to take him in."

"No," Caffery said. "But he knocked one of the men to the ground and stole his weapon and used it to shoot the other marshal in the leg."

"But not in the head, Benjamin," Adkins said. "And believe me a head shot would have been easier for him than you can possibly imagine."

Langdon gazed at Adkins as if he were seeing his DCI for the first time. He nodded. "Mr. Adkins, you're fired. Your deputy director will take over on an interim basis."

This hadn't come as a surprise to any of them, but of the men in the room, Shapiro seemed to be the most smug.

"Leave us now. Clean out your personal items from your office, return your laptop and secure telephone and security badges and any files or other documents you might have in your possession."

"It's already been taken care of, Mr. President."

"A release document under the Secrets Act is ready for your signature. Mr. Whittaker has it for you," Langdon said. He got to his feet and extended his hand. "On behalf of a grateful nation—"

But Adkins just looked at him. "I'm truly sorry, Mr. President, but you have no idea who you're dealing with or the serious nature of the problem he's been trying to work out for his country."

"If it's found that you've withheld information, you will be prosecuted," Shapiro told him.

"You haven't a clue, do you," Adkins said. "Well, neither do I. But I think if you press him people will get hurt."

"If he contacts you we want to know," Caffery said.

"I'm sure you'll be monitoring my phone lines."

"Of course," General Reed said.

"God help you all," Adkins said, and he turned and walked out of the Oval Office.

PART

TWO

The Following Days

THIRTY-ONE

☐

McGarvey flew a U.S. Airways flight out of Baltimore's Thurgood Marshall Airport a few minutes after five in the afternoon as a U.S. Marshal, touching down in Orlando at eleven-thirty. Rencke had arranged everything and the captain and crew thanked him.

"Makes us feel a lot better having you guys aboard," one of the flight attendants said, flashing him a smile.

But he was focused and had simply nodded, and went inside where he took the train to the main terminal and the rental car counters where Rencke had arranged for a car under the same work name—Joshua Taylor—but with no reference to him as anyone other than a private citizen.

He was out of there by midnight heading down I-4 to Tampa and the Gulf Coast, where he would take I-75 south to his home on Casey Key. But it didn't seem like coming home to him. All of Florida was empty now, devoid of any life, or any purpose of any happiness. It was just another place he was traveling through, because when this business was finally over and done he would never come back.

Traffic was light at this hour and he made good time. Once he reached the outskirts of Sarasota he called Rencke on the sat phone.

"Any trouble?" Rencke asked.

"None so far. Have you heard anything from the seventh floor?"

"Dick Adkins was fired. Apparently he and Langdon had it out, and on Shapiro's strong recommendation, Dick was given the boot."

"Has anyone been appointed interim DCI?"

"Dave Whittaker. The White House doesn't want to put someone new in place until you're brought in."

"Is anyone looking for you and Louise?" McGarvey asked. It was the only thing left he had to worry about, except for his granddaughter. But whatever happened she was safe at the Farm.

"Not officially, but Tommy Doyle has sent out a number of posts on a couple blogs I check out from time to time."

Doyle had been the deputy director of intelligence when McGarvey was DCI. He retired a few years ago, so it was tough to figure if he was trying to make contact with Otto on his own in order to find McGarvey, or if Whittaker or someone at Langley had put him up to it. Either way it would be too dangerous to respond to his queries and Otto agreed.

"The Bureau has two guys at your house, three teams rotating every eight hours. The off-duty guys are staying at a Holiday Inn up in Venice. I didn't get any names, but their shifts start at oh six hundred, so if you mean to get in sometime this morning the guys on the twenty-two hundred shift should be getting bored and tired around four in the morning. It'd give you two hours to get in and get back out."

"The timing's right," McGarvey said, thinking ahead. The closer he got the odder it seemed to him that he was going to break into his own house. It wasn't real. When it was over he would go back to Greece, at least for the interim, until he healed. If ever.

"Honest injun, Mac, these are the good guys. Louise is right, you can't go in there and do something . . . stupid."

"Don't worry," McGarvey said. "I won't hurt anything but their pride."

"That's bad enough."

The village section of Siesta Key with its restaurants, bars, and nightspots, one barrier island north of Casey Key, was lit up and busy as normal on an evening, but the residential areas, especially south of the village, were dark and quiet as was also usual for this time of night.

It was past the tourist season, and many of the houses on the Gulf side of the island as well as the Intracoastal Waterway side were closed down, no one in residence until sometime around Thanksgiving. McGarvey had no trouble finding a stretch of half a dozen such houses on the ICW that were dark, and he shut off his headlights and pulled into one of the driveways.

The house next door had a small inboard/outboard powerboat on a lift out of the water. McGarvey jimmied the lock on the back door of the house, first making sure there wasn't an alarm system, and in the kitchen found the boat's keys, and in the garage found a couple of jerry cans of gas and after a couple of minutes searching a roll of duct tape.

Ten minutes later he had the boat cover removed, had lowered the boat into the water, had gassed it up and started the engine, which kicked into life on the third try. Since it was an I/O, its exhaust and engine noises were quieter than those of an outboard motor hanging on the transom. It was a small bit of luck.

Easing away from the lift, he gingerly made his way across the shallow water of Little Sarasota Bay to the green 57 ICW marker and turned south in the middle of the channel before he turned on the boat's navigation lights and increased the throttle. It was just coming up on three-thirty in the morning, the air perfectly still, the overcast sky pitch black except for the glow of Sarasota.

His house, about four miles south, was just north of the smaller swing bridge at Blackburn Point. These were waters he knew well. Besides their sailboat, which they kept in downtown Sarasota at Marina Jack, they had a small Boston Whaler runabout that he and Katy often took up the ICW as far as Anna Maria or sometimes down to the Crow's Nest in Venice for leisurely Sunday brunches.

Just now the two houses north of his on Casey Key and several to the south were empty for the summer. All of them maintained private markers leading to small backyard docks.

Twenty minutes later he throttled back to idle, switched off the boat's nav lights, and angled west to the island just after marker 37, no need to raise the engine because water depths here in the channel were three feet at lower low tide right up to the docks, less than five hundred yards outside the channel.

From here he could see the red and green lights on the Blackburn Point bridge and make out the silhouette of his house, and the spindly outline of the gazebo in the backyard where Katy had loved to have a morning cup of tea or an early-evening glass of wine.

At the last moment he cut the boat's engine and drifted to the dock two houses up from his, and tied bow and stern lines to the cleats. He speed-dialed Rencke's number, and Otto answered on the first ring.

"I'm tied up just north of my place. Can you cut the house alarm system?"

"Stand by," Rencke said.

Now that the boat's engine was off, the night had become silent, except for the frogs and other animals and the sounds of what was probably a night hunting bird in the distance.

"Done," Rencke said.

"I'll let you know when I'm out of there," McGarvey said, and he broke the connection.

Pocketing the duct tape, he jumped up on the dock, and headed through the sea oats and tall grasses at the water's edge to the edge of his property. Only a few people had put up fences or security walls down here, which was just as well because McGarvey had a clear sight line, and he spotted the Bureau agent sitting in the gazebo almost at the same moment he smelled the man's smoke and saw for just a brief moment the glow from the tip of the cigarette.

It was damn sloppy, but it told McGarvey that at least this man wasn't expecting trouble, which in a slight way was troublesome. If the Bureau didn't expect McGarvey to show up here, why had they posted guards, at least one of whom was lax?

He waited in the darkness a full five minutes to make sure the second man wasn't on this side of the house, and that no communications passed between them, then he angled away from the water, his path between the house and the gazebo.

The agent, stood up, took a last drag on his cigarette and flicked the butt out into the water, and McGarvey silently raced the last five yards, leaped over the gazebo's low rail and hit the man low in the back with enough force to knock him down, but not enough to break his back.

McGarvey put pressure on the man's carotid arteries and within seconds the agent was out. Working quickly McGarvey slapped a piece of tape over the agent's mouth, then taped his wrists and elbows behind his back, his ankles and knees together and finally his torso and his legs to the gazebo's rail.

The agent was beginning to come around when McGarvey disappeared up to the house, opened the rear door, and slipped inside, into the kitchen where he was brought up short.

He could smell Katy's scent, and he stepped back, the same dark rage from Arlington threatening to blot out his sanity. It had only been a few days since they had left for Washington to see about Todd, yet it was a lifetime, ten lifetimes ago. But she was here.

He stayed at the kitchen door for a full minute, before he was able to rouse himself enough to go upstairs to the master suite, which was even worse for him than the kitchen. Katy was everywhere here. Her clothes, the bed, the bathroom, photographs of her on the walls, on the bureau were almost overwhelming even in the dark. He could almost expect to hear her voice telling him to stop brooding and come to bed.

Taking a small, red-lensed pen light from the dresser drawer on his side of the bed, he was about to turn and get his things from the secret floor safe in the walk-in closet when the small, framed photograph of him and Katy on the top deck of the Eiffel Tower, taken when they were very young, before Liz was born, caught his eye. Another tourist had agreed to take it, and looking at the image now McGarvey was brought back to that simpler, happier time. Nothing had ever been the same again.

He pocketed the photograph and went into his closet where he switched on the pen light. The floor safe was open and empty.

Rearing back he switched off the light, and went to the windows that looked down on the pool, the gazebo, and the dock. They had expected him to come here to retrieve his things; money in different currencies, passports and ID sets under four different work names.

But they'd gotten sloppy, waiting.

He hurried downstairs, mindful of the corners, expecting an armed man to materialize out of the darkness, yet he didn't pull his gun. These were Bureau agents. He wasn't going to be placed under arrest, nor was he going to hurt anyone beyond what was necessary.

Outside, he hurried across the yard to the next-door neighbor', keeping in the deeper shadows as much as possible and well away from the gazebo.

A few minutes later he was aboard the boat, had untied the dock lines, and using the emergency oar poled himself on an angle to the north out to the ICW before he switched on the engine, and idled a half-mile farther, before he switched on the nav lights and increased his speed.

No one else was out here on the water this early in the morning, and most of the houses along the shore were in darkness, but it wasn't until he reached the dock on Siesta Key, had replaced the boat on to lift and had re-covered it, and was in his car heading off the island did he take a deep breath.

When he reached I-75 on the mainland he turned south and merged with the very light traffic before he called Rencke.

"I'm away," he said.

"Nobody got hurt?"

"No. But they knew I was coming. They searched the house and cleaned out my safe. I don't have anything now except for what you got for me."

"You're heading south," Rencke said. "Good. I want you to go to Miami. I'll book you a room in the Park Central under your Taylor work name; it's still safe and so's the car."

"I didn't want this."

"None of us did, Mac. But it landed in our laps and now we'll deal with it," Rencke said. "Do you remember Raul Martinez?"

"Your contact in Little Havana. He arranged for me to see General Marti last year."

"Right. He'll be showing up at your hotel within the next thirty-six hours. Just sit tight until then."

THIRTY-TWO

Robert Foster's sprawling eighteenth-century home on a sloping hill above the Potomac River between Fort Hunt and Mount Vernon, about fifteen miles south of the White House, was aglow the next evening as S. Gordon Remington and his wife, Colleen, arrived in their Bentley.

Remington had preferred to drive himself, rather than be chauffeured. Some outings were better left away from prying eyes, even sympathetic ones. And he had remained sober all day, a fact Colleen had noted and appreciated, because she, too, was aware of just how much actual power Foster and his Friday Club wielded in Washington. This was no group to be trifled with. And the fact that she and her husband had been invited for cocktails and dinner topped even the A list, the only invitation better was to the White House.

They were admitted by a large, stern-looking man in a broadly cut suit, which Remington figured concealed a pistol in a shoulder holster, and were directed to the pool area in the backyard. Soft jazz was piped from several speakers as a dozen well-dressed couples circulated between a self-service bar and a table laden with hors d'oeuvres centered by an elaborate ice sculpture. Notably missing were the musicians, a bartender, and servers.

"He likes his parties lean and mean," Colleen said as they headed to the bar.

"I would have been disappointed if his house staff had been on hand tonight."

Colleen gave her husband a sharp look. "What's that supposed to mean?"

And he smiled at her. "This is the inner circle, sweetheart. All of us can discuss anything we want without fear of being overheard and misunderstood. Keep your ears open and your mouth shut."

Colleen started to bridle when a stern man who could have passed for a minister, a plain, almost mousy woman at his side, came over and stuck out his hand.

"David Whittaker, acting DCI," he said. "I'm pleased to meet you finally. Bob has told me about you and your work for the club. We appreciate your efforts."

They shook hands and introduced their wives.

"I wasn't aware you were a member," Remington said. Sandberger had warned him about sticking to a fine line between familiarity and awe. These were Washington's true power brokers, but Admin, in Roland's words, was "covering their asses."

Whittaker smiled faintly. "Charter member, actually. Bob's an old friend; he and I go way back together."

"He's not here yet?"

"He'll be down in a bit," Whittaker said. "Likes to make his entrances. His only fault, I suspect, but he's a bit of a showman, if you know what I mean." He spotted someone just coming in. "Please, enjoy yourselves," he said. He nodded to Colleen and he and his wife went to greet the new arrivals, Dennis Tressel, the assistant adviser to the president on national security affairs, and his wife.

"You never told me about this," Colleen said, reprovingly yet with a bit of admiration.

Remington got two glasses of champagne and they stepped aside.

"Actually, the Club is a new client. Roland knows more about them than I do. We're just stand-ins tonight."

"I approve, Gordo," Colleen said. "These people need to be our group, if you know what I mean."

"Perfectly—" Remington said, but his wife had spotted someone she evidently knew, and she waved and walked off, just as the armed man from the front hall who'd directed them back here approached.

"Mr. Foster would like to have a word, sir," the bodyguard said. His accent was Cockney and it grated in Remington's ears.

"My wife?"

"You won't be long, sir."

Remington noticed Whittaker and a couple of other men, including Tressel, disappearing through the pool doors back inside the house. "Of course."

"Just this way, then, sir," the bodyguard said, and Remington followed the man back into the house behind the others, who'd obviously been here before and knew the way.

Upstairs and down a short hall, the bodyguard stopped at double doors and stepped aside. "Mr. Foster is expecting you, sir."

"Royal Marines?" Remington asked.

"No, sir," the bodyguard said. "United States Marines, Gunnery Sergeant Thomas Schilling." He turned lightly on his heel and walked back past the stairs and went through a door at the end of the hall.

Remington hesitated for just a moment. This was his initiation, something Roland had mentioned. "Tell it like you see it. Don't be an asshole, but remember Foster hired Admin because of our track record. They need us more than we need them."

Remington knocked once, and went in.

Robert Foster, seated on a couch in the middle of the tastefully furnished, book-lined room, was a man in his mid-sixties, short, somewhat stocky with the build of a midwestern farmer, who touted himself as nothing more than a "servant of the common man."

Seated on the couch with him and in chairs across a coffee table, were Whittaker and Tressel, plus Air Force general Albert Burnside, who was the chief political adviser to the Joint Chiefs.

Foster was as far right a conservative as was possible, with exceedingly strong views on everything from the role of religion in government, to abortion, states' rights, the Constitution and the makeup of the Supreme Court, and the powers of the executive branch versus a meddling, ineffective Congress. And he was a multi-millionaire with a law degree from Florida's Stetson University and an MBA from Harvard.

To this point in his career he'd made his money as an economic adviser to several foreign governments, including South Korea, Japan, Australia, and the Czech Republic, but most notably Mainland China in the mid-nineties. The last had taken his supporters somewhat by surprise, until they realized that an emerging China would be needed to shore up the U.S. government, which would, in Foster's estimation, be faced with a financial meltdown. It was because of his advice that China had become a major bondholder for the U.S. In some circles he had come out the hero—America's savior, or so the conservative think tank Arnault Group had labeled him. But Democrats, except for the ones he had bought and paid for, were dead set against him, calling him "America's Judas Iscariot, the man who sold his country for silver."

Foster looked up and smiled. "Gordon, welcome to my home. I assume you know most of the others here tonight?"

"Good evening, sir," Remington said. "Some only by reputation, I'm afraid."

"Well you know David and Dennis but perhaps not General Burnside."

"I've read his position memos you were kind enough to share with Admin," Remington said. "I assume these gentlemen have been briefed on our contract with you."

"Roland is a regular," Foster said. "Normally he would be here this evening, but since he's out of the country I invited you."

"May I ask the reason?"

Whittaker got up and poured a glass of champagne for Remington. "This is a council of war, Gordon. And since Admin is on the front line we thought it best that you were briefed."

"Are we talking about Kirk McGarvey?" Remington asked. The champagne was first-rate. Cristal or Krug, he guessed.

"Indeed we are," Foster said. "And by the way, David is the CIA's new director."

"I heard," Remington said. "Dick Adkins's resignation came as a surprise."

"Langdon fired the fool for standing face-to-face in the Oval Office and defending McGarvey."

"Actually did us a service," Foster said. "With Adkins gone Mr. McGarvey doesn't have many friends. And witnessing the deaths of his family at Arlington has unhinged the man."

"He's dangerous," Remington said.

"Yes," Foster said.

"But he knows nothing," Whittaker said. "He suspects there may be a connection between the incidents in Mexico City and Pyongyang, but he can't prove a thing."

Remington had a fair guess what they were talking about, something of the smuggling of radioactive material across the border from Mexico and less than one year later the assassination of a high-ranking Chinese intelligence officer in North Korea's capital had been in the news. But Sandberger had not briefed him on what role, if any, the Friday Club had played in the incidents, and he held his tongue.

"The man is a bulldog," Foster said. "He'll never give up. Especially now."

"We've anticipated just that," Remington said. And all eyes were turned toward him. "Roland is remaining in Baghdad for more than contract negotiations. He's there because we think McGarvey will come after him. And Baghdad is Admin's city, where accidents can and do happen."

"None of you still know the measure of this man," Whittaker said.

"He's just that," Remington disagreed. "Just one man, while we have in excess of one hundred highly motivated, highly trained shooters on the ground, along with a sophisticated infrastructure of weapons, surveillance, and communications. When he shows up in Baghdad he will die. At this moment he is Admin's number one priority."

"There you are, gentlemen," Foster said. "Thank you, Gordon. We have the utmost confidence in your company. Now, please, rejoin your wife and the others outside. We'll finish up in here in a couple of minutes and have something to eat."

When Remington was gone, Foster turned back to the others. "McGarvey may be Administrative Solutions' top priority, but I'm afraid we'll have to turn to even more drastic measures."

"What do you have in mind, Bob?" General Burnside asked.

"Neither the Mexican nor the North Korean missions had the desired effect."

"Because of McGarvey," Whittaker suggested.

"In part," Foster agreed. "Once he's out of the way, we'll need to look to Taipei to meet our objective. Hong Kong is too small, only Taiwan will do. And it may be up to our navy to trigger the spark. The pressure will fall on the Pentagon's shoulders."

"I've already begun to put some pieces into play," General Burnside said.

"Tell us," Foster said. "And leave nothing out."

THIRTY-THREE

On the beach in front of the Park Central Hotel, McGarvey stopped a moment and looked back at the balcony of his fifth-floor room. He thought he'd spotted a movement, but then it came again, a random breeze fluttering the drapes on the partially open patio window and he relaxed a little.

He'd checked in late, and if anyone at the desk remembered him, but under a different work name from last year, they didn't show it. The Park was one of the older, refurbished hotels in the heart of Miami's art deco district, the last place anyone, especially the FBI or someone from Admin, would look for him.

For the moment he was reasonably safe here, but he was chafing at the bit to get started. And it was next to impossible for him to erase the vision of Katy's limousine exploding in front of him. He couldn't put out of his head the last touch, the last kiss, the last words, and it was driving him nearly insane; his rage was a barely controlled thing just beneath the surface.

He'd gotten up before dawn, and waited until the gift shops along Ocean Drive opened. He bought a pair of swim trunks and a beach jacket, and went across to the ocean where an attendant brought him a beach chair. He'd left the jacket behind and went into the water, warm at this time of the year, and began swimming straight out to sea. His stroke was strong, even, measured and he let a slight rip current help carry him farther.

At one point he thought he'd heard a lifeguard's whistle, but then it faded and he put more effort into his stroke until looking over his shoulder he could see the buildings, but not the beach itself, and he rolled over on his back and floated on the long, gentle swells.

Otto would get him to Baghdad in such a way that Sandberger and his people wouldn't know about it until it was too late. There was a connection between Admin and the Friday Club and he was going to find out about it, whatever it took. Afterward he would take whatever leads he could extract and go after them until he reached the end.

It didn't matter, now, who he brought down. But someone was going to pay for Katy and Liz and for Todd, and pay dearly.

Forty minutes later he was back on the beach, where he dried off, got his beach jacket, gave the attendant a twenty-dollar bill, and walked back across to his hotel and up to his room.

He'd left a couple of obvious fail safes, including a hair across the door seam, and the carpet scuffed in a certain way just inside the door, that would have easily caught even an amateur's notice, but the smudge on the inside door handle was hidden, and might have been missed. But nothing had been disturbed. So far he'd attracted no notice.

He stripped and took a long hot shower, followed by a cold one, then shaved and got dressed in a pair of jeans, a khaki sport fisherman's shirt, untucked, and a pair of deck shoes. When he came out the missed call light on his encrypted sat phone was blinking.

It was Otto and he answered as usual on the first ring. "Are you okay?"

"I went out for a swim."

Otto was silent for a beat. "Oh, that's good," he said. "But now you need to keep a lower profile. A federal judge signed a warrant for your arrest and the Bureau has issued an APB, with emphasis on central and southern Florida. They figure you're still in the state, because they know what you were looking for in your house, and probably why. So they're backtracking to find out what ID you used to get down there and when they get that they'll have you."

"I'll need to get out of here sometime tonight."

"Sooner than that. Martinez will get your package in a few hours, and he'll come over to the hotel for the delivery. I'm still working on some of it, but I'm taking my time. This has got to be right the first time, because after your deal in Frankfurt they've gotta expect you'll go up against Sandberger again. This time in Baghdad. So they'll be looking for you."

"What do you have in mind?"

"First off you'll have to change your appearance, but nothing drastic. Martinez will have everything you need. I've lifted two of your ID photos from your Company file and altered them. You'll see from what I've done what you'll have to change. Hair dye, skin tone, that sort of thing."

"We've been through it before."

"Yes," Otto said. "I thought about getting you out under a diplomatic passport, but I think that's just what the Bureau might be expecting. Homeland Security has probably been notified, which means the TSA guys at every airport in the country will be on the lookout for someone with your general build traveling under the ID of a State Department FSO."

"No weapons."

"That would compound the troubles, and it's also something they expect. I'm working on getting you two sets of legitimate passports and IDs. Maybe one as a contractor and the other as a journalist. I'm working on that part."

"What about out of Kuwait?"

"You'll need a guide."

"I don't want to involve anyone else," McGarvey said. People close to him tended to get themselves killed. He didn't know if he could handle much more of that.

"You don't have much of a choice, kemo sabe. The situation out there is too fluid for you not to rely on local knowledge. Hell, just getting from Kuwait City to Baghdad is a tough nut to crack even for a convoy. You gotta listen to me, Mac."

But it was hard. He wanted revenge, and yet he knew that he wasn't thinking straight.

"Pull your head out, Mac. Honest injun. This is too important to screw up. You and I both know that Mexico City and Pyongyang were connected and there's more to come."

"How's Audie," McGarvey asked, changing tack. Otto was correct, there was no getting around it. He'd always considered himself a loner, but almost from the beginning he'd had Otto's help. Only it wasn't until now that he really understood just how much help his friend had given him.

"She's fine, and she's going to stay put until we get this shit settled. Are you with me?"

"Yeah," McGarvey said. "I'll need to know who Sandberger's surrounding himself with, the layout of where he's staying, and my chances of getting to him when he's least protected."

"What I can't come up with before you head out this afternoon I'll have waiting for you in Kuwait," Otto said. "Question."

"Go ahead."

"What if Sandberger and Administrative Solutions are nothing more than they advertise themselves?"

"That's not true."

"Goddamnit, Mac, isn't there anything Louise or I can say to make you back off just for a little while until I come up with something concrete?"

"No," McGarvey said, a coldness closing over his heart. "It's too late for that now."

Otto was silent for a long moment, when he was back he sounded resigned. "Your call, kemo sabe. I'll do everything I can from this end to get you the intel you need."

"As you always have."

"But I need you to listen to me—really listen to me, no shit. I'll give you the truth. I'll never blow smoke up your ass. My promise. And you'll have to promise me that you'll listen back."

McGarvey looked out the window. The morning sky over the Atlantic was perfectly clear. *When the sun is shining anything is possible.* It was one of Katy's favorite sayings. She hated dark, cloudy, rainy days.

"Promise," McGarvey told his old friend.

THIRTY-FOUR

☐

Dick Adkins had never been much for confrontations, nor had he ever been much of a spy, in the sense of a field agent, or a special operative like McGarvey. But he was a good administrator and while under his watch morale at the CIA hadn't been given much of a boost, yet it had not sagged with the economy and political tides as other agencies, in particular FEMA and Homeland Security, had.

But pulling up at the security gate at CIA Headquarters he wondered if coming back to confront Dave Whittaker made any sense, or would make any difference. He was certain that the only man who had any real inkling of what Mexico City and Pyongyang meant, and what was still coming after them, was McGarvey. And the Company needed to cut him some slack.

The guard recognized Adkins, but for just a moment he seemed unsure of what to do. He glanced at something to his right, then looked back, smiled and nodded. "Good afternoon, Mr. Director," he said, and he waved Adkins through.

Evidently word had not filtered down to the security personnel that Adkins no longer had access. It was something he'd counted on.

He drove up the curving road to the Old Headquarters Building, past the visitors' parking lot around to the gated entrance to the executive underground parking garage. He'd neglected to turn in his security pass and it still worked to raise the barrier. Down on the third level he pulled up beside the DCI's slot, occupied now by Dave Whittaker's dark green Chevy Impala.

His pass also worked in the private elevator to the seventh floor, and stepping off the car he was taken aback for just a moment. A long-standing tradition had been for all the doors on the seventh floor to be left open. Everyone up here was cleared for just about everything that went on. And every DCI, back as far as Adkins could remember, had liked to come out of their offices and wander up and down the corridors to see what was going on. The only doors left closed were the ones to the director's office and to his private dining room.

But this afternoon every door on the seventh floor was closed. That fact seemed somehow ominous to Adkins as he walked down the hall to the DCI's office and went in.

Dahlia Swanson, the secretary Adkins had inherited from McGarvey, had already been replaced by a much younger woman with her dark hair up in a bun, reading glasses on a gold chain perched on the end of her nose. She looked up in momentary surprise, but recovered nicely.

"Mr. Adkins," she said pleasantly. "Do you have an appointment with Mr. Whittaker?"

"Is he in?"

"Yes, sir."

"Good," Adkins said, and he went around to the door to the DCI's office and let himself in before the secretary could pick up her phone.

Whittaker was seated at his desk, his back to the door. He was staring out the windows at the softly wooded, gentle West Virginia hills, and it was a second or two before he swiveled around, and his right eyebrow twitched.

"Thought I'd come by for a chat," Adkins said, dropping into a chair in front of the desk.

"You're a surprise, Dick. How did you manage to get in?"

"My security passes have not been invalidated yet. You might want to have a word with Housekeeping, they tend to drag their feet unless given a nudge now and then."

"What do you want?"

"That's the rub, then, isn't it? You have your hands full trying to satisfy a president who, like most presidents before him, doesn't want to listen to the truth, while at the same time you're trying to rein McGarvey in without forcing a bloodbath."

"Trying to save your friend?"

"Save him from what, Dave?" Adkins asked. "The Bureau has been given a warrant for his arrest. Are they really expecting casualties?"

"I'm sure it's something they're considering. He took down the two marshals at Arlington."

"He didn't kill them."

Whittaker hesitated a moment, a disagreeable expression on his long face. "What's your point? What are you doing here?"

"You no more believe Mac is a traitor than I do. It means you have to find him before the Bureau does, and definitely before the marshals do, because if someone makes a mistake—and it won't be Mac—someone could get hurt."

"You came here to help me?"

"To advise you, unless you still think Van Buren's death was a random act, and that Mac's wife and daughter were blown up by terrorists with no specific target in mind. Just mayhem at Arlington."

"We have no other supporting evidence, Dick. You know that. Christ, I wish it were different."

Adkins had wished his coming here wasn't an exercise in futility, but he was beginning to seriously wonder. "IED's have moved from Iraq and Afghanistan to America. A lot of people are asking why the hell the government isn't doing something about it."

"Homeland Security—"

"Bullshit. These weren't homegrown terrorists, and everyone knows it. Puts the pressure square in your lap. Or are you still blaming McGarvey for the deaths of his wife, daughter, and son-in-law?"

"I'll ask again, what's your point?"

"Connections."

Whittaker shrugged. "I'm sorry, I don't follow you."

"Mac went to Mexico City to figure out what a Chinese intelligence officer was doing down there, and he found out a lot of polonium-210 was being smuggled across our border. And it disappeared. Less than one year later a Chinese intelligence officer is assassinated in Pyongyang and when Mac unravels that mess—averting an exchange of nuclear weapons in the region—we find out that our deputy director of operations was involved in both operations. And when all was said and done, Mac was accused of being a traitor to his country. Now you tell me what's bullshit and what's not. Because there're damn well some connections there that need the light of day."

Whittaker got very still.

"You know that I still have some political capital left," Adkins said. "How about if I hold a news conference and lay out what I know and suspect about Mexico City, Pyongyang, and Arlington? You'd have the media crawling all over this place, but more importantly all over the White House. I wonder what Langdon's reaction would be, considering his energy bill is falling apart, and we've had the first serious terrorist attack on our soil since nine/eleven?"

"One call and you'd be stopped."

"I didn't get the word until it was too late. Anyway, once the cat's out of the bag it's too late."

"One last time, Dick. What's your point? What do you want?"

"Has anyone seen Otto Rencke lately?"

Whittaker was startled. "No," he said. "Is that significant?"

"I'd think so," Adkins said. "Instead of trying to find Mac and corner him, look for Otto. If Mac fights back someone will get hurt."

"If Rencke fights back the son of a bitch could do us a lot of harm."

"At least no one would get physically injured," Adkins said. "Find him and you'll find Mac."

"And then what?" Whitttaker asked.

Adkins got to his feet. "Maybe you'll find the connections. Mexico City to Pyongyang and to whatever else Mac is looking for." At the door Adkins looked back. "It's important."

Whittaker nodded. "I'll do what I can. No promises."

"Good enough."

T H I R T Y — F I V E

McGarvey's sat phone rang. It was Otto. "He just pulled up in front of your hotel."

"Did he come in clean?" McGarvey asked. He'd been here, in one place far too long to trust anything.

"I haven't picked up traces of anyone interested. But you might want to take a look down his track."

McGarvey broke the connection, slipped out of his room, and as one of the elevators started up from the lobby, he ducked into the alcove containing the ice and vending machines, pressing back into the corner.

At this hour of the early afternoon the hotel was not very busy, and the car came directly to the eighth floor. Moments later a slender man, with a narrow, clean-shaven, olive-complected face, dressed in a European-cut suit, carrying an attaché case in his left hand walked by. McGarvey didn't think he'd ever met the man, and he pulled out his pistol and chanced a quick look out into the corridor.

The man stopped at the door to McGarvey's room, and knocked. In the meantime the elevator continued up.

McGarvey stepped out of the alcove and keeping the pistol at his side moved toward the man, who suddenly stopped knocking, but did not turn away from the door.

"It's me," the man said as McGarvey reached him, and his voice was vaguely familiar.

"Who are you?" McGarvey said, as he patted the man down for a weapon.

"Raul Martinez. We met a couple of years ago, here in Miami. You were here to see General Marti about his daughter."

"You look different."

"Everyone needs a little change every now and then," Martinez said. "Otto asked me to tell you that Audie is just fine. She's safe at the Farm." He turned finally to look McGarvey in the eye.

The last time McGarvey had seen Martinez, the CIA operative could have been out of central casting for a *Miami Vice* episode; peg-legged slacks, embroidered Guayabara shirt, pencil-thin mustache, and slicked-down shining black hair. He looked like a lawyer or businessman now. But the eyes were the same: cool, assured, haughty, on guard. McGarvey relaxed.

"You ought to think about becoming a spy."

"Too dangerous," Martinez said.

"I've heard," McGarvey said, holstering his pistol. He let them into his room, relocking the safety bar.

"With all the heat out there, I made sure I came in clean," Martinez said, laying the attaché case on the bed.

"Have I been traced here to Miami?"

"No, but the federales are beating the bushes across the entire Southeast, but mostly here in south Florida. The U.S. Marshal and Bureau guys are practically tripping over one another. But they'll get their shit together soon enough, and then it'll become a little rough for you to stick around."

"I want to get out of here this afternoon."

"You'll just make it if we work fast," Martinez said, and he opened the attaché case and started pulling stuff out. "United leaves MIA at ten after five, gives you about three hours."

He took out an eight-by-ten photograph of a McGarvey with short, gray hair, glasses, and a ruddy complexion, and laid it on the bed. "Tony Watkins, a freelance journalist accredited with the U.S. Army." He handed McGarvey a pair of barber shears, and a bottle of hair dye and a couple of brushes, one of them small, and nodded toward the bathroom. "Better get started. We'll talk while you work."

McGarvey pulled off his shirt, tossed it aside, and went into the bathroom, where he propped the photo on the counter, and started to work on his hair.

"The small brush is for your eyebrows," Martinez said from the bedroom. "I have lotion for your face and the backs of your hands that will age you a few years. We don't want to overdo it."

McGarvey had gone through these kinds of routines before, it was all standard tradecraft that even the kids at the Farm were taught from the get-go.

"I'm laying out all your paperwork for you, including your passport, D.C. driver's license, health insurance cards, Army credentials, credit cards, even photos of your wife and kiddies, plus a portfolio of your work and a small digital video camera."

"When do I get to Kuwait City?"

"Tomorrow afternoon, quarter after five. It's the best we could do on such short notice. Miami to Orlando, then Washington's Dulles and finally across the Atlantic. But your layovers are short."

McGarvey had been on those kinds of interminable trips before. He'd catch up on his sleep, because he was sure he'd need it once he was boots on the ground. "What's the drill in Kuwait City?" he asked, matching his appearance in the mirror with that in the photograph. He was close.

"You're booked at the Airport Crowne Plaza. A little rich for a free-lancer, but you're a successful journalist," Martinez said. He came to the bathroom door. "That's close enough. Use the dye."

McGarvey put down the shears. "Don't check me out of this hotel until the last minute. I'd like at least a twelve-hour head start."

"That's what Otto figured. Once you're gone I'll clean up the mess, and get rid of your old work name credentials. And your weapon. You'll have to travel bare this time. Lots of suspicious people in Kuwait."

McGarvey didn't like it, but he understood the necessity. "What comes after the Crowne Plaza?"

"Khalid Hadid will pick you up in front sometime before midnight for the run to Baghdad. He'll have some new clothes and field gear for you, including a helmet and Kevlar vest, which you might need, along with a weapon or weapons. We're leaving it up to his judgment what's best up there, but it'll probably include a Kalashnikov."

"Who is this guy?" McGarvey asked, brushing in the hair dye, and it began to work almost immediately, lightening his brown hair, and blending the gray at the sides.

"He's one of ours. A NOC from the old days. Just before the end he was one of Uncle Saddam's Republican Guards. Had a couple of really good chances to whack the bastard, but he was told to back off."

McGarvey looked at Martinez's reflection in the mirror. "It was a war we wanted."

"Something like that. Anyway, he knows what he's doing, so he'll be an asset."

McGarvey concentrated on the hair dye for a minute or two, making sure he'd covered everything, including his eyebrows. The chemical stung his scalp but it was fast-acting.

"I'll put the Do Not Disturb sign on the door, and lock the safety bar before we clear out. I'll drive you to the airport, but we'll leave by a service exit in back. My car's parked just around the corner."

When he was done with the hair dye, McGarvey stripped and showered off the excess chemical. When he was finished, he applied the lotion to his face and the backs of his hands, which gave his skin a slightly red and mottled cast, as if he'd spent too many years outdoors in harsh conditions.

Martinez had packed everything except McGarvey's khaki slacks, a white pullover, blue blazer, shoes, and a change of underwear, plus the portfolio and digital camera.

"Look, Mr. McGarvey, for what it's worth, I think it's a bunch of bullshit what they're trying to do to you," Martinez said as McGarvey was getting dressed. "The word's gotten around headquarters what's going on and everyone's behind you. Especially after your wife and daughter, and son-in-law."

"They're charging me with treason," McGarvey said, putting on his blazer and pocketing his new IDs, passport, and airline tickets. "If the media picks it up there'll be a firestorm. Those guys are a hell of a lot more tenacious than the Bureau. So if it happens, keep your ass down."

"Do you have a timetable?" Martinez asked.

"No. But I suspect the shit will begin to hit the fan a lot sooner than we want."

THIRTY-SIX

At that moment Remington, still in his pajamas and robe with his family's monogram on the right breast, put down the encrypted telephone in his study and sat back for a moment to admire the view of his backyard.

Sandberger was in Baghdad settling the details for Admin's new, lucrative contract with State, and nothing other than the McGarvey issue was pressing at the moment in the office, so he'd opted to stay home for the day, all his important calls rolled over to his home phone.

Roland had once told him that the Brits, especially the gentry, were not exactly lazy, but they did know how to relax. It was something Americans had never learned. Another reason they'd made such a good pair, opposites were complementary.

McGarvey had apparently shown up in Miami for whatever reason and he was flying to Kuwait this afternoon. Presumably he would make his way to Baghdad from there, though Remington's contact didn't know all the details yet, nor did he know if McGarvey would be traveling under a work name. But he was on his way, as they expected he would be, to confront Roland. And it was exactly what they wanted.

He telephoned the office and was connected with Gina Ballinger, Admin's housekeeper who provided cover identities for Admin's contractors who needed anonymity, as well as their travel arrangements and whatever other equipment or services they would require at both ends of the assignment.

"Two for Baghdad," Remington told her. "Tim and Ronni this time."

"Certainly, sir," Gina said. She'd been an accountant and had the rare ability to keep her eye on the details—all the details, all the time.

"We'll need speed, luv."

"Do you want them staged through Kuwait, or will this be direct from Frankfurt to Baghdad?"

"Keep them away from Kuwait. Frankfurt would be best. And send them first class this time."

"Equipment?"

"The usual in Baghdad. This will be a surgical strike. We have word on the whereabouts of Muzammil Suhaib."

"He's not coming up on my database," Gina said after a moment's hesitation.

"This is something new."

"Shall I add his name?"

"That won't be necessary for the moment," Remington said. The Suhaib name was a code word that would eventually be used for records and payroll after McGarvey had been taken down and Kangas and Mustapha were back in the States. It would give them time to sanitize the operation. It was something that Gina had done before. Often.

"I understand," she said. "Will they be coming into the office, or should I arrange for a drop at the airport?"

"A drop would be best," Remington said. "I'm going out in a few minutes. As soon as you've made the arrangements, text me. All I need are the flight number and time."

"Dulles?"

"I don't see any reason why not," Remington said, and he broke the connection and sat again for a minute or so contemplating not only the chances for their success against a man such as McGarvey, but the consequences if they failed.

His opinion had been to sidestep the issue. McGarvey was already under suspicion of treason; it was a charge the White House wanted to press. And his actions at Arlington and his disappearance afterward were not those of an innocent man.

With Foster's connections McGarvey wouldn't have a chance in hell to prove his innocence, especially if he took down more U.S. Marshals or perhaps a couple of Bureau agents. It was even likely that he would be shot to death attempting to escape.

But Sandberger had been adamant. "I want the son of a bitch taken down, Gordo. And I don't give a damn what it costs. Everything else is secondary."

McGarvey's arrogant appearance at the Steigenberger had so infuriated Roland that, in Remington's estimation, he wasn't thinking straight.

He telephoned Kangas, who answered on the first ring. "You and Ronni are leaving this afternoon. Meet me in front of the Lincoln Memorial in forty-five minutes."

"Free the slaves, is it?" Kangas replied.

Remington bit back a sharp retort. They were expendable. No matter what happened in Baghdad, it would be their last assignment. They were getting out of control. It was the same reason why they'd been fired by the CIA. Free the slaves, indeed.

Remington finished his coffee, got dressed, and left his house, cabbing over to the Mall, getting there a full twenty minutes early. His tradecraft was a little rusty; it had been years since he'd taken part in a field operation, but old habits died hard, and there were some survival skills you never forgot.

The day was bright and warm, and a lot of tourists were in town, which was why he had picked this place. Depending on what happened in Baghdad, Kangas and Mustapha might attract the wrong sort of attention. Meeting anonymously like this the same day they left the country would provide some deniability later if questions were to be raised.

He walked down from the foot of 23rd Street where the cab had dropped him, and around the circle toward the Reflecting Pool, intending to wait there to see what developed when Kangas and Mustapha arrived, but they were already there.

Vexed, he walked down to them. "I said forty-five minutes."

"Insurance," Kangas said insolently. "You can never tell what'll happen, so you cover your bases." He glanced down toward the Vietnam Memorial, the black wall filled with the fifty thousand plus names of war dead. "Don't want to end up like those poor bastards."

"We all die sooner or later."

"I meant wasted," Kangas said. "What's our assignment?"

Gina had texted him with the flight information on the way over. "McGarvey's in Baghdad. I want him taken down."

"There'll have to be a bonus," Mustapha said.

"Another one million dollars."

"Another two million dollars," Kangas said. "Each."

Remington was momentarily taken aback, but he managed to smile. "Of course. The first half will be in your accounts by the time you touch down." It wouldn't matter, because recovery of Admin's funds from dead men's accounts was SOP. There were no next of kin benefits in this business, and everyone understood it. The idea tended to sharpen up the average contractor.

"Baghdad's a dangerous place, we'll need some gear, and some intel. How long has he been in country?"

"Our intel says he's not there yet. We think he's going through Kuwait and then presumably by ground transportation the rest of the way. We're sending you through Frankfurt and from there direct, so you'll be in place at least six, maybe twelve hours before him."

"Equipment?"

"You'll be met at Dulles with your instructions, including the name of your contact in country, and any updates we have on Mr. McGarvey's itinerary. You're flying United 8826, leaves at quarter to six."

"What about ground support?"

"You're on your own after you've met your quartermaster," Remington said. "Which means you are to have no contact whatsoever with anyone working for us or any other contractor service. If you do, the deal is off, you'll forfeit your bonuses and you will be terminated. Can you handle it, or should I send someone else?"

"We can handle it," Kangas said, his eyes narrowed.

"Don't miss this time."

THIRTY-SEVEN

A couple of hours out of Kuwait, McGarvey ordered a bloody Mary from one of the business-class attendants and settled down to familiarize himself with the material Otto had sent to him via Martinez.

Besides the name Tony Watkins, a freelance journalist who had published articles in the *Washington Post* and *New York Times* as well as journals such as *Jane's Defense Weekly*, which Otto had included for McGarvey to read, he'd memorized the man's background—place of birth, education, family. All of it was manufactured, of course, but convincing enough even if someone curious were to search out the published stories under his name.

Everything was going to happen very fast once he was on the ground, so even if someone started poking around it would already be too late. He would be gone, headed back to the States under a different work name.

Watkins was an expert on weapons including all types of hand-guns and personal defense weapons such as the Heckler & Koch MP5 room broom, and on IEDs. According to the legend Otto had built for the character, Watkins had apparently witnessed several IED incidents, in one of which he'd lost someone close.

When he came to that part, McGarvey looked up and stared out the window for a long moment, seeing the explosion at Arlington, seeing and knowing that his wife and daughter were dead, completely beyond saving. He closed his eyes, the cruelty of what Otto had done beyond belief. But it was just for a moment, until he understood that if for whatever reason someone on the ground questioned him about his background, he wouldn't have to lie about his loss. He would be convincing. And a part of him, the professional part, had to admire the touch, and he suspected that it could not have been easy for Otto to include it.

It was around four in the afternoon in al Kuwait, but only seven in the morning back in Miami. He'd actually gotten a couple hours of sleep, and for once since Arlington he'd not had the dream. He'd become super-focused on the job ahead. Confronting Sandberger was only the first part of what he wanted to do, because he was certain that threads had to go back to Foster and the Friday Club. But untangling that mess wouldn't be easy, or clean, in part because he suspected that the incident in Mexico City and the one in Pyongyang were connected.

Foster had some goal in mind, some reason for the operations and for the killing of Todd and Liz and Katy. And there was no power on earth that was going to stop him from finding out what that was.

But the threads went to the CIA itself, and even the White House, as if Givens had been correct in fearing there might be some sort of a shadow government in Washington.

The question always in McGarvey's mind throughout his career was who to trust. There weren't many people left for him.

. . .

The Crowne Plaza with its soaring atrium lobby and glass elevators was just a few minutes drive from the airport, and could have been in just about any country. Airport hotels everywhere had the same general look and feel to them.

In the cab on the way to the hotel Otto called him on the sat phone. "Any trouble with customs?"

"No, everything went smoothly," McGarvey said. "Has anything new developed in Washington?"

"If you mean with the Friday Club, no. And, man, I'm telling you they're tight. Getting intel on them beyond their public persona is impossible. I mean, I get their social security numbers and tax returns, I even get the position papers Foster and some of the others have written, but everything else is a blank. I can't even come up with a members list."

"No connections between them and Mexico City or Pyongyang?"

"Not so far, but I'm working on it, trust me."

"Anything else on Sandberger and his people on the ground in Baghdad?"

"Aside from the fact that he's surrounded himself with more muscle than usual, nothing. Except that his contract negotiations with the State Department finished two days ago, but he's stayed there."

"He knows I'm coming."

"Yeah," Otto said, and he sounded glum. "Go ahead and unpack, then get something good to eat, but you're leaving everything behind, except for your IDs and Army passes and accreditation cards. Hadid will be picking you up around nine."

"What about the background files Martinez gave me?"

"They're all printed on smart paper," Otto said. "Soon as you leave the hotel, I'll send a signal and erase the imbedded memory. And once you're done in Baghdad and on the way back out I'll erase the rest of your documents."

"That'll put me in Hadid's hands."

"He's been risking his life for us for a long time. He's a good man who's willing to go back into Iraq even though the Sunnis have a contract on him."

"What about in Baghdad?"

"That'll be up to you, Mac," Otto said. "He's willing to do anything you want him to do. But he's putting himself in a tough position."

"I'll need him to stay put, out of my way. I'm handling Sandberger myself."

Check-in went without a hitch; upstairs McGarvey unpacked his things and distributed them around the room and in the bathroom as if he were planning on staying for the four days the room had been booked. He laid the files in plain sight on the desk, and went downstairs to the Fauchon's of Paris restaurant in the lobby, getting a table near the back but from where he could watch the front entrance.

He was served a good rib eye steak, no beer or wine of course, and when he was finished it was a couple of minutes before nine. As he signed the check a slightly built man, dark eyes and hair and thin mustache, handsome as many Iraqis were, sat down across the table from him.

"Tony, good to see you again," he said jovially, his English good. "Did you have a pleasant flight over?"

The waiter collected McGarvey's check. "Would the gentleman care for something?" he asked Hadid.

"A dry martini, straight up, very cold."

The waiter turned and stalked off.

"He'll remember you," McGarvey said.

Hadid smiled. "But not you." He stuck his hand out. "Khalid Hadid. Are you ready to rumble?"

"Any time," McGarvey said, and he started to rise but Hadid motioned him back.

"Wait for one hour, then come out. We'll be in a dark blue Range Rover, soft top."

"We?"

"Yes, my son Saddam is making the trip with us," Hadid said, grinning broadly. "His name is a joke, but Hussein thought it was kind of me to name my only boy after him."

"It was a dangerous game."

"All life is a danger, Mr. Tony, you of all people should know this. Anyway, my Saddam is sixteen today and this is his first trip. Someone might be expecting you. But not an entire family."

Before McGarvey could ask another question Hadid turned and headed across the busy grand lobby.

THIRTY-EIGHT

The moment Sandberger found out that McGarvey had landed in Kuwait under the name Tony Watkins, he telephoned Stuart Marston, the U.S. envoy from the State Department he'd worked with on the new contracts. Marston was a player, his father a family friend of Foster's.

"There's been a new development. The one we talked about a few days ago. I'll have to remain here in the city for a day or two, possibly longer."

"I heard the rumors," Marston said.

"It's true, the son of a bitch is coming here gunning for me. But he's in for a nasty surprise."

"I don't know what you're planning, but you'd better be damned careful if you're contemplating any sort of gunplay. Right now the situation is relatively calm. Better than it's been since the beginning. Shooting an American will be dicey."

"The man's been accused of treason."

"But not indicted," Marston said. "And he was the director of the CIA. Not every president hated him."

"You tell me, Stu, am I supposed to simply sit on my ass and let the man kill me? It won't happen. I have people who'll take care of the situation."

"I'm not telling you what to do, that's not my job. All I'm saying is that if you get yourself involved with McGarvey, and the situation goes south—if civilians get in the way and are hurt—Admin's contracts would be in serious jeopardy."

The man was an ass licker in Sandberger's opinion. The only reason he was given a seat, and only on the sidelines, with Foster was because his old man had been a powerful senator from Montana, and his uncle had been one of the biggest cattle ranchers in that state plus Wyoming and Colorado. Money had always been the real raison d'être in Washington.

But Sandberger forced himself to calm down, putting aside for the moment the incident with McGarvey in Frankfurt. "What do you suggest?" he asked.

"I think we can kill two birds with one stone, if we're smart about it," Marston said.

"I'm listening."

"Do you know Mustafa Kabbani?"

"He's chief of Baghdad police, but I've not had any direct dealings with him. Admin's contracts have always been with the State Department."

"From what I'm told McGarvey almost always works alone. So when he shows up here he'll be armed but on his own. The FBI has a warrant for his arrest, and if the Baghdad police were to take him into custody and let the Bureau transport him back to Washington it'd be a feather in their cap. And a feather in yours for showing restraint."

"I see your point," Sandberger said.

"I'll arrange a meeting for you."

"When and where," Sandberger asked without hesitation.

"One hour from now at the Babylon."

. . .

The Babylon Hotel on the banks of the Tigris River in the Zuweia District was unique in that manager and staff didn't seem to mind that most of its guests arrived heavily armed. AK-47s were as common as attaché cases. And alcohol was served, though usually only in the guest rooms from minibars. But exceptions were made.

Sandberger went straight through the lobby to the patio and pool area that overlooked the river, to where Captain Mustafa Kabbani, drinking beer from a frosted mug, was seated alone at a small table. He was a big barrel-chested man, in his late forties, with thick, salt-and-pepper hair, a large mustache, and long delicate fingers.

He looked up and nodded toward the chair across the table.

"Thanks for agreeing to see me on such short notice," Sandberger said, sitting down.

"We have mutual friends, and perhaps a problem that will result in a mutual benefit to both of us. What is it that you want? Exactly."

The waiter came and Sandberger ordered a cold beer then outlined what probably would happen in the next twenty-four hours or so. "Do you know McGarvey?"

"I've heard of the man. But why is he coming here to assassinate you? And what has he done that his government is charging him with treason?"

"He wants me dead because he believes I murdered his son-in-law. Which is a lie, I was here in Baghdad at the time. But exactly why he's being charged with treason I'm not sure. I only know that the FBI wants him for questioning, as does the U.S. Federal Marshal's office. Apparently he shot a marshal when he escaped a few days ago."

Sandberger's beer came, and Kabbani turned to look at something across the river. He remained silent like that for several long moments before he turned back. "Which would be more to your advantage? Kill him or arrest him?"

"That's totally up to you, Captain. But if only half of what I've heard about him is true, it might be easier all around to shoot him as he was trying to escape." Sandberger looked across the river, but he couldn't make out anything that might interest the policeman. "I'm sure his U.S. warrant has shown up on Interpol's net, which you should have access to. I suggest you print out the warrant and photo or photos and watch for him."

"Will he have help here?" Kabbani asked. "Does he have contacts with the military, or perhaps with the State Department?"

"None that I know of."

Again the policeman hesitated. Clearly he was weighing his options. "At one time Mr. McGarvey was the director of the CIA. It is a powerful position. He must still have many friends in Washington."

"Undoubtedly."

"Killing him will not be without political risk."

Sandberger sat back. "I was told that you would help."

"Such an operation could bring about certain expenses not in my budget," Kabbani said, leaving the thought hanging.

Sandberger smiled. "Something will be arranged. I signed a new contract for services."

"Yes, I know. Could you be more specific?"

"How many men will you require?"

"I think six—"

Sandberger interrupted. "Make it twelve. But the Basra Highway from Kuwait will have to be watched. We don't think he'll be flying in."

"Then I will send some men out to meet him. Not policemen. Perhaps we will be able to deal with the problem before it arrives here."

"Call me as soon as you have the situation in hand," Sandberger said. He got up and started to leave, but Kabbani stopped him.

"McGarvey's wife and daughter lost their lives in an IED explosion at Arlington Cemetery," the policeman said. "It is a very bad business involving a man's family."

Sandberger started to protest, but Kabbani held him off. "I will take care of this problem for you. Administrative Solutions will be here for at least one more year. It could be I will require a favor in that time."

"All you have to do is ask, Captain," Sandberger said, and he turned and walked back across the lobby and out of the hotel, where a valet parker brought his Humvee.

Driving away he promised himself that Chief of Police Mustafa Kabbani would lose his life in an unfortunate accident before the month was out, that is if McGarvey didn't kill him first. It was a matter of sanitation.

THIRTY—NINE

☐

Kuwait International Airport was ten miles south of the city center, and the highway leading from the hotel branched east toward the Persian Gulf and west toward the city of al-Jahrad, at the head of al-Kuwait Bay, before it turned due north through the oil fields toward the border with Iraq.

It was getting dark when McGarvey emerged from the Crowne Plaza and walked across the broad driveway covered by a canopy to the dark blue soft-top Range Rover, and got in on the passenger side, Hadid at the wheel. The backseat was empty.

"I thought your son Saddam was coming along," McGarvey said.

"Wait," Hadid said, and he pulled away from the hotel, down the long driveway, and out onto the west highway, the airport lit up behind them; the city of al-Kuwait sparkling to the east.

Traffic was heavy, and everything seemed to move at breakneck speed. But there were no military vehicles, nor could McGarvey pick out any obvious signs of damage from the first Gulf War. Kuwait was a tiny but modern oil-rich country apparently no longer affected by what was happening in Iraq.

Once they had reached the head of the bay and made the turn

north, the border fifty miles away, everything changed. From here nearly everything moving on the road was a military supply transports of one sort or another, many of them eighteen-wheelers, all of them traveling in groups of eight or ten vehicles accompanied by several RG-33s, which were mine-resistant, light-armored vehicles equipped with M2 heavy machine guns. The peace had been all but won, but the road to Baghdad was still dangerous and would remain so for the foreseeable future.

"Are you expecting trouble tonight?" McGarvey asked.

"If we were military we might expect something interesting, Mr. Tony, but since we're simple civilians we will be reasonably safe from the insurgents," Hadid said. "Our only real concern will be bandits."

"Have they become a problem?"

"Always a problem," Hadid said, checking his rearview mirror, and he slowed down and pulled off to the side of the road, nothing in any direction out here except the waste gas flames atop oil rigs in the distance.

A minute later one of the convoys passed, raising a storm of dust.

When they were gone Hadid powered down the soft top, jumped out, and went around back where he opened the rear hatch to an empty space.

McGarvey got out and came around to the back as Hadid undid a pair of concealed fasteners and the carpeted floor slid out revealing a long space the width of the car and all the way forward to just behind the front seats. A young man with the wisp of a beard on his chin nimbly hopped out, a big grin on his face, his dark eyes large and round.

"Good evening, Mr. Tony," he said, his English passable. "I am Saddam." Like his father he wore a dark robe and headdress, sandals on his feet.

Hadid reached inside the dark space and helped a slightly built figure out and over the lip of the rear bumper. For a moment McGarvey thought it was another, much younger son, until he realized it was a woman.

"My wife, Miriam," Hadid said proudly.

Her face was perfectly round, her complexion smoky, her smile as bright as her son's. "I'm pleased to meet you, Mr. Tony," she said, her accent British. She, too, was dressed in a dark robe, her hair covered.

McGarvey suddenly had a very bad feeling. Inside the hidden compartment he could make out at least three AK-47s, and a couple of canvas bags that almost certainly held spare magazines. "I appreciate the help, but I don't think this is such a good idea," he said.

"Is it my son, or are you a chauvinist American?" the woman asked.

McGarvey nodded toward the weapons. "I don't want to be the cause of a woman going into harm's way. I'll get to Baghdad on my own."

"Then you are merely a sad American. We heard of your loss. It must be terrible."

"We will present less of a threat, a family traveling with an American journalist," Hadid said.

"People are expecting me in Baghdad. There'll be trouble."

"Once we get you there you'll be on your own until it's time to return," Hadid said. "You'll stay at the Baghdad Hotel, while we'll stay with my wife's uncle. When it's time for you to leave we'll come back in the same fashion, but you will cross the border with a new identification, and appearance."

McGarvey looked over his shoulder the way they had come, and he could see the glow of al-Kuwait on the horizon. Getting back to the city would be a problem, but he'd faced worse. Once back at the Crowne Plaza Otto could arrange for something else. Anything else.

"What explanation will you give when you are picked up by a military patrol, unless of course you are murdered first?"

"We'll take your wife back to the city, and start over," McGarvey said.

"Have you been to Baghdad before?" Miriam asked.

"Once, a long time ago."

"But not since the war, and the chaos left behind when Uncle

Saddam was caught and executed. You don't know the full extent of the troubles between the Sunnis and Shi'ites."

"Believe me, Mr. Tony, my wife and I have worked together ever since our marriage sixteen years ago," Hadid said. "She is an unusual woman for an Iraqi. She was educated in England, and her father was a general in Saddam's army. She knows her way around. In the beginning it was I who was learning from her. She worked on the outside of the palace while I worked on the inside. We are a team."

"It will be better for you if we do this together," Miriam said. "And if I thought the danger would have the possibility of becoming overwhelming, do you think I would allow my son to ride with us?"

"Be sensible," Hadid said.

The situation sounded anything but sensible to McGarvey, but it was far too late for him to back down. Sandberger was the tie to Foster and the Friday Club. Almost nothing else mattered.

"Do you have a weapon for me?" he asked after another hesitation, and Hadid looked relieved.

"You may have your sat phone now, you will have your weapon once we cross the border."

The last thirty miles up to the border was heavy with traffic, only one vehicle out of fifty a civilian car. The Baghdad road wasn't exactly the gateway to the country. But it was bandits who gave civilians trouble, while it was the Sunni and Shi'ite radicals who targeted the military and Iraqi police.

"Saddam and I are actually quite good marksmen in our own right," Miriam said conversationally at one point.

"Unusual for an Iraqi woman," McGarvey said.

"Not as unusual as you might expect, but we don't parade in the streets firing into the air like the men. When we shoot it's from concealed positions at a specific target."

A conglomerate of lights in addition to the red taillights of the trucks heading north, and the headlights of vehicles heading south, straddled the highway. Northbound traffic was backed up for one hundred yards or so, which according to Hadid was nothing compared to the delays during daylight hours when most convoys preferred to run. Then traffic could be backed up for miles.

"Are your passport and Army credentials in order?" Hadid asked.

"Yes," McGarvey said, uncomfortable that he wasn't armed.

"You will need to show them to the Kuwaiti Army patrol on this side of the border and then to the Iraqi police on the other side."

"What about the Americans?"

"Delta Company, First Light Armored Recon Battalion. But they're on standby with fifty-caliber Sasser sniper rifles in case someone tries to make trouble."

"You have good information," McGarvey said, impressed.

"It's my part of the world," Hadid said. "My life depends on good information."

They moved forward slowly, until ten minutes later they reached the border crossing and a pair of Kuwaiti army border guards, armed with American M16s, asked to see their papers.

Hadid's and his family's papers raised no interest, but McGarvey's passport and especially his U.S. Army credentials did, and one of the Kuwaiti border guards took the documents across the road to a low concrete block building, with machine-gun emplacements looking north on the roof.

Traffic began to back up behind them, and a U.S. Army captain jumped out of his RG-33 at the head of a convoy and came up to them.

"What's the trouble up here?" he demanded, and he spotted McGarvey in the backseat. "Who the hell are you?"

"I'm an American freelance journalist," McGarvey said, meeting the officer's eyes.

The captain held out a hand. "Let's see some ID."

"No," McGarvey said. "And I suggest you get back in your fucking thirty-three until we're cleared here."

At that moment a Kuwaiti officer came from the concrete block building, and ignoring the American officer, looked in at McGarvey. "You have an American Army pass. Why is it you didn't fly direct to Baghdad?"

"I'm doing a piece on convoys traveling the Baghdad Road," McGarvey said. He glanced at the captain. "And the men running them."

The Kuwaiti officer handed McGarvey's papers back. "You may pass," he said, smiling slightly. "Good luck."

"Is there something we should be aware of tonight?" Hadid asked, but the Kuwaiti had turned and headed away.

"Maybe I'll see you in Baghdad, Captain," McGarvey told the American. "What's the name of your CO?"

The captain turned and stalked off, and Hadid moved past the barrier where they were stopped by a pair of Iraqi police who inspected their papers. When they looked at McGarvey's he was sure they recognized the name, but they handed the papers back, stepped aside, and waved them through.

"They might be expecting me," he told Hadid when they were on the other side and accelerating into the dark night.

"I saw it, too," Hadid said. "But I have a few tricks up my sleeve, you'll see."

FORTY

□

Kangas and Mustapha had flown first class from Washington and had fully indulged in the free bar service, so that by the time they touched down at Baghdad's International Airport, if not drunk they were certainly less than sharp.

Their contact man at Dulles had assured them that McGarvey was traveling undercover as a freelance journalist by the name of Tony Watkins, and was driving up from Kuwait, which gave them a twelve-hour head start. They weren't worried. It wasn't often that the cheap bastards handling travel arrangements for Admin sprung for first class, and they'd meant to enjoy every minute of it, because once they got to Baghdad they figured they'd be put up in some shit hole of a hotel.

It was early evening and the airport terminal was fairly busy. Since the so-called peace, a lot of international business was returning to the country, especially people interested in oil.

Through passport control and customs a young man came up to them and without a word handed Kangas a thick manila envelope then turned around and walked away, lost in the crowd almost immediately.

"Welcome to the hot zone," Mustapha said. "Make sure it isn't a fucking letter bomb, because that kid was for sure not our quartermaster."

"Too light," Kangas said, and he and Mustapha went down the corridor to an empty boarding area and opened the envelope. Remington had provided them with five thousand in U.S. currency, mostly hundred-dollar bills, a pair of presumably untraceable credit cards, and confirmed reservations for a suite at the new Baghdad International Airport Hotel and Business Center, along with a photo of Harry

Weiss, their on-the-ground Admin contact, who would meet them once they checked into the hotel.

"This keeps getting better," Mustapha said.

"There's always a catch," Kangas said. He was beginning to get a seriously bad feeling between his shoulder blades. He'd never really trusted Remington, and with this added luxury he was becoming even more distrustful.

"Yeah, taking McGarvey down," Mustapha said. "We've already seen the bastard in action."

"He won't be expecting us," Kangas said, but he wasn't so sure.

The hotel was on the airport property and just down a walkway from the terminal. Big and ultra modern, especially by present-day Iraqi standards, the place reminded Kangas of hotel/business centers in places like Dubai. Everyone was in a hurry, everyone seemed to have bags of money, and everyone smiled at everyone else without meaning it. It was, he suspected, a dangerous place. But it was handy to the airport, so once their business in town was finished they could get back here and get out on the first available flight. Admin had provided them with open-ended tickets, which meant they could hop aboard any flight. Their first-class status gave them priority.

The lobby was plain and functional, yet luxurious at the same time. The clerks, almost all of them young, dressed in identical gray blazers with gold buttons, bustled seemingly everywhere.

The clerk at the reception desk brought their reservations up on his computer, printed out the arrivals document, and had Kangas sign it. "Welcome to the Baghdad International Airport Hotel, gentlemen. A credit card will not be necessary, your firm has arranged for all of your expenses."

"Right," Kangas mumbled.

The clerk handed them each a key card. "Will you be needing help with your luggage?"

They had each carried only a single overnight bag. They'd be staying only as long as was absolutely necessary. Hopefully they'd be in and back out in twenty-four hours or less. "Not necessary," Kangas said.

They took the elevator up to their twelfth-floor suite, the balcony looking toward downtown Baghdad, about fifteen miles away. In addition to a pair of bedrooms with king-sized beds and separate Jacuzzis, the sitting room was well furnished with a modern couch and chairs, a desk, a large HD plasma television, and a well-stocked minibar. A guest half bath was just inside the entry hall.

The red message light on the telephone began blinking at once and Kangas answered it.

"Message from Mr. Weiss. Please meet him in the lobby bar at your soonest convenience," a recording of a woman's voice said. "If you would like to hear this message again, please press one."

"Our quartermaster wants to meet downstairs in the bar," Kangas said hanging up.

"That was quick," Mustapha said.

"The sooner the better."

Although security at this hotel was probably reasonably tight, this was Baghdad, and Kangas felt vulnerable without a weapon, something he expected their quartermaster was going to fix first thing.

They used the stairs to the tenth floor, where they made sure the corridor was empty before they took the elevator to the lobby. It was an old survival trick they'd learned in the CIA. Never willingly give up any information about yourself. In this case, by taking the elevator from the tenth floor, anyone spotting them emerging into the lobby wouldn't necessarily know they were staying on the twelfth. It was minor, but such little things in the field added up.

They recognized Weiss, seated at a booth in the far corner of the lobby lounge, from his photograph. Kangas thought he looked like a poofta, the same as Remington: narrow, sloped-shoulders; light, sand-colored hair; and tiny round face with droopy eyes that seemed to see nothing.

But he looked up from his drink as Kangas and Mustafa came over, and motioned for them to sit across from him. "You assholes look like shit," he said.

"Pleased to meet you, too," Kangas said, letting Mustapha slide in first. He never liked for his movements to be confined.

"First class doesn't mean you show up drunk. Do you have any idea who the hell you're going up against?"

"We've seen him in action, we know," Mustapha said. "But he won't be here until sometime tomorrow. By then he'll be road weary, but we'll have had a good night's sleep and a big breakfast."

"And this city belongs to Admin," Kangas added.

"I speak the language, do you, prick?" Mustapha said.

Weiss sat back. "Okay, if this weren't so important to Roland I'd tell you guys to get the fuck out of here first thing in the morning. As it is I hope you go up against McGarvey one hundred percent. If you miss the smallest step he'll have you for lunch."

"We'll take care of our business," Kangas said. "What about our equipment?"

"In a leather satchel at my feet. Wait five minutes after I'm gone, then pick it up and take it to your room."

"Where will he be staying?"

"The Baghdad Hotel where a lot of journalists who don't care to stay in the Green Zone hang out," Weiss said. "Give me the photo you got at the airport."

Kangas had figured Weiss would want it back. He handed it over. "Not a very good likeness."

Weiss gave them both another appraising look, before he got up. "Stupid bastards."

As soon as he'd left, Kangas reached under the table for the satchel, then slid out of the booth, Mustapha right behind him, and they left the lounge, holding up just at the entrance to see which way their quartermaster was heading. But Weiss was nowhere to be seen.

"Not bad," Kangas had to admit. The man might have looked like a poofta but he knew his tradecraft.

FORTY-ONE

Heading north from the border away from the head of the Gulf, toward Basra, the night turned warm, even sultry. This, Hadid explained, was the region of the famous Fertile Crescent, the confluence of the Tigris and Euphrates, near the Garden of Eden.

More oil rigs dotted the horizon, and to McGarvey the area seemed anything but fertile. It was mostly desert now, and when a breeze blew it stank of oil and natural gas.

"We'll have no trouble until after Basra," Hadid said, checking his rearview mirror often. "It starts to get bad once we get near An Nasiriyah. The convoys take the route on the west side of the river, but we'll cross over and take the eastern route. It's about the same distance, but I know it better."

"Wouldn't we be safer traveling in the middle of a couple of convoys?" McGarvey asked.

Hadid glanced at him and shook his head. "No," he said, and he checked his rearview mirror again.

For the moment they were alone on the road, though in the distance behind them they could make out the lights of an oncoming car or perhaps the convoy that had been directly behind them at the checkpoint. It was time for the weapons.

Hadid pulled over and they all got out and went around to the back of the car where Hadid opened the lid and brought out a Glock 17 for McGarvey with a silencer and three magazines of ammunition plus three AK-47s with the satchel of spare magazines, which went to McGarvey, Saddam, and the woman.

They all piled back inside the car and Hadid pulled away before the oncoming lights had reached them.

Saddam and Miriam both handled the AKs with practiced ease, checking the actions, loading the weapons, and racking rounds into the firing chambers as McGarvey was doing the same.

The woman looked up, catching McGarvey watching her. "Little children know how to use this weapon," she said.

"Have you ever killed a man?"

Her lips compressed, but she didn't look away. "More than one," she said. "I didn't care for it each time."

"Most people usually don't," McGarvey said.

They had switched positions at the stop; McGarvey now riding shotgun in the front seat with Miriam and her son in the back, watching for trouble on either side of the road and to the rear.

The night was pitch black here, except for the Range Rover's headlights. And it was beginning to cool down.

Miram said something to her husband in Persian, and Hadid looked in his rearview mirror. "Someone back there seems interested in us, I think."

McGarvey looked back and he could see that the headlights were moving up on them very fast. "I don't think it's the convoy."

"No, it's only one maybe two pairs of lights," Hadid said. He was searching for something on either side of the road.

Miriam said something else, her tone urgent.

"This will do," Hadid said. "Hold on, it's time to give them a little surprise."

He jammed on the brakes suddenly, doused the lights and swerved off the road to the right, across a shallow ditch, and headed for a small concrete block structure, just reaching it as a Toyota heavy-duty pickup truck roared up and without slowing down careened off the road.

"Shoot now," McGarvey shouted, and he opened fire with the AK-47 at two figures dressed in black braced in the bed of the pickup truck with what looked like an M249 squad automatic weapon, which was a Belgian-made 5.66mm light machine gun mounted on a pedestal. One of the guys was a shooter the other the loader.

Miriam and Saddam began firing at the pickup truck at the same moment the M249 began banging away, several rounds slamming into the rear of the Range Rover before Hadid hauled the car behind the building, and there was no target for several beats.

"I'm going to try to get behind them," Hadid shouted, as they reached the far end of the building and he hauled the big SUV around the corner.

The Toyota was right on their tail, but didn't have as tight a turning radius, so the rounds from the M249 went wild out into the desert night.

Two seconds later, Hadid shouted something in Arabic as they came back to the front of the building, where another Toyota heavy-duty pickup truck was waiting in ambush just off the side of the road, and he swerved hard to the right.

"Stay on our rear," McGarvey shouted to Miriam and the boy at the same moment they started taking incoming fire from the second pickup truck. McGarvey opened fire with his AK-47, walking the rounds across the field as Hadid jinked left and right, in an attempt to keep out of the line of fire.

For just an instant the Range Rover and second pickup truck were in perfect alignment, and McGarvey hit the shooter and loader and walked his rounds forward to the driver and passenger, taking them out, running dry in the next instant.

The first pickup truck had careened around the corner from behind the building and opened fire as McGarvey reloaded, and swung around to fire toward the rear.

Miriam and the boy were both down, blood everywhere, and once again Hadid swung hard right putting the Toyota in a perfect firing position. McGarvey took out the shooter and loader in the bed, and emptied the remainder of the AK-47s thirty-round magazine into the cabin.

The pickup truck suddenly swerved sharply to the left, its front left fender slamming into the side of the building, slewed away and rose up on its right side flipping over, its engine screaming up the scale until something loud popped and the Toyota ended up rocking on its roof.

Hadid jammed on the brakes and pulled to a stop, the night suddenly very quiet.

He pulled out a pistol, jumped out of the Range Rover, and started toward the upside-down pickup truck.

McGarvey put down his weapon and reached over the back of the seat, making a quick check of the woman and boy. They were both dead. Miriam's chest was blown half away by the machine gun's rounds, and Saddam's face had been destroyed, the back of his head completely gone.

"Khalid," McGarvey called, a great sadness coming over him, along with a deep, deep bitterness. All such a terrible waste.

McGarvey turned around as Hadid fired once into the cab of the pickup truck, then reached inside and dragged out a body. He said something, and then spat on the body.

McGarvey got out of the Range Rover and walked over, as Hadid went around to the other side of the Toyota.

"Sunnis," Hadid said, looking up. "The bastards will do anything to break the peace. They have no morals, Mr. Tony. No real religion."

"Your wife and son are dead," McGarvey said. There was no way of softening the blow. The situation was what it was.

Hadid shook his head, his mouth open, but then he went back to the Range Rover and stood at the rear passenger door. He dropped his pistol on the ground and began to beat his chest with his right hand, a high-pitched keening wail coming from the back of his throat.

McGarvey walked back to him. "We'll return to Kuwait now so you can attend to your family."

After a long time Hadid looked at him, shook his head, then gazed at the bodies of his wife and son. "They were Sunnis and they have no morals," he said. "They cannot be allowed to win this war."

The Sunnis felt the same about the Shi'ites, but McGarvey said nothing. The deep division between the two Muslim sects was something a westerner could not really understand. The rift was even deeper than between the Catholics and Protestants in Northern Ireland in the sixties and seventies.

"I will take them to the home of Miriam's uncle in Baghdad. They will receive a proper burial before the sun goes down," Hadid said. "If you will help me we will place them in the secret compartment in the back. Hopefully there will be no further trouble for us tonight."

FORTY-TWO

Sandberger, having drinks with a couple friends from a rival contractor service, Decision Infinity, looked up as Harry Weiss came into the barroom of the new Ritz-Carlton Baghdad in what had been the Green Zone. It was around ten in the evening and he'd been expecting his point man on the McGarvey issue about now, but he didn't much care for the look on Weiss's face.

"Sorry, gentlemen, but business calls," he said. He finished his martini and got up.

Jerry London, DI's CEO grinned. "Trouble, I hope," he said, and his exec, Ken Brody, glanced over at Weiss standing at the bar and raised his glass.

"Bloody well hope old Harry has brought you shit news, you son of a bitch," he said, laughing.

"I hope you get syphilis and your dick rots off," Sandberger replied and the two men laughed.

"The game starts in my suite at midnight," London said. The CEO and execs of most of the contractors usually got together at least once a week for high-stakes poker, courtesy of Uncle Sam.

"Wouldn't miss it," Sandberger said and he walked over to where

Weiss was waiting, and the two of them left the bar, crossed the lobby, and took the first elevator up to the eighth floor.

Neither man spoke until they were safely inside Sandberger's suite. Contractor firms were under fire again in Washington, and the CIA sill maintained a strong presence in Iraq, and especially here in Baghdad. No public spaces—barrooms, dining rooms, elevators, and even corridors—were ever completely safe from electronic surveillance. Only individual rooms and suites that were swept on a regular basis, as was Sandberger's, could be considered private.

"They're here," Weiss said. "Drunk, as you figured they might be."

"I don't care unless they get themselves in trouble tonight," Sandberger said, but in fact he did care. McGarvey was no one to screw around with. Captain Kabbani had been so self-assured that it had been obvious he had no real idea what the former CIA director was capable of. And there was a very real possibility that his people would have failed tonight, and McGarvey would actually be showing up here sometime in the morning.

"They're a couple of loose cannons, but I think they understand who they're up against. They oughta be sober and rested by morning, unless they're complete idiots."

"They know their tradecraft, and neither of them has ever been afraid to pull the trigger."

"Do you think McGarvey will make it this far?" Weiss asked.

"I think it's a possibility that we have to consider," Sandberger said.

"What can I do?"

Weiss was Admin's on-the-ground CO here in Baghdad, and to date he'd done a credible job. Such a good job in fact that Sandberger was torn between bringing him back to Washington to take overall command of operations or leaving him here. He would decide after the McGarvey business was settled and Foster finally got off his back. But Weiss would have to name his own successor, and it would have to be someone good.

"He has reservations at the Baghdad Hotel. Go over there and keep your eyes open. I want to know not only if he shows up, but if he's alone."

"If I have the chance I'd like to take him out myself," Weiss said.

"No," Sandberger shot back. "Kangas and Mustapha are expendable, you're not."

It was a little past two-thirty in the afternoon in Washington when Sandberger used his encrypted sat phone to reach Remington at his home, and he was more than a little angry that his partner wasn't in the office, and he said so.

"I've never punched a clock, and I don't intend to begin now, old man," Remington replied. "Is there anything that I've mishandled to this point for the company?"

The man's British sarcasm rankled, but Sandberger held his temper in check. Remington had been a steady if unimaginative hand from the beginning. "Your people are here, and drunk."

"Not surprising. But they have a twelve-hour head start. And I think they're smart enough to sober up in the meantime."

"Don't you think first class was a little excessive?"

Remington chuckled, his English superiority showing again. "Last banquet for the condemned men," he said. "They haven't strayed from their quartermaster have they?"

"Not yet. But I've put someone else on the job. Could be McGarvey will never reach Baghdad."

"That might not have been the best call, Roland," Remington cautioned. "It's not our people, I hope."

"Captain Kabbani is handling it for us."

"The man's a buffoon."

"Yes, and just as expendable as Kangas and Mustapha, and a hell of a lot less expensive. We're not running a goddamned charity."

"Don't lecture me," Remington shot back. "You're gone and I covered for you at the Club. That's what partners are for. And we *are* partners, unless you want to dissolve the arrangement, a move I would not strenuously object to."

Sandberger realized that once again he'd gone too far, but the Foster contract had been a constant drain on his nerves from the start nearly two years ago. If he had known then what he knew now, he would have turned it down, no matter how fabulous the money was. But now he and Remington were in it up to their necks, and they would have to see the business through until Foster reached his ultimate goal— something that gave Sandberger nightmares.

"Sorry, Gordon, it's the pressure," he said.

"I understand," Remington said reasonably. "By this time tomorrow the issue will be resolved."

One way or the other, Sandberger thought but didn't say. "I'll call you."

"Do," Remington said and he rang off.

Leaving Sandberger to pour a stiff brandy and stare out the window at the river and try to quell his rising concern that this business with McGarvey and the Friday Club was a very long way from any sort of acceptable resolution.

A couple of minutes before midnight, as Sandberger was getting set to go up to the poker game in Jerry London's suite, Captain Kabbani called on the house phone.

"I'm in the lobby. We need to talk."

"Is there trouble?" Sandberger asked, a tightness gripping his chest.

"It's better if you come downstairs."

"I'm on my way," Sandberger said. He went to the bureau in the bedroom, and got his SIG-Sauer P226 pistol and shoulder holster. If they were going to talk it would not be in the one of the hotel's public spaces, nor was he having the captain up here. It meant the streets, and for this business he would go without his bodyguards, as he had when he initially met the cop.

Kabbani, dressed in robes instead of his khaki policeman's uniform, was seated near the doors, and Sandberger passed him without a greeting and walked outside and headed down the street.

The cop caught up with him half a block away. "I received word a half hour ago that eight Sunni rebels working for Saddar Mukhtar were found shot to death on the north road outside Basra."

Sandberger had almost expected the news. But eight-to-one odds were too lopsided even for McGarvey. "He must have had help."

"Almost certainly. And it could have been a trap if there was a leak in your company. This man could have been waiting for them."

"If there's any leak it's in your police barracks," Sandberger retorted angrily. "But there wasn't any. The people you hired were not good enough. And I warned you."

"What about my money?" Kabbani said. "I have debts."

"So do I."

"This is still my country, my city. Accidents do happen."

At this moment they were alone on the sidewalk, though there was traffic on the street.

"What the hell's that supposed to mean?"

"You know exactly what I'm saying, Mr. Sandberger," Kabbani said. "And this evening you do not have your bodyguards with you. Perhaps that was a mistake."

Sandberger lowered his eyes and nodded. "I thought it might come to this with a bastard like you."

"It's the cost of doing business in Baghdad since the war and the pullout of most of the American soldiers. Not so easy for men such as yourself to call for help."

"The cost of doing business in Baghdad," Sandberger repeated. He glanced up as a police car, its blue lights flashing passed by without slowing.

Kabbani pulled out a pistol and pointed it at Sandberger's chest. "I hope for your sake that you brought my money with you."

Sandberger smiled inwardly, but he nodded, a grim set to his lips. "As a matter of fact, I thought it would come to this," he said. "But not out here in plain sight. And put that gun down, as you say my bodyguards aren't with me and I'm not armed."

Kabbani concealed the pistol in a fold of his robes and motioned toward a narrow alley nearby. "In there," he said, glancing around to make sure no one had spotted the exchange so far. But except for the traffic on the street, no one was nearby.

The narrow alley was dark, littered with garbage and the burned-out remains of an automobile chassis that had been dragged off the street a couple of weeks ago.

"Here," Sandberger said reaching into his jacket. He pulled out his pistol and before Kabbani could react he shot the cop once at point-blank range in the forehead. The man fell backward, dead before his body hit the ground.

Sandberger waited several seconds to make sure no one had heard the shot and was on the way to investigate. But Baghdad was still in a state of siege. Gunshots in the night were common, even in the peace. Curiosity was practically nonexistent.

Holstering his pistol, Sandberger went through the cop's robes to see if he'd been carrying a wire or anything else that might incriminate Admin. But he'd not even carried his police card. Just the pistol and a set of car keys.

Sandberger slipped out of the alley and headed back to the hotel, satisfied that he would only be fashionably late for the poker game.

FORTY-THREE

Hadid said nothing for the remainder of the trip up to Baghdad, which they finally reached late in the morning. Instead of driving straight into the city, Hadid headed west through Saddam City to a neighborhood called Quds. The busy streets were rat warrens of narrow lanes that twisted through mostly one- and two-story ramshackle concrete-block buildings. Most of them were private homes and some had small gardens off rear courtyards, others had retail businesses on the ground floors.

He called someone on his cell phone and at the end of one very narrow street he stopped at a corrugated-metal gate, blew the horn once, and moments later the gate swung inward and Hadid drove through into a dusty courtyard. He turned around so that the nose of the Range Rover was pointed toward the gate being closed by an old man with a Kalashnikov slung over his shoulder.

"That is my uncle Fathi," Hadid said. "I told him about Miriam and Saddam and he has agreed to help. His wives will make my family ready for burial, which must be completed before sundown today. You understand?"

"Yes," McGarvey, thinking about the funeral for his wife and daughter. "What can I do to help?"

"Nothing, Mr. Tony. You will remain here in the car, you will speak with no one, you will make no eye contact, you will make no moves. Do you understand this completely?"

"Yes."

"This will not take long and then I will take you to the al-Zuhoor where you have a suite."

"I thought it was the Baghdad Hotel."

"It is the same. But the name in Arabic is The Flowers Land. And it is in its own compound along with the Hamara Hotel, where most of the western journalists who do not want to stay in the Green Zone have rooms. It is also where many of the contractors stay. And for that I have a plan."

His uncle came over with three other men as Hadid got out of the Range Rover and went around back and opened the hatch. No one looked at McGarvey in the passenger seat. Before they had entered the city, Hadid had stopped and raised the top.

"Do we need to hide the weapons?" McGarvey had asked.

"Here it is not necessary," Hadid had told him, and once inside it became obvious why. Every third or fourth person seemed to be carrying a weapon of some sort, either a pistol or a Kalashnikov. The peace was still an uneasy one.

The four men removed the bodies of Hadid's wife and son and carried them gently across the courtyard and into the house. The Range Rover's windows were down and McGarvey heard a keening wail coming from inside, and he understood what these people were feeling now; he really understood them, and it hardened his heart further for the business ahead.

Hadid came out of the house, his face an unreadable mask, got in the car, and started it as his uncle came out and opened the gate. "Now it is time for you to go to work, or rest if need be. But if I may suggest, you should complete your business as quickly as possible. This evening. And I will come back after the funeral."

"No," McGarvey said. "The rest I will do alone until it's time to leave the city."

The al-Zuhoor was a shabby six-story hotel at the end of a street partially blocked by two concrete blast walls, almost directly across the Tigris River from the Green Zone. Next to it, but behind the same blast barriers, were the two large buildings of the Hamara Hotel.

Hadid slowed down at the gap in the walls, and eased through the opening and stopped. A pair of stern-looking men armed with Kalashnikov rifles materialized, one of them on the driver's side, the other a few feet and slightly behind McGarvey.

"What do you want?" the guard asked Hadid in English.

"I am this man's driver. He has a reservation here."

"Name?"

"Mr. Tony Watkins. He is a freelance journalist."

"American?"

"Yes."

"Release the hood and rear hatch," the guard said, which Hadid did. Two other men came over, one of them searching under the Range

Rover's hood and in the back, while the other checked the undercarriage with a slanted mirror attached to the end of a long aluminum
pole as the two armed guards stayed where they were.

The man at the back of the car said something, and the guard near
Hadid raised his rifle a fraction. "There is blood in the back."

"We were on the road from Basra last night," Hadid said. "There is
blood and shell casings in the backseat, and, as you can see, bullet
holes in my car. But no explosives."

The hood and rear hatch were closed and the men with the rifles
stepped back.

Hadid drove up to the glass-fronted entrance, next to the restaurant. A big awning covered what had apparently once been a sidewalk
from the street that was now blocked off by a chain. No one seemed
to be around, and the restaurant was empty.

"Take one of the rifles and a couple magazines," Hadid suggested.

"Let's save them for the return trip," McGarvey said. He had the
Glock, the silencer, and three magazines of ammunition. Enough for
tonight.

Hadid nodded. "I will wait for your call, Mr. Tony. Good luck."

"I'm sorry about your wife and son."

"They are in Paradise now, waiting for me."

McGarvey's reservation for five days was in order, and the bald clerk
sitting on a stool behind the counter in the tiny lobby checked him in
and handed him a key. No porters were around, and except for the
clerk and one man who was a westerner in jeans and a light sweater
sitting reading a New York Times, the lobby was deserted. The man
never looked up.

His suite on the sixth floor, had a view of the concrete blast barriers,
and consisted of a sitting room, small bedroom, and bathroom. The
place was shabby but fairly clean, and the wheezing air conditioner
kept the rooms reasonably cool.

McGarvey laid his overnight bag on the bed and phoned Rencke, who answered, as usual on the first ring.

"Oh, wow, you made it," he said. "Louise said that one of her KH-elevens picked up some trouble on the Basra Highway about the time you should've been there."

"That was us. Hadid brought along his wife and son, and both of them were killed. Did you know him?"

"Not personally. But he's done work for us since before the first Gulf War. He came highly recommended. Are you okay?"

"Yes," McGarvey said. "I just want to do what I came to do and then get the hell out of here. Where's Sandberger staying?"

"He has a suite in the new Ritz-Carlton. Eight-eleven. But he almost always surrounds himself with bodyguards. And honest injun, kemo sabe, if you get into a shoot-out you'll be outnumbered and outgunned."

"I want to get his attention," McGarvey said. "I want him to know that I'm here, and why. And I want that to get back to the Friday Club in spades."

"Go easy."

"I want to hurt him," McGarvey said.

"Jesus."

McGarvey broke the connection then lay down on the bed to get a few hours' rest, something, it seemed, that he hadn't gotten for a very long time. But this evening he would need to be in top form.

FORTY-FOUR

Sandberger had just sat down for lunch alone at a table in the Ritz-Carlton's dining room and ordered a Bombay martini straight up with a twist when his encrypted sat phone vibrated in his pocket. It was Weiss calling from the Baghdad Hotel across the river.

"He showed up a couple of minutes ago," he said. "I waited to see what room he was given. He's in suite six-oh-seven."

"Did he come in alone?" Sandberger demanded.

"Wait, there's a lot more. You said he was coming in under the name Tony Watkins, a freelance journalist, right?"

"Yes."

"I would never have recognized him from the photographs I've seen. He's in a disguise and a damned good one. Not so obvious so you wouldn't take a second glance. I was close enough to the desk to hear the name, otherwise I would have missed him."

"Did he make you?"

"He glanced over at me, but there was no reaction that I could see. He just got his key and went up. Elevator straight to the sixth floor, no stops in between."

"Was he carrying any hardware that was obvious?"

"Probably a pistol, unless he's crazy. But his only luggage was a small nylon overnight bag."

"What else?"

"He came into the hotel alone, but I got a look at the car and driver who dropped him off. Didn't get the tag number, but the guy driving was obviously an Iraqi."

"Anyone we know?"

"I never saw him before. Anyway he just dropped McGarvey off in front and then drove off. The car was a Range Rover and shot up pretty good. Holes looked recent. Still shiny metal. Bandits on the Basra Highway, I imagine."

Sandberger gripped the telephone a little tighter, checking his anger. It was the outcome he'd expected, because Kabbani had been an incompetent fool. Now the police chief was dead, the people he'd hired down south probably dead as well, and McGarvey was here in Baghdad. But it was not the outcome he'd hoped for.

"What do you want me to do?"

"Call Kangas and Mustapha. But wait until nightfall. I don't want them doing a daylight operation. They can go in after dark. But you'll have to stick it out there to see which way McGarvey moves, and keep us advised. But I'd rather you lose him than have him spot you. Are you clear on that point?"

"Yes, sir," Weiss said. "But you have to understand that if I do lose him, and our guys miss, he'll come after you."

"Not the worst-case scenario," Sandberger said, and he glanced over at his personal bodyguards, Carl Alphonse and Brody Hanson, seated at one of the tables by the entrance. Unlike the idiots Kabbani had sent to ambush McGarvey, and even Kangas and Mustapha, the two men with him now were among the best he'd ever worked with. Tough, ruthless, and, above all, capable. If they had any fault it was their arrogance. But they had the skills and experience to back it up.

McGarvey was here and he would not live through the night. Sandberger found that he was looking forward to getting back to Washington. He and Gordon would have to make a decision about Foster and the Friday Club. The money was fabulous but the risks were beginning to rise to an unacceptable level. Time to get out, he decided. But in order to do that Admin would have to manage a number of erasures.

Kangas and Mustapha were about to go downstairs to the bar for a couple of drinks and something to eat when the phone in their suite rang. This day had been long and boring, and at one point Mustapha had suggested they say the hell with it and head back to the States. Kangas answered and he recognized Weiss's voice.

"He's at the Baghdad Hotel as we thought he would be. He's in six oh seven."

"Did he come alone?"

"An Iraqi driver brought him in, but left immediately. And it didn't look as if he was carrying any heavy hardware, though he's almost certainly armed."

"Where are you?" Kangas asked. He snapped his fingers and gestured to Mustapha that the mission was a go.

"Somewhere near enough so that I can watch his movements. He went upstairs around noon, and he hasn't come down since."

"Did he spot you?"

Weiss had supplied them with Knight's Armament PDWs that, on full automatic, fired the 6×35mm cartridge at seven hundred rounds per minute, and three thirty-round magazines each. With the stock folded and the suppressor removed the super-compact weapon was less than eighteen inches long. Mustapha was fixing his weapon diagonally across his chest with a big Velcro pad.

"He saw me, but I don't think he felt that I was any sort of threat or he would have done something about it by now," Weiss said, and he gave Kangas a description of McGarvey's new look.

Kangas had another thought. "Where will Mr. Sandberger be tonight?"

"That's none of your goddamn business."

"Yes, it is. This guy came here to take him out. If we get over to the hotel too late he might be on his way over to wherever the boss is staying."

"Mr. Sandberger is well protected."

"Yeah, so was the pope."

Mustapha was wearing a Kevlar vest and he pulled on a dark blue Windbreaker, which he zipped up. It was obvious he was carrying, but then so were a lot of others in the city.

"He's staying at the Ritz-Carlton in the Green Zone."

"Good. Tell him to stay there until we're finished," Kangas said. "We're on our way."

"Not until tonight."

"We'll handle this now," Kangas said and hung up.

FORTY-FIVE

□

Well rested after sleeping all afternoon, McGarvey took a shower and dressed in blue jeans, a dark pullover, and dark blazer. The Glock 17 Hadid had supplied him with went in a holster on his hip, beneath the jacket, and the silencer and spare magazines in a pocket.

He went to the window and looked at the lights in the Green Zone across the river. Many sections of the city were dark or nearly dark, like his mood he thought. Otto was a friend, but he didn't understand loss and rage. Nor should he need to understand.

Rencke called on the sat phone, just as McGarvey was about to walk out the door. "You may have more trouble coming your way."

"What is it?"

"A pair of Admin's tough guys showed up in Baghdad yesterday evening. Timothy Kangas and Ronni Mustapha. Ex-CIA NOCs. They were fired a few years ago for using excessive force, operating outside their charters, and more or less telling the establishment to screw itself. One of my programs monitoring Sandberger and his people tripped, but I didn't catch it until a few minutes ago."

"Are they staying with Sandberger, or Admin's people?"

"No, and that's what triggered the search engine. They're staying at the Baghdad Airport Hotel, and they have open-ended first-class tickets on United, which was another trigger."

"They know I'm here and they were sent over to take me out," McGarvey said. "It makes getting a message to Sandberger that much easier."

"I looked at these guys' jackets, Mac. They're good. And I suspect they've been ordered to stay away from Admin's operations in the city. You're a separate contract. But it doesn't mean they won't call for help if they think they need it."

"It'll hinge on what they know. My work name and this hotel."

Rencke hesitated a second or two. "If they have that info it means we have a leak here. And it'd have to be someone fairly high up in Ops. Maybe even the seventh floor."

"Work out a sting."

"Shit, shit. I hope to hell I'm wrong, kemo sabe. Honest injun."

"Contact Hadid and tell him I'll need a ride out of Dodge in about two hours," McGarvey said.

"Where do you want him to pick you up?"

"Have him circle the block around the Ritz-Carlton. I'll find him."

"Watch your ass, Mac," Rencke said.

McGarvey broke the connection, pocketed the phone, and looked around the suite. He wasn't coming back, and there was nothing else he needed to take with him except Watkins's passport. It didn't matter about his fingerprints; even if some Iraqi investigator did lift them, the FBI wouldn't cooperate with an identification, nor would the CIA.

Downstairs, the lobby was deserted except for the same bald clerk as before. When McGarvey approached the desk, he looked up, his eyes watery. "Sir?" he asked.

"Two friends of mine may be looking for me. If they show up tell them that I've gone next door to the Hamara Hotel to have a drink."

"Of course, sir. Your name?"

"Tony Watkins," McGarvey said and he walked out and started down the path over to the much larger hotel, when something out of place caught the fringes of his attention, and he turned suddenly to go back as if he had forgotten something. The same westerner who'd been sitting in the lobby at noon was now sitting behind the wheel of a fairly new C class Mercedes sedan, parked to one side of the concrete blast barrier. It was a different pair of armed guards on duty this evening. They were sitting on lawn chairs in front of a pile of rubble ignoring the man in the Mercedes, nor did they bother to look up when McGarvey, apparently changing his mind again, turned back and headed to the Hamara.

Portions of the long walkway between the hotels were in darkness, and McGarvey picked a spot where he could wait in the shadows from where he could see anyone coming from the Baghdad Hotel, yet they would not be able to see him.

He'd thought at the time that it was odd that a man was seated alone in the lobby of the hotel, but since there'd been no contact, he'd all but put it out of his mind. Now he knew that the man was a spotter, sent by Admin to keep tabs on him. As soon as the muscle that had been sent over to deal with him showed up, the spotter would direct them to the Hamara.

And he only had to wait five minutes before two men came up the path. They looked like NOCs, anonymous, not particularly large or beefy, and they moved easily on the balls of their feet, their attention in all directions, like rotating radar beams. They were expecting trouble.

McGarvey eased a little farther back into the shadows so that he was partially hidden behind the bole of a palm tree.

The two were dressed nearly alike, baggy khakis and dark Windbreakers with more bulk than was likely. They were wearing vests under the jackets, and by the look of it even in the dim light McGarvey could tell they were carrying some heavy hardware strapped to their chests. The Windbreakers were zippered, which was a mistake on their part. It would be awkward for them to draw their weapons.

McGarvey waited until they were just past then drew his pistol and stepped out on the path. "I expect that you're looking for me."

They both reached for their weapons.

"I have no intention of killing you this evening, unless I'm forced into it," McGarvey told them, and they stopped. "Please turn around."

They did as they were told, their jackets half unzipped, and he saw their weapons.

"Knight PDWs. Nice. Which one of you is Tim Kangas?"

The one on the left pursed his lips.

McGarvey nodded pleasantly toward the smaller man on the right. "That means you must be Ronni Mustapha. Former NOCs, and I'm told quite good, though you had a little trouble with discipline and following orders."

"We're here," Kangas said. "What do you want?" He showed no fear, only a wariness; he was looking for an opening.

"You were sent here by your boss at Admin to kill me. Fair enough. But I'm here just to gather some facts. Maybe we can work something out."

"What's in it for us?" Muataspha asked.

"Your lives, of course," McGarvey said.

"What do you want?"

"Someone placed an IED at Arlington Cemetery. Was it on Admin's orders? Roland Sandberger or Gordon Remington?"

"We don't know," Kangas said.

McGarvey suddenly raised his pistol to point directly at Kangas's head and took several steps closer. "I asked you a question. The people killed in that explosion were my wife and daughter. I'm motivated."

"We know about you, Mr. McGarvey, but it wasn't us at Arlington. And if it was Admin we were not told." No fear showed in his eyes, just the same wariness.

"Why were you sent here to assassinate me? Who ordered it?"

"Our boss, Mr. Remington."

"Why?"

"You've been declared a threat to our operations," Mustapha said. "I'm sure the order originated from Mr. Sandberger because of an incident between the two of you in Germany."

"Toss your weapons in the bushes," McGarvey said, and he watched their eyes as they very slowly did as they had been told. They were professionals. They knew how to back away when the odds were not in their favor so that they could live to fight another day.

"Now what?" Kangas asked.

"Go back to the airport hotel, and in the morning get on your United flight back to the States," McGarvey said. "My issue is with Sandberger, not with his foot soldiers. But if I see you again I'll kill you. Do we have an understanding?"

"Yes," Kangas said, and McGarvey stepped back off the path to let them pass. "What do you want us to tell Mr. Sandberger?"

"Whatever you want," McGarvey said, and he watched as they walked back the way they had come, his body bathed in sweat. It had taken everything in his power not to kill them. But they were just foot soldiers, and he wanted word to get to Sandberger.

FORTY-SIX

Sandberger was in a booth at the bar in the Ritz-Carlton when Weiss phoned to tell him what had happened on the path between the two hotels, and for several long seconds he could not answer. His throat was constricted and the muscles in his face were rigid.

The American call girl he was seated with turned pale.

"Mr. Sandberger?" Weiss said.

"Just a moment," Sandberger said, coming down. He laid the phone on the table, pulled a hundred-dollar bill out of his pocket and handed it to the girl with a smile. "Next time I'm in town," he said.

The girl took the money, grabbed her purse, and slid out of the booth, her short skirt riding up. She had great legs and a tight ass. "Sure thing," she said, and she left.

Sandberger picked up the phone. "Tell me everything," he said, his voice even. He was back in control.

"McGarvey came out of the hotel and headed over to the Hamara about five minutes before our guys showed up. I told them where he'd gone, and they went after him. A couple of minutes later they came back in a big hurry, without their weapons. I told them to go back to their hotel and fly out first thing in the morning. We don't need them here now that McGarvey's made them."

"How do you know they had no weapons?"

"Their jackets were open, the Velcro pads were empty, and no shots had been fired," Weiss said. "What do you want me to do?"

"They didn't say anything else to you?"

"They didn't even want to look at me."

McGarvey was a sharp bastard, easily still as good as his reputation, and he didn't know that Kangas and Mustapha had been the triggermen on his son-in-law and for the IED at Arlington, otherwise he would have killed them.

"Stay where you are," Sandberger ordered. "He's probably coming over here next. I want to know when he leaves."

"Yes, sir," Weiss said. "I'd still like to take the bastard out myself, if the opportunity is there."

Sandberger was about to tell him no, but he realized all of a sudden that he was being stupid. "If you get the chance, do it," he said, and he broke the connection.

His bodyguards, drinking Cokes, were seated together at a table near the door. He waved them over.

"Kangas and Mustapha screwed up," Sandberger told them. "McGarvey will be coming here tonight."

"When?" Alphonse asked.

"I don't know yet. But I have a spotter watching him."

"What do you want us to do?"

"Station two of our people on each side of the driveway. He'll probably be showing up in a cab, and I'll have the tag number for our guys. I want him taken down, priority one."

"What about us?" Hanson asked. He looked as if he were itching for a fight.

"You're sticking with me, because I think we might have underestimated the son of a bitch. And if he actually makes it this far, I wouldn't put it past him to know my room number."

"There are two stairwells plus the elevators. We'll need an extra hand if we're to cover all three," Alphonse said.

"I want one of the stairwells wired. One pound of Semtex should be enough."

"Could be collateral damage."

"We'll blame it on McGarvey. He's a ruthless son of a bitch who's practically under indictment for treason, and who's unhinged by the deaths of his wife, daughter, and son-in-law."

"When do you want it done, sir?"

"Wait until we find out if he's gotten past our people and is actually inside the hotel," Sandberger said.

"Where will you be?" Hanson asked. "In case we have to fall back for some reason."

"In the suite with a surprise, because if he gets that far it'll mean at least one of you is down."

Hanson smiled. "Not a chance in hell of that happening, Mr. Sandberger," he said.

FORTY-SEVEN

McGarvey had walked the rest of the way up the path to the Hamara, but instead of going inside he handed the doorman a hundred-dollar bill and had him call for a taxi, which had just come through the blast-barrier entry that served both hotels.

"Where would you like to be taken, sir?" the doorman asked.

"The American embassy," McGarvey said, and got in the cab.

Before the driver had got the cab turned around, McGarvey held another hundred-dollar bill over the seat. "Do you understand English?"

"Yes, sir," the cabbie said. "Very much."

"This is yours if you do exactly as I say with no questions."

The driver looked uncertain for just a second but then he nodded and snatched the hundred. "Where do you want to go?"

"Not far. And when I tell you to stop, do it immediately. I'll get out and you will drive away. Do you understand? There'll be no shooting."

"Yes, sir. Perfectly."

McGarvey slid over to the driver's side of the rear seat and unlatched the door but did not open it. "Now, head to the exit, slowly."

The driver did as he was told, and at the end of the Hamara's driveway McGarvey sat back so that his face and shoulders were in deeper shadow. "See the Mercedes parked by the blast barrier?"

"Yes, sir."

"Drive close to it, slow down so I can get out, and then leave."

The cabbie glanced in the rearview mirror for just a moment, and once they were out in the Baghdad Hotel's driveway, still moving slowly, he swung close to the Mercedes and pulled up short.

McGarvey slipped out of the cab and drew his pistol as the driver immediately made for the exit through the concrete barriers.

Keeping low McGarvey used the retreating cab as a shield until at the last second he ducked around the trunk of the Mercedes and yanked open the passenger-side rear door, and slipped inside, laying the muzzle of the big pistol in the side of the spotter's face.

Weiss was reaching for something on the console beside him, but McGarvey jammed the pistol harder.

"Do exactly as I say or you die now."

Weiss stopped short.

"If you were reaching for a pistol, pick it up by the barrel and hand it back to me."

For just a beat Weiss hesitated, but then he slowly handed a standard U.S. military-issue Beretta 92F 9mm autoloader over the seat.

McGarvey pocketed the weapon. "I assume that you work for Admin, and it was you who brought Kangas and Mustapha over to take me down on Sandberger's orders."

"I don't know what you're talking about," Weiss said.

"If you know who I am, you'll know what I've gone through, and you'll have to guess that I don't give a shit who I take out," McGarvey said, his voice reasonable.

"Okay."

"Was the IED at Arlington planted on Admin's orders?"

"I don't know," Weiss said, but McGarvey slammed the muzzle of his Glock hard against the man's cheek, opening a two-inch gash, which immediately began to bleed. "Christ!"

"Tell me what you do know," McGarvey said.

"You can beat on me all you want, you bastard, but I don't know," Weiss said. "If it was a Admin operation it could only have been authorized by Mr. Sandberger or Mr. Remington. No one else in the company has the power to make that kind of a decision."

McGarvey glanced over at the armed guards sitting just inside the blast barriers, but they hadn't moved from their folding chairs. "Why were Kangas and Mustapha brought over here?"

"To kill you."

"On Sandberger's orders?"

"Yes."

"Why?" McGarvey asked.

"Mr. Sandberger thought that it was likely you were coming here to assassinate him."

"And why do you suppose I'd want to do something like that? What do you think I have against your boss?"

"Because you think he ordered the assassination of your son-in-law. And maybe had something to do with the Arlington thing."

"You're learning," McGarvey said. "And you know goddamned well that your boss ordered the hits on my son-in-law and the newspaper reporter because they were getting too close to the Friday Club. And the IED at Arlington was meant for me, but a mistake was made."

Weiss said nothing.

"Call Sandberger and tell him that you spotted me leaving in a cab, but that you have no idea where I was going."

Sandberger was still in the booth when Weiss called the second time. Since then the bar had filled up, and he'd switched from martinis to Bud Lite. Four of his people were outside watching the driveway, and Alphonse and Hanson were nursing their Cokes across the barroom near the door.

"He just left in a cab."

"Which way is he headed?"

"I didn't see."

"Aren't you following him, for Christ's sake?" Sandberger demanded, his voice rising.

"It happened too fast. By the time I realized it was McGarvey in the back of the cab, it was out on the street and for some reason the stupid bastards at the barrier wanted to check my ID."

Suddenly nothing was making sense to Sandberger, and he had a strong premonition that wherever Weiss actually was at this moment, McGarvey was there with a pistol to his head. Weiss was too good to have been taken like that, but he was also smart enough to give some sort of a clue if he got any opening. "Who was the lead man on the barrier? Was it Johnny Karp?"

Weiss had no reason to know the names of the contractors guarding the hotel entrance. They operated out of a small and not very well known company headquartered in Los Angeles.

"Johnny left around four, I don't know who the hell this guy was," Weiss said.

That was it, McGarvey was with him. "Okay, I want you to get back here as fast as you can. I think McGarvey's probably going to back off for now, but I want to talk to you." He motioned Alphonse and Hanson over.

"I think you're right. He might even be trying to catch up with Tim and Ronni."

"I'll be in my suite," Sandberger said. "Come right up."

"Yes, sir," Weiss said and the connection was broken.

Alphonse and Hanson slid in the booth across the table from him. "I just got off the phone with Harry. I think McGarvey got the drop on him and they're on their way over. Alert our people outside—Harry's driving a dark blue Mercedes C class—I want them both taken out. Then get upstairs and wire the east door. I'll be in the suite with a little surprise."

His two bodyguards got up and left the bar.

Sandberger finished his beer, laid a couple of twenties on the table, and went out to the elevators just off the lobby. He'd always been of the opinion that second-rate personnel were not capable of handling first-rate problems. Sometimes the only way to make sure that a job was done right, was to do it yourself.

The McGarvey problem would end tonight.

FORTY-EIGHT

They crossed the Tigris above the section known as Babil, and Weiss kept nervously glancing over at McGarvey. The Ritz-Carlton tower rose above most of the other buildings in the Green Zone and traffic here had dramatically increased. Baghdad wasn't back to normal yet, but the city's people seemed to want to head that way, and McGarvey hoped the lives we had given up to topple Saddam Hussein's regime were worth the results.

"Look, you know you won't get within a hundred yards of Mr. Sandberger," Weiss said. "He knows you're coming."

"Your little play with the hotel guard's name was obvious," Mc-Garvey said.

"I meant that Tim and Ronni must have called him by now."

McGarvey shook his head. "I think they went back to their room in the new airport hotel, and they'll be on the first United flight back to the States. Theirs was supposed to be an independent operation. With the deals on the table for Admin from State, your boss doesn't want to take any chances of a shoot-out except in self-defense."

"What the hell are you talking about?"

"I'm talking about the Friday Club, and I'm here for the answers. But I don't think your boss is going to be very happy how I ask."

"You're crazy."

"Certifiable," McGarvey said, his anger in check, his level of aware-ness tuned to everything around him, inside and outside the car. He was going to have one chance to get Sandberger alone long enough to find out who had killed his son-in-law and Katy and Liz. To do that he figured he was going to have to either take down whatever assets Sandberger had put in place, or sidestep them if possible. Probably shooters in front of the hotel, on either side of the driveway. Maybe a spotter in the lobby. And certainly men in the eighth-floor corridor, at the stairwells and elevators, because he was pretty sure that Sand-berger would have retreated to his suite where it would be much easier to defend himself than out in the open. The man would be treating this affair like a military operation. But all battles had losers as well as winners.

A block from the hotel McGarvey had Weiss pull over and stop at the curb. This close inside the zone traffic, most of it civilian, was heavy. "You have a choice," he said. "I'm getting out of the car and you're free to go. But if you want to try something stupid I will take you out."

Weiss licked his lips but said nothing.

"If you do drive over to the hotel, I'd advise that you keep your head down, because I'll kill anyone who gets in my way. My only interest this evening is Sandberger. Clear?"

Weiss nodded, but held his silence.

McGarvey opened the door and started to get out of the car when he felt Weiss make a sudden lunge. Dumb, but not unexpected. Sandberger's orders would be for his people to take whatever opportunity came along.

"Bastard," Weiss grunted.

McGarvey slipped out of the car and slid half a step to the right as he turned and brought his pistol to bear. Weiss had grabbed a spare pistol, another Beretta 9mm, from probably under the seat, and was raising it when McGarvey fired one shot, catching the man in the middle of his forehead and slamming him back against the driver-side door.

The noise, partially contained inside the car and muffled by the sounds of traffic, went unnoticed. None of the cars or trucks passing slowed down.

Slipping his pistol into the holster beneath his jacket McGarvey closed the car door, and headed down the street to the Ritz. Other people were on foot, some of them in western dress so he figured he wasn't terribly obvious.

About fifty yards from the hotel's sweeping driveway that led up to the entrance portico he pulled up and slipped into the shadows of a line of small shops, shuttered now, in the lee of what was probably a building containing some Iraqi government function. Such places were scattered all across the Green Zone.

He watched for a full five minutes as cars and cabs came and went, spotting a pair of men stationed in the driveway leading to the hotel's entrance, and another pair on the opposite side for vehicles leaving. Dressed in the near standard contractor's uniform of jeans, dark shirts, and Kevlar vests with a lot of pockets, they were waiting for Weiss to show up, presumably with his passenger, and their orders were to take out both of them.

It was a little risky to stage a shoot-out these days, but before the cops showed up they would probably plant some explosives in the car. They were simply doing their jobs, protecting the hotel from suicide bombers.

McGarvey moved back until he was clear, then ran down the street, keeping to the shadows as much as possible, until he found a service driveway that led to the rear of the hotel.

When he was out of sight of anyone on the road, he took out his pistol and screwed the silencer onto the end of the barrel.

Sandberger eased the door open and looked out into the corridor. Alphonse leaned against the wall a few feet from the elevator, which meant that Hanson was just around the corner from the east stairway door.

"Keep on your toes," he told his bodyguards. "If McGarvey's going to show tonight, it'll be within the next half hour, or less."

Alphonse nodded, and Sandberger closed his door, keeping it slightly ajar with a book of paper matches. He went across to the sliding door that led onto the small balcony and opened it. The cool evening air with the sounds of traffic and the smells unique to Baghdad—rotting garbage, diesel fumes, and a hint of cordite—were immediately there.

Before he switched off the lights he removed the silenced Sterling submachine gun's thirty-four-round box magazine, checked one last time that it was full, and slammed it back home. The unique weapon, which used nonsubsonic 9×19 mm Parabellum ammunition, had been used by British special forces, including the SAS. It had been one of Remington's suggestions that Admin's people might find the weapon handy in special circumstances.

Like now, Sandberger thought as he waited half inside and half outside the slider.

McGarvey was good, if even half of what he'd heard was true. He had gotten past Kangas and Mustapha, and had somehow gotten the drop on Weiss. However unlikely it might be, it was possible he would get past the four men watching the driveway, and perhaps even Alphonse and Hanson up here.

But anyone coming through the door would take the full thirty-four rounds. Survival this up close and personal would be impossible.

A delivery van was backed up to the loading dock and an older man in Arab dress was pulling out plastic flats filled with bundles of cut flowers and carrying them inside through the open roll-up door.

McGarvey waited until the florist went inside, then ran around to the end of the loading dock and ducked down in the shadows in the corner. Five minutes later the man came out, closed the delivery van's doors, and left.

As soon as the van was out of sight, McGarvey jumped up on the delivery dock and peered around the corner into the receiving area, where all the supplies for the hotel were received and processed. Two men were directly across a fairly large space where they were loading the flats onto a pair of hand trucks. When they were finished they pushed the carts off to the left where they boarded a service elevator.

When the doors had closed McGarvey hurried after them, and waited, until the car stopped at the lobby level. Sandberger's suite was on the eighth floor. He would have people watching the stairwell doors and the guest elevators. But he might have overlooked the service elevators, which the maids, room service people, and maintenance crew used.

McGarvey brought the elevator down then hit the button for the eighth floor. He suspected that the doors would open not onto the main corridor but onto a service corridor, and when the car reached the eighth floor he was proven right. This corridor, which ran the length of the hotel along the rear walls of the rooms, was unpainted concrete walls and floors, with minimal lighting from basic ceiling fixtures.

Several doors opened onto the main guest corridor, one at each end opposite the emergency exits, and one at the vending machine alcove.

McGarvey went to the west emergency door and examined the hinges. It was wired, a small grey mass of Semtex molded into the jamb about chest high. It came to him that only the two bodyguards from Frankfurt would be up here, one on the elevators and the other on the stairwell door.

He turned and hurried back the way he'd come, past the service elevator, which had been recalled to the kitchen level, to the door opposite the east emergency exit.

Opening the door just a crack he saw a man in a contractor's uniform leaning against the wall less than ten feet away. The man spotted the open door immediately and he reached for his pistol holstered high on his right hip.

McGarvey pulled the door all the way open and raised his pistol. "I'll kill you right now," he said in a low voice.

The contractor's hand stopped just above the butt of his pistol. He was weighing his options, and it was obvious in his eyes.

"Who else is up here with you?"

"I'm alone," Hanson said.

"You had a partner when I saw you in Frankfurt," McGarvey said. "Where is he?"

"I don't know."

"As you wish," McGarvey said, and slipped out of the service corridor to where the contractor stood, batted the man's hand away from his gun, and pulled it out of its holster. It was a 9mm SIG-Sauer. McGarvey dropped it to the carpeted floor and kicked it away.

"Now what?" Hanson asked, tensing his muscles, getting ready to spring.

"We're going for a walk," McGarvey said, roughly hauling the man around, and shoving him from behind.

"Bloody hell," Hanson said, but McGarvey jammed the muzzle of the big silencer hard against the base of the man's head, and they headed slowly to where the corridor turned right.

At the corner, McGarvey suddenly shoved Hanson away and stepped to one side as Sandberger's other bodyguard stationed at the elevator realized that something unexpected was happening, and he grabbed for his pistol.

McGarvey fired two shots, both hitting Alphonse in the head, knocking him backward against the wall where he collapsed to the floor, leaving a bloody streak as he fell.

Hanson spun on his heel and started to charge, when McGarvey turned and pointed the gun at the man's head, and the contractor pulled up short.

"Lie to me again and you're dead."

"You're going to kill me anyway," Hanson said.

"No need for it, unless you were personally involved in the murders of my son-in-law, wife, and daughter."

"No," Hanson said, and McGarvey believed him.

"Your boss has the answers. So what we're going to do, is knock on his door and you'll tell him whatever you need to say to get him to open up. Then you can go."

"Right."

"I have no beef with you. Unless you do something stupid you can walk away from this thing. But time is short, so make your decision."

"No choice, do I?"

"No," McGarvey said.

"You can't be lucky every time, you bastard," Hanson said, but he headed down the corridor, past Alphonse's body lying in a heap, to Sandberger's suite. He started to knock on the door, but then backed off.

McGarvey saw that the door was open and he pulled Hanson back. "Tell him I'm down."

Hanson was clearly nervous now. But he turned back to the door. "Mr. Sandberger, it's me, Brody. We got him."

No one answered. Hanson started to turn back but McGarvey bodily shoved the contractor into the suite, and stepped aside out of what he expected would be the line of fire. And he was right.

Something that sounded like a silenced, heavy-caliber automatic weapon opened up, the bullets slamming into Hanson's bulletproof vest, but at least one hitting the contractor in the leg and another in the face just above and to the right of the bridge of his nose.

The firing stopped, and McGarvey stepped over Hanson's body and entered the room. Sandberger at the open slider was trying to reload, but McGarvey, still moving forward, fired one shot, hitting the man in the right thigh, dropping him to the floor.

"There'll be people all over the place up here, because someone must have heard something," McGarvey said. "So I don't have much time. Does Admin have a contract with the Friday Club."

"Fuck you," Sandberger said.

McGarvey fired a second shot, this one destroying the man's kneecap, and Sandberger cried out.

"Who killed my family?"

"You're a dead man."

McGarvey stepped closer and placed the muzzle of the silencer on Sandberger's forehead. "Your people did it to cover up whatever the *Washington Post* reporter found out about Foster and his group. Is that worth dying for?"

"You'll never take me back to Washington, and even if you did it wouldn't do you any good. I have friends—"

"You're right," McGarvey said, and he fired one shot.

Sirens were approaching from the north by the time McGarvey made it down to the service floor and out onto the street. Before the police arrived at the hotel Hadid pulled up with the Range Rover, and McGarvey jumped in.

"Time to leave?" Hadid asked.

McGarvey nodded. "Time to leave."

FORTY-NINE

It was one in the afternoon in Washington when Remington and his wife, Colleen, met for lunch at the George Hotel just down from Union Station. She'd remarked that it was an odd choice, but he hadn't explained that he wanted to come here to satisfy a perverse curiosity to see where the *Washington Post* reporter had met with McGarvey's son-in-law. The dining room/bar area was faintly art deco and nice, though not grand. Not up to Colleen's usual standards.

But she hadn't complained, and in fact had stopped all her complaining after the dinner party at Foster's home. She'd been impressed with her husband, and he'd even cut back on his drinking—because of the crisis mode Admin was in—which impressed her all the more.

"What made you think of this place?" she asked when their martinis came.

The dining room was nearly full, but the service was good.

Remington shrugged. "Someone mentioned the place. Thought we should give it a try."

She looked around, and smiled. "I approve. Anyway, Gordo, I'm famished."

Remington's sat phone vibrated in his pocket and he hesitated whether to ignore the call, but with everything happening here in Washington and in Baghdad, he answered it. "Remington."

Colleen shot him a disapproving look.

"We're in deep shit over here, sir." It was Peter Townsend, Sandberger's administrative assistant, who'd done all of the nuts-and-bolts negotiations with the State Department reps in Baghdad. A lawyer by training, he'd served one term as a junior congressman from the Russian River area of California. He sounded shook up.

"What is it?"

"Mr. Sandberger was shot to death in his suite about an hour ago."

Remington was struck dumb for just a moment, and it must have showed on his face because Colleen put down her drink and gave him a concerned, questioning look. "What about Hanson and Alphonse?"

"They were taken out, too, but it looks as if Mr. Sandberger killed Brody. It's not making any sense to me, because Harry Weiss was found shot to death in his car a block from the hotel. What the hell is going on? I wasn't told that we were facing any sort of a threat of this magnitude."

It was McGarvey, of course. Couldn't be anyone else, but for now they needed to do some serious damage control. "Okay, listen up. I'll come there as quickly as possible, but it probably won't be until tomorrow. In the meantime you're the on-site supervisor as of this moment. I want the mess cleaned up before I get there. Get in touch with Captain Kabbani, he's been of some help in the past."

"His body was found in an alley a block from the hotel. He'd been shot to death at close range. You have to tell me what the hell is going on if you expect me to take care of this shit, because I have no idea what's coming next. And what do I tell our guys that'll make any sense?"

Remington didn't have a clue, but Townsend was waiting. All of Admin was waiting because he'd just become president of the company. The easy way, he couldn't help but think, and he smiled for just a moment, and his wife's right eyebrow shot up.

"Goddamnit, I'm in the hot seat. I'm not a contractor, I'm a negotiator, a lawyer."

"Do you know Stuart Marston?" Remington asked.

"Yes, of course I do. He's been our point man at State. Helped put the deal through for us."

"Call him, set up a meeting and tell him what you know—"

"I don't know shit," Townsend shouted.

"Calm down, and let me finish," Remington said. Colleen was watching him, hanging on every word. "Tell Stu that we think it was

Kirk McGarvey. The man's gone over the edge, and he had some sort of a personal vendetta with Roland."

"Holy shit," Townsend said.

"Get a hold of yourself, Pete. Until I get there you're Admin in Baghdad. Work with Marston. Work the problem, don't let it work you."

Townsend was silent for several beats, and when he came back he sounded as if he was coming down. "Do I mention McGarvey's name? I mean the guy was the DCI at one time."

"The FBI is looking for him, and Justice is considering bringing him up for treason," Remington said. "So definitely mention his name. It's something that guys like Marston understand."

"It's late here, I'll call him in the morning."

"Call him now. He needs to hear about this from us, not the Iraqi police."

"You're right."

"I'll get there as soon as I can. But keep in touch."

"Will do," Townsend said and he rang off.

Remington broke the connection and lowered the phone.

"Talk to me, Gordo," Colleen said, keeping her voice low.

"Bit of a muckup over in B-town," Remington said. "Roland and a couple of his people have been shot to death."

"Good Lord," Colleen said, but then he could see in her eyes that she understood the consequences as well as he did. "Do you actually have to go over there?"

"We'll see," Remington said, and he dialed Robert Foster's private number, which would be rolled over to wherever the man was. Anywhere in the world.

On the third ring it was answered by a voice mail message. "Leave your name and number after the tone." But before Remington could leave a message, Foster came on.

"Good afternoon, Gordon. Is something bothering you that you called this number?"

The waiter came over to take their order, but Remington waved him off and waited until he was out of earshot.

"I just received word that Roland was assassinated in Baghdad about an hour ago. His bodyguards were taken out, as was Baghdad's chief of police."

"That's certainly a stunning development. Do you know who was behind this and why?"

"It was McGarvey," Remington said. "Our operations over there are facing a potential meltdown. I'm flying over tonight to straighten it out."

Foster's reply was immediate. "No. I want you to remain here in Washington. Business as usual. Do you have any idea where Mr. Mc-Garvey is at this moment? Certainly not still in Baghdad?"

"I'm not sure, but I believe he'll try to get out of the country, probably either through Kuwait, the way he got in, or perhaps across the border into Turkey."

"Is he receiving help from the CIA?"

"Unknown, but I'd say it's fairly unlikely considering the charges Justice is preparing to file against him."

"I was under the impression that you had arranged for some of your people to take him out."

"Apparently they failed."

"Are they dead?"

"I don't know, they haven't surfaced yet. Last I heard they had reached Baghdad."

Foster was silent for a moment. "This is what we're going to do. I'm going to arrange for your contract over there to go to Decision Infinity. They can use the money. I need all of your attention devoted to the McGarvey problem."

"That would put Admin in a bind," Remington protested, even though he had to agree with what was coming next. "We're carrying a large salary and training budget."

"We'll take care of your company," Foster said. "Your main objective now is to kill Mr. McGarvey as soon as possible. I don't care where or how, just get the job done, Gordon, and you will be a busy man, because we have the main issue to contend with."

"I wasn't in on that loop," Remington said. "Roland never discussed it with me."

"Conclude the McGarvey business, and you will be brought into the loop, as you call it."

"I'll do my best," Remington said, but he was talking to a broken connection.

FIFTY

The sky to the east was just beginning to lighten when Hadid slowed down and pulled off the highway a few miles outside of Az Zubayr, a small city just north of the border with Kuwait and barely twenty miles from Basra.

"It's too dangerous to cross the border now," Hadid said. "It's what the authorities will expect Mr. Tony to do. We'll stay here until nightfall, when Mr. James will spring into existence."

The battery in McGarvey's sat phone had worn down, and the Range Rover's cigarette lighter receptacle didn't work, but Hadid had promised that when they finally stopped, the phone's charger could be directly connected to the battery under the hood.

They followed a dirt track for a few miles out into the desert until they came to what at one time in the past might have been a farm or more likely a small sheep station. A main stone building in absolutely horrible condition, a gaping hole in one of the walls, and half the roof missing, sat at the edge of a small dried-up stream. Several other, much smaller buildings in even worse condition made up what would have been a small compound, sections of a stone wall visible here and there.

"This belonged to one of my uncles, but during the first war the U.S. Army based three tanks here. They didn't leave much."

"Who owns it now?"

"The family, so this in some respects belongs to me," Hadid said. "But no one cares. There is no oil just here." He drove around to the back of the main structure and backed the Range Rover inside, where most of the roof was intact, then shut off the ignition.

It was a good spot, covered from the air and from the highway or anyone coming up the dirt track. Getting out of the car McGarvey felt a sense of sadness for the people who had lived here, their shattered lives. Maybe they had dreamed of cashing in on the oil revenues that had never materialized. All that had shown up on their doorstep were Iraqi tanks and American ordnance.

Hadid had opened the hood. He took the sat phone charger, cut the wires from the plug with a penknife, and peeled them back so they were long enough to be wrapped around the battery terminals. He plugged the other end into the phone, and a second later the charge indicator lit up, and he grinned. "Now we will spend the day here—you and I plus the battery—recharging."

They sat on the open tailgate and ate their breakfast of flat bread, figs, goat cheese and American vinegar, and sea salt potato chips. Hadid had brought several bottles of sweet tea for himself, along with several liters of water and two cans of Heinekin for McGarvey.

"After the last twenty-four hours you've had I thought beer would be better than tea."

"No worse than yours," McGarvey said, opening one of the warm beers. "What's next for you?"

Hadid smiled wistfully. "The sadness is leaving, Mr. James. They are waiting for me in Paradise. This I truly believe and it gives me comfort."

There was nothing to be said in reply.

"After you are safely back at the Crowne under your new identity, I'll return to my duties in Baghdad. And for you, did you accomplish what you came here for?"

"A part of it."

"But there is more back in Washington?"

"A lot more," McGarvey said looking away.

"Revenge is never the just thing," Hadid said. "But very often it is the only thing for the soul. I hope you finally find what you are looking for."

McGarvey was dead on his feet, and bunked out in the rear of the Range Rover he managed to sleep through most of the day, although he continued to have dreams about the explosion that had killed Katy and Liz, and about Todd's battered body covered by the sheet at All Saints. And on waking around four in the afternoon the images didn't want to fade.

Hadid was already up, and he was in the front room of the house, looking through a pair of binoculars up toward the highway. "I thought we might be having some visitors," he said, not looking over his shoulder.

"Civilian?" McGarvey asked. He thought it was a good possibility that either the Baghdad police or more likely Admin would have sent someone after them.

"American military. But why they got off the highway is a mystery."

"They're gone?"

"Yes," Hadid said, lowering the binoculars. "We have a few more hours to wait. There's more food and water, but no beer."

McGarvey went back to the car, got the things Hadid had brought for him, and using the door mirror on the passenger side dyed his hair dark brown, darkened his complexion with one of the chemicals Martinez had supplied him with in Miami, and finally placed contact lenses in his eyes to change their color from gray green to blue. When he was finished he exchanged the passport and other documents that identified him as Tony Watkins a freelance journalist, with the papers of James Hopkins, a contractor with Decision Infinity.

He got dressed in khaki slacks, a black short-sleeved polo shirt, and a bush jacket with a lot of pockets. A nylon sports bag contained a few toiletry items, a week-old *New York Times* with an article about DI, and a fresh shirt, underwear, and socks. Hopkins was nothing more than a tired contractor going home on leave.

Hadid had disconnected the sat phone from the battery and laid it on the seat. When McGarvey was finished he switched it on. It showed a full charge but no missed calls. By now Otto would have heard about Sandberger and the others at the Ritz, but he was holding back, knowing what else had probably happened overnight.

Hadid was looking at him. "You look the same, but different. I would never have picked you out in a crowd as the same man who was Mr. Tony. Whoever arranged this disguise for you was very good. It's subtle."

"Let's hope the people at the hotel, and especially the customs and passport people at Dulles, think the same thing."

"They'll be watching for you?"

"Absolutely."

FIFTY-ONE

It was nearly nine in the evening in Washington, which put it around five in the morning in Iraq, when Remington, calling from his office just inside the Beltway in Alexandria, finally managed to reach Tim Kangas at the Baghdad airport hotel.

"What the hell happened?" he demanded.

"The son of a bitch got the drop on us, which means he must have spotters here on the ground."

"We have big problems coming our way, tell me everything," Remington said, and Kangas did.

"You wanted us to keep a low profile here, arm's length from any Admin personnel other than Harry Weiss. He told us to come back here and fly out on the first available flight. Which we're planning on doing. Leaves at six local."

"I still want you back here as soon as possible, but everything's changed," Remington said. Admin was in crisis mode, and he'd required that the five office staff remain until he could fully brief them and give them orders that would make sense. First he had to gather the facts.

"What's happened?" Kangas demanded, his voice suddenly guarded.

"Weiss is dead, shot to death by McGarvey because you failed to do your job."

"Bastard. He's gotta have help here on the ground."

"That's not all. There was a shoot-out at the Ritz last night. Alphonse and Hanson are dead, and so is Mr. Sandberger."

The connection was silent for a long time, and when Kangas finally came back he sounded shook. "We don't need this shit. With all due respect, Mr. Remington, we're bailing. You can take this job and shove it."

It was about what Remington had expected. "The contract still stands. Two million for each of you when you take McGarvey down."

The hesitation was shorter this time. "Do you want it done here?"

"McGarvey's probably already on his way back here, either through Kuwait or possibly across the border into Turkey. Either way you're too late to catch him. But if you're on the next flight back, you'll beat him here. You know what he looks like and unless you don't know it yet, he's traveling under the work name Tony Watkins, as a freelance journalist. Once you're on the ground call me, and I'll tell you what flight he took and when to expect him."

"We're supposed to take him down at the airport?"

"Only if he's not taken into custody, which is a possibility. If the FBI picks him up, you can back off. If not, you can take him just like you did his son-in-law."

"What about equipment?"

"Something will be arranged."

"Wait one," Kangas said and the connection went quiet. He came back ten seconds later. "All right, we're in. But we want our backs covered, so make damn sure he won't have help at Dulles."

"Don't worry, Admin takes care of its own," Remington said, and he broke the connection and sat back. The beauty of the situation was that neither Kangas nor Mustapha could prove that they'd been ordered to assassinate McGarvey. Their orders had been verbal. Nothing written and neither of them had been wearing a wire. And they would never allow themselves to be taken into custody. Their backgrounds were too dirty, and by the time the FBI came looking, Admin's records would show they'd been terminated months ago.

He got up and went out to the operations room where the five office staff were waiting. They looked up with interest because they knew that something important was happening.

"I need to make one more call, and then I'll brief you in the boardroom and you can go home and get a few hours' sleep."

"What's going on Mr. R.," Calvin Boberg, the operations manager, asked. He'd been with Admin from the beginning, and was irritated that he'd been told nothing.

Remington held up a hand. "Five minutes, please."

Boberg wanted to argue, but he shrugged. He was tired and he and the others wanted to go home.

Remington telephoned Ivan Miller, his contact at the FBI, who worked as the acting assistant director of the Bureau's Domestic Intelligence Division. Remington didn't know for sure, but he was convinced the man had a connection with the Friday Club, because he had landed in Admin's lap within one week of the Friday Club contract.

His wife called him to the phone, and he sounded guarded. "Good evening, Gordon. Not a social call, I suspect?"

"You may have heard that we ran into a spot of trouble in Baghdad."

"Just found out about it before I left the office. Could it have involved McGarvey?"

"We have that as fact," Remington said. "He gunned down Roland and at least three of our people. Now he's on his way back here."

"I'm told that a Baghdad police captain may have been involved as well?"

"I just learned about that myself, and there's very little doubt that McGarvey was the triggerman. The captain was Admin's liaison for security measures."

Miller hesitated for a moment, and Remington could hear music playing in the background, and maybe the sound of young voices. Miller had two teenaged children at home. "What can I do for you, Gordon?"

"This time it's what Admin can do for the Bureau."

"I'm listening."

"McGarvey is definitely coming home. But you might not know he's traveling on false papers and with a pretty fair disguise. It's possible he could walk right past your Homeland Security TSA people."

"Tell me," Miller said.

"He's traveling as a freelance journalist under a U.S. passport in the name of Tony Watkins."

"How do you know this?"

"Two of our people had contact with him but managed to get away undamaged."

"Lucky."

Remington gave him the Tony Watkins description. "I think Admin can give the Bureau convincing evidence of McGarvey's involvement with the shootings."

"Roland was more than a partner, he was a personal friend from what I understand," Miller said. "You must be shocked."

"Devastated," Remington said. "Do us a favor and pick him up. Or, better yet, shoot the man as he tries to escape."

"You'd like that."

"We all would," Remington replied.

Boberg, Admin's secretary Sigurd Larsen, the firm's equipment specialist Roger Lewis, their computer expert David Thoms, and their in-house travel agent Gina Ballinger sat around the table in the conference room. They looked up with interest and a certain amount of concern when Remington walked in.

"Mr. Sandberger along with two of his bodyguards and Harry Weiss were shot to death last night in Baghdad."

"My God," Sigurd gasped. "Insurgents?"

"No. It was a man named Kirk McGarvey."

"Son of a bitch," Boberg said. He was a short, narrow-hipped man who was hard as bar steel. Remington had personally recruited him from the British SAS. "Have we got someone on the ground to take him down?"

"He's on his way back here, and I have two angles covered," Remington said. He explained about Kangas and Mustapha and about the FBI that would have agents in place to grab McGarvey traveling as Watkins the moment he stepped off the jetway. "But there still could be a mistake, so I'll need a spotter out there."

"Harry was a good friend," Boberg said. "I'll take care of it myself. Just in case."

"If he's taken into custody he'll likely face treason charges. But he mustn't be allowed to make it away from the airport and go to ground. At all costs."

"Understood," Boberg said, softly.

FIFTY-TWO

Despite the fall of Saddam Hussein's regime and the end of organized fighting in the north, the Kuwaiti military maintained a strong presence on the border with Iraq, mostly to intercept insurgents who might want to send suicide bombers across.

A few kilometers north of the Iraqi town of Safwan, which was on the main north-south highway, Hadid pulled off the paved road, doused the headlights, and headed east into the desert toward the even smaller town of Umm Qash.

"I have a cousin there," Hadid said. "He and his two brothers and one cousin, my wife's nephew, all work in the oil fields across the border."

"Are we going to cross with them?" McGarvey asked.

Hadid shook his head. "Too dangerous for them, and I promised they wouldn't become involved. But I know this border area. The crossing will be easy."

The two towns were only twenty-five kilometers apart and yet after fifteen minutes of driving fairly fast, there were no signs of lights out ahead, though to the south waste gas fires from wellheads lit up the night sky with an eerie glow. This place was otherworldly and had been ever since the first Gulf War, when the invading Iraqi army had set most of those wells on fire. The air tasted of crude oil.

At one point the rough track dipped down into a shallow valley and Hadid stopped. "We'll bury your weapon and old papers here, but you may keep your satellite telephone."

He took a small shovel and a Kuwaiti Gulfmart Supermarket plastic bag from the back of the Range Rover, and dug a shallow hole in the sand a few feet away. He put McGarvey's things into the bag, tied it shut, and buried it.

"Will you come back for at least the pistol?" McGarvey asked.

"No need, Mr. James. Guns are plentiful here." He grinned in the darkness. "Maybe in five thousand years an archaeologist will dig it up and it will be placed in a museum of antiquities." He laughed.

It struck McGarvey that Hadid was trying very hard to find something to laugh about after having lost his wife and son. But there was nothing more to say, and he couldn't find the will yet to look for humor in his own life. But then he didn't have Hadid's faith in a Paradise.

Back in the car, they waited with the engine running. Ten minutes later Hadid glanced at his watch, and two minutes after that they spotted the glow of a pair of headlights traveling east to west in the general direction of Safwan.

"That is the Kuwait Army patrol," Hadid said. "Five minutes late."

They waited another full five minutes, before Hadid put the Range Rover in gear and they continued down the valley for about five or six kilometers until a hundred meters from an oil rig they bumped up onto a dirt road and turned west toward the highway back down to Kuwait City, reaching the pavement ten minutes later.

McGarvey powered up the sat phone and when it had acquired a bird, phoned Otto, who answered on the second ring. The man never slept. "You made it across the border."

"We're on our way down to Kuwait City. What's the word on the ground in Washington?"

"All hell is breaking loose on just about every site on the Internet. We're in lockdown mode here, and the entire country is in an uproar about the president's lack of a strong response over the IED in Arlington."

McGarvey's hand tightened on the phone. "Any leads on who did it?"

"None," Otto said. "But the Bureau is taking big heat from the

White House because they haven't bagged you yet. It's the only thing Langdon can do, except wring his hands. His advisers have convinced him that you're a traitor over the Pyongyang thing last year, and nothing any of us can say to him makes any difference. It's spooky, Mac, honest injun."

"Anything about the situation in Baghdad?"

"The Bureau had it eight or nine hours ago, which makes me think someone in Sandberger's outfit has a friend in the building. They even knew about your Tony Watkins ID, and they're waiting for you right now at Dulles."

"I've already switched IDs to Hopkins."

"How does Hadid think you look?"

"Good enough," McGarvey said.

"I can book you into LaGuardia if you want to avoid a possible hassle," Otto suggested.

"Make it Dulles. I think I can get past the Bureau guys, but I'm pretty sure that Admin will have someone posted out there as well, and I want a shot at spotting them."

"Give me a minute or two and I'll see what I can do," Otto said, and he was gone.

Traffic was picking up now the closer they got to al Kuwait, but almost all of it was convoys headed north. It was a never-ending stream 24/7.

Hadid glanced over at him. "Was that Mr. Otto?"

"Yes."

A big grin crossed Hadid's face. "I met him last year in Washington. He is a strange and wondrous creature. Very brilliant. Very . . ." He searched for the word. "Exotic."

"Eccentric," McGarvey said.

Otto was back. "Can you make it to the airport by ten-thirty?"

McGarvey relayed the question to Hadid who nodded vigorously and sped up. "Just."

"We'll make it."

"I'm booking you first class on United 981. Leaves at eleven forty-five your time, and touches down here at six forty-seven tomorrow morning."

"Good enough," McGarvey said. "They'll be watching for Tony Watkins, and someone's bound to sit up and take notice if he doesn't show."

"Get me a minute, I'm looking at the passenger manifest and pulling up passports. My darlings are looking for a reasonable match with Tony Watkins." Rencke's darlings were his custom-designed computer programs.

The lights of al Kuwait lit up the night sky and the tops of some of the taller skyscrapers were beginning to dot the horizon.

"Okay, I have a match, but I won't put it into place until you guys are aboard and airborne. Real name's Fred Irwin, works for State as a deputy assistant secretary for communications. When he gets off in Washington he'll be pegged as Tony Watkins. Should tie everybody up long enough for you to get clear. But it won't take long for the Bureau guys to realize who he really is, so you'll have to hustle."

"Have a rental car waiting for me," McGarvey said.

"Too slow. I'll pick you up myself."

"Bring me a weapon, and a silencer."

"Will do," Otto said. "And you better get some sleep on the flight over. I think you're gonna need it."

Hadid pulled up at United's departures area five minutes after ten-thirty. The long sweep of the driveway was busy with cars, taxis, and buses. A lot of flights heading west across the top of the African continent left around this time, for arrival in New York, Washington, Atlanta, and Miami first thing in the morning. The fourteen-hour nonstop flight was grueling for coach, but actually pleasant in business class and especially in first class.

McGarvey gathered his overnight bag. "Thanks for your help," he said.

Hadid shrugged and smiled shyly. "It was for a good cause. My family's cause. I am getting paid very well."

McGarvey nodded. "I'm sorry about your wife and son."

"But you don't understand, Mr. Kirk, a Muslim's grief is short-lived because it is tempered by joy. Go in peace."

"*Insh'ah Allah*," McGarvey replied.

PART

THREE

The Next Day

FIFTY-THREE

☐

Kangas and Mustapha touched down a few minutes before six a.m. at Andrews Air Force Base outside Washington, in a State Department Gulfstream IV arranged by Stuart Marston in Baghdad. Remington had called just before they boarded and warned them to stay sober and get some sleep. They would need their wits about them in the morning. And it was exactly what they'd done.

The aircraft taxied immediately over to a VIP hangar where they were met by a bird colonel who didn't bother introducing himself. A new Ford Taurus was parked nearby.

"The car's a rental, not expected back for five days," the Air Force officer said. He was of medium height and build, probably around forty or forty-five years old, and he had a thousand-yard stare. At one time in his career he'd been there and then some. "When you're finished wipe it down and leave it on some side street."

"Yes, sir," Kangas said, and he was about to ask about their equipment, but the officer turned away, got into a staff car, and drove off. No one else was around.

"Typical," Mustapha said.

They tossed their overnight bags in the backseat. Mustapha got behind the wheel and started the engine as Kangas slipped in on the passenger side.

The sat phone rang. It was Remington. "I assume you're on the ground and have the car."

"Just got it," Kangas said. "What do you have for us?"

"You need to get over to Dulles on the double march. McGarvey's coming in on United 981, scheduled to land in less than an hour."

Kangas put his hand over the mouthpiece. "Dulles and hustle," he said, and Mustapha drove out of the hangar and headed toward the main gate. "That was quick. What about our equipment?"

"Standard-issue Berettas, a couple of spare magazines and silencers for each of you under the seats. But don't take them into the terminal. If McGarvey somehow manages to get past the Bureau agents, you'll have to get on his trail and run him down. I want no gunplay anywhere in or near the terminal. Make damn sure of it."

"Will someone backstop us?" Kangas asked. "Because we can't leave the car in short-term parking, wait to see where McGarvey is off to, and then get back to it before he's out of sight."

"Cal Boberg is already in place. If need be he'll tail McGarvey while you get your car, and give you the details by phone."

"Why don't we just wait in the garage?"

"Because I want two extra sets of eyes to watch what happens," Remington said, and he sounded vexed.

Limey bastard, Kangas thought. "Once we've finished this business and get paid, we're retiring."

"That will be for the best," Remington said. "Just see that you finish the job this time. It was because of you that Roland was gunned down."

Maybe there would be just one more job after McGarvey, Kangas thought, breaking the connection. Remington had been asking for it for a long time now.

They were waved through the gate by an air policeman, and just off base got on I-495, the Beltway, and headed west, early-morning traffic still light but beginning to build.

"What's the situation?" Mustapha asked, and Kangas told him.

"Boberg is already out there to act as a spotter once McGarvey shows up."

"Then we take him down if he makes it past the Bureau guys?"

"Just like his son-in-law," Kangas said. "Nothing fancy."

"What about equipment?"

"Berettas under the seats."

Mustapha glanced at his partner. "No screwups this time."

"No," Kangas agreed. "Not this time. We can't afford to have the bastard come gunning for us."

"And we have two million each on the line."

"There's that, too," Kangas said, but mostly he was thinking about McGarvey and Baghdad. The son of a bitch could have shot them both dead and thought nothing of it. And he would have, had he known who'd put the IED at Arlington. "First things first," he said.

"I hear you."

Traffic began to pick up the closer they got to Dulles, most of it cabs, buses, and the occasional hotel van all coming to meet the dozen or more incoming international flights. Kangas and Mustapha reached the short-term car park just as United 981 was touching down, and they hustled into the main terminal where they took up positions across from the corridor leading out of the Customs and Border Protection Center. They were near one of the gift shops not yet open for the day, so they could look at the reflections in the glass as if they were window shopping.

The main hall was fairly busy now, because in addition to the incoming international traffic, domestic flights were beginning to accept passengers. But it was easy to spot the pair of FBI agents by their uniforms: dark blue suits, the jackets cut a little large to accommodate the bulge of their pistols, white shirts, ties correctly knotted, and earpieces. They stood on either side of the customs exit.

"If they recognize him he won't make it out of here," Kangas said.

"Unless he takes them down," Mustapha said.

"Won't happen. That treason shit is just some sort of cover."

"For what?"

"Beats me. But there's not a chance in hell of McGarvey taking out Bureau guys or cops."

"We're different," Mustapha said. "If he makes us he'll know why we're here."

It was something Kangas hadn't understood, because Remington wanting two extra pair of eyes here made no sense. Not unless he *wanted* McGarvey to spot them, which made even less sense.

Five minutes later a man leaning against a wall next to a men's room, not twenty feet from the Customs exit, lowered the newspaper he was reading, and Mustapha spotted him.

"There's Calvin."

Kangas looked over and Boberg raised his paper.

Twenty minutes later, when the first of the international passengers began straggling out from Customs, the main hall was busy enough that Kangas and Mustapha could afford to turn around and watch with little likelihood they would be made.

Most of the people coming out were businessmen, carrying laptops and hauling roll-about luggage, a few couples, one woman with three young children, an older woman toting a dog carrier while hauling a very large roll-about on which she had stacked two small bags.

A gray-haired man, fairly husky, a hanging bag over his shoulder, emerged from customs, glanced up at the overhead signs pointing toward ground transportation, and started to talk away when the pair of FBI agents fell in step beside him, and grabbed his arms. The man struggled at first, trying to pull away, and said something, obviously angrily.

"That's not him," Kangas said. "What the hell are they doing?"

One of the agents flashed his badge, and, suddenly subdued, the man allowed himself to be led away back into the Customs area.

Boberg lowered his newspaper, shrugged, and started to walk away, but Kangas shook his head. Urgently. And Boberg stopped.

Two minutes later another man, husky, but with a darker complexion than the first man, his hair dark brown, emerged from Customs.

He carried only a small nylon bag and he was dressed like a contractor, which was the only reason Mustapha spotted him.

"It's him, the guy in the bush jacket just coming out."

Kangas saw the resemblance at once. The clever bastard had changed his disguise and papers. He made sure that he had Boberg's attention and he nodded toward McGarvey.

Boberg did a double take, and when he looked back Kangas nodded again, and he and Mustapha headed back to short-term parking as quickly as they could without attracting any attention.

FIFTY-FOUR

At the curb outside the main terminal building Louise pulled up in her Toyota SUV, and McGarvey walked across to her, but before he opened the passenger-side door he glanced at the reflections in the car window in time to spot a dark, slightly built man in a tan jacket suddenly pull up short and turn away.

He wasn't surprised that the Bureau had shown up, he and Otto had expected it, nor was he surprised that he'd picked up a tail. A local Admin hand, no doubt. But the fact that all three of them, and whoever else would be coming after him, knew the flight he was coming in on had to mean there was a leak at the CIA. Someone senior in Operations, or possibly even someone on the seventh floor.

Most likely the Friday Club had people imbedded in the Company, probably the FBI, and almost certainly in Congress and the White House. Something serious was happening in Washington, or was about to happen. Maybe it wasn't as fanciful as what was on the disk that Givens had supposedly handed over to Todd, but it was big enough to maneuver a charge of treason against a former CIA director, and then send someone gunning for him.

He got in on the passenger side. "Where's Otto?"

Louise glanced in her rearview mirror, pulled out, and headed away. "At home trying to figure out how much damage your escapade in Baghdad did to your case." She glanced at him. "Are you okay? We were worried."

"They knew I was coming and they had a couple of guys waiting for me just outside my hotel," McGarvey said. "Slow down."

"What?" Louise asked, not quite sure that she'd heard right.

"Slow down, but don't make it too obvious. I think we're going to have some company."

She glanced in the rearview mirror, but slowed down by a few miles an hour. Otto had complained that Louise was a manic driver with a lead foot. She couldn't stand to be passed. Slowing down meant that she was now going the same speed as just about everyone else.

"Did you bring me a weapon?"

"In the glove compartment," Louise said, glancing in the rearview mirror again. "I'm a photo interpreter and image analyst, how am I supposed to know someone is following us?"

"I'll take care of that part," McGarvey said. He pulled a Wilson 9mm Tactical from the glove compartment, along with a suppressor, and three extra magazines of ammunition. The pistol was loaded and ready to fire.

"It could be anybody," Louise said.

"Just drive."

"Where?" she asked, alarmed.

"Soon as we pick up our tail, I want you to speed up and head back to Georgetown, to Rock Creek Park." He used the control button on the center console to turn the door mirror on his side to a position that would enable him to watch the road behind them. "At some point I'll have you slow down so that I can hop out and then you can take off. Drive around until I call for you to come back and pick me up. It'll be safe by then."

She was clearly upset now. "Otto says they've branded you a homicidal maniac because of Baghdad. Did you kill an Iraqi police captain?"

"No."

"Well, somebody at the State Department got a report from its people on the ground over there, that's exactly what you did."

"Any witnesses?"

Louise opened her mouth to say something, but then she shook her head. "If there were, Otto couldn't find any mention."

"I took Sandberger and three of his people down. Any witnesses who can place me at the Ritz?"

She shook her head again. "But State knows that you were there and the shootings couldn't have been coincidental."

"The Bureau had two agents waiting for me."

"Otto told me about switching identities. A State Department FSO. They're not going to be very happy."

"No, but the other guy waiting for me also knew what flight I was coming in on," McGarvey said.

"A leak?" Louise asked. "Otto was worried about it."

"Was he expecting it?"

She nodded glumly. "Can you tell me what's going on? Who the hell are these guys and what do they want? They have to be more than lobbyists."

"Sixty-four-dollar question," McGarvey said, watching the mirror. A dark blue Taurus had pulled up from way behind as if the driver had been in a big hurry, but then had slowed down, keeping up a position three cars back. "Switch lanes right now and speed up," he told Louise.

She glanced in her rearview mirror and suddenly pulled into the next lane left and hit the gas. The big Toyota surged forward, and a hundred yards later she had to move left again to pass a cab.

The driver of the Taurus managed to keep up, while maintaining his position three cars back. McGarvey could make out two figures in the front seat, but they were too far away for him to make any sort of identification. But he knew damned well they were Admin muscle.

"They're back there, in the dark blue Ford," he said. "You can drive normal now."

"You're going to kill them," Louise said, glancing nervously at him again.

"Not unless I have to," McGarvey said. "I need answers not bodies." He'd seen enough bodies lately to last three lifetimes. And yet it wasn't over, and possibly would never be over. Plato had said that only the dead had seen the end of war. Maybe his turn was coming.

Traffic on the Airport Access Road all the way down to where it crossed beneath the Beltway and finally the off ramp to I-66 was busy as usual, but the blue Taurus managed to keep up even though Louise drove erratically, always searching for the fastest lane.

At one point she glanced nervously in the rearview mirror. "They're still back there."

"Otto was right, you drive too fast."

"Makes him crazy," she said smiling. "Should I slow down?"

"No, you're doing just fine. Those guys probably think you're trying to shake them, which is what I want them to think."

She took the ramp to the Key Bridge, and as they crossed the river directly into Georgetown, McGarvey pocketed the three spare magazines of ammunition and screwed the silencer on the end of the Wilson's barrel.

Louise was glancing at him, clearly frightened now. "I don't know if I can lose them long enough for you to get out."

"I want them to see you dropping me off," McGarvey said. "That's the whole point."

"They'd be stupid to try to come after you. Why not grab me?"

"They're Admin shooters and they want to take me out," McGarvey said. It was the next step after Baghdad. He'd definitely got their attention, and now they were going to make the next series of mistakes that would lead him directly to the Friday Club. He just had to stay alive and out of custody until he could find out what was going on. What had been going on since the operations involving Chinese intelligence in Mexico City and Pyongyang. Those had been difficult and very expensive operations, neither of which had produced any visible results, other than having him branded as a traitor.

It made no sense. And situations that made no sense bothered McGarvey to no end.

Across the river, Louise turned east on M Street NW until the off ramp into Rock Creek Park, just at the beginning of Pennsylvania Avenue. Suddenly they were on the winding road that led north nearly two miles all the way up to Connecticut Avenue, crossing and recrossing the creek twice as it meandered through the sometimes densely forested park.

This morning traffic on the road was light, and only a few joggers and bicyclists were out and about, and none of the benches or picnic areas was occupied. On the weekends the park was always busy, but on weekdays most people were either at work by now or on the way.

Which was perfect as far as McGarvey was concerned, because he definitely did not want any collateral damage if shots were fired.

"Where do you want this to happen?" Louise demanded, her voice shrill now.

They had already reached the first bridge across the creek and for the next stretch the park area was very narrow, not enough room to maneuver.

"We're going to cross under Massachusetts Avenue. A little past that there's another bridge. I'll get out there."

"Jesus Christ," Louise said, her hands tight on the steering wheel.

Two minutes later they crossed under Massachusetts Avenue and almost immediately the second bridge was just ahead.

"Now," McGarvey said.

Louise jammed on the brakes and McGarvey popped open the door and jumped out even before the Toyota came to a full stop.

"Go," he shouted over his shoulder, and darted off the road about ten yards into the woods, where he stopped and looked back.

Louise was gone, and the blue Taurus had pulled over to the side of the road and two men were getting out. The same two from outside his hotel at Baghdad. It was perfect.

FIFTY—FIVE

Kangas and Mustapha stood at the edge of the road looking down the hill into the denser woods. The rising sun was in their eyes, but they knew that McGarvey had to be somewhere close, they'd seen him jumping out of the Toyota.

"There," Mustapha said suddenly, and Kangas looked where his partner was pointing in time to see McGarvey disappearing farther down the hill.

"That's the bastard," Kangas said.

"Whoever the broad was probably brought him a weapon," Mustapha said. "Could be a trap. He jumps out, and like complete idiots we run after him."

"That's exactly what this is. But we'd be bigger idiots to turn down three mil each."

"Won't do us any good if we're dead. I say we turn around and get the fuck out of here right now. You know what this guy is capable of."

"Yeah, but he doesn't know us, now, does he," Kangas said. "And I'm not ready to walk away from a pile of money."

"You'd do it even if there was no money at stake," Mustapha said, and Kangas grinned.

"Payback time for Baghdad."

"Sandberger . . ."

"Fuck Sandberger, this is for us," Kangas said. "Go left, I'll go right. We'll catch him in our cross fire."

Mustapha nodded. "Careful what you shoot at."

Kangas took the silencer out of his pocket and screwed it onto the end of his Beretta, and headed down the hill into the woods, slightly to the right of where they'd last seen McGarvey, at the same time Mustapha headed at an angle the other way.

Back at the airport they had just reached their car when Boberg called and described the Toyota SUV that had come for McGarvey. "Some woman driving, but she's not on any of our lists. I checked."

"Anyone else with her?" Kangas had asked as Mustapha headed down the spiral ramp to one of the cashier gates at the bottom.

"Not unless they were hiding in the backseat."

"Did he spot you tailing him?"

"I don't know," Boberg said. "But I think it's a good possibility. He was looking at something in the passenger-door window. Maybe at the woman, but he could have been looking at the reflection in the glass."

"If he spotted you he'll be expecting someone from Admin to be on his ass," Kangas said. It had been a stupid mistake on Boberg's part that just made their jobs a lot tougher. "Thanks."

"Take the bastard down anyway you can. That's priority one after what he did to us in Baghdad. We'll pick up any loose ends afterward."

"Could be collateral damage."

"I couldn't care less," Boberg had said. "Get the job done this time."

Ninety seconds from the moment they'd come within tailing distance, the Toyota had suddenly sped up and the woman had driven like crazy into Georgetown and the park.

The bastard had definitely set a trap for them, and when he saw it was them he would shoot first and ask questions later. Only this time Kangas had a bargaining chip. One that McGarvey wouldn't be able to resist.

FIFTY-SIX

□

From where he stood behind the bole of a large tree McGarvey heard the two men coming down the hill and knew they had separated, as he expected they would. Once out of sight from the road he'd headed off to the right, well away from the line the first of them had taken, putting him on their right flank, not between them.

Theirs was a good tactical move, but they hadn't counted on the unexpected, and they were walking into a trap. It was something that happened when the operator underestimated his opponent.

A couple of minutes later he spotted a figure moving through the trees about forty yards beyond where he figured the first guy was coming down the hill. But the first one had stopped. He was smart, possibly suspecting something.

"Mr. McGarvey," a man called out, off to the right, perhaps ten yards away. "We know you're down here somewhere. It was very smart of you to take our fight away from the road where innocent bystanders might get hurt. Very smart."

McGarvey moved halfway around the tree to where he had a better sight line up the hill and to the right, and he caught just a flash of something dark, perhaps the sleeve of a jacket or shirt.

"But there's no need for gunplay this morning. Because we have something that you want. And we're willing to trade."

The bastards hadn't flown commercial back from Baghdad. Probably hitched a ride on a military transport, or perhaps a private jet one of the oil or reconstruction firms operated.

"Mr. Kangas, I told you that I would kill you if I saw you again," McGarvey said. "And that goes for your partner out to your left."

"We know about you. What you're capable of, and I'm not ashamed to admit that we made our mistakes in Baghdad, but now everything has changed. Mr. Sandberger and a couple of his personal bodyguards, plus Harry Weiss, are all dead, and Admin is in pretty tough shape."

"I'm listening," McGarvey said. He stuffed his pistol in his belt, and got down on his hands and knees, below the level of most of the brush and tall grasses, and careful to make absolutely no noise began edging his way back up the hill.

"We lied to you in Baghdad. Admin was responsible for your son-in-law's death and the IED at Arlington. It was meant for you. Mr. Sandberger wanted you dead to protect one of his clients."

McGarvey stopped. He was less than five feet from Kangas, who was looking in the general direction of the big tree. It took everything within his power not to shoot the contractor in the back of the head, right now.

"Listen, we want to make a deal with you. We're getting out of Admin, too much shit is going to hell. It's no longer healthy for us."

McGarvey took out his pistol, suddenly stood up and in two steps was on Kangas, jamming the muzzle of his silencer into the side of the man's head. "Drop your pistol now."

Kangas hesitated for just a second, but then did as he'd been told.

"Tell your partner to drop his weapon and come closer so I can see him."

"Ronni stay where you are, he has me," Kangas shouted. "Sorry, Mr. McGarvey, but you'll have to be satisfied with just me."

A black rage threatened to block McGarvey's sanity, but he forced himself to calm down. This was business, nothing more. These guys were only a means to an end. "Who were the shooters who took out my son-in-law and the newspaper reporter and his family?"

"Just one gun. Ex Green Beret, works out of our Washington office. He's Mr. Remington's right-hand man. He was our spotter at the airport when you came in. Short, dark."

"Name?"

"Calvin Boberg. Lives down in Arlington."

"Why are you telling me this?" McGarvey asked.

"Because if it was my family that got wiped out I'd go after the bastard who did it, and nothing could stop me."

"How do I know it wasn't you?"

"We're contractors, which means we don't kill women and children. But that's what Admin's come to, and now that Mr. Sandberger's dead it's going to get a hell of a lot worse, because Remington is a crazy son of a bitch."

"But you were sent to Baghdad to kill me, and now you're here," McGarvey said. "Why specifically?"

"Because of what your son-in-law probably told you on the phone after meeting with the reporter."

"The Friday Club?"

"Yeah, Mr. Foster, he's one of our biggest clients, and he wants you dead."

"Why?"

"I don't know, and I swear to Christ it's the truth. But Remington and Sandberger were both worried that you would probably get too close for comfort. You were the company's top priority."

What Kangas was saying had the ring of truth to it, but there was more, just out of reach. McGarvey could feel it.

Something moved a little higher up the hill toward the road, but still to the left, but then stopped. Kangas had heard it and he stiffened.

"Tell him to walk away or I'll shoot you right now and it'll be just him and me," McGarvey said.

"You're going to shoot me anyway."

"No need, I got what I wanted."

Kangas shifted his weight to his left leg and started to swivel away from the gun pointed at the side of his head. The man was good, his movement sudden and swift, but he'd tensed the instant before he started to turn and McGarvey had felt it, and followed to the left, the pistol never leaving the contractor's jawline.

"Your choice," McGarvey said, jamming the pistol even harder.

"What do you want me to do?" Kangas asked, resignation finally in his voice.

"Tell your partner to toss his gun out where I can see it and walk back up to the car and wait for you."

"Ronni," Kangas shouted.

"I heard him," Mustapha said from maybe only a few yards farther up the hill. "I can take him out from here."

"Don't miss," McGarvey said, and he pulled the pistol's hammer back. It was not necessary but the sound was distinctive.

"Do what he says, goddamnit, and we get to walk out of here alive!"

"I heard what you told him," Mustapha said. "If Remington goes down, what about the money?"

"Screw the money."

Mustapha was silent for several seconds.

"Come on, man," Kangas said. "Just do it."

Mustapha stepped into view, his hands in plain sight out to the sides. He let his gun drop to the ground. "If you're going to shoot me it'll have to be in the back," he said. "But it wasn't us who wiped out your family, you have my word on it." He turned and started back up the hill.

When he was gone, McGarvey stepped back. "Go."

Kangas didn't bother turning around, just headed up the hill after Mustapha.

When they were both gone, McGarvey followed them, coming within sight of the road just as they were getting into the Taurus. A minute later they drove away, and McGarvey called Louise's cell.

"Can I bum a ride?" he asked when she answered.

FIFTY-SEVEN

□

Remington was fifty years old, the same age his father had been when he'd hung himself from a ceiling light fixture, the only decisive thing the man had ever accomplished in his miserable life. And at this moment Remington figured that he had come to his own crossroad. Either the McGarvey situation would be resolved and Admin would continue its work in Baghdad for the State Department and here in Washington for the Friday Club, or everything would fall apart.

The cab had taken Colleen over to Reagan National Airport an hour ago, and before she'd walked out the door she'd kissed him, something she had not done in private for a very long time.

"It's the shootings in Baghdad, isn't it," she'd said. "Roland was assassinated and you think you might be next?"

She was a bright woman, and never missed much, but he'd just smiled. "Anything's possible, my dear. Might even get run over by a bus."

"But you're sending me up to New York just in case. How terribly romantic."

"Just for a day or two."

She gave him a double take. "You're actually worried something like that could happen here. I mean just now that you've been handed the company practically on a silver platter. Doesn't seem fair somehow."

Remington had wanted to tell her to shut her mouth, but he'd held his smile. "Have a good time in New York."

She'd given him a last, searching look. "Always do," she said and she left.

It was quiet on Wednesdays, when the house staff had the day off.

The only one left was Sergeant Randall, his driver and personal body-guard, who had his own apartment in the carriage house above the garage at the rear of the property.

Remington stood by the French doors in his study looking at the rose garden. At this moment the bushes were bare, and looked dead. But in two months the garden—his personal project—would be magnificent. If everything held together that long, and he was here to see it.

It was coming up on nine-thirty, time to leave for the office, and yet the only word he'd received had been from Boberg who'd confirmed that McGarvey had shown up in disguise.

"A woman picked him up at the curb in a Toyota SUV," Boberg reported. "But the plates matched some French doctor supposedly out of the country right now."

"What about Kangas and Mustapha?"

"Last I heard they were following the Toyota into the city. Haven't you heard from them yet?"

"No."

"I'm in the office now, do you want me to try to reach them? Find out what's going on?"

"I'll take care of it myself from here," Remington said. "But listen, Cal, I'm putting you in total charge of Admin for the next couple of days. I'm going to be busy soothing some ruffled feathers."

"He hasn't called here yet," Boberg said, referring to Robert Foster.

"He's waiting for me to take care of the situation. So just sit tight."

"Business as usual?"

Remington laughed despite himself. "Or the illusion thereof," he said. "Something comes up, call me."

"Will do."

Remington called the sat phone Kangas had been using since Baghdad, and it was answered on the second ring.

"It was a bloody fucking circus," Kangas shouted.

Remington could hear the sounds of people and traffic in the background. "Where the hell are you?"

"On the Mall, in front of the Vietnam Memorial. Figured we

needed to be around a lot of people. The son of a bitch is good, and we're going to need some serious help if you still want him taken down."

Remington held the phone tightly to his ear, but his other hand was shaking. He hadn't had a drink in two days, and he needed something now. "What happened?" he demanded.

Kangas settled down and went over everything that happened from the moment McGarvey showed up and Boberg told them about the Toyota SUV. "The bitch driving stopped up in Rock Creek Park and McGarvey jumped out and ran into the woods. It was a setup."

"Which you must have guessed."

"Right. But the guy knows his stuff."

"Why didn't he kill you?" Remington asked, afraid that he already knew the answer, and knew he wouldn't like it.

"He wanted us to take a message back to you."

"Me, personally?"

"He mentioned you by name, and he also said he knew about Foster and the Friday Club. Said he was coming after everybody because of what happened to his son-in-law and wife and kid."

"He knows Admin was involved? That you and Ronni were the triggermen?" Remington asked, astounded.

"He knows Admin was involved, but I sure as hell wasn't going to tell him what part we played," Kangas said. "So what's next? If you want us to go after him again, we'll need more money, but we'll arrange for our own extra muscle."

Remington's stomach was sour. "What's next, you pricks?" he practically shouted into the phone. "You're fucking fired, that's what's next. And you'll have more to worry about than McGarvey, because every contractor on our payroll will be gunning for you. And I'll make goddamned sure that every other service knows how incompetent you are."

"Just maybe you're our next target," Kangas said.

"In your dreams," Remington shot back. But he was talking to dead air. The connection had been broken.

He slammed the phone down, and went to the wet bar where he picked up the brandy decanter, but after an intense moment put it back. "Not now," he muttered. "Not like this."

It had been the worst possible news. Sandberger, and now this. And for the first time since he'd gotten out of the service, just before he'd teamed up with Roland to start Admin, and before he'd married Colleen and her money, he felt as if his back was truly up against the wall. He imagined that his father had felt the same thing at the end. But the old man had run out of options; no place to go and no money with which to get there.

Remington went back to his desk and sat down. It was different for him. He had set aside a fair amount of money—some of it siphoned from Admin and some of it from Colleen—and he owned a pleasant eighteenth-century villa in the south of France, just a few kilometers inland from the Med. Life could be comfortable there.

A new life, he thought. But first he had to cover his back. Maintain the illusion that Admin was still up and running and very much on track, which would give him time to slip well clear before he was missed. Twenty-four hours, tops.

Reluctantly he called Foster's encrypted number, which wasn't answered until the fourth ring.

"I expected a call from you much sooner, Gordon. What is the current situation vis-à-vis Mr. McGarvey?"

"I sent two shooters after him here in Washington this morning."

"But they failed again, is that what you've telephoned to tell me?" Foster asked.

"Yes, sir. But it's worse than that. Apparently McGarvey not only knows that Admin engineered the deaths of his son-in-law, wife, and daughter, but all of it was at the behest of the Friday Club. At your behest." Remington hoped the bastard was squirming. That all of them in the man's little group of tin-pot lobbyists were. None of them had any class that only centuries of English breeding could produce.

"How could he know such things unless someone from your staff said something. How about your two shooters?"

"They don't know that you are a client. Only Roland and me and a few key people know about it."

"It's possible somehow they found Givens's real CD and it's also possible that Roland opened his mouth to try to save his life," Foster said. "But it doesn't really matter at this stage, because Mr. McGarvey has no proof. Couldn't possibly have."

"Perhaps you should see that the FBI takes a more active interest in arresting him. Maybe there could be an unfortunate shoot-out."

"No," Foster said flatly. "Your firm was hired to take care of just this sort of thing, and will continue to do so. Whatever it takes, no matter how much money you need, no matter how many Admin personnel it takes, I want McGarvey eliminated."

"That may be messy."

"Handle it."

"McGarvey will almost certainly come after you, and quite soon I would think. Probably tonight. I'll be sending Cal Boberg out to your place. He's one of our best. He'll handle it, as you say."

"I'll be expecting him," Foster said. "But Gordon, I have my own security measures out here. Make sure he's forewarned. His only mission will be to provide an outer layer of defense should McGarvey be foolish enough to come all this way."

"Yes, sir," Remington said.

After he hung up, he thought about his next moves. He would be out of here no later than midnight and on his way first to Atlanta aboard the company jet, as a diversion, and then off to Paris, commercial, and his new life. Long before his rose garden bloomed he would be eating clementine oranges from his own trees.

He telephoned Boberg at the office. "A change of plans, Cal. I have a new assignment for you."

FIFTY-EIGHT

□

On the way back to the Renckes' brownstone in Georgetown Louise was silent, almost as if she were afraid to ask the one question that had been on her lips the moment she'd seen him waiting by the side of Rock Creek Road.

And he was glad for it, because he felt battered, physically as well as emotionally. Admin had killed just about everyone he truly loved on the orders of the Friday Club. Robert Foster's orders. S. Gordon Remington's orders. Roland Sandberger's orders.

But just before Louise pulled into the driveway back to the garage in what once upon a time had been a mews of carriage houses with apartments above, she glanced at him. "Are you okay?"

He shrugged. "I've been better," he said. He felt that a great weariness was falling on him because of what he knew, and because of what would have to happen next.

"Did you kill those two guys?"

"No need for it," he told her. "I wanted information and they gave it to me. It was a part of the bargain, so I had them toss their weapons and let them drive away."

"Will they come back?"

"Maybe," McGarvey said. "And if they do I'll kill them."

Louise said nothing, just shook her head and parked the car. They went inside together and Otto came to the head of the stairs. His operational headquarters, as he called one of the front bedrooms filled with computer equipment, was on the second floor. He'd spent most of his days and nights up there since Todd's funeral and the explosion afterward.

"How'd it go," he asked.

"He didn't kill them," Louise said. "Anybody hungry for break-fast?"

"Sure," McGarvey said. "Then I'll need to borrow your car."

"Where're you going?"

"Wherever Gordon Remington is holed up. Because if the two con-tractors at Rock Creek report in, he'll go to ground. Might run anyway because of Baghdad, and I definitely want to catch him before he gets too far."

Louise looked up at her husband. "You'd better tell him," she said, and she went down the hall to the kitchen.

"Tell me what?" McGarvey asked, going upstairs.

Pete Boylan stood at the open door to Otto's workroom. She was dressed in jeans and a light sweatshirt, the sleeves pushed up, and even though her face was bruised, and she had a bandage on her left arm, she still looked fetching. "You're a popular guy, Mr. Director," she said. "You might think about hanging out here until after dark, less chance of you being spotted."

"I walked right past the two Bureau agents at the airport."

"Yeah, and they're mad as hell," Otto said, and he led McGarvey back to his workroom. Two long tables filled with large wide-screen computer monitors, keyboards, and several pieces of equipment that prevented electronic eavesdropping, prevented virus infections, and allowed an undetectable wireless connection through the system at a Starbucks half a block away had been set up in a long V shape.

"You need to take a look at something," Pete said. She sat down at one of the keyboards and pulled up the FBI's For-Internal-Use-Only Persons of Interest page. The first name on the list was McGarvey's. Included was a lengthy file with photographs of him in various dis-guises and in various locals including Frankfurt, and most recently Baghdad—but none showing him at any crime scene.

"They know you were there," Pete said. "But take a look at this."

She brought up the rest of his file, including his bio and a fairly complete rendering of his CIA jacket from day one right up to the Mexico City and Pyongyang incidents.

"All classified top secret or above," Pete said.

"I've been looking, Mac, but I have no idea how that stuff got to the Bureau," Otto said. "No traces were left behind in any of the Company's computer systems. So if someone hacked our mainframe they were better than me."

"It was probably done the old-fashioned way," Pete said.

And McGarvey saw it before Otto, who was too tied into his computer world to think along a parallel line. "Someone copied the paper files and hand-carried them across."

"Someone with access," Pete said. "Someone on the seventh floor."

Otto saw it, too. "This proves it," he said. "We thought McCann was working with someone else in the company," he explained to Pete. "Maybe someone he was reporting to."

"Well, he's still there, and he's trying to bring you down, Mr. Director," Pete said.

"Show him the rest."

"Okay, so the Bureau is looking for you, but so is the U.S. Marshal's Service." She brought up the Service's internal-use files and came up with the same dossier on McGarvey. "And the State Department's Bureau of Intelligence and Research, D.C.'s Metro Police, and just about every law enforcement agency—state, county, and municipal—in a several-hundred-mile radius. Homeland Security has you on its watch list. And just this morning Baghdad police were seriously looking for you, and Iraq's ambassador to the U.S. filed a formal complaint."

Nothing was a surprise to McGarvey except the speed at which everything was happening. "Foster must be getting nervous to go to these lengths," he said.

"I came over last night and Otto briefed me," Pete said. "But we still don't have enough proof that Foster's Friday Club has anything to do with this, or with the Mexico City or Pyongyang incidents. Leastways nothing we can take to the Justice Department."

"How'd you find this place?" McGarvey asked.

"I sent an e-mail to Otto's home account and he answered me within ninety seconds."

"Untraceable," Otto said.

"Most of the people I talked to on Campus think someone is gunning for you, but their hands are tied. They're afraid for their jobs. It's scary over there. Morale has never been so low."

"Technically makes you a traitor," McGarvey said.

She smiled. "Just doing my job, Mr. Director."

"Might be easier if you started calling me Mac. My friends do. The ones in this house at least."

"You'd be surprised how many friends you have in this town," she said.

"And just now too many enemies," McGarvey said. "But you're wrong about proof, I've got all I need." And he told them about Kangas and Mustapha in Baghdad and again in Rock Creek Park this morning. "Admin is right in the middle of it."

"On the Friday Club's orders," Otto said. "But the stuff on the disk they found in Todd's car is worthless. So right now all we have is your word that a couple of Admin contractors at gunpoint told you everything." Otto shook his head. "We need more than that to convince just about everyone in Washington including the president's staff that you're no traitor."

"We can go after these two guys," Pete said. "Present them as material witnesses."

"They're just shooters, not planners. They heard stuff, but they probably had no direct contact with Foster and his group," McGarvey said. "It's why I went to Baghdad, to see what Sandberger had to say. But he was willing to take a bullet rather than tell me anything. Which leaves us Remington."

Otto was clearly worried. "What do you have in mind?"

"Find out where he lives, find out what security measures he has in place, and if he has bodyguards, and then I'll go over to see him."

"And if he's willing to take a bullet the same as Sandberger, that'll leave us with squat," Otto said. "Admin killed Todd and Katy and Liz.

We already had that pretty well figured out. But as bad as it is you gotta calm down and think it through. Honest injun."

"Goddamnit, I'm not going to walk away," McGarvey said, his entire body numb. Killing Sandberger had been satisfying. Too satisfying, and yet Otto was right, killing Remington would do nothing for them.

"Okay, so if you get nothing out of Remington, what next? Foster?"

"Yes."

"And after him you'd be gunning for some top people in this town," Otto said. "Think it out. Where does it end? And more important than that, where's the connection between Mexico City, Pyongyang, and now? Because I don't see it."

"You still need material witnesses," Pete broke in. "One material witness who would be willing to testify against Foster to save his butt. S. Gordon Remington."

"That's right," McGarvey said.

"To save his butt from you," she said quietly. "There's no way you can run around Washington on your own—especially not during the day—no matter how good your disguise is."

Louise was at the door. "She's right. I recognized you because we're friends. Could happen again if you're in the wrong place at the wrong time."

"Otto can check out Remington's house and security measures and I'll go over there myself later, around dinnertime, and ring the doorbell," Pete said. "I'm not very threatening-looking, and he wouldn't be expecting someone like me to show up."

"He's ex-SAS," McGarvey said. "Sandhurst."

"No offense, Mac, but he's an old guy who probably hasn't been on a field assignment in years. And I'm pretty good. I think I can take him down, and bring him back here, and we'll have our foot in the Friday Club's front door."

It made sense but McGarvey didn't like it. "That puts you on the firing line."

"I didn't lose a child or a spouse, but I did lose a partner who was my friend. And I've been on the firing line before."

"You can't go on a field ops with an empty stomach," Louise said. "Breakfast is ready."

FIFTY-NINE

Pete Boylan had wanted to be a tomboy all her life, but her good looks had made that nearly impossible, and at thirty-three she was just as frustrated as she'd ever been. Men tended to fall into two groups: those who were intimidated by her and those who trivialized her. Neither type of man had ever interested her, so she was still single, and hating that, too, which sometimes, like this evening, lent her a mean streak. She wanted to hit someone.

She cruised slowly along Whitehaven Street in her personal car, a red Mustang convertible, top up, past the Danish embassy and then the Italian embassy, Remington's upscale house with the tall iron gate at the front entrance sat between them.

Otto had set her up with a one-piece voice-operated wire that looked like an in-the-ear-canal hearing aide. "Just drove past his house," she said softly.

"Any visible activity?" McGarvey's voice was soft but understandable in her ear.

"Lights on upstairs and downstairs, and a Bentley parked in the driveway, trunk lid open, no trunk light." It was past eight and dark already.

"He's going someplace."

"Looks like it," Pete said. "I'm at Massachusetts Avenue now. Soon as the light changes I'll drive up to Thirtieth and make a U-turn."

"How's traffic?"

"Not bad," Pete said. The light changed and she made a left then almost immediately a right, and made a sharp U-turn in somebody's driveway. Two minutes later she was across Massachusetts Avenue and heading back to Remington's house.

She missed Dan, and wished he were here with her right now. He was bright, kind, and above all understanding, just like her father had been in Palo Alto when she was growing up, especially when she'd gone through her teen years. But he'd had a heart attack when she was in her first year of pre-law at USC, and by the time she'd made it home he was gone. There wasn't a day when she didn't think of him, and it would be the same with Dan for the rest of her life.

She pulled up to the curb and parked, blocking Remington's driveway. "Okay, I'm here, still no activity."

"If he's heading out, it means he's probably desperate," McGarvey said. "So watch your back."

"And don't forget about his driver, Sergeant Randall," Otto's voice came through the earpiece. "Ex-Sandhurst and SAS along with Remington. Probably tough as nails."

"As far as they're concerned I'm coming from the CIA to conduct an unofficial briefing on the Baghdad situation for Mr. Remington."

"He'll ask you on whose orders," McGarvey said.

"I'm not allowed to give you that information, sir."

"If something goes bad it might take me ten or fifteen minutes to get to you, so keep on top of it. Give us a clue."

"Will do," Pete said.

She took out her CIA identification wallet, got out of her car, and went to the front gate where she pushed the button for the bell, aware that a closed-circuit television camera was pointed at her. A few seconds later an overhead light came on.

"What is it?" a man's voice came from the speaker grille. He sounded English.

Pete held her ID up to the camera. "Pete Boylan. CIA. I've been sent to brief Mr. Remington on the situation in Baghdad."

"We're aware of the situation."

"Some new facts have just come to light, and it was thought that you should have this information immediately. It'll only take a couple of minutes, sir."

"Who sent you?"

"I'm not at liberty to give you that name. But he said you would know who it was."

"Just a moment."

If Remington called someone over at Langley the game would be over before it began. But the gate lock buzzed and she went through and up the walk to the red front door with a brass knocker, which opened as she approached.

A short man, craggy face, definitely not Remington, wide brown eyes, narrowed now with suspicion, looked at her. "Let me see your identification."

She held it out for him, but when he reached for it she pulled back. "You may look, Sergeant Randall, but you will not touch."

"Are you armed?"

Pete almost smiled. "Of course."

"I'll have your weapon, then."

"Not a chance, Sarge," Pete said. "Inform Mr. Remington that I've returned to the Campus." She turned and started away, but Remington came to the door.

"It's all right. Come back, please, I need to know what you brought for me."

Pete turned back. Remington was dressed in a European-cut dark blazer with the family crest on the breast pocket, a white shirt, and club tie. "Are you going out this evening, sir?"

"To the office. We're in crisis mode."

"It's why I was sent, sir," Pete said.

He stepped aside for her to enter the stair hall, long crystal chandelier, ornate side tables, a pristine white marble floor, and a large painting of a man in formal dress on one wall opposite a mirror in an ornate gold frame. Sergeant Randall had stepped back a few feet, but he was super-alert.

"This is for your ears only, sir," Pete said.

Remington was looking at her breasts. "Give us a minute, Sarge."

Randall hesitated for just a moment, but then turned and disappeared down the corridor to the rear of the house.

"I have to tell you that I've never seen a prettier CIA officer," Remington said. "But were you in an accident recently?"

Pete reached inside her jacket and withdrew her 9×19 mm compact Glock 19 pistol, fitted with a short barrel silencer and pointed it at Remington, who reared back, and stumbled away a couple of steps. But Pete followed him, keeping just out of his reach. If he lunged she meant to switch aim and shoot him in the kneecap. The whole idea was to get him back to Georgetown alive.

"I'm not here to assassinate you, Mr. Remington, but if you cry out or in any way try to alert Sergeant Randall, I won't hesitate to pull the trigger."

It took Remington several beats to understand something of what he was facing. "You're not really from the CIA."

"Yes, I am. Housekeeping actually."

"Then why are you here pointing a pistol at my head?"

"Somebody wants to have a chat with you before you leave town."

The rest of it came to Remington. "McGarvey," he said. "I'll take my chances here." He started to turn around.

"One step and I will shoot you," Pete warned.

Remington stopped, his back to her. "If I go with you, McGarvey will kill me anyway, so I'm a dead man."

"You have one option."

"Which is?"

"Help us prove what Foster and his Friday Club are up to; what Joshua Givens evidently found out about and passed to Todd Van Buren that resulted in their deaths."

Remington's shoulders sagged, and he turned around. "It's bigger than you can imagine," he said. "There'd be no place safe for me."

"If you don't cooperate do you think McGarvey will back off? He knows your company was involved in the deaths of his son-in-law and the *Post* reporter. And he knows your people killed his wife and daughter."

"And he killed Roland without hesitation because of it."

"Only because your boss chose to take a bullet rather than cooperate," Pete said.

Remington's lips parted slightly at the same moment Pete became aware of the distant sounds of traffic as the front door opened. Sliding to the left and swiveling on one heel she was in time to see Sergeant Randall coming through the door, his gun hand rising. With no time to assume the proper two-handed grip and solid firing stance, she pulled off two snap shots, one smacking into the wall, but the other hitting the sergeant in center mass and he fell back, bouncing off the door frame and crumpling to the floor.

Before she could recover her balance Remington was on her, his superior weight bulling her to her knees. Instead of resisting, she went with his forward momentum, ducking down so that he came over the top of her back, and she grabbed the material of his jacket with her left hand and helped him the rest of the way over.

She scrambled away on her butt and heels, and got to her feet as Remington turned over and tried to reach Randall's pistol. But he was too old, and too slow, and Pete was on him before he got two feet, and jammed her pistol in the back of his neck at the base of his skull.

"Now that the situation is stabilized and your sergeant is dead, give me one good reason not to pull the trigger," she said. McGarvey and Otto were listening, and she'd just told them that she was okay.

"We want him alive," McGarvey said.

"We have a safe house for you," Pete said.

"What about afterward?" Remington asked, looking over his shoulder from where he was sprawled on the marble floor.

"If you mean your house in France and your secret bank accounts in Switzerland, Guernsey, and the Caymans, that will depend on how well you cooperate. We can take the house and drain your accounts easier than you think."

"Flash drive," Remington said.

"What about a flash drive?"

"The Friday Club. All of Admin's records. Names, financial dealings. Everything. You can't imagine."

"Everything on the Friday Club?" Pete asked, for McGarvey's benefit.

"Anyone else in the house?" McGarvey asked.

"Not that I know of."

"Make sure you have the flash drive and then get him out of there, right now. His sergeant might have called for backup," McGarvey said. "I cheated. I'm five minutes away."

SIXTY

□

The Toyota SUV moved quickly in the night up the Rock Creek Parkway, and past the spot where Louise had dropped McGarvey off early that morning. Now, except for the streetlights, the park was mostly in darkness and all but deserted.

"Do you really think his sergeant called for help?" she asked.

"I think that it's likely if they got suspicious," McGarvey said.

Otto had fitted him with the same earpiece comms unit that Pete was using, except his had a lapel switch that in one position was a party line connecting him with Otto and Pete, while in the other only he and Otto could talk.

He flipped the switch that excluded Pete. "Were you able to intercept any calls to or from Admin's offices?" he asked.

"Several since this afternoon, but just about everything in or out is heavily encrypted with some really good shit. My darlings are working on it, but it might take more time than we have."

"No calls to Metro D.C. police?"

"Not to Remington's address."

McGarvey flipped the switch. "You don't have to answer unless you're in trouble. I want you to get out of there as fast as possible and head up to Massachusetts Avenue, take the first right, and then the next into Rock Creek Park. We'll run interference from there. If that's a roger, cough."

Pete's cough came out clearly.

"Have you got the flash drive yet? One cough yes."

"Okay so it's encrypted," Pete said. "We'll need the key." She was talking to Remington.

"The key will save time, but Otto can crack it," McGarvey told her.

"Which makes you our next best bet," Pete said. "Now, nice and easy, we're going out to my car and take a little drive. Do as I tell you, and you just might survive to make it to France."

"Make sure the street is clear before you leave the house," McGarvey told her.

They came around the last long sweeping curve before Massachusetts Avenue and Louise pulled over to the side of the road, and switched off the headlights. "Do you want me to turn the car around?"

"No, don't turn the car around yet," he told Louise, but for Pete's benefit. "Not until we're sure she's clear and on her way."

"Hold up," Pete said.

McGarvey could visualize her at the front door, using Remington's much larger bulk as her cover. She wasn't a field officer, but she was a smart woman and well trained. She knew what she was doing, but

McGarvey was anxious. If something were to go wrong, it would happen within the next sixty seconds.

"We're clear," Pete said into his earpiece.

McGarvey flipped the transmit switch back to Otto-only. "Anything from Admin, or D.C. Metro?"

"Nada," Otto said.

"Son of a bitch," Pete swore, and McGarvey flipped the transmit switch.

"Talk to me," he said.

"Dark blue or black Ford, maybe a Taurus, coming on fast. Halfway to my car. No other cover." She was out of breath.

It was Kangas and Mustapha, back for revenge. They wouldn't give a damn about Pete. They wanted to take Remington down. "We're on our way right now, Pete. Get down! Get down!"

Louise flipped on the lights and rocketed to the red light on Massachusetts. There was a break in traffic so she blew through it and accelerated across the bridge to Whitehaven a little more than a block away.

"Shit, I'm hit!" Pete shouted. "Remington's down. Two guys with silenced automatic weapons just jumped out of the Taurus. I'm returning fire. Get here now, Mac!"

They had to wait for several precious seconds for traffic until Louise could turn onto Whitehaven.

"Kill your lights," McGarvey told Louise. He had his pistol out.

As soon as the Toyota's headlights were out, they could see muzzle flashes a hundred yards away.

"Pull over here," he told her. He didn't want her in the line of fire. She wasn't a field officer.

"No time," Louise said and she headed directly for the blue Taurus.

SIXTY-ONE

☐

Hunched down behind her Mustang, Pete ejected the empty magazine from the handle of her pistol, slammed another in its place, and charged the weapon. Remington was down, and definitely dead. He had taken several rounds to his torso and at least two to his head.

His body lay a few feet back on the sidewalk.

But she had managed to get off fifteen rounds on the run over the top of her car, and nearly made it to cover when she'd been hit in the left hip. The initial shock had stung like hell and knocked her to her knees. But she was sure it was just superficial, though her butt and upper leg were numb.

The two men from the Taurus who'd opened fire were somewhere in the road, maybe behind their own car. Evidently they'd been taken by surprise when she had returned fire. But a Glock 19 compact pistol was no match for a pair of automatic weapons. She didn't recognize the sound, but the guns were effective.

She ducked down so she could see the street from beneath her undercarriage, but nothing was there except for the ford. No feet on ankles.

"They've gotta be close, so watch yourself," she said softly.

"Keep down, I'm right on top of you," McGarvey told her.

Suddenly she heard a car coming up the street at a high rate of speed, and someone firing what had to be a nine-millimeter pistol.

She pulled herself up to a crouch so she could see over the hood of her car. One of the shooters hidden behind the Taurus was aiming his weapon at the oncoming car when Pete fired one shot catching him in the side, knocking him down.

To her left the Toyota screeched rubber, braking to a halt, and she had just a split second to see a dark figure jump out of the passenger side and disappear behind a line of parked cars ten yards away, when the shooter down behind the Taurus opened fire.

She turned and fired two shots, the first ricocheting off the pavement, the second catching him in the side of the head or throat, and he fell back and was motionless.

"One down—" she said, when a figure came running out of the darkness to her right.

"Bitch," he shouted, practically on top of her.

"Damn," she said, turning, trying to bring her pistol to bear, but she was too late and she knew it.

Her hip gave out and she lurched against the hood of her car and began to fall as someone behind her fired three shots, all of them connecting with the man who fell backward, almost in slow motion, his silenced weapon discharging a volley of shots in an arc up in the air.

All of a sudden she was sitting on her butt on the curb, the night silent, her head buzzing, a pool of blood slowly gathering under her.

McGarvey loomed above her. "You're hit," he said, and she could hear his voice coming from his lips as well as in her earpiece.

"Not bad, I think," she mumbled.

McGarvey holstered his pistol then rolled over on her side. He undid her jeans and pulled them down around her hips then yanked off his jacket, balled it up and pressed it against the wound in her hip. "Hold this in place," he said, guiding her hand to it.

He opened the door of the Mustang, then picked her up and gently put her in the passenger seat.

"I'm taking Pete to All Saints. Tell them we're coming in. I'm driving Pete's car."

"How bad is she?"

"She's losing a fair bit of blood."

"They might tip off the Bureau that you're on the way," Otto said.

"I'll take the chance," McGarvey said. "Have Louise follow us."

Pete was hearing all of this and when McGarvey got behind the wheel she wanted to tell him that she would get there herself, but her focus went soft gray and nothing was making sense.

At All Saints Hospital the gate opened for them and they drove inside and around back where a pair of nurses waited with a gurney. As soon as McGarvey pulled up, they eased a semiconscious Pete out of the car and helped her up onto the gurney.

"Are you hurt, Mr. Director?" one of them asked.

He had a lot of Pete's blood on him. "I'm fine," he said.

"Dr. Franklin's standing by upstairs for her. He says that you were never here. So go."

"What about her?"

"She was never here either. So just go. And leave her car."

They wheeled Pete inside the hospital, and McGarvey hesitated a few moments before he walked back to Louise waiting in the Toyota. So much history here, he thought. Some of it with good outcomes, but other bits not so good. He could see Todd's shot-to-hell body lying on the stainless-steel table. Nothing he could have done to prevent it. Nothing.

PART

FOUR

That Night

SIXTY-TWO

☐

Louise was shaking and subdued when they got back to the brownstone and Otto gave her a hug, and then held her until her shivers subsided. "You did good," he told her.

"I'm sorry I put you through something like that," McGarvey told her.

They were standing in the stair hall, and Louise looked at him. "Pete will be okay, won't she?"

"She lost a bit of blood, but she'll be fine by morning. It was nothing serious."

Louise shook her head and then looked from McGarvey to her husband. "You two have been doing this for a lot of years."

Otto just shrugged.

She shook her head again. "I never imagined what it was like for real, until tonight," she said.

"Are you okay?" Otto asked.

"I just need to clean up," she said, and she went upstairs.

"It was Kangas and Mustapha, the guys from Baghdad and early this morning in the park," McGarvey said. "They're both down, and so is Remington and his driver."

"Metro D.C. cops are all over it, and so is the Bureau," Otto said. He was excited. "But you got Remington's flash drive from Pete?"

She had handed it to him before she passed out. McGarvey gave it to Otto and they went upstairs to his computers, where Otto plugged it into one of the machines and brought up the drive. It was encrypted as Remington had said it would be, but Otto brought up one of the decryption programs he'd devised for the CIA and National Security Agency about nine months ago and set it to work on the drive. The sensitive program had never been meant to leave either agency, but Otto backed up everything he did. Always.

"This could take awhile," Otto said.

"How long?" McGarvey asked. "With Sandberger and Remington both down, Admin has to be hurting, and Foster and his crowd will be getting nervous about now. I want to finish this tonight."

"Could be a matter of minutes or days. I don't know how good his algorithms are."

"Better than your stuff?"

Otto grinned shyly. "There's always a first, ya know."

McGarvey glanced at the monitor. Line after line of figures marched down the screen, the pace accelerating. "I need to take a shower and change out of these clothes. I got Pete's blood on me putting her in the car."

Otto's eyes were wide. "What you told Louise is true, right? She's gonna be okay?"

"Unless she has broken bones, or the bullet in her hip hit a major artery, she should be up and around by morning. Franklin's a good doc."

"The best," Otto said, and he turned back to his computers.

McGarvey went to the room they'd set up for him, took a shower, changed into jeans, another dark pullover, and dark boat shoes. He field stripped his Wilson, cleaned it with the kit from his bag, reloaded the one magazine he'd used, and holstered the pistol at the small of his back.

All of that had taken less than fifteen minutes, and when he got back to the computer room, Otto was hopping from foot to foot, grinning ear to ear. "Am I good, or am I good? You tell me, kemo sabe."

"You cracked it?" McGarvey asked.

"Bingo," Otto said, and he suddenly became serious. "And you're not going to believe this shit. Foster has everybody involved, and I mean *everybody*."

"Someone else in the Company other than McCann?"

"David Whittaker, our acting DCI," Otto said. "How about them apples?"

"It had to have been someone near the top," McGarvey said, but still he was amazed and a little bit saddened. He'd worked with Whittaker for a number of years when the man was the assistant deputy director of operations, under McGarvey, and the head of operations when McGarvey had briefly run the Agency. When Adkins had taken over the top job Whittaker had become the number two man.

"Can you hack into David's computer?"

"The one connected to the mainframe, but not his laptop unless he's online."

"Keep an eye out for it," McGarvey said. "Who else is on the flash drive?"

"How about Dennis Tressel and Air Force general Albert Burnside and Dominick Stanford and Charles Meyer, and about thirty-five others? All men, and except for Whittaker, the number two or three at their respective agencies."

"I don't know these people."

"Tressel is the assistant to Frank Shapiro, the president's adviser on national security affairs; Burnside is the chief political adviser to the Joint Chiefs of Staff; Dominick Stanford is the assistant to the State Department's deputy under secretary for economic affairs; and Meyer is one of the chief policy advisers to Senator Walter Stevens."

"Never heard of them."

"Nobody knows who they are. And that's the entire point. All of them are under the radar, and yet they're the ones who really run the show. They're the guys who feed policy to their bosses, the ones who actually steer their agencies."

"To do what?" McGarvey asked. "It can't be anything like what you found on the disk that Givens supposedly gave to Todd."

"The names are on the drive along with the financials—who was getting paid and how much, but not for what operation. That's something Remington apparently hadn't known."

"Did McCann's name show up?"

"Yeah. The Friday Club passed him eleven million dollars over a two-year period, which matches the Mexico City and Pyongyang operations."

"But not the reasons?"

Otto shook his head. "Nor Foster's ultimate aim."

"There has to be more than that, goddamnit," McGarvey said, struggling with his anger. "How about other payouts? Can we match who the money went to and then work from there to see what happened?"

"I'm on it," Otto said. "But simply matching McCann to the money he got from the club wouldn't have pointed toward either Mexico City or Pyongyang. We got those leads from Turov's computer that you liberated in Tokyo."

McGarvey turned away for a moment. "Nothing else on the drive?"

"No. Means Remington didn't know what Foster was really aiming at, and Sandberger probably didn't either."

"But Admin was on the payroll."

"Right."

McGarvey turned back. "To do what?" he asked. "What did Foster hire Admin to do?"

"It's not on the flash drive."

"My name didn't show up?"

"That's one of the first things I looked for," Otto said. "If we could have connected Foster with orders to have you assassinated it would have been something solid to use against him. As it stands now he can claim he was a lobbyist just doing his job. A lot of the guys in the club would take a fall, there'd be a lot of dirt stirred up, and there would be a congressional investigation, the attorney general would probably get into it, but in the end we'd be no nearer to learning what he's really been up to than we are right now."

"If Remington knew what was going on he would have put it on his flash drive. He was buying himself some insurance in case he got himself into a corner. But Sandberger knew."

"It would have to be something big for the man to risk getting shot to death."

"He thought I was going to take him back to the States, and let the Bureau or the CIA or somebody interrogate him. He knew that once he got back here he'd be safe. Foster's group would have protected him."

"It's big," Otto said. "We already figured that out. Otherwise they wouldn't have taken the risk to assassinate a newspaper reporter and a CIA officer, especially not your son-in-law."

"They made a mistake," McGarvey said.

"Yes, they did," Otto agreed.

"And we're going to capitalize on it. Tonight."

SIXTY-THREE

Boberg passed through the town of Mount Vernon on the Potomac's north shore a few minutes before ten in the evening. Traffic on the GW Memorial Parkway at this hour was practically nonexistent, and the moonless night was just as dark as his mood.

On the way down from Alexandria he'd tried twice to reach Remington without luck. And just across a creek that fed into the river, he pulled up short of the driveway to Foster's estate and parked at the side of the highway, shutting off the lights and engine.

He was starting to get a seriously bad feeling that things were beginning to fall apart for Admin. The center could no longer hold with Sandberger down and especially not if Remington had taken a runner. Or if McGarvey had gotten to him.

He tried the phone one more time, and it was answered on the third ring by a man's voice he didn't recognize.

"Who's calling?"

Boberg could hear something going on in the background, footsteps, other voices. Official-sounding voices. The cops, he realized, which meant McGarvey *had* been there.

He broke the connection and sat thinking. All of Admin's phones, including everyone's personal cell phone and the encrypted sat phones they used in the field, were untraceable, so he had no worry that his name would pop up on some computer screen. But with Remington out of the picture, if he were, the company had no future. No leadership. No contacts.

But the company was small, much smaller than most of the other contractor services, some of which had upwards of two thousand employes. Admin had eighty-eight on the payroll until Baghdad, and now probably four or possibly five or six less than that. And although the company no longer had the State Department Baghdad contract, it still had the Friday Club.

"Lean and mean, Cal," Remington had preached when he offered him the job. "We can do things the bigger services can't handle."

"Mobility," Boberg remembered saying.

"Spot on. First in, first to get the job done."

In that respect nothing had changed except for the company's leadership. And since he was senior now, the job of keeping Admin up and running had fallen on his shoulders. He let a small smile curl his lips. Lean and mean it was.

He wrote a note that he had car trouble and had gone for help, stuck it under the windshield wiper, and hefting the small shoulder-bag of extra ammuniton, a red-lensed flashlight, Steiner mil specs binoculars, and a few other things, headed through the woods up the hill parallel to the driveway and about ten yards away.

Before driving out he'd studied the sketch diagrams of the property's security arrangements that Sandberger had entered in Admin's files just after they'd signed on with Foster. What had surprised him was the relative lack of surveillance and warning systems. There were no razor wire–topped electric fences, no gate guards, no dogs patrolling the estate, just the long driveway with pressure pads that reacted when a vehicle drove over them, motion sensitive lights around the house and the helipad fifty yards to the east, and a few closed-circuit cameras.

Someone approaching on foot wouldn't run into trouble until the last thirty yards across the clearing in which the house stood. And even then, darting from tree to tree, and keeping to the shadows of the Greek and Roman statues that dotted the lawn, it would be possible to get right up to the house without being spotted.

It was something that McGarvey was good at. Which was why Remington wanted someone out here just in case it happened.

"Why the hell haven't we insisted on tighter security?" Boberg had asked a couple of months ago. "I mean, it's our arses on the line if something goes down."

"He doesn't think something like that will ever happen," Remington had told him.

"What, his connections, money, and reputation are going to protect him? Is that what he thinks?"

"That's exactly what he thinks."

"Christ," Boberg had muttered, and here he was at the edge of the clearing, with a path up to the house through the shadows so easy that even an amateur second-story man would have no trouble.

As he settled down to wait to see what might happen, he studied the house, which was lit up as if a party was going on. But the driveway was empty, so if Foster were entertaining tonight, it was only himself and his staff, unless his guests' cars were parked out of sight in the back.

In his early days as an SAS leftenant he and his surveillance unit of four men had been sent to the mountainous border between

Afghanistan and Pakistan to be on the lookout for Osama bin Laden. They and other British surveillance teams had worked in conjunction with the CIA on the top-secret mission, with orders to take the al-Quaida leader down, no questions asked, and no need for permission to go hot. They had never spotted bin Laden in the three months they'd been in the field, but they had learned patience.

Surveillance was something Boberg neither liked nor disliked. It was nothing more than a simple job. And all jobs came to an end sooner or later.

Waiting, he began to assess his feelings about losing Sandberger and Remington, and he found that he didn't care. Just like his attitude toward surveillance, he was totally indifferent. It was the main reason his wife of three years had left him. According to her he'd been the coldest most distant man she'd ever met. Not cruel, not mean; he'd not been a wife beater, he'd just never been there in spirit for her. No flowers, no presents, no caresses, yet he'd been there for her financially. A Rock of Gibraltar. But as she'd told him: "Who wants to love a bloody rock?"

And when she'd left him, he'd been nearly indifferent. He was what he was.

A noise came to him from somewhere to the northwest. Faint at first, on the slight breeze, but then louder, and he recognized it as an incoming helicopter. A light machine, definitely not military. He pushed away from the tree, all of his senses alert. He'd not expected this.

A minute later he picked out the navigation lights and strobe of the chopper as it descended toward the helipad, which suddenly lit up. A moment later the lights around the exterior of the house came on. Any approach on foot now was next to impossible.

It was a safe bet McGarvey wasn't aboard, so it had to be Foster's friend or friends coming out here in reaction to what had happened in Baghdad, or most likely what had probably happened to Remington within the past couple of hours.

Very possibly whoever was coming to see Foster could affect

Admin's future position. And like many men in Boberg's profession, he'd set aside enough money in offshore accounts, plus an emergency traveling kit of a few thousand dollars in cash along with three extra passports and other IDs, so that if the need ever arose he could drop everything and disappear immediately.

The helicopter finally came into full view as it flared over the landing pad, and Boberg recognized it as an Italian-built AgustaWestland AW-139 VIP machine. The CIA had recently purchased three of them.

He pulled the binoculars from his bag, and when the chopper came to rest on the pad he trained them on the hatch as it opened.

A tall man wearing a dark Windbreaker and plain dark baseball cap got out, and hunching over moved away from the slowly rotating main blades.

A golf cart came from behind the house and headed to the helipad at the same moment the man turned so that Boberg could see his face. It was David Whittaker, the interim director of the CIA.

No real surprise there, except that McGarvey had seriously stirred the pot at the highest level, as he'd done before. And Boberg settled back to see how the evening turned out. At the very least it would be interesting, he thought.

SIXTY-FOUR

David Whittaker had been running on pure adrenaline ever since Admin's shooter had taken Todd Van Buren and the *Washington Post* reporter down. He'd warned Foster that if McGarvey got involved, and he certainly would, the dynamics would change and there'd be no way to predict the outcome.

Foster's bodyguard, Sergeant Schilling, had driven out to the helipad with a golf cart and brought Whittaker over to the house, where Foster waited drinking a cognac in the living room.

"Your visit is not totally unexpected this evening. Have you brought news? Good, I hope."

"Not good," Whittaker said. "And remember, I warned you that the situation could get out of hand."

Foster shrugged. "Nothing that can't be dealt with. Would you care for a drink?"

"I don't believe I'll be having anything to drink until this business is resolved and we can get back on schedule. McGarvey has been a thorn in our side ever since Mexico City."

"We all agree, just as we all agree that he is to be dealt with, which is exactly what Administrative Solutions is doing for us at this moment."

"Evidently you've not heard the latest."

"Roland and some of his people were shot to death in Baghdad. Yes, I have. And the FBI has a warrant for McGarvey's arrest. But Gordon assures me that he would not live to be taken in."

"Remington was shot to death in front of his house, not two hours ago," Whittaker said, and he was satisfied to see that he'd finally gotten to Foster, whose lips tightened. "McGarvey was almost certainly involved but it's not entirely clear how it all played out."

"Meaning what?" Foster asked.

"Remington may have been gunned down by two of his own people, who were in turn shot to death on the street. His bodyguard was found shot to death inside the house."

Foster turned stiffly and poured another cognac. "Are you sure you won't join me? It's Black Pearl, brand new from Rémy Martin. Frightfully expensive, but definitely better than Rémy's Louis XIII."

"Goddamnit, Bob, you're not listening to me," Whittaker shouted. "This has the potential to ruin everything we've worked for."

"Don't raise your voice, David," Foster warned. "Nothing will be ruined. We had Mexico City and Pyongyang, despite Mr. McGarvey's interference. And our last step, the Taiwan initiative, will go as planned. China will take the fall. The United States will not be brought down by a nation of rice-eating peasants who are merely clever at flooding the market with cheap products."

Whittaker had heard all of this many times before; it had been Foster's mantra from the very beginning eight years ago when the Friday Club first came into prominence. The United States had only two enemies: the old Soviet Union, which lost the economic race because of Reagan's Strategic Defense Initiative, and now China, which seemed to be winning. Something had to be done before being American became synonymous with being a second-class citizen. Spain, Portugal, Great Britain all had their empires, and now it was America's rightful time in history.

We had the nuclear weapons, the missiles, the submarines, the aircraft carriers—more aircraft carriers in our fleet than every other nation combined. But even more than that, Foster argued, the U.S. had the industrial might, the resources, the facilities, and the most highly skilled workers in the world. It was something the Japanese hadn't fully understood in 1941 when they attacked Pearl Harbor. The sleeping giant had indeed been awakened.

And it would happen again. Given the right conditions, the right push in the right direction, China would fall by the wayside as the last real enemy of the United States.

But after eight years, Whittaker wasn't so sure that he believed in the message as strongly as he had at the beginning. He wasn't so sure he wanted to help with the business of empire building. That tack had nearly embroiled the country in a global thermonuclear war with the Soviet Union, in part because of Kennedy's stand over the Cuban missile business.

And now China had an even more potent weapon to use against us: money. Beijing didn't need bombs and rockets because it practically owned us. Besides the growing trade deficit, we were nearly one trillion dollars in debt to China. That was more than four times the money we owed all the oil exporters in the world.

What China held were mostly Treasury securities, which they could call due or simply dump. Either way the U.S. economy would take the biggest hit it had ever taken—much bigger than the Great Depression—and it would literally bring us to our knees. Factory closings; bankruptcies, for which there would be no money available for help; unemployment lines, for which there were no jobs and no unemployment checks.

"Worst-case scenario," Foster had pounded home his point. "Social Security and Medicare would fail. That cannot be allowed to happen. At all costs."

All true, Whittaker agreed. Especially now when the U.S. was in the midst of the biggest bailout in history. Something had to be done.

"McGarvey could stop us," he said, but Foster shook his head.

"One man, David."

"Look what he's done to us already."

Sergeant Schilling came to the door. "Admin's man has shown up, sir," he said.

"Where is he at this moment?"

"Just within the woods about ten meters west of the driveway."

"What is he doing?"

"Surveillance, I would imagine, sir. Waiting. I have his cell phone number, shall I make contact?"

"Yes, tell him we know he's here," Foster said. "It's possible that Mr. McGarvey may show up tonight. Mr. Boberg can watch from outside, and you can monitor the situation from inside. Shouldn't be too difficult to catch him in a cross fire."

"Yes, sir. Shall I prepare your safe room?"

"Not necessary," Foster said, and the sergeant left.

"A safe room wouldn't do you any good, because if McGarvey somehow gets his hands on the proof of what we've been doing, even a shred of proof, all of us will take the fall."

"But there's no proof to be had, David. It simply doesn't exist. We don't have a manifesto, nothing has been written. All we have is an agreement among gentlemen that something needs to be done to save America. What fault can be found with that?"

"No manifesto, I agree," Whittaker said. "But what if he actually manages to get to you, and holds a pistol to your head, will you take a bullet to defend your idealism?"

"It won't come to that."

"It's why I flew down here tonight. I have a CIA jet standing by at Andrews to fly you to a safe house on La Croix in the U.S. Virgins. And you'll have plenty of people down there to take care of you until McGarvey is resolved."

Foster looked amused. "While I'm scurrying off to the tropics, where will you be?"

"At home tonight, and in my office first thing in the morning as usual. He has no reason to suspect that I'm involved in any of this. We'll let the FBI and the U.S. Marshal Service take care of him."

Foster sipped his cognac. "Are you carrying a pistol tonight?"

"Yes, I am."

"Good. Then stay with me. If McGarvey does get this far, you can shoot him dead. You'll be a national hero. I'll see to it, personally."

Whittaker shook his head. "I'm not getting into a shooting match with that man. You have no idea what he's capable of doing."

But Foster merely smiled. "You have no choice, David. Call your helicopter pilot and tell him to leave."

"I'll tell him to stand by."

SIXTY-FIVE

☐

McGarvey and Louise stood looking over Otto's shoulder as he hacked into the CIA's feed from the latest generation of Keyhole surveillance satellite systems, this one the KH-15, designated Romulus, with a full range of optical abilities from infrared to near ultraviolet with a resolution under good conditions of less than 0.04 meters, in the range of less than one hundredth of an inch, about the thickness of a piece of paper.

"I have the bird, receive only," he said.

"Right," Louise said, and she sat down at another keyboard and in a few keystrokes brought up the logo for the National Reconnaissance Office. As chief of the NRO's imagery analysis section she had her own set of passwords that not only allowed her to tap into the product any surveillance satellite in orbit was producing, she could also, supposedly if she had with proper orders, reposition any satellite and change its values and modes.

She brought up the North American KH-15 that Otto had captured and then looked up at McGarvey.

"Your call, Louise," he told her. "Could mean your job, maybe even jail time."

"But we need this, right? To rescue the fair maiden and save the planet?"

McGarvey had to smile. "It'd help."

"What the hell," she said, and she entered a series of passwords, which brought her past a number of security messages against unauthorized use, each warning of harsh penalties including fines and imprisonment.

The KH-15 technical page logo came up followed by a split screen, one half showing what the bird was looking at and the other a control panel. At present the satellite was looking at an inbound ship off the U.S. East Coast about two hundred miles southeast of New York City.

"Just need to borrow you for a minute or two," Louise muttered. She touched the command and control tab on the screen, and a drop-down box appeared asking for a password, which she entered.

"Okay, you're in," Otto said.

"And we're near enough so I don't have to reposition, just change the angle."

On the current setting the satellite was showing a swatch of Earth less than five hundred meters on a side. She increased the view to fifty kilometers then touched another tab that lit up a small icon in the middle of the map, which she dragged with her finger toward the northwest, picking up the coast just south of Atlantic City, lit up like a sparkling diamond in a sea of jewels. Farther southwest she picked up the upper Chesapeake, then straight across the Maryland peninsula to the Potomac.

"Alexandria," Otto said.

Louise reduced the area to a five-kilometer square and now they could pick out lights on I-495 and other highways as she followed the river south. At the town of Fort Hunt she reduced the area to one kilometer and followed the GW Memorial Parkway west, about a mile.

"That's his place," Otto said.

They were looking at Foster's house all lit up in the middle of a lot of darkness. Louise started to move the icon away from the road, but McGarvey stopped her.

"Stay on the driveway and tighten up."

She brought the area down to one hundred meters, then fifty then forty. A car was parked on the side of the road just to the west of the driveway.

"Get the tag number, I'll run it," Otto said.

Louise tightened up the image so that only the front end of the car was showing. She adjusted the lo lux levels, adjusted the focus, and the license plate number became clear.

"Virginia," Louise said, and she read off the numbers for her husband.

"Half a mo," Otto said.

"Anybody in the car or nearby?" McGarvey asked.

Louise pulled the image back a little so they were looking at the entire car, and adjusted the light values again. "No," she said. She touched another tab and the hood of the car came up a soft red. "Hasn't been there long. Engine's still warm."

"Calvin Boberg," Otto said. "And take a wild-ass guess who he works for."

"Administrative Solutions," McGarvey said.

Louise made another adjustment to the satellite's infrared capabilities. "Here we go," she said excitedly. "See the faint red smudges leading way from the car and into the woods."

"Footprints?" McGarvey asked.

"Heat signatures," Louise said, absently, and she moved the icon to follow the trail, finally coming to the edge of the woods just before the clearing up to the house, and Boberg's heat output stood out brightly against the cooler trees and ground.

"Waiting for you?" Otto asked.

"Be my guess," McGarvey said. "Pan out wider."

Louise did, and started the icon toward the house, but something at the edge of the screen caught her eye. "Hold on," she said, and she moved to the right, to the helicopter pad.

"That's one of our choppers," Otto said.

"Whittaker?"

"Yeah. But what's he doing? He's gotta know you're on the way."

McGarvey stared at the machine on the pad for a moment. Its rotors were not moving. "Tighten up, I want to see if the pilot is still aboard."

She did; the pilot was in the left seat and the door was open. He was smoking a cigarette.

"He's waiting for Whittaker to come back," Louise said.

"Check the status of our VIP jets at Andrews," McGarvey said.

"I'm on it," Otto said. "But if he runs, especially with you still on the loose, it'll look damned suspicious."

"Not him," McGarvey said. "He's come to convince Foster to get out of town."

"St. Croix," Otto said after a few seconds. "One of our Gulfstreams manned and standing by in the ready hangar. Two passengers on the manifest. Robert Foster and David Whittaker."

"Take a look at the house."

Louise panned left, brought the area out to forty meters and toned down the light input because of the outside floods. "Looks like they're expecting company."

"They have Admin's guy out front, and Schilling inside." He said, "Foster's probably not a shooter, but David is."

"He started out as a field officer. Expert marksman on the pistol range," McGarvey said. He remembered telling his staff, when Whittaker was promoted to deputy director of operations, that David was one of the few men in that position to really know what it was like to pull out a pistol and actually fire it with some expectation of hitting the target. "I'm going out there."

"I have to switch the bird back out to the ship," Louise said, "in case some supervisor notices it's off target."

"Can you get back to Foster's from time to time?"

"Every five minutes or so," Louise said.

"Good enough, but keep in touch if anything changes."

"I'll go with you—" Louise said, but McGarvey cut her off.

"I need you here to keep tabs on the house and grounds."

A nightlight plugged into a socket across the room suddenly started to blink. "Someone's at the door," Otto said and he doused the room lights, and pulled up the camera concealed in the eaves.

Pete looked up, grinned at the camera and waved.

"She was wounded," Louise said.

"That she was," McGarvey said, putting his gun back in its holster. "Let her in."

Otto buzzed the lock. "We're upstairs," he told her on the intercom. He flipped on the room lights.

Pete came up, in fresh jeans and a dark pullover and dark jacket, CIA stenciled on the back. She'd cleaned up and brushed her hair, and she was still grinning.

"How did you get past Franklin?" McGarvey demanded.

"I have a gun and he didn't," Pete said. "No bone chips, no major arteries. Just a heavy graze. He sewed me up and pumped a pint of O-positive into me, nothing but a local anesthetic and a butterfly bandage."

"What are you doing here?" McGarvey demanded.

"I expect that you're going after whoever's name came up on Remington's flash drive. Probably Foster, and I'm coming with you."

"Not a chance in hell."

"Give me one good reason."

"You're wounded."

"It stings, nothing more."

"No," McGarvey said.

"Sorry, Mr. Director, but if you rightly remember you *are* my prisoner."

Louise shook her head. "You're nuts, do you know that? All of you are certifiable."

SIXTY-SIX

They took Louise's Toyota SUV, Pete behind the wheel after assuring McGarvey three times that she was okay to drive. "Like I said, Mac, it just stings a little, and I'll have a major bruise on my ass by morning. But Franklin's a good doc."

"He's patched me up more than once," McGarvey said, his thoughts back to Katy and Liz and Todd. He'd never be able to think of All Saints without seeing the look of devastation on his daughter's face when he and Katy had shown up the morning after Todd had been shot to death. It was an image that, along with the one of the limo, bearing Katy and Liz exploding, would stay with him for the rest of his life.

They took the Key Bridge across the river and headed east, where they picked up U.S. 1 that led south, eventually to Fort Hill Road and the town of Fort Hunt.

"Where do you think this is heading?" Pete asked.

"I'm not sure, but it started in Mexico City a little over a year ago, and then Pyongyang was a part of it somehow," McGarvey told her. He briefly went over his actions in both operations. "The only connection other than the Friday Club is China."

"Okay, so whatever they're up to involves the Chinese. And they're not done, which is why you have to be eliminated at all costs. So it's big. But what?"

"That's what I want to ask him and Whittaker tonight."

Pete shot him a double take. "The DCI?"

"His name was on Remington's flash drive," McGarvey said and he gave her some of the other names.

"Jesus," she said softly. "You're on the hit list of a bunch of important people."

"Yeah. And by tagging along with me tonight you just painted a big target on your back."

"Then we'd best do it right," she said.

"I'm back to Foster's house," Louise said in McGarvey's ear. "Nothing's changed."

"How about the chopper pilot?"

She came back a few seconds later. "He's a chain smoker."

"Stick with it."

"Will do."

McGarvey telephoned Dick Adkins's home phone. The former DCI answered after three rings. "Yes."

"Do you still have your encrypted phone?"

It took a moment for him to reply, and when he did he sounded cautious. "Yes."

"Turn it on, I'll call you in five minutes."

Adkins broke the connection.

"Who did you just call?" Pete asked.

"Adkins."

Pete shook her head. "All this should be taking my breath away, but I read most of your jacket and I *was* warned." She concentrated on her driving for a bit. "Whittaker's on the list, but there's no chance of him being in his office tonight, and Dick's passes might still be valid."

"You'd make a good field agent," McGarvey said, but Pete shook her head.

"Louise was right. You guys are nuts. It's just that I'm not quite that crazy."

McGarvey called Adkins at the encrypted number.

"I didn't expect you to call me."

"You stuck out your neck for me with the president, so I figured I owed you one," McGarvey said.

"Don't do me any favors," Adkins replied. "I don't suppose you'd be willing to tell me where you are, or what part you played in a shooting this evening on embassy row. D.C. Metro is apparently having a fit."

"I took out one of the shooters who killed Remington, and right now I'm headed to Robert Foster's estate down around Mount Vernon. I need your help."

"I thought you might say something like that," Adkins said. "But first do you mind telling me what the hell is going on?"

"I found a bridge between Mexico City and Pyongyang."

"Yeah, China."

"Foster's Friday Club financed both operations through Howard McCann."

"That's too far-fetched," Adkins objected.

"Something else is in the works, and whatever it is will be big," McGarvey said.

"We've already gone over this, Mac. All of it was on the disk we found in Todd's car. Utter nonsense."

"It was a fake. But I have a flash drive we got from Remington with a list of card-carrying members of the Friday Club. McCann had help inside the Company. Someone who had complete access to my files, someone who could track my movements."

Adkins was very quiet.

"David's a member," McGarvey said. "From the looks of it he was in from the beginning. Eight years ago."

Adkins was silent for a long time, and when he came back was subdued. "Who else?"

"Foster's got guys just about everywhere, DoD, State, the Bureau, and even the White House. All of them were in on Mexico City and Pyongyang."

"Maybe Todd's disk wasn't so far-fetched after all if what you're telling me is true," Adkins said. "What do you want me to do?"

"Do you still have your building passes?"

"I haven't turned them in, if that's what you mean. But I suspect they've all been deactivated by now. David would have been a fool not to."

"He's been distracted lately."

"Yeah."

"I want you to go out there tonight, right now. If you get in talk to the guys on the Watch and find out if they're seeing anything developing in China, or Hong Kong, maybe Taiwan or the Strait. Chinese naval maneuvers, missile readiness drills. Anything involving Beijing, and especially their intelligence services, military and civilian."

"Where are you going with this, Mac?"

"Right now I'm just fishing. But Foster has people inside the Pentagon. See if we're planning anything in the region. Something that only the Watch might have been warned about."

"Right," Adkins said. "I'll try to find out where David is. If he's off campus I'll try to get into his office. Maybe he hasn't changed his passwords." Adkins chuckled. "Maybe I'll get lucky, or maybe someone will send for security and they'll shoot me."

"David's at Foster's right now," McGarvey said. "He showed up a half hour ago in a Company helicopter, and he's got one of your Gulfstreams standing by at Andrews to take them down to St. Croix."

"It's going to happen tonight?"

"I don't know," McGarvey said. "But I have a feeling that I've forced their hand and ready or not they're going to launch."

"Launch what?"

"I'm going to ask Foster and David just that."

"Seriously, watch your back," Adkins warned. "The Bureau and the U.S. Marshals are gunning for you. And I mean that literally. Comes from Justice through the White House. Langdon has developed a personal interest in you, and he wants you stopped no matter how they do it. The body count is just way too high."

"Yeah," McGarvey said. "Todd, Katy, and Liz. Way too high."

"I'm sorry, Mac."

"If you get into Whittaker's office forget his main computer, but if his laptop is there, and you can get online, send a message to Otto, and just walk away, but leave the computer on." McGarvey gave him Otto's untraceable e-mail address.

"What if his laptop is password protected, which I'm sure it will be?"

"Call Otto," McGarvey said. And he gave the phone number.

"I'll try," Adkins said.

☐

SIXTY-SEVEN

Two cars had passed in the last hour. Boberg had seen the flash of the headlights through the woods below, and watched as they moved away. The night was still, except for the cry of a distant night bird, and at regular intervals he spotted the glow of a cigarette from inside the parked helicopter. Typical government service, he thought. Just like the military: hurry up and wait.

He looked over his shoulder as another set of headlights approached, these from the east, but instead of passing, the lights slowed and suddenly went out. It had to be McGarvey. According to Foster's sergeant, no one else was expected out here tonight.

Taking care to make absolutely no noise, Boberg moved to a position from where he was still concealed and yet had a decent view of the driveway, the open field up to the house, and the edge of the woods leading around to the helicopter on the pad.

He called the house and Sergeant Schilling answered on the first ring. "What is it?"

"Someone pulled up and parked just below on the highway. It's probably McGarvey."

"Do you have decent sight lines on the possible approaches?"

"Yes, I do."

"Good. Take him out if you have a chance."

Boberg was about to say that was the idea, but the sergeant had already rung off. "Prick," he said under his breath.

It would be tough to keep Admin together with both Sandberger and Remington gone. There would be no problem organizationally, it had been his job from the beginning to attend to the day-to-day details of the firm. Nor was Admin so large that it couldn't be handled by one man and a dedicated office staff. The trouble would come from the field commanders who might not be willing to put their loyalty on the line for a new headman. It was possible that Admin would fall apart because several of the field guys might feel that they were more qualified to run the company, and an internal fight might take place.

If that were the case, Boberg decided, he would take what money he could grab and bail out. His loyalty was to himself, as it always had been and always would be.

He caught a movement out of the corner of his eye, at the edge of the woods at least one hundred yards to the east. He grabbed his binoculars and trained them on the field, picking up a pair of figures coming up behind the helicopter. Unless the pilot leaned out of the cockpit to look toward his six he wouldn't have a clue someone was back there.

One of them was much larger than the other, and he got the impression that the shorter, slighter of the two might be a woman, though he couldn't be sure who either of them were.

For a moment he debated calling the house, but decided against it until he had his shot. Keeping out of sight just within the woods he hurried over to the driveway and across and into the woods on the other side.

If the chopper pilot could keep them engaged for just a few minutes, Boberg figured he could come up behind them and take the two easy shots. If one of them were McGarvey, and he manged to take the guy down, taking over Admin would be a pice of cake, because he would have Foster's blessing.

SIXTY-EIGHT

The twin-engine helicopter was modern and sleek. The helipad lights had been switched off but the strong floods spilling across the lawn from the house reflected off the bright paintwork.

From twenty feet away they could smell cigarette smoke, and as they got closer McGarvey could see that the instrument panel lights were switched off. It would take several minutes for the machine to be started and readied for takeoff, which was the break he'd hoped for. If Boberg had spotted them they would need a diversion to get over to the house.

"I think he's coming through the woods behind us," Pete whispered.

"What's Boberg doing?" McGarvey spoke softly.

"Two seconds," Louise's voice came back. "I'm moving from the ship."

"He won't try a shot now for fear of hitting the helicopter," McGarvey told Pete.

Louise was back. "Okay, if that's you and Pete just behind the chopper, he's about twenty yards almost directly behind you in the woods."

"Go back to the ship," McGarvey said. "He's twenty yards behind us," he told Pete.

He pulled out his pistol. Holding it in his left hand out of sight at his side, he moved forward, his right hand trailing on the fuselage.

The pilot looked up, startled, and then he reared back, his eyes wide. "Son of a bitch, you scared the shit out of me, Mr. Director." His plastic name tag was readable in the bright lights from the house.

"Didn't mean to sneak up on you, but what the hell are you doing out here, Cardillo?"

The pilot shook his head. "Listen, I don't want any trouble, Mr.

McGarvey, but as far as I was told just about every LE officer in the area is looking for you."

"That's what you were supposed to be told. It's a cover. Now what the hell are you doing out here?"

The pilot was skeptical. "I flew Mr. Whittaker down from the Campus."

McGarvey turned to Pete. "Another comms screwup," he said, and she nodded.

"You have to get out of here right now," she told the pilot.

"What about Mr. Whittaker?"

"We'll have to take care of him," McGarvey said. "But you guys stumbled into the middle of a Bureau-Company ops we're running on one of Robert Foster's people. I'm surprised that Dave didn't get the word. Damned sloppy, because this whole thing was his call from the beginning."

"I'd better call him," Cardillo said, reaching for a phone.

"And warn the house?" McGarvey demanded. "Hell no, I just want you out of here as quickly as you can get this thing running."

The pilot was confused. "That's going to take a few minutes."

McGarvey motioned him to get on with it. "Our people are moving in right now, and we don't have time to screw around." He held out his hand. "I'll take the cell phone."

The pilot hesitated for a moment, still extremely skeptical, but he handed over the phone.

"Go," McGarvey said.

The pilot began flipping switches and the helicopter's lights began coming on, first on the control panel and then the nav lights on the fuselage and tail section.

"Stand clear," he shouted, and he closed the door and the engines began to spool up.

McGarvey and Pete hurried around to the front of the chopper, ducking low as the main rotor began turning. "Louise, we're going to try for the house, and I want to keep the chopper between us and Boberg. Give me bearing."

"Stand by," Louise said.

The main rotor was building up speed, and McGarvey had to cup a hand over his earpiece.

"You're good to go on a straight line from the nose of the chopper to the east side of the house," Louise's voice was faint over the noise. "Is the chopper getting set to take off?"

"Any minute."

"Then get the hell out of there right now."

McGarvey glanced over his shoulder. The pilot was looking at them, and he was shaking his head. He made a slashing gesture at his throat and the engines began to spool down. McGarvey turned and pointed his pistol at the man's face.

For a second nothing happened, but then the engines roared back to life and the main blades began to spin up.

"I think he got the message," Pete shouted.

"Stay low and move fast," McGarvey told her. "Boberg's right behind us."

He turned and sprinted toward the house, Pete right behind him.

SIXTY-NINE

Adkins had never wanted to be a spy, but he was a damned good administrator because he knew how to manage people while at the same time balancing the complex relationships between the Company, the White House, the director of National Intelligence, and, in some ways most important, Congress.

Pulling up at the CIA's main gate was the first test of how good a spy he actually was, because if he were stopped here the mission would be a bust, and McGarvey, a man for whom he had an immense amount of respect, would most likely end up dead or in jail.

One of the guards came out of the building and over to Adkins's car. "Good evening, Mr. Director, back again so soon?" He could have been a Dallas Cowboys' linebacker; he had the size and the look.

"I have a couple of things to take care of. Couldn't wait."

The guard hesitated, but then nodded. "I'll have to make note of your entry, sir."

"Of course," Adkins said, and the guard stepped back.

Driving up toward the OHB, Adkins kept glancing in his rearview mirror expecting to see flashing lights, but nobody was behind him and the guard had gone back inside the reception building.

It was nothing short of amazing that Whittaker hadn't yanked his credentials. It was a stupid lapse of security procedures that even the gate guard had recognized.

The parking area in the front of the building was practically deserted, and so was the VIP parking garage where his entry pass worked, as it did in the elevator. He had debated arming himself, but decided against it, because there was no way he was going to get into a shoot-out with security. If he was busted he could make the argument that his clearances were still intact, and he'd merely come back one last time out of simple nostalgia. No one would believe him, but they wouldn't be able to prove anything different.

Unless he was caught in Whittaker's office.

The seventh-floor corridor was deserted, all the doors closed, unlike when he had been the DCI, and McGarvey before him. Under Whittaker, morale at the Company had already dropped, and the word was that everybody was busier watching their own backs than actually doing any real or creative work.

Halfway down the corridor he stopped at the DCI's door, swiped his pass, and entered the old four-digit code he'd used before the president had fired him. The lock clicked softly and he was in. Whittaker was a fool. And if what McGarvey had told him was true, David was also so arrogant that he'd felt no need to take ordinary precautions.

He passed through the outer office, the only illumination from the tiny green indicator on the emergency light in one corner up near the ceiling, and into the DCI's office. The blinds were open and before Adkins turned on the desk lamp he closed them against the faint possibility that someone outside might know that Whittaker was not in the building and wonder why a light had just come on in his office.

The main computer on the desk was in standby mode, but Whittaker's Toshiba laptop on the credenza was closed. Adkins sat down, opened the laptop, and powered it up. As he'd suspected it was password protected. Whittaker wasn't a complete idiot.

Using his cell phone he called the number McGarvey had given him, and Otto answered after the second ring.

"Oh, wow, I know where David is right now, so this has gotta be Dick Adkins calling from the DCI's office."

The man was a genius, but he was spooky. "Mac told me to call if I ran into trouble getting into David's laptop."

"Did it boot up?"

"No. All that's on the screen are two boxes: User ID and password."

"It's a Toshiba, right?"

"Yes."

"Look on the bottom and give me all the numbers you see."

Adkins turned the laptop over. "There's a bunch of them."

"Find the Toshiba pin number. It'll be printed right under a bar code."

"Got it," Adkins said and he read it.

Otto laughed. "I built that machine. Okay now find any label that says service."

"There's only one. Two sets of numbers."

Otto laughed even harder. "Dumb," he said, and he read off both set of numbers.

"That's it," Adkins said.

"My service numbers. He hasn't changed a thing."

"Mac said he's been distracted."

"He's going to get even more distracted any minute now," Otto said. "User ID, whittakercia. Password: tk%//7834ps."

Adkins entered both, and the computer booted up. "Okay, it worked."

"Of course," Otto said. "If Mac gave you this number he must have given you my e-mail address. Get online, type in my address, and hit send, and then get out of there. But leave the machine turned on."

"First thing in the morning somebody—his secretary at least—will come in here and find out someone hacked his computer."

"It'll be all over by then, Mr. Director, and you'll have a bunch of work to do, 'cause the president is going to reinstate you. Honest injun."

"Jesus," Adkins muttered, but he did as Otto had asked.

"Good work. I'm in. Now beat feet."

By the time Adkins shut off the desk lamp and opened the curtains every file on Whittaker's laptop was being downloaded at lightning speed.

He let himself out into the still-deserted corridor, and hesitated for just a second before he headed down the hall to the Watch, which was housed in a long room, one end of it glassed in for added security. Manned 24/7 by a watch commander and five people, including a National Geospatial Analyst, anything that was happening anywhere in the world that had any effect or even the possibility of an effect on U.S. interests was monitored here. With direct links to the National Security Agency, the National Reconnaissance Office, and just about every other surveillance system, the people who worked here considered themselves to be information junkies. They had an almost compulsive need to know what was happening on a real-time basis everywhere.

And like air traffic controllers who never saw the light of day during their long shifts, and who had the indoor palor and thousand-yard stare of people who'd worked too long and too hard at something that was nearly impossible to comprehend, analysts in the Watch always looked as if they were on the verge of a nervous breakdown, and loving it.

Adkins swiped his pass on the reader, entered his code, and the lock clicked softly. Everyone looked up from what they were doing, and all the wide-screen monitors on the walls above each position went blank, and a red light on the ceiling began flashing.

Ron Loring, the watch commander had been leaning against his desk, his jacket off, his tie loose, and he immediately came over before Adkins could take more than two steps into the room. "What are you doing here, Mr. Director," he said softly, but urgently. "You have to leave, immediately."

"McGarvey sent me to talk to you. It's important."

Loring shook his head and stepped back. "I've got to call security. You know the drill, sir."

"Something big is about to go down. Maybe even tonight. And it has something to do with the Chinese."

A flicker of interest crossed Loring's eyes. "What are you talking about?"

"I don't know for sure, but Mac has made a connection between what happened last year in Mexico City, and a few months ago in Pyongyang, with China. And with the Friday Club here in Washington."

Loring turned away for a second. All his analysts were looking at him and Adkins. "I don't know what you're talking about, Mr. Director. But I'll give you a head start before I call security."

"You know damned well what I'm talking about. Goddamnit, I can see it all over your face. What is it? What's happening over there?"

Again Loring shook his head, trying to come to a decision. "You never heard this from me. But we're getting set to send a courier over to the White House."

"Why?"

"China has been warming up its short-range missiles since about sixteen hundred zulu." Loring looked up at one of the wall clocks. "Almost two hours ago. Then, at about seventeen thirty, Taiwan started doing the same thing with their missiles, and placed their armed forces at Defcon two."

"They're seriously expecting that China is going to attack them?"

"It's a possibility. We're starting to get inputs from the Pentagon and State and we're putting the package together for the president."

"What's Dave Whittaker's input?"

"We haven't reached him yet. Apparently he's not at home, and his cell doesn't pick up."

"Christ."

"Now get the hell out of here, please," Loring said. "We need to get back to work."

"Right," Adkins said, and he felt a little sick to his stomach.

"Tell Mac good luck," Loring said.

"Security wants to know what's going on up here," one of the analysts called out across the room.

"Use the VIP elevator, I'll stall them for as long as I can," Loring told Adkins.

SEVENTY

Sergant Schilling came to the living room door at the same moment Whittaker was trying to reach his pilot by cell phone. It had to have been McGarvey's doing, sending the helicopter away. But Cardillo was one of them, ferrying members of the Friday Club with no questions asked.

"The two cameras in front went down, and the lights are going out one at a time," Schilling said.

"Something wrong with the power?" Foster asked.

Cardillo's cell phone rang.

"I believe Mr. McGarvey shot out the cameras and is doing the same with the lights."

"He's right outside the house, then."

"Yes, sir. But the only way in is through the front door, which I'll cover."

Cardillo's cell phone rang a second time.

"Let Boberg know what's going on."

Cardillo's phone was answered on the third ring. "Yes."

"Why the hell did you leave?" Whittaker shouted, but all of a sudden he realized that he wasn't hearing the helicopter's cabin noises.

"Because I didn't want you to get away before I had a chance to talk to you and Foster," McGarvey said.

Whittaker was shaken, but not surprised. "The FBI is on its way out here in force," he said. Foster and Schilling were staring at him.

"Not yet, David," McGarvey said after a slight delay. "We're monitoring calls from the house, including your cell phone."

Whittaker held his hand over the cell phone microphone. "It's McGarvey on my pilot's cell phone. Can he get inside the house?"

"Only with explosives," Schilling said.

"Unless you brought some Semtex you're not getting in here."

"I saw the bars on the window," McGarvey said. "Makes you wonder what Foster is trying to protect. But I don't need to blow my way inside, because you and Foster are going to let me in."

"The hell you say."

"We deciphered a flash drive that Remington gave to us before he was gunned down by his own people. It's a Friday Club membership list. Impressive."

"You've got nothing, you son of a bitch. You're a traitor to your country."

"We have the information on your laptop. Stupid to leave it in your office for just about anyone to grab. Otto told me that he built the machine, and he knew your user ID and password. Whittakercia? Come on, David."

Schilling had stepped out into the stair hall, and he came back. "Boberg is on the way. Keep McGarvey talking."

"All you have are the names of a number of American patriots who love their country enough to form a club, just like Kiwanis or Rotary."

"Except Rotary wasn't involved in Mexico last year or in Pyongyang a few months ago. Rotary hasn't involved the Chinese in some kind of plot."

"You're talking nonsense," Whittaker practically shouted, but he was rocked to the core. He knew what McGarvey was capable of. He had tried to warn Foster and the others, but none of them would listen, and now it was too late, unless McGarvey could be killed.

"There never was any polonium in Mexico, and none ever came across the border in Arizona. And we know that the shooters who took out the Chinese general in Pyongyang were South Koreans working for a Russian expediter in Tokyo who'd been hired by Howard McCann. And Howard was getting money from your club of patriots."

Schilling switched off the living room lights and those in the stair hall. He was armed with a Franchi SPAS-12 automatic shotgun capable of firing four rounds per second. It was a devastating weapon at close range. "Stay in this room," he said, and he disappeared into the darkness in the stair hall.

"Even if what you're telling me was only partially true, it still proves nothing. How do we know this flash drive you mentioned was Remington's?"

"I think Otto could make a case for it," McGarvey said. "The only thing we haven't figured out yet is what you people are really up to. Whatever it is involves the Chinese, of course. But to what purpose?"

Whittaker said nothing.

"So here's what we're going to do. If Mr. Boberg manages to kill me in the next few minutes, you will have won. But if I survive, I'm coming inside and you and I and Foster will have our little chat. Fair enough?"

Whittaker broke the connection. "He wants us to let him in so he can ask us about China."

Foster was unfazed. "Fine."

"Don't be a fool," Whittaker said, and he speed-dialed the CIA's on-duty security officer, and he didn't give a damn if McGarvey's freak friend Otto Rencke was somehow monitoring his call.

The number didn't answer until the fourth ring. "Security, Donald Briggs."

"This is David Whittaker. I want someone to go up to my office right now, and check my computers."

"Somone's already on the way up, sir."

"Why? What's happening?"

"I'm not sure, Mr. Director. But one of the watch officers called and said there might be a security issue."

"What sort of an issue?"

"Unknown."

"I'll hold," Whittaker said, but then he knew what the issue was, and he knew that it had been his own sloppiness that made it possible. "Have there been any visitors to the building tonight. Within the past half hour or so?"

"Other than Mr. Adkins, I don't know. But his passes were all still valid. I'll have to check the log at the Reception Center."

"Is Adkins still in the building?"

"I don't know, sir."

"Well, find out, you idiot! And if he's still there, arrest him!"

"I'm on it, sir."

Whittaker broke the connection. "Dick Adkins was in my office and it's unlikely, but possible, he managed to get into my private laptop."

Foster nodded. "Anything that would hurt us?"

"Names, dates."

"No manifesto, I would hope, David."

"No."

"Well then, I think it's time we telephone our friends at the FBI and the Marshal's office," Foster said. "Let them know that Mr. Mc-Garvey is here to assassinate me, and that you came to warn me, and protect me. With your life, if need be."

SEVENTY-ONE

☐

McGarvey was crouched in the shadows on the west side of the house from where he had a good sight line all the way along the front wall, and down the hill toward the woods.

"Did you get any of that?" he said into his comms unit.

"Yeah, I managed to tap into the cell phone you took from the chopper pilot," Otto replied. "It's one of ours, standard issue for housekeeping and security. But Whittaker also called Campus security and he knows about Dick."

"Has he made it out of there?"

"He hasn't called me back so I don't know. But I've got everything from David's laptop."

"Anything interesting?"

"Pretty much the same info from Remington's flash drive. A few more names, some dates, and banking stuff. We can use it."

"Mac," Louise broke in. "I can't see your heat signature. Where are you?"

"On the east side of the house, right up against the wall."

"Is Pete with you?" Louise asked. She sounded strained.

"No, she's on the other side of the house," McGarvey said. "Where's Boberg?"

"I had to switch back to the ship for a minute or two, and when I

got back just now he was gone. The only place he could be is somewhere inside the heat signature of the building. But I'm painting the
remnant heat of his footprints leading up to the house. To the west
side of the house."

Pete didn't have a comms unit so there was no way for Louise to
contact her.

McGarvey turned and sprinted toward the rear of the house. "I'm
on my way," he whispered.

"I have to get back to the ship," Louise said.

"Do it, and then get out of the program. Security's been alerted
and the Campus will probably go into lockdown. Every system out
there is going to come under scrutiny any minute now."

"I can slow it down," Otto said.

McGarvey held up at the back wall and took a quick peek. The rear
of the house was lit up, but no one was in sight, so he eased around
the corner and, keeping below the level of the windows, hurried toward the west side of the building.

"Too dangerous," he whispered. "It could interfere with ongoing
operations."

"Let's hope Dick managed to get out of there," Otto said, but Mc-
Garvey had reached the west side of the house and he didn't reply.

Pete had shot out the cameras and lights on this side of the house,
so it took a full minute for McGarvey's eyes to adjust to the darkness
before he saw her shoved up against the wall near the front veranda.
Boberg was in front of her, his pistol less than two feet from her face.

McGarvey switched his pistol to his left hand, and pulled a spare
magazine out of his pocket with his right. Hiding the pistol behind
the back of his leg, he stepped around the corner. "I think it's me you
want," he said.

Boberg turned and looked at McGarvey, his pistol never wavering
from Pete's head. "You're damn right I do. Throw your gun down."

McGarvey tossed the magazine to the ground. It was dark and the
distance was great enough that the Admin contractor could not have
gotten a very good look.

"I said throw your gun away."

"I just did, you stupid bastard," McGarvey said. "Do you want me to pick it up and bring it to you?"

Boberg glanced at Pete and then back. "Come closer, I don't want to miss."

"Sure," McGarvey said, starting toward the two of them. Pete was looking at him, trying to signal something. "But you should know something before you decide to shoot either of us."

"I've already decided."

"We have your name. We know everything about you and Administrative Solutions. About your work in Iraq, but mostly about the company's assignments for the Friday Club. Payoffs. Bribery. Assassinations. The jobs are pretty impressive, and so are the names. Sandberger is at the top of the list, next is Remington, and third is Calvin Boberg. What are you, the company's operations manager? Or should I have said *were?*"

"Bullshit," Boberg said, but it was obvious even in the dark from fifteen feet away that he was agitated. He kept glancing at Pete.

"We have a KH-fifteen satellite watching us in real time. We saw where you parked your car just to the west of the driveway. Infrared sensors picked up your footprints through the woods where you stopped just before the clearing. We watched you coming up behind us as we sent the chopper away. The satellite caught everything. Kill us now and you're screwed."

Boberg was smart enough to know or at least guess that the NRO had put up a new version of the Key Hole system.

"Lower your weapon, turn around, and get out of here," McGarvey said, and he stopped about ten feet away.

"How do I know you won't shoot me in the back?"

"No need. It was Tim Kangas and Ronni Mustapha who killed my son-in-law and my wife and daughter. Not you."

"They're dead."

"A lot of people are dead, Cal. And now I'm going to take Foster and his Friday Club down. If you want to take the fall with them, stick around. I don't give a damn one way or the other."

"You're lying," Boberg said, his gun hand shaking. He looked at Pete.

McGarvey winked at her and raised his pistol as Boberg was starting to turn back. She jerked her head a few inches to the left, and McGarvey fired one shot, catching the Admin contractor in the temple. Boberg's pistol discharged as he was shoved sideways, the shot smacking harmlessly into the clapboard siding.

"You're right, I lied," McGarvey said.

Pete kicked the pistol away from Boberg's reach, but the man was dead.

"Your timing was perfect," she said, her chest heaving. "I never heard him."

"We're good here," McGarvey said softly. "Boberg is down and Pete's good to go."

"You've about run out of time, Mac," Otto said. "Foster called his friends at the Bureau and the Marshal's Service. Both of their names are on Remington's list. They'll have SWAT teams heading your way by chopper within a few minutes."

"I'm sending Pete back to you, and then I'm going inside to finish this once and for all."

"I'm staying with you," Pete objected.

"I'm going to get arrested tonight by Foster's people, so I'm going to need you with Otto for backup. This is going to get ugly real fast."

"Shit."

"No matter what happens, no matter what you have to do, get back to Otto's."

"Tell her to call me on her cell phone," Otto said into his ear. "Louise is still on the KH-fifteen, and we can relay a safe route for her if need be."

McGarvey told her that, and she shook her head again, but she got her pistol from Boberg's jacket pocket, and walked over to McGarvey and kissed him on the cheek.

"That's twice tonight you've saved my butt."

McGarvey smiled. "And a nice butt it is."

"Sexist," Louise said in his ear.

"Go now," McGarvey said, and Pete turned and sprinted back to the woods.

SEVENTY-TWO

Adkins reached the main gate down the long driveway from the OHB, his hands shaking on the steering wheel. Administration was his thing, not running around stealing secrets, telling lies. And yet he felt just a little sense of exhilaration for pulling it off, and dread about what was happening between China and Taiwan.

The possibility that somehow Foster, who had never been anything more than a well-connected, high-priced lobbyist, and his group could have fomented trouble over there was unbelievable, even monstrous.

If the missiles started to fly a lot of people would die. And for what?

The same linebacker security guard who'd signed him in, came out of the Reception Center and ran into the road, frantically waving his hands for Adkins to stop.

Evidentally Loring hadn't been able to stall whoever had come up to the seventh floor to see what was going on, and word had been sent down here.

Adkins swerved sharply to avoid hitting the man and jammed his foot to the floor, his E class Mercedes taking off like a rocket. He glanced in the rearview mirror in time to see the guard race back inside. It would only be a matter a minutes now before the highway patrol had a description of the car and its tag numbers.

At the bottom of the hill, Adkins slowed down and drifted through the stop sign then headed to the Parkway south, merging with the fairly light evening traffic.

He took out his cell phone and called Otto. "I'm on the Parkway, but they knew I was up on the seventh floor, because they sent someone up. And one of the Reception Center security guys tried to stop me from leaving."

"They'll be calling the highway patrol about now, so you're going to have to come here."

"I can't outrun a cop. I mean my car is capable of it, but I'm not."

"I want you to cross the median as quickly as possible and head the other way."

"Back toward the Company?"

"Nobody will expect it, and by the time they realize they've been outsmarted you'll be across the river at Turkey Run Park."

"Hold on," Adkins said, and he put the phone down. A maintenance road crossed the median, and making sure that traffic was clear and no flashing lights were approaching from either direction, he slammed on his brakes, crossed over to the other side of the Parkway, and accelerated.

He picked up the phone. "Okay, I'm heading north."

"Did you find anything else in Whittaker's office?"

"I didn't check his desk or try the safe. I didn't think he'd keep anything incriminating on paper, but I went down to Watch and talked to Ron Loring. Something is apparently starting between Mainland China and Taiwan. The Pentagon is in on it, and so is State. Ron said they were sending a courier over to the president tonight."

"Did he tell you what it was?" Otto asked. He sounded excited.

"He didn't want to say anything at first. Not until I told him that Mac had connected Mexico City and Pyongyang with the Friday Club, and it involved the Chinese government."

"Are you telling me that China is going to attack Taiwan?"

"Two hours ago the Chinese started warming up their short-range missiles, and shortly after that Taiwan began spinning up their missiles. Their military was placed at Defcon two."

"China wouldn't gain a thing," Otto said.

"No, and Beijing knows it," Adkins agreed. "Something else has to be going on over there. A trigger of some sort."

At least a half-dozen police cruisers, lights flashing, had pulled up at the access road into the CIA, and as Adkins passed on the opposite side of the Parkway, two of the cruisers headed south at a high rate of speed.

"Cops are all over the place," he told Otto. "That was really fast."

"You're only a couple of miles from the bridge. Anyone taking an interest in the north-bound lanes?"

Adkins checked his rearview mirror. "Not yet."

"Won't take them long," Otto said. "Once you get across I want you to head up to State Road One-ninety, it's just a little past the Cabin John Parkway. Turn east toward Somerset and the highway changes to River Road."

"Is that where you are?"

"No, we're in Georgetown. But I want you to come here clean, so I'm going to keep track of what the cops are doing. If anyone gets close I'll redirect you to another route. So keep your phone on."

"I don't know about this, Otto."

"Piece of cake, Mr. Director, you're doing just fine."

"Are you going to work the China thing?"

"I'm already on it," Otto said.

"Keep me posted."

□

SEVENTY-THREE

McGarvey held up at the side of the house until Pete disappeared into the woods. She'd been limping, and he figured that her wound had to hurt like hell. But she was dedicated; she believed in the mission in a way McGarvey wasn't so sure still existed for a lot of people in the Agency.

"Pete's on her way back to you," he said. "Anything from Dick?"

"He got out with Security right on his tail," Otto said. "But he's clear and I'm talking him in."

"I'm going to talk to Foster now and try to see what's going on. But I won't have a lot of time, because as soon as the Bureau and Marshals get out here they're going to arrest me, and I'm not going to run or resist. We need the situation to come to a head."

"It is, Mac," Otto said. "Dick talked to Ron Loring who's the Watch commander tonight. They're monitoring a situation between Mainland China and Taiwan. All the missiles out there are being spun up, and everybody's at Defcon two. Could get real hot any minute."

"We knew it was going to involve China again, but there'd have to be a trigger before anyone would actually launch. Beijing's not going to risk attacking Taiwan unless it had a good reason to do so. They'd end up the pariahs of the world. Probably slam their economy back fifty years. We'd certainly stop trading with them."

"Maybe it's just that simple. Maybe that's exactly what Foster wants to happen."

"Still wants for a trigger," McGarvey said. "Go back to Remington's list, and whatever you downloaded from David's computer, and run all the names from the State Department and especially the Pentagon, see what those guys have been up to."

"I'm on it," Otto said, and McGarvey could hear the strain in his friend's voice.

"We've come this far, we're not backing down now."

"Watch your back, kemo sabe, I shit you not."

"Keep me posted," McGarvey said and he called Whittaker's cell phone.

"I'm listening."

"Boberg is down, and my partner has left. It's just me now."

"Turn around and walk away, Mac, and you just might live to see the morning," Whittaker said. "There's nothing here for you now."

"I know that the Chinese and Taiwan militaries have gone to Defcon two. Their missiles are being warmed up right now."

Whittaker didn't reply.

McGarvey stepped around the corner and walked to the steps leading to the veranda, his pistol in plain sight. "I'm coming to the front door. If someone is watching from inside, you'll see that I'm tossing my pistol onto the ground."

"Do it," Whittaker said.

McGarvey ejected the magazine, tossed it off the porch, then ejected the single shell and tossed it and the gun away. "If you shoot an unarmed man you'll have a tough time explaining it, no matter how many friends you think you have in high places. I just want to talk to Foster before I'm arrested." He turned away as he pocketed the still connected cell phone.

The night was very quiet, no wind, no traffic noises, no boat horns in the river. Katy had always liked this time of the evening, just before bed. She said she'd never been afraid of the dark; in fact, she'd always felt cocooned, protected, safe, ready to dream.

It would take everything within his power not to kill them all, starting with Foster. Vengeance never solved anything, Louise had told him, but he didn't know if he could believe it, or if he had ever believed it.

The door opened inward to a dark stair hall. "Keep your hands in plain sight and come in," Whittaker said.

"First turn on the lights."

"No."

"Then you'll just have to shoot me," McGarvey said. "You're a good shot, and I'm sure Sergeant Schilling is an expert marksman. The advantage is yours. And you'll even get credit for stopping me. I just want to talk."

A moment later the lights in the living room came on and spilled into the stair hall. Whittaker stood back from the open door, a standard military-issue 9mm Beretta in his hand, no silencer to degrade its accuracy.

There was no sign of Foster or of Sergeant Schilling.

"You wanted to talk to Mr. Foster, and he agreed," Whittaker said. "Come in, Mac."

"Only my friends call me that," McGarvey said, and he walked into the stair hall and stopped just a couple of feet from Whittaker, whose gun hand was rock solid.

Foster stood just within the living room to the right, a disdainful but curious expression on his round, almost bulldog face. He had no intention of talking, and it was obvious by the way he held himself: tense, his eyes narrowed.

Sergeant Schilling stood just beyond the living room entry, in the lee of the grand staircase. He was pointing the Italian-made Franchi SPAS-12 shotgun in McGarvey's direction. Even in the hands of an amateur the weapon was lethal out to a range of more than forty yards, and Schilling looked like anything but.

McGarvey took a step forward and to his right putting Whittaker between him and Schilling.

"You should have left when you had the chance," Whittaker said.

"You knew I couldn't leave it."

"The hell of it is that I always liked you. All of us did when you were the DCI."

"But why Arlington, David? Can you just tell me that much?"

"We never meant to hurt Kathleen or Elizabeth. The IED was meant for you."

McGarvey nodded, because he knew that Whittaker was telling the truth. "What about China?"

"Enough," Foster said.

Whittaker raised his pistol so that it was pointed directly at McGarvey's face.

"I'm wearing a wire," McGarvey said softly. "Otto's recorded everything including our telephone conversations, and the two calls made from the house phone to the Bureau and the Marshals. Maybe you want to make a deal before it's too late."

"He's lying," Foster said.

Whittaker shook his head, a sick look on his face. "No, he's not."

"Anything new?" McGarvey said.

"One of our B-52s made an emergency landing at Hsinchu Air Base about six hours ago," Otto came back.

"Who's he talking to?" Foster demanded.

"Hsinchu Air Base, Taiwan," McGarvey said. "Ring a bell?"

Whittaker went visibly pale. "Christ."

"The crew off-loaded something into one of the 499th Tactical Fighter wing's hangars," Otto said. "Could have been missiles."

"Is it possible that Chinese intelligence saw what was going on?" McGarvey asked.

"That'd be as close to a hundred percent as you could get."

"Otto has found out about the B-52s emergency landing out there. Whatever the crew off-loaded could have been nuclear missiles, or at least that's what Beijing probably believes."

"Enough," Foster roared. "Get that thing from him!"

Whittaker stepped forward and Schilling shouted something, but McGarvey moved left, away from the Beretta's muzzle and snatched the pistol from the acting DCI's hand.

Schilling fired three shots, the lead pellets shredding Whittaker's back, destroying most of his spine, and violently shoving him forward.

McGarvey fell back, using Whittaker's body as a shield, as Schilling fired at least six more times; a few of the pellets hit McGarvey's left shoulder and arm before he managed to fire two snap shots, one going wide, the other hitting the sergeant in center mass.

SEVENTY-FOUR

□

Pete had just about reached the highway where she'd parked Louise's SUV when she heard the gunshots, including what sounded like an automatic shotgun, and she pulled up short and looked back.

The night was suddenly very silent, and she swayed on her feet trying to come to a decision. Mac could be down; in an unknown situation inside the house the odds stacked against him. And leaving him like this wasn't an option. She'd lost one partner she didn't want to lose this one.

She took two steps back the way she had come, but stopped.

"Goddamnit," she muttered. This was bad, had been from the get-go. The man had lost his entire family; saw them murdered right in front of his eyes. And now she was supposed to turn her back on him?

She turned around again and ran the rest of the way through the woods to the Toyota, where she got her cell phone from her purse and called Otto.

"He made me leave, but there was gunfire," she blurted.

"Mac's okay for now," Otto said. "He took out Foster's bodyguard, and Whittaker is down. No one else is at the house."

"Does he need help?"

"No. But the Bureau and Marshals are on their way, so you've got to beat feet right now. Please tell me that you're in the car, or close to it, and not still up at the house. We don't know where you are. Louise had to switch the satellite back to the ship, someone was getting snoopy."

"I'm in the car," Pete said.

"Then get back here as fast as you can."

"Jesus."

"Yeah," Otto said. "Some really bad shit is just about ready to happen. Maybe a shooting war between China and Taiwan."

SEVENTY-FIVE

McGarvey disentangled himself from Whittaker's ravaged body, got to his feet, and, throwing Foster a quick glance to make sure the man wasn't armed, cautiously approached Schilling's inert form, and kicked the shotgun away.

"He's dead," Foster said. "Both of them are."

McGarvey safetied the Beretta and laid it on the hall table. "You must have expected casualties, otherwise why did you hire Administrative Solutions?"

"I underestimated you, Mr. McGarvey. We all did, except for poor David. But he was in over his head, and I think he was probably getting cold feet at the last minute."

The front door was still half open and in the far distance McGarvey heard sirens, and perhaps the rhythmic thump of helicopter rotors.

"China," McGarvey said.

"It's too late to be stopped, you know," Foster said. "Has been since before Mexico City." He was dressed in a natty blue blazer, khaki slacks, and an open-neck white silk shirt. He'd been drinking, his square-jawed face flushed. "In any event, what's about to happen has been inevitable, actually, for a number of years. When the Soviet Union disintegrated under the weight of historical pressure, China was next. Always had been next."

"Why? To what point do you risk innocent people, perhaps millions, or tens of millions?"

"There are no innocents."

McGarvey had to wonder about Foster and his type, because Osama bin Laden had told him the very same thing shortly before 9/11. What did they believe in? Certainly not religion, leastways not in bin Laden's case. Was Foster's god, money?

"You've come this far and you still don't understand, do you?" Foster said. "I can see it written all over your face. You're confused. You of all people . . . you've spent just about all of your adult life fighting for the same things I'm fighting for. And you've sacrificed more than any man should be able to bear. You've defied your superiors time and again because you knew you were right and they were wrong. You felt it in your gut because you have an extremely strong sense of fair play. You've even gone against the direct orders of the president. Why? Just answer that."

The sirens were much closer now, and the helicopters—he could make out two of them—were coming in for a landing.

"If China actually attacks Taiwan this evening, what advantage will it bring you?"

"Not me, Mr. McGarvey. The United States."

"China is no military threat to us."

"No, but they are on the verge of buying us. Purchasing the resources of a nation teetering on bankruptcy. They've already started. And for pennies on the dollar, a fact that most Americans are not aware of. How many people in Iowa or New Mexico or New York, for that matter, can name China's top ten cities and where they're located? How many of our citizens are totally ignorant of China's long, rich history?

How many know the threat they pose to our oil supplies? Or to a host of other natural resources we cannot do without?"

"You don't want to work it out in the marketplace," McGarvey said. The helicopters were on the ground now, and he could hear people just outside. "You never did. Mexico City, Pyongyang, and now this incident with the B-525 unloading something in Taiwan for the benefit of Mainland China's intelligence apparatus was meant to shove Beijing so hard it had no other choice but to react. Stupidly, blindly, but it had to do something."

"And it's working," Foster said, triumph in his eyes.

"But we know about it." he said.

"You're the only man who could have stopped us, and now it's too late for you. Far too late."

McGarvey turned toward the front door as FBI agents in SWAT team dark camos, automatic weapons at the ready, poured inside.

Steve Ansel and Doug Mellinger, the two U.S. Marshals he'd taken down at Arlington after the explosion, came in, their pistols drawn. Mellinger was wearing a knee brace and he walked with a heavy limp. They both wore dark blue Windbreakers with U.S. Marshals Service in yellow on the back.

Mellinger came right up to McGarvey. "Innocent until proved guilty, that was your line after we picked you up at Andrews."

McGarvey just looked him in the eye, but said nothing.

"Turns out we didn't have to prove anything," Mellinger said, nearly shaking with anger. "You did it for us." He smashed the butt of his pistol into McGarvey's jaw.

"Doug, for Christ's sake," Ansel said, and he grabbed Mellinger's arm and pulled him away.

McGarvey had expected the blow, and he had rolled with it as best he could, but he saw stars in his eyes, and tasted blood in his mouth.

"No need for any of that," Foster told them. "Who's in charge here?"

"We are," Ansel said. "Are you all right, sir?"

"A little shaken, but as you can see my bodyguard has been shot to death, along with Mr. Whittaker, and you'll find another body outside somewhere, Calvin Boberg who was employed by Administrative Solutions to provide me with security."

"The Bureau's forensics people are en route, and we're going to keep this as a federal crime scene. No locals."

"Very well. They will have my complete cooperation."

"Ask him why I'm here," McGarvey said.

"The man is wearing a wire, though I'm not quite sure who is monitoring it," Foster said.

"In my left ear," McGarvey said, and Mellinger yanked it out, pulling the wires from the control pack behind his ear.

"He came here to assassinate me, because for some reason he got the notion that the unfortunate terrorist attack at Arlington Cemetery in which his wife and daughter were killed was ordered by me personally." Foster shook his head. "The man is obviously deranged."

"Yeah," Mellinger said. He holstered his weapon and cuffed McGarvey. "I told you before that I didn't like traitors," he said. "I like them even less now. Especially guys like you who had it all."

"And you might search the grounds for a second gunman. I think he indicated that he had help."

"Who came with you?" Mellinger asked.

"Aren't you going to read me my rights?" McGarvey said. "You're just doing your job. And if it's any consolation, I'm sorry about your leg, but I wasn't thinking very straight just then." He turned and looked at Foster. "It's almost over for you and your Friday Club. We have most of the names and we know what you're trying to do." He smiled. "It won't work."

"I don't like traitors who hate their country either," Foster said. "Kindly remove this piece of garbage from my house."

Ansel took him from beneath the elbow and they walked out of the house, and across the lawn to the helicopter pad where two machines—one the FBI's the other the U.S. Marshals'—were idling. He only hoped that Pete was able to get clear and that she and Adkins would make it to Otto's. Everything was riding on them now.

SEVENTY-SIX

□

It was late when Pete finally showed up at the brownstone, and Otto buzzed her in after she parked the Toyota in the back, out of sight from the street. Adkins had already arrived and was hunched over Otto's shoulder studying something on the monitor, and Louise was seated at one of the other monitors.

They all looked up when she walked in.

"Is he okay?" she asked. She was dead tired, and her hip and leg were on fire.

"The Marshals took him, presumably to a holding cell somewhere in D.C., but he's not showing up on any of my search engines," Otto said. "He sounded good before they took his comms unit and found the cell phone in his pocket."

"Did he actually get to talk to Foster?"

Otto nodded. "Yeah, and the guy comes across as a wacko, but he has so many friends that no one has been willing to challenge him."

"He's sending the message that people want to hear," Adkins said. "No one trusts their government any longer, and that's not just the president's approval rating, it especially includes Congress. Most people think they're a bunch of crooks."

"And in a lot of instances, that's true," Louise said. "You read about it in the newspapers and see it on television practically every day."

Pete was havng trouble keeping on track. "So he's got the message. What are we doing to find Mac?"

"He's okay for now," Otto said. "He's in federal custody, no one is going to hurt him."

"Come on, you said yourself you can't find him. If Foster is as crazy as you say he is, why wouldn't he order his people to shoot Mac in the back of the head while trying to escape? Problem solved."

"Too many witnesses who are not in the Friday Club," Otto said. "There's only about three dozen of them and they're spread out. So take it easy."

"Who were the arresting officers?"

"As far as I can tell Douglas Mellinger and Steven Ansel. Mellinger's on the list we got from David's computer and Remington's flash drive."

"They'll kill him," Pete said.

"No," Otto said. "Ansel's clean, and he's just doing his job because so far as he knows Mac will be indicted for treason, and there was a warrant for his arrest. Same with the FBI guys who made the bust."

"Shit," Pete said, turning away for a moment. She felt overwhelmed. It had become a nightmare at Arlington when her partner had been killed in the blast and McGarvey had gone on the run. Bodies had piled up all over the place, and now with a possible shooting war between China and Taiwan, which made absolutely no sense, the numbers could rise astronomically.

"He knew that he was going to get arrested," Otto said, and Pete turned back to them. "By walking in there and confronting Foster he gave us the last pieces of the puzzle."

"He solved it for us," Adkins said.

She shook her head. "I don't see any of it," said. "Solved what?"

"What Foster was trying to do," Adkins said.

"Push China into starting a war, but how's knowing that going to help Mac?"

"There's going to be no war," Louise said. "Never was."

Pete's head was buzzing. "You're making no sense."

"Mac saw it before I did," Otto said, smiling. "Think about who Foster is. What he is. What he's always been."

Pete spread her hands. "I don't know. A lobbyist?"

"Right," Otto said. "So instead of trying to find out how he was trying to spark a war, I looked for how he was making his money. Starting with the polonium thing. A Chinese intelligence officer, supposedly under orders from Beijing, used Mexico as a staging ground for what looked like a series of terrorist attacks against the United States. Made Mexico look as if Beijing had played it for the fool."

"Foster's a lobbyist for Mexico?" Pete asked.

"Definitely not," Otto said. "Pemex, which is the Mexican government–owned oil and gas monopoly, was on the verge of signing a trillion-dollar oil deal with the Chinese. Oil that we needed. But Foster had enough of his people in the White House and Congress and State—all over Washington—so he could pull this off for the Department of Energy and a few key congresmen who didn't want to see Mexico sell its oil to China."

"We never found that any polonium crossed the border," Adkins said. "It was his first major scam. And except for the people who lost their lives over it, the U.S. came out on top. Pemex canceled its contract with China and the oil came to us instead."

"The guy really is nuts," Pete said. "So who paid him?"

"I don't know that part yet," Otto said. "But it was someone on this side of the border."

"What about Pyongyang? How did he make money by nearly starting a nuclear war between China and North Korea?"

"Think of who would have had the most to gain by getting rid of Kim Jong Il, and possibly even reunifying the Koreas."

"Us, I suppose," Pete said. "Certainly would have helped reduce tensions over there if the nuclear issue had been solved."

"There wouldn't have been a war," Louise said. "Nobody, not even Kim Jong Il, and especially not the Chinese, are that crazy. That never was the real issue. But by driving a wedge between North Korea's only ally it strengthened South Korea's bargaining position to build automobile factories in the north, something the Chinese wanted to do."

"Beijing is rushing full tilt into the twentieth-first century, and the only way they can keep up the pace is to find new markets for their products," Adkins said. "They're approaching saturation level here, and each time we have an economic downturn the U.S. debt China holds looks less and less promising. So they create new markets in places where workers earn enough income to afford the cars and televisions and stereos."

"North Korea is poor," Pete said.

"Build factories for them and the workers will earn the money to buy Chinese products," Adkins said. "Simple economics."

"China was stopped again, so who paid Foster?"

"At this point it looks like a consortium of South Korean car makers to the tune of fifty million dollars," Otto said.

"They were willing to risk nuclear war for the sake of money?" Pete asked. "Or am I being too naïve?"

Louise smiled. "Naïve, and that's not such a bad thing."

"And Taiwan?"

"Haven't got that one totally figured out yet," Otto said. "Except that the B-252 didn't have an actual emergency landing, they were on a training mission to deliver spare parts, not missiles—although a Chinese sleeper agent was fed that info, and China began rattling its sabers. Something it's been doing for a long time."

"Who paid Foster?"

"Probably a cabal in Taiwan very similar to the one Foster ran here: Taiwan for the Taiwanese. It's too dangerous to go head-to-head with Beijing on a political level, so Foster was able to engineer something like this to give China another black eye."

Pete was amazed. "People died for this nonsense. Money. Position. And if things had gotten out of hand in Mexico City, or Pyongyang or Taipei, we might have gotten embroiled in some sort of a nuclear exchange."

"Wars have started for less," Adkins said.

"Still leaves Mac in jail, and Foster's people on the loose to figure out their next scam," Pete said. "What can we do about it?"

Otto and Adkins exchanged a glance, and Otto touched a finger to the send box in the header of what looked like an e-mail message. "Just did it."

"Did what?"

"We wrote an e-mail detailing everything we just told you, and sent it to every name from Remington's flash drive and Whittaker's laptop."

"Don't you think they'll fight back?"

"With what?" Otto asked. "We have the proof, and Mac got it for us."

"Now we wait," Adkins said.

PART

FIVE

Thirty-six Hours Later

SEVENTY-SEVEN

□

At the Central Detention Facility, known as the D.C. jail, McGarvey sat on his cot, his back against the dirty concrete wall. His clothing had been taken from him when he'd been admitted thirty-six hours ago, and he was dressed now in jeans, a light blue denim shirt, and black shoes, no laces.

He was in a special holding cell away from the general population used for prisoners on suicide watch, prisoners who were in danger from the other inmates, and occasionally a special case like McGarveys ordered held by the Bureau or the U.S. Marshal Service.

So far no one had come to talk to him, and the jailer who delivered his meals had said nothing, merely sliding the metal plate, tin cup of Kool-Aid, and the spoon through the slot in the metal door, and returning in twenty minutes to retrieve the dirty dishes.

The single light set behind a grille in the ceiling never went out, and there was no window.

Everything hinged on Otto, as operations in the past so often had, but he hoped that Dick Adkins and Pete had managed to make it to safety and keep their heads down until the dust settled.

There were going to be repercussions, and it was almost certain that Foster would fight back using whatever connections were left in place and still loyal to the cause. But it was anyone's guess how it would turn out.

During the first night, and all yesterday, he'd had plenty of time to think about Katy and Liz and Todd, and what his life was going to be without them. But he'd come to no conclusions. Too soon, he supposed. And he was numb, a feeling he'd never really known to this depth. It was as if a very large part of his body and his mind had been cut out and disposed of. No ceremony. No time to prepare. No time to mount some sort of defense or counterattack. They were there in his life, and then they were gone.

He'd also thought about the day Katy had given him the ultimatum, her or the CIA, and he'd been so stupid that he'd walked out the door and had taken up an existence in Switzerland. But even that separation, that distance had never been final in his mind. There'd always been at least a glimmer of hope, a possibility for reconciliation that was missing now. And he was still angry. Almost shaking with anger.

The door locking mechanism was thrown back, the door swung open, and Ansel was there, holding what looked like a clear plastic dry cleaner's bag over his shoulder, his thumb hooked in the curve of the hanger.

McGarvey sat up. "Where's your partner?"

"He didn't show up for work this morning," Ansel said.

"No one knows where he is?"

Ansel's eyes narrowed. "That's right," he said. "Anyway, all charges against you have been dropped, but there'll be a coroner's hearing. A lot of dead bodies scattered around that need answering for." He came in, laid the bag at the foot of the cot, and stepped back out of the cell as if he were wary of getting too close. "Your clothes have been cleaned and pressed. Soon as you're dressed I'll get you out of here."

"What about my shoes?"

"With your other things up front."

McGarvey got up and began changing out of the prison garb. "Anything else been going on around town overnight? Disappearances? Resignations? Suicides?"

"You knew all along that something like this was going to happen, didn't you?"

"Not at first. But the deeper I got into the mess the more likely I thought Foster and his people would fold if they were given a nudge. Like a house of cards."

"Well, Foster's car was run off the road early this morning and he was shot to death. No witnesses."

"Anyone with him?"

"No. He was driving. As it is we'll probably never find the killer. It was professional."

"It'll turn out to be an Administrative Solutions shooter. They've got a grudge."

"Against you," Ansel said.

"Foster owed them a lot of money. I didn't," McGarvey said. "Who else?"

Ansel shook his head. "I don't know, I don't think anybody does yet, but the media is all over it. One of Langdon's advisers resigned, along with a couple of guys from the State Department, one at Justice, and maybe someone at the Department of Energy. A general who was an adviser to the Joint Chiefs was found shot to death in his office last night. A suicide."

"All Foster's people," McGarvey said. "Just like your partner probably was."

"I don't know what you're talking about," Ansel said. "And I don't think I want to know. But I expect that's exactly what the president is going to ask you."

McGarvey shook his head. "I don't have anything to tell him that he doesn't already know by now."

"No choice, Mr. Director. Technically you're still under arrest until I drop you off at the White House."

The D.C. jail was way out by RFK Stadium, and during the long drive over to the White House Ansel didn't say a thing, but he let McGarvey use his cell phone to call Otto.

"I'm on my way to the White House, the president wants to talk to me. Did our friends make it okay?"

"It's not your cell phone. You can't talk."

"Right."

"I'll take care of it. But yeah, they made it just fine. Have you been told what's been happening around town?"

"Some of it. How many from the lists?"

"So far twenty-three out of thirty-seven, and without Foster the rest of them won't get very far," Otto said. "You heard that he was murdered?"

"Yes. Where was he going?"

"Looks like he was headed to Dulles. He keeps a corporate jet out there."

"Flight plan?"

"Zurich."

And so it was over and done with, or very nearly so. "What about you guys?" McGarvey asked. "Are all of you in the clear?"

"Pete's going back to work tomorrow, debriefings probably for at least a week. Louise and I will do the same, but not until Monday, gives us a few days to clear out of here, pick up Audie, and get back to our old apartment."

"And Dick?"

"DCIs serve at the president's pleasure, with congressional consent," Otto said. "What about you?"

"I hadn't thought about it," McGarvey said. "I suppose I'll bunk with you and Louise for a day or two and then go to Casey Key and start closing down the house and getting rid of the sailboat."

"You're not going to move back?"

"No," McGarvey said.

"The phone you're using is a U.S. Marshal Service issue. Soon as you hang up, I'm going to fry it. Might be a recording device inside, memory, something, ya know. Can't be too careful."

"You're right."

"Louise and I have a few things to do yet, but Pete's coming over to pick you up. She'll be waiting at the West Gate. We're all going to have pizza and red wine. Lots of red wine."

Ansel dropped him off at the White House west portico. "I'm sorry that things worked out the way they did for you, Mr. Director," he said. "Your wife and daughter and son-in-law. This stuff should never involve families."

"Not in an ideal world," McGarvey said, and he got out of the car and didn't look back as Ansel left.

He was met by a presidential aide who escorted him down to the Oval Office without a word. President Langdon was seated in an easy chair facing his National Security Adviser Frank Shapiro, seated on the couch.

"Good, you're here at last," the president said. "We have to clear up a number of things before your news conference. I'm appointing you as interim director of the CIA, just until this mess is straightened out."

"No."

"No, what?" Shapiro asked sharply. He was angry, and looked a little like a frightened man.

"No, sir, I'm not going back to work for the CIA, nor am I going to hold a news conference."

"I understand how you must feel," Langdon said. "But your country needs you. I need you, because we're facing a set of very serious problems, and the Chinese government is demanding some answers. Immediate answers."

"No, sir," McGarvey said.

"Well at least sit down and hear me out," the president said, his voice rising in anger.

"I'm not staying, Mr. President," McGarvey said. "I came here because I was ordered to, and because I wanted to tell you that I don't like you, I never have. I don't believe in most of your policies or most of the people you picked for your advisers."

Shapiro got to his feet, but Langdon waved him back.

"Mr. McGarvey is exercising his right as a citizen. And as it turns out I don't like him, never have, never have agreed with how he did things." He looked McGarvey in the eye. "But I believe that there is no man alive who loves his country more than you do."

"No, sir," McGarvey said. "That man had better be you, or we're all in trouble."

EPILOGUE

Several Months Later

It was noon, and, shirtless, McGarvey was running along the rocky path above the Aegean Sea on the Greek island of Serifos, pushing himself as he had since coming back to the same island, the same converted lighthouse he'd run to a number of years ago.

That time John Lyman Trotter, a close friend, had turned out to be a mole within the CIA, and in the end McGarvey had been forced to kill him, getting seriously wounded himself. He'd found this island, this refuge in the middle of nowhere, and started the healing process.

Only now he wasn't bouncing back quite as fast, and this time he was alone, truly alone except for his granddaughter, who Otto and Louise had brought here six weeks ago for a visit.

And seeing her, being with her, was wonderful and sad all at the same time because Audie was the spitting image of Liz, who'd been the spitting image of Katy. A lot of memories had come to the surface making it next to impossible to keep smiling and keep it light.

Already she was forgetting her parents. It was something Otto and Louise wanted to correct. They wanted to show her the pictures, a few videos that Todd had made and tell her about them.

"Later, when she's older," McGarvey had told them after they'd put her to bed. The night had been soft, the kind Katy had always loved. "She wouldn't understand. And you're her parents now. Just love her, it's all she needs."

Reaching the west side of the island, he came in sight of the white-tiled patio at the base of the lighthouse one hundred yards below, and pulled up short. The figure of a man was leaning on the railing looking down at the sea, one hundred feet below.

Apparently he'd walked up from town, not an easy task.

McGarvey had switched back to his Walther PPK, more out of sentimental reasons than any other, and it was holstered at the small of his back. He never went anywhere without it these days.

So he started down the path toward the lighthouse wondering who the man was, because he wasn't familiar, and why he had come.

And McGarvey was curious, so his step quickened just a little.